"With mastery and grace, Ann's gentle prose woos us back to a simpler time with a simply beautiful love story. Truly, *When the Heart Heals* is sweet tonic for both the heart and the soul."

—**Julie Lessman**, award-winning author of the Daughters of Boston and Winds of Change series

"*When the Heart Heals* is sure to grab your attention. Rosemary is a memorable heroine in an intriguing story that left me glad I'd read it and looking for more Ann Shorey novels."

—**Lauraine Snelling**, author of the Red River series and the Wild West Wind series

Praise for *Where Wildflowers Bloom*

"The authenticity of *Where Wildflowers Bloom* transported me straight to post–Civil War times, yet the characters—their hopes, dreams, conflicts, and fears—all rang contemporarily true. Another winner from Ann Shorey!"

—**Christina Berry**, Christy-nominated and Carol Award–winning author of *The Familiar Stranger*

"*Where Wildflowers Bloom* invites you to settle down over by the checkerboard at Lindberg's Mercantile Store and get to know the people of Noble Springs as they put the sorrows of the Civil War behind them and embrace life and love anew. Ann Shorey has come up with an appealing mix of history and romance that readers are sure to enjoy."

—**Ann H. Gabhart**, author of *The Blessed* and *Words Spoken True*

When the
HEART
Heals

Books by Ann Shorey

When the HEART Heals

A NOVEL

Ann Shorey

R
Revell
a division of Baker Publishing Group
Grand Rapids, Michigan

© 2013 by Ann Shorey

Published by Revell
a division of Baker Publishing Group
P.O. Box 6287, Grand Rapids, MI 49516-6287
www.revellbooks.com

Printed in the United States of America

Library of Congress Cataloging-in-Publication Data
Shorey, Ann Kirk, 1941–
    When the heart heals : a novel / Ann Shorey.
        pages cm. — (Sisters at heart ; #2)
    ISBN 978-0-8007-2073-5 (pbk. : alk. paper)
        1. Nurses—Fiction. 2. United States—History—1865–1898—Fiction.
    I. Title.
    PS3619.H666W475 2013
    813'.6—dc23   2012040322

Scripture used in this book, whether quoted or paraphrased by the characters, is taken from the King James Version.

This book is a work of fiction. Names, characters, places, and incidents are the product of the author's imagination or are used fictitiously. Any resemblance to actual events, locales, or persons, living or dead, is coincidental.

The internet addresses, email addresses, and phone numbers in this book are accurate at the time of publication. They are provided as a resource. Baker Publishing Group does not endorse them or vouch for their content or permanence.

13 14 15 16 17 18 19   7 6 5 4 3 2 1

To nurses everywhere,
with appreciation for your
skills and commitment

NOBLE SPRINGS, MISSOURI
FEBRUARY 1867

*R*osemary Saxon startled awake. Downstairs, her dog sounded like he was attempting to burst through the front door. His bark was one continuous "rawr rawr rawr," interspersed with deep growls.

A glance out the window told her daylight waited somewhere beyond the horizon. She flung her wrapper over her shoulders and tiptoed down to the entryway. Her heart thudded in her throat at skittering noises on the porch.

Crouching next to Bodie, she placed her hand on the raised fur along his back. "Shh. We're fine." She inched to the window and peered through a corner of the lace curtain. Blackness.

Bodie growled low in his chest. Her pulse gradually slowed as she stroked his velvety ears, reassured by his solid presence next to her. Anything that got through her locked door wouldn't get past Bodie.

"I hope you didn't wake me because you smelled a raccoon."

The dog relaxed against her and licked her fingers. After a moment she turned and walked to the kitchen, her steps sure in the darkness.

She struck a match against the surface of the cookstove and lit a lamp, then returned to the sitting room to glance at the case clock atop a bookshelf.

"Oh, Bodie, why today? It's five in the morning." She massaged her temples. "I need to be alert when I call on the doctor." A ripple of nervousness tingled across her chest. So much depended on Dr. Stewart's response.

Resigned to wakefulness, Rosemary opened the firebox and tossed several chunks of wood over the banked coals. As soon as the sky lightened, she'd step out the front door to investigate the reason for Bodie's excitement.

She considered the possibilities. This section of the state remained in some turmoil since the war, with refugees occasionally coming through town seeking assistance. Maybe someone had stopped to ask for help.

"At this hour? I doubt it." She rubbed the dog's ears. "Most likely one of those critters you like to tree."

When dawn approached, she padded to the entryway, slid the bolt aside, and opened the door. She glanced up and down the deserted street. The houses across the way remained dark.

A scrap of paper protruded from beneath the rug she kept on the porch for Bodie. When she bent to retrieve it, she noticed footprints in the frost that bristled on the wooden porch. A trail led from the gate in her picket fence to the door and away. Someone *had* been outside. Those weren't animal tracks.

Rosemary grabbed the paper and backed into the house, slamming and bolting the door. With shaking hands she unfolded the wrinkled brown page.

I no wat yore up to with yore witchs brew. Be warned!

Shocked, she stared at the message. What witches' brew? Someone went to a great deal of trouble to deliver a warning to the wrong person. She'd lived in Noble Springs for over a year and no one had gone this far to make her feel unwelcome.

She paced to the window and watched the day awaken. Thin sunshine touched the frosted landscape with tentative fingers, as though one willful storm cloud would be all the discouragement it needed to disappear. After a moment, Rosemary shrugged. She had more to do today than worry about a misdelivered, misspelled message. Later she'd go to Lindberg's Mercantile and show the paper to her sister-in-law, Faith Saxon. Now she needed to prepare for her call on Dr. Stewart.

After letting Bodie back in the house following his morning romp, Rosemary climbed the steep staircase to the second floor, rehearsing what she'd say to the doctor. Everything depended on his opinion of women as nurses. *Please, Lord, give him an open mind.* She'd had enough disrespect from Dr. Greeley, the town's elderly physician, to last her for eons.

She dressed carefully in a dove-gray watered silk dress with a high white collar. Seeking a practical look, she arranged her thick black hair in a bun at the back of her head, careful to pin loose strands in place, then settled her gray spoon bonnet over her coiffure.

After a final check in the mirror, she wrapped a green paisley shawl around her shoulders and descended the stairs. Bodie sat next to the door.

"Not now, boy. You wait here."

Rosemary straightened her shoulders and stepped into the frosty morning. Despite shrugging off the message, she examined the area for strangers before leaving the security of her picket-fenced yard. A horse-drawn buggy clipped by on the frozen road. No threat there. She strode toward Second Street, chiding herself for being overcautious.

When she reached the corner, she turned south toward the railroad tracks, her destination a building that had been the quartermaster's headquarters during the war. Now converted to business space, a new doctor had set up an office at the east end, facing the railroad tracks.

ELIJAH STEWART, PHYSICIAN, OFFICE HOURS 8:30 TO 5:00, MONDAY THROUGH FRIDAY was painted in black on the white-washed wall next to his door. Rosemary paused and drew a deep breath before stepping inside.

On her right, a stove threw off waves of heat. A sofa upholstered in horsehair sat under a window at the rear of the room. Uncomfortable-looking wooden chairs shoved against the windowless left wall faced two closed doors. She supposed one led to the doctor's private office and the other to an examining room. A murmur of voices seeped from behind one of the doors.

Rosemary settled on the sofa, pushing her toes against the floorboards to keep from sliding forward on the slippery covering. Her hands perspired inside her tight gloves. To calm herself, she closed her eyes and rehearsed what she'd say when her turn came.

After several minutes, the door closest to the entry opened and a youth limped into the waiting room.

A burly man wearing a black waistcoat over rolled-up shirt-sleeves followed him. "Keep a fresh bandage on that cut, and stay off your feet as much as possible."

"Thanks, Doc." The young man tipped his hat at Rosemary as he left.

"I'm Dr. Stewart. Sorry to keep you waiting, miss." The doctor gestured toward the open door. "If you will step inside, we can discuss your complaint."

A shock of recognition rippled through her. Dr. Stewart had been a surgeon at Jefferson Barracks during her first weeks as a nurse. He'd been there only a short time before being called to the front lines, but she remembered his distinctive height, his mop of curly hair, and his eyes, so dark they were almost black.

"Miss?"

She rose and extended her hand. "My name is Rosemary Saxon, and I didn't come with a medical complaint."

He took her hand and bowed. "Miss Saxon. Then how may I assist you?"

"I'm here to offer you my assistance." She held her voice steady. "I spent the war years as a nurse, and now I'm seeking employment as such." She pasted a determined expression on her face.

He crossed to the second door and swung it open. "Come into my office and tell me why you think I should employ a nurse in my practice." One wall of the room was lined with glass-fronted bookcases. A skeleton hanging from a hook on the wall took up space between the window and what had to be the interior door to the examination room. Dr. Stewart flung himself into an oak armchair on casters and pointed to a straight-back chair facing his desk.

Rosemary settled herself, folding her hands in her lap and willing them not to tremble. "As I said, I have several years of hospital experience in tending to wounds, administering medicines, and assisting doctors. I do not faint at the sight of blood."

"Neither do I, Miss Saxon."

"I believe there's a need for a woman's presence when doctors have female patients, and that's where I'd be most valuable. Of course, I'd be prepared for any other duties as necessary."

"You must know this is irregular." He rocked back in his chair with his arms folded across his broad chest. "I called on

Dr. Greeley when I first contemplated Noble Springs for my practice. He doesn't employ a nurse, neither male nor female."

"If I may be blunt, Dr. Greeley is an old man who's been a physician practically since the turn of the century." She sat straighter. "The war has changed many things, but Dr. Greeley isn't one of them. He believes women have no place in medicine. I disagree."

His lips twitched. "Miss Saxon, although you present a good appearance, I don't know you. You could be seeking access to my laudanum supply."

"Dr. Stewart! I assure you—I have no need of laudanum."

He waved a hand at her, chuckling. "Please excuse my humor. With your permission, I'd like to speak to someone who could vouch for you, then we'll talk again."

"I have a brother here, and the pastor of our church knows me." Her confidence wavered when she realized how weak that sounded. Of course her brother and her pastor would speak well of her. She dropped her gaze to her lap. "If you're seeking a professional recommendation, I could write to my supervisor from the Barracks. She remained in St. Louis after the war." Mentally, she berated herself for not thinking of this long ago. She should have had the information ready for him.

She knew why she hadn't. That part of her life had ended. Or so she'd believed.

After Rosemary returned home, she exchanged her silk dress for a serviceable blue and gray plaid wool skirt with matching bodice. Unless Dr. Stewart hired her, which seemed unlikely, she'd continue to volunteer her mornings at Lindberg's Mercantile while she searched for a salaried job. She heaved a deep sigh. Tonight she'd compose a letter to Alice Broadbent, and pray for a speedy response.

Bodie bounced and wiggled next to the door when she prepared to leave. She smiled at his enthusiasm.

"Of course you're coming with me. You'd be missed if I left you behind."

The air held the biting snap of a forthcoming snowstorm. Iron-gray clouds smothered the horizon. Grateful she had only two blocks to walk, Rosemary wrapped her cloak around her and covered the distance between her home and the store with rapid strides.

When she entered the building, she didn't see Faith in her usual place behind the counter. On her left, colors from bolts of fabric on display brightened the area under one window. Two cookstoves shared space with new plows in the center of the rectangular room.

Faith's "woodstove regulars," Mr. Grisbee and Mr. Slocum, looked up from their checker game next to the box stove. They'd been fixtures at the store long before Rosemary arrived in Noble Springs. Mr. Grisbee lived up to his name, with grizzled whiskers and a growly manner. In contrast, Mr. Slocum kept his gray beard neatly trimmed, and his thinning hair was regularly barbered. As Faith's grandfather's friends, they took it upon themselves to act as substitute uncles.

"Morning, Miss Rosemary," Mr. Slocum said. "You looking for Miss Faith? She's in the storeroom." As he spoke, he rose and strode to the burlap curtain hanging across the opening in the rear wall. Poking his head around the door frame, he called, "Miss Rosemary's here. You can quit your worrying."

Faith bustled past the curtain. "When you didn't arrive at nine, I was afraid you were ill. I was planning to call on you during the dinner hour."

"I went to see Dr. Stewart first thing this morning. I'm sorry to worry you." Rosemary hung her cloak on a peg and tied an apron around her waist.

Faith's lake-blue eyes widened with concern. "You went to see the new doctor? What's wrong? Why haven't you said anything?" She gestured toward the front counter. "Come and tell me."

Gratitude for her friend swept over Rosemary. "I'm healthy as a horse." She followed Faith past shelves stacked with cookware and china. Once they were out of earshot of the woodstove regulars, she lowered her voice and said, "I went to see Dr. Stewart to ask if he'd hire me to assist him as a nurse."

"A nurse? You said you'd put all that behind you."

"I know, and I meant it at the time, but now that you and Curt are married, I want to earn my own living. Curt's salary from the academy should go for the two of you, not to keep a roof over my head."

"We'd love it if you'd move in with us. I've told you that before."

"Your house is already overflowing."

"Just Grandpa and Amy and Sophia," Faith said, referring to the young widow and her child who stayed with her grandfather while she and Curt were at work.

"Plus you and Curt. That's a houseful."

Faith's expression brightened. "The mercantile is doing fairly well. I'll pay you for your help."

"I told you from the beginning I didn't want to be paid. Besides, that would be no different than taking part of Curt's salary." She squeezed Faith's hand. "I love spending mornings here. But I need to look after myself. Nursing is what I know."

"When does Dr. Stewart want you to come to work?"

Rosemary looked down at their clasped hands. "Never, I'm afraid. He didn't seem to take my request seriously. Then when he asked for recommendations, I couldn't think of anyone but Reverend French and Curt. Not very impressive."

"Did he say that?"

"No. He just said he'd let me know soon. I think that was a polite way to get me out the door."

"Let's say you're right, and he doesn't hire you. There are bound to be places in town where you could work. Why don't we make a list?" Faith leaned on the counter, winding a loose strand of her straw-blonde hair around one finger. "How about a paid companion for an elderly lady?" She scribbled some notes on a sheet of paper.

"What elderly lady? I don't know any."

"Could you be a seamstress?"

"I hate sewing."

"You're a wonderful cook."

"None of the ladies who could afford a cook would want

me. Most everyone who knows I was a nurse thinks I'm vulgar for having touched men's bodies."

"That's bound to pass in time."

Rosemary slid an arm around Faith's waist. "I'll think of something. Please don't worry."

The bell over the door jingled as Mrs. Raines, one of the mercantile's steady customers, entered. Her gaze slid past Rosemary and settled on Faith. "Mrs. Saxon, the druggist told me you have several excellent shaving soaps. Mr. Raines would like to try something different."

Rosemary watched while Faith showed the woman an assortment of round pots, each bearing the name of the company that produced the soap. She thought of the shaving compound she prepared for Curt. Maybe she could . . . No. She'd have to sell dozens each week. As if that were likely to happen.

Rosemary drew the hood of her cloak around her face as she made her way home through blowing snow. Frozen droplets struck her nose and cheeks, melting to run down her neck. Bodie trotted at her side, his eyes squinted against the swirling flakes. His feathery collie-like fur hung in limp strings. She'd stayed longer at the mercantile than she'd planned and now dusk had settled over the streets. Even the horses that passed on the road seemed in a hurry to get out of the storm.

She paused in front of the barbershop at the corner of Second Street and peered in the direction of her house. A shadowy figure moved eastward beyond her fence, then disappeared into the gray twilight. Bodie growled low in his throat.

"That's enough. We're almost there." The last thing she needed was to have her dog chase after a fellow pedestrian.

Bodie didn't weigh more than forty pounds, but he didn't know that.

Rosemary crossed the street and covered the remaining distance to her front gate, stepping with care over icy patches on the boardwalk. When she unfastened the latch, her gaze fell on fresh tracks leading to her porch and back to the street. The person she'd seen must have been inside her yard.

Drawing her cloak to one side, she placed a foot inside one of the tracks. The outline dwarfed her small boot. A man's shoe, no doubt. But who? If Curt had stopped by, he would have waited.

Shivering, she followed Bodie up the brick pathway to the porch steps, then paused at the foot of the stairs. Another set of footprints led around the house. Partially filled in by snow, they remained distinct enough for her to see they were made by a smaller shoe. Two people inside her fence. Three if she counted her predawn visitor. A chill ran down her spine that had nothing to do with the snowy evening. She dropped her hand to Bodie's collar and held him close until she had locked and bolted her door.

With shaking hands she built up the fire in the kitchen, then draped her cloak over a chair to dry. She'd been on her own since Curt and Faith married last October. Until today, she hadn't given much thought to her vulnerability. Perhaps Faith was right. She could join them in the large home at the west end of town and give up her notions of independence.

Rosemary sank into a chair and rested her chin on her closed fist, considering the idea. If she moved in with her brother and his wife, how long would it be before people pitied Curt for being burdened with his spinster sister?

She shook her head. She would take care of herself. By herself.

Water bubbled from the spout of the teakettle and sputtered

on the stovetop. She stepped into the pantry and brought out a glass jar containing a special jasmine tea mixture that she used when she needed to focus her thoughts. After measuring leaves into a white porcelain teapot, she poured hot water over them, savoring the perfume-like fragrance of jasmine flowers.

Bodie had wriggled behind the cookstove and lay there panting with contentment. The sable patch around his left eye gave him a mischievous appearance. Rosemary grinned. As long as she had her watchdog, she'd stay right where she was. If the Lord wanted her to have a husband, he'd send someone her way. And if not, she believed he'd show her how to support herself without burdening her brother.

The dog stirred and pricked one ear up. Growling, he crawled out from his retreat and darted to the front door. His deep barks shattered the fragile peace.

Elijah Stewart took a step away from the door. From the sound of the barking, Miss Saxon must keep bulldogs in her sitting room. Footsteps approached. In a moment the door opened a crack and she peeked out at him.

"Dr. Stewart?" Her voice rose to an incredulous pitch. "What are you doing here?" Face reddening, she stepped back, motioning him to enter. "I mean, I didn't expect to see you."

A sable and white dog stood at her side eyeing him, hackles raised. The animal looked smaller than his bark. He held the back of his hand toward the dog's nose, then moved with caution into the closet-like entryway. A flight of enclosed stairs rose directly in front of him. To the right, a lamp burned on a table in the tidy sitting room.

Miss Saxon gestured toward a pair of cushioned chairs beneath the front window. "Please, sit."

He removed his hat and settled onto one of the chairs. She

opened the curtains, then remained on her feet, facing him. Surprised, he raised an eyebrow. "Am I to be on display?"

"I'm alone here. It's not proper for me to entertain a gentleman caller. With the curtains open, anyone can see we're not behaving in an unseemly fashion. It's a beastly night, or we would have talked on the porch."

"You didn't tell me you lived alone."

"You didn't ask," she said, with a testy edge to her voice.

Prickly women made him nervous. Turning his hat in his hands, he surveyed her plain wool dress. So she didn't spend her days dressed in silks—that much was to her credit. "I stopped by a bit earlier, but no one was home. I apologize for not leaving my card."

She nodded. "As I said, I didn't expect you at all after our meeting. I've had no opportunity to contact my supervisor."

"It doesn't matter."

"I thought not. Well, thank you for hearing me out this morning. I wish I could offer you some refreshment before you leave, but I've only just returned from town." She moved toward the door.

He shook his head at her haste to send him away. "Do you always jump to conclusions?"

"Pardon?"

"I came here to tell you I'm willing to give you a try as a nurse in my practice. Of course, most of the time you'll be occupied with duties other than nursing. Preparing medications, keeping records current, tidying the office." He waved a hand. "Things like that."

Miss Saxon left the doorway and sank onto the chair facing him. "Tidying the office? You want a housekeeper, not a nurse."

Elijah ran his finger under his too-tight collar. Definitely a prickly woman. Her words about being present when he saw female patients had convinced him he needed her help, but if she was going to work for him, she needed to understand who was in charge.

"Miss Saxon, as you no doubt experienced at Jefferson Barracks, nurses were called upon to do everything from writing letters to changing soiled linens and scrubbing floors. If you're willing to perform those same duties in my office, you're hired." He rose and replaced his hat. "I'll expect you at half past eight on Monday morning. If you have any qualms, then I wish you well in your future endeavors. Good evening."

*R*osemary rummaged in a back corner of her wardrobe and removed a rust-colored calico dress. The sight of the plain frock brought the smells and sounds of the Barracks hospital to her memory. She bit her lower lip, wishing she knew another way to support herself. Any acceptance she'd gained since arriving in Noble Springs would surely disappear once word spread that she was employed as a nurse.

The winter chill in her bedroom offered little incentive for reflection. She dropped the gown over her petticoats and fastened the buttons on the bodice, then dashed downstairs to her warm kitchen. The dried thyme and rosemary hanging from the ceiling beams lent the room a savory aroma. She sniffed with appreciation, pinching a bit of her namesake herb between her fingers to stir into her breakfast cornbread.

As she slid the pan into the oven, she heard the sound of a key in the lock. Bodie scooted out from behind the stove and ran into the sitting room, his tail fanning the air. Rosemary hurried after him.

"Just a moment. I need to move the bolt," she called.

Her brother, Curt Saxon, bent to kiss her cheek after the

door opened. "I stopped by to wish you well." He stepped back, his large hands gripping her upper arms. "Are you sure you're ready to do this?" A corner of the faded scar on his neck showed above the high collar of his shirt. His dark brown hair bore the fresh tracks of a comb.

She hid a thankful smile. His teaching job at the academy had done wonders for his spirit, shattered after wartime experiences.

"I'll be fine. A local practice won't be anything like hospital wards." She took his hand and led him to the kitchen, talking as she went. "I don't know about Dr. Stewart, though. I think he studied arrogance in medical school."

He snickered. "As long as you keep a tight rein on your temper, all should be well."

"I told you what he said when he was here Friday evening. If he continues to talk to me like that, I can't guarantee anything." She placed two cups on the table and poured tea for both of them.

He inhaled the steam rising from his cup. "Chamomile. This should help keep you calm."

"Stop teasing. I'm not that bad."

"Sorry." He sipped his tea, a slight frown creasing his forehead. "Why did you have the door bolted? Usually you have trouble remembering to lock it."

Rosemary stood and lifted a flowerpot from the windowsill. She removed the folded piece of brown paper tucked beneath the pot and handed the scrap to Curt. "This was left on my porch before daylight Friday morning. I think whoever wrote it has mistaken me for someone else. Regardless, the thought of a trespasser frightens me. So I bolt the door."

He scanned the brief message. "Witches' brew, eh? No wonder you're frightened. The writer sounds unhinged. I wish you'd agree to come and live with us."

"I don't want to be dependent on anyone. You know that."

"This changes things." He tapped the message.

"No it doesn't." She locked eyes with him. "Give me a year. Then we'll discuss this again."

"A year from when Faith and I were married, not a year from today."

"Promise you won't bring up the subject in the meantime?"

Curt stood, blowing out an exasperated sigh. "Maybe." He winked. "But the offer stands, anytime you change your mind."

"Get on with you." She gave him a mock shove. "Your students are waiting."

After he left, she ate a quick breakfast, left Bodie in the house, and headed for Dr. Stewart's office. She needed to prove herself to her brother, as well as to her new employer. It wouldn't do to be late.

The doctor met Rosemary at the door, impressive in a black coat and dark gray waistcoat. "So you decided to take the job. I wasn't sure."

She stifled the tart reply that rose to her lips. "I appreciate the opportunity. Thank you. Now if you'll show me my responsibilities, I'll begin."

"We discussed your responsibilities on Friday evening. What we didn't discuss is salary. Will you accept twenty percent of what comes in every week?" A rueful smile crossed his lips. "Sometimes I'm paid with a ham or venison. You'd get a share of that too."

"A percentage would be satisfactory. Thank you." The piddling amount she received from her grandparents' trust fund covered her rent but didn't leave much for food and other necessities.

"Excellent." The doctor exhaled with a huff. He sounded like he'd been holding his breath.

He pointed to a small slant-top desk that had been added to the room since her visit. "This will be your station unless I need your direct assistance. Last week's receipts are in the drawer and need to be entered. That's the ledger on the corner of the desk."

His face took on a boyish look and he grinned at her. "I hope you're better with figures than I am. I can compound medications all day, but my brain reels at columns of numbers."

"My brother is a mathematician. Some of his skill has rubbed off on me." She fought down disappointment. She'd expected to don an apron and assist him with patients, not to act as a clerk tucked away in a corner. Still, if she wanted to live without being dependent on others, she couldn't let pride stand in the way of employment.

Dr. Stewart must have sensed her inner struggle. "Never fear. When ladies seek my advice, I'll summon you to the examination room immediately. In the meantime, please tap on my door when a patient arrives."

"Yes, Doctor."

When the door to his office closed, she hung her cloak on a hook and tied her apron over her dress. She'd be ready when she was needed.

Rosemary settled behind the desk, realizing he'd positioned her against a windowless wall. A lamp hung from the center of the ceiling. The flame threw light in a broad circle but left her work area in shadow.

After studying the area, she decided to move the desk under the rear window and place the sofa against the wall. She rose and shoved against its horsehair-upholstered back. The ball feet screeched across the floorboards as the couch traveled to the center of the room. Leaving it there, she pushed up her sleeves and steered the desk toward the window.

The door to Dr. Stewart's office flew open. "What are you doing?" His eyes widened when he saw the disarray in the waiting area.

She gestured toward the window. "If I'm to work with figures, that light is far better."

"Miss Saxon . . ." He shook his head. "You haven't been here for half an hour, and you're assuming control. I wanted you against the side wall so you could greet patients when they entered."

"This is a small room. No one is going to sneak past me." She hoped her amusement wasn't noticeable.

Apparently she didn't succeed, because he shot a sharp glance in her direction. "Anything else you want changed while I'm here?" His voice carried an edge of sarcasm.

"No."

In moments the doctor had moved the sofa from the room's center to the wall opposite his door. After arranging her desk under the window, he gave a mock bow. "I trust this is to your liking. Now if you'll excuse me, I do have more important things to attend to."

Her hospital training rescued her. "Thank you, Doctor," she said, keeping her tone respectful.

"You're welcome." A glint of humor flashed in his eyes before he turned away.

On Thursday, near the end of Rosemary's first week as Dr. Stewart's nurse, the entry door opened and a middle-aged man entered the reception area, holding his right arm close to his body. His hand was bound in cloth strips.

She jumped from her chair and hurried toward him. "My goodness. What happened?"

"Burned myself. You ain't the doc, are you?"

"No. I'm his nurse." A sense of pride swept through her as she said the words. She *was* a nurse, and a good one. Her service during the war had proven the fact. "Please have a seat. Dr. Stewart will be with you in a moment." She tapped on the door to his office before returning to her desk.

He chuckled. "Figured you was too pretty to be named Elijah."

"I'm Miss Saxon." She opened the receipt book to a new page. "May I have your name?"

"Eldridge. We're new here." He raised his bandaged hand. "I was trying to burn some brush behind the house. Shouldn't of threw kerosene on it."

"If you can find comfrey growing around, make a poultice of the root for your burn. It will help with healing."

Dr. Stewart stood in the doorway of the examination room. He fixed her with a stern gaze. "If you're quite through dispensing medical advice, I'll see the patient now."

Mr. Eldridge rose. "She wasn't doing no harm, Doc. My granny used comfrey. Worked good." He preceded the doctor into the room.

Toward the end of the afternoon, Rosemary tidied her desk and prepared to leave. If she hurried, she'd have time to stop at West & Riley's for a few groceries before dark. She suppressed a groan when the exterior door opened. A young woman stood silhouetted on the threshold.

As soon as the caller stepped inside, Rosemary recognized her. "Cassie Haddon. It's been weeks." Rosemary hurried across the room and seized Cassie's hands.

"I'm so glad I found you. I went to the mercantile and Faith said you were employed here." Her gaze took in Rosemary's plain dress and severe hairstyle. "As a nurse?" Her voice spiked higher.

"Yes. Whenever possible. Most of the time I'm a clerk." She tried to keep from sounding offended at her friend's incredulous tone. "Please sit and tell me what brings you all the way across town."

"Mother sent me on an errand." She twisted her hands together. "I don't have much time. My stepfather will expect me at the mercantile by half past five. I don't dare keep him waiting." Her green eyes misted, reflecting the color of the emerald ribbons on her bonnet. "Mother needs more of that tonic you prepared for her. Living with Mr. Bingham is . . . difficult."

"I can have some ready for you tomorrow."

Cassie shook her head. "At best, it will be next week before I can ask to come to town again."

"Then I'll bring it with me on Monday." She patted her friend's hand. "Suggest to your mother that she take long walks. Fresh air—"

"Are you treating my patients again, Miss Saxon?" The doctor stepped into the reception area.

Rosemary jumped to her feet. "Miss Haddon is a friend of mine, Doctor. This is a social call." She sucked in her lower lip. He had the most irritating habit of popping out of his office at awkward moments.

Ignoring her, he nodded in Cassie's direction. "Is your mother in need of medical attention? If necessary, I'll pay a visit to your home."

Cassie paled and scrambled for the door. "No. She's fine." She cast an anxious look at Rosemary. "I'll be here Monday." She whipped through the door in a whirl of green plaid taffeta.

Dr. Stewart stared after her, then ambled to the sofa and

settled against the cushioned back. He waved a hand at Rosemary. "I need to get to know folks here. Sit a moment and tell me what that was all about." In shirtsleeves, with his hair rumpled, he looked far less imposing than he had when she first called at his office.

"I met Miss Haddon and her mother last summer. They were passengers on a train that derailed. They stayed with me and my brother while the tracks were repaired." She leaned forward in her chair, caught by the interest in his dark eyes. "After they returned to St. Louis, I thought I'd seen the last of them, but by a strange coincidence, this past July Miss Haddon's mother married Elmer Bingham, a local farmer, so here they are again."

"From Miss Haddon's demeanor, it would appear all is not well?"

She stared at her hands, hesitant to gossip. "The Binghams' courtship was quite brief and their sudden marriage took place in St. Louis. From what Miss Haddon has said, she and her mother were not exactly welcomed by Mr. Bingham's servant when they arrived here. The man treats them as interlopers. As a result, Mrs. Bingham apparently suffers with nervous spells from time to time."

He stretched his legs out, crossing them at the ankles. His black boots were scuffed and well-worn. "So you're prescribing long walks? Then why is Miss Haddon coming back on Monday?" The tone of his voice was casual, interested.

"I prepared a tincture of valerian root for her in the past. My friend reports it had a calming effect on her mother."

His eyebrows shot up. "You can't use my practice as a dispensary for your home remedies. What if someone sickened from their use?"

"I've never sickened anybody." She stalked to the center of the room and faced him, hands on hips. "If it'll put your mind at ease, I'll tell my friends to come to my house and not endanger your precious practice." Rosemary swept her cloak from its hook on the wall and flung it over her shoulders. "It's past five. I'll see you tomorrow morning."

He stood, towering over her. Up close, she noticed gray strands woven through his hair. The war had taken a toll on the young doctor she remembered. His dark eyes smoldered at her.

"Your friends may visit here at any time. Just leave your potions at home."

4

uming, Rosemary marched the two blocks from Dr. Stewart's office to West & Riley's. Darkening clouds overhead mirrored her stormy thoughts. She never should have mentioned the tincture. For the moment, she'd forgotten his position and considered him a friend. She wouldn't make that mistake again.

When she entered the grocery, the aroma of roasting meat coming from the restaurant side of the building made her mouth water. As soon as she had the funds, she'd visit a butcher for a piece of beef chuck. For now, she'd make do with pea soup and cornbread.

Mr. West called to her from behind a counter. "Evening, Miss Saxon. Have you got a list for me?"

"Not today. I'll be back for a larger order when Curt brings me in the buggy." She didn't say that day would come after she'd paid the rent and knew how much money she had left. "For now I need salt, two pounds of cornmeal, and two pounds of dried peas."

He filled bags from barrels next to the counter, weighed them, then placed a box of salt next to the bags. "Hang on a minute—got something in the kitchen for your dog." His black moustache lifted when he grinned. "Be right back." When he returned, he gave her a lumpy package wrapped in paper and tied with string.

"Thank you." From the shape, she knew it was a bone. "Bodie will appreciate this." She added it to the purchases in her carryall, then handed him the coins to pay for her order.

Mr. West leaned against the counter. "Don't see you much these days. Heard you had a job with the new doc. Next thing we know, you ladies are going to be running the town." He chuckled.

"That day's a long way off, I'm afraid. First we have to get you gentlemen over the idea that women shouldn't leave the home."

After Miss Saxon's angry departure, Elijah Stewart stepped into his private office, shaking his head. He'd never met a woman so quick to take offense. She reminded him of a nurse who'd arrived at the Barracks soon after the war started. The other physicians warned him to mind his manners with her. No orders without a "please." No task performed without a "thank you." He'd been sent to a battlefield hospital shortly after her arrival, so had been spared much contact. He smiled at the memory. She'd probably married a wounded soldier and had several children by now.

A gust of cold air blew into the room. He poked his head into the reception area and saw a tall man wearing a lawman's badge pinned to his coat. "Hope you don't mind seeing patients after hours. Heard you got Miss Saxon working for you and figured she'd be gone by now." He extended his hand. "Thaddeus Cooper. I'm the sheriff here." His firm grip matched his steely expression.

Curious, Elijah studied the thin-faced man. "Excluding Augustus Greeley, you're the first person I've heard speak unfavorably about Miss Saxon. What do you have against her?"

The sheriff tugged at a corner of his drooping moustache. "It's the other way around. She can barely tolerate me."

"So a big fellow like you goes around avoiding a slip of a woman?"

"It's a long story, and I didn't come in to jaw. Need you to look at the back of my neck. Got a real tender spot."

Once Sheriff Cooper sat on the examination table and removed his shirt, Elijah probed an angry boil below his hairline. "This'll have to be lanced to get the poison out. Might hurt a bit."

"Hurts now. Get on with it."

"Stretch out on your stomach. This'll take a few minutes." He draped a sheet over the sheriff's shoulders, then opened a drawer in a side table containing surgical instruments and removed a scalpel. A pitcher and basin sat near jars of remedies and clean bandages.

The sheriff sucked in a breath when the scalpel penetrated the angry flesh.

An ooze of blood and pus welled from the incision. "Once this is cleaned out, I'll apply a bandage. You'll want to change the dressing every day. There's a better chance of healing if you keep this clean." He poured water into the basin and swabbed the cavity with a piece of cotton toweling.

"How much longer are you gonna take?" Sheriff Cooper gripped the edge of the table, his knuckles white.

"Not long." He dropped the soiled rag into a pail for Miss Saxon to wash. After bandaging the wound, he removed the sheet. "You can get up now. We're finished."

"Thanks, Doc." The sheriff buttoned his shirt and then flexed his shoulders. "Feels better already." He shoved his thumbs in his front pockets. "You usually go home for supper? Got a wife waiting?"

"No, and no. I've been eating at that restaurant attached to the grocery store—West & Riley's. They serve a fair meal."

"Want company? I got no wife waiting either. Not yet, anyway."

When the two men reached the corner of King's Highway, they nearly collided with Miss Saxon. Elijah whipped off his hat. "I didn't expect to see you out at this hour. It's growing dark. May I escort you home?"

She pointed to the picket fence in the middle of the block. "Thank you. I'm only two doors away." She gave him one of her rare smiles, then her gaze slid to the sheriff, and her smile disappeared. "I won't keep you gentlemen. I'm sure you have important things to do." Swinging her carryall, she strode down the board sidewalk.

Sheriff Cooper turned to cross the street, but Elijah lifted a hand, signaling him to wait. He watched until Miss Saxon entered her house. "She lives by herself," he said. "Just making sure she got inside safely."

"I wouldn't worry overmuch about that one. Her and that sister-in-law of hers could move a mountain if they put their minds to it."

Elijah smiled to himself, recalling her determination to move the heavy sofa in his office. "Could be. But my mother taught me to look after womenfolk—even headstrong ones."

Bodie frisked around Rosemary's feet as she walked through the house. "Do you smell what I brought you?" She plunked her bag on the kitchen tabletop and rubbed his ears. "First you need to go outside, then supper." After unlocking the back door, she shooed him off the porch.

While he sniffed around the makeshift greenhouse Curt had built for her, Rosemary reentered the kitchen, leaving the door open a crack so the dog could come back inside. She stored her purchases in the pantry, then unwrapped the bone. Tears blurred her vision when she saw the generous amount of meat clinging to the shank. Enough for a hearty soup.

Judging from their heft, Mr. West had given her more than two pounds each of cornmeal and peas as well. Her cheeks burned with embarrassment in spite of her gratitude for his kindness. There was no denying he'd seen through her excuses for not making larger purchases.

She added wood to the coals in the firebox and scooped a dollop of lard into a deep skillet to melt. After cutting the meat into chunks, she chopped an onion, tossing the raw ingredients into the heated grease. Savory steam rose to perfume the room.

Bodie trotted inside and butted his head against her leg. When she paid no attention, he whined.

She closed and locked the door. "Ready?"

Rosemary dropped what was left of Mr. West's gift under his nose. Wagging his tail, he snatched the bone and retreated behind the stove. She smiled at his delight, then turned back to the stove to add water, thyme, and a scoop of barley to the browned mixture.

While the soup simmered, she took a pen and a sheet of paper from a drawer. A polite thank-you to Mr. West was in order, but she needed to discourage him from thinking of her as impoverished.

"This is for you," Rosemary said to Mr. West, handing him the note she'd written.

He smiled at her, his teeth white against his darker skin.

"You're early this morning. Did you forget something yesterday?"

"No. I wanted to thank you properly for your generosity."

"It was nothing." He unfolded the note and read it aloud. "'Dear Mr. West. Many thanks for the gift of food.'" He flattened his "A's" and dropped the "R" at the end of words, reflecting his eastern roots. Just where in the east, she wasn't sure. "'I enjoyed a fine meal, and so did Bodie. However, please don't consider me as needy. I'm well able to take care of myself, and shall continue to do so. Most sincerely, Rosemary Saxon.'"

He lowered the paper, his face crinkling into a smile that lit his coffee-brown eyes. "A correction, if you don't mind."

Surprised, she nodded.

"You've been shopping here for months. Call me Jacob. Mr. West makes me think of my father."

She ran her eyes over his wavy black hair, his unlined face, and down his broad-shouldered frame. Definitely not an old man. Perhaps a year or two older than Dr. Stewart, no more.

"Jacob it is." She smiled. "I'm Rosemary."

"*Miss* Rosemary." He cleared his throat. "Sharing isn't the same as charity. Next time I have extra, hope you won't object to taking it off my hands. You'd be doing me a favor."

She dropped her gaze, wishing she didn't find it so difficult to accept kindness. "All right. Under those conditions. Thank you."

When Rosemary entered Dr. Stewart's office a few minutes later, a fire had been lit in the stove and the room was warm. Both interior doors were closed, and the sound of voices emanated from the examination room. She hurried to her desk. The receipt book lay open to a new page, with a man's name written on the first line. She knew she'd allowed plenty of time to visit the grocery before arriving at her job. The doctor must have started his day earlier than half past eight.

She thought of Mr. West's reaction to her note. To her shame, she'd been guilty of thinking of him simply as the grocer. Today he'd become a person. Jacob.

The outside door opened, admitting a woman wearing an indigo print skirt topped by a flared rusty red jacket. "I . . . I need to see the doctor." Her thin lips were pale to the point of whiteness. Darkened circles rimmed her eyes.

Rosemary dashed to her side, afraid she would faint. "Please have a seat. Dr. Stewart is with another patient at the moment." She guided her to the sofa, then tapped on the doctor's door and returned to her desk.

Flipping to a new page in the receipt book, she asked, "May I know your name?"

"Miss Jolene Graves." Her voice trembled. "I've never been to a doctor before. Girls in town told me this one's nicer than the old one—Dr. Greeley. Is he?"

"Definitely." She smiled reassurance, recalling the town's senior practitioner's opinionated personality.

After several silent minutes, Dr. Stewart emerged and escorted his patient to the exit, then turned and nodded at Rosemary. "Please show this young lady into the examination room."

Jolene blanched.

"Don't worry, ma'am. My nurse will stay with you." He stepped to the open door and stood to one side. A lamp glowed on the side wall, casting yellow light over the long table under a curtained window.

Rosemary took Jolene's arm and led her to one of two chairs inside. Stepping back, she waited under a second window while Dr. Stewart closed the door behind them.

"This is Miss Graves, Doctor," Rosemary said.

He straightened his black coat. "What can I do for you, miss?"

"I've been terrible sick. Can't keep nothing down. Took everything I've got to get dressed and come here today." She sucked in a deep breath and held it for a moment. "I can't hardly do my work at Miss Lytle's Millinery—can't do nothing."

Rosemary stifled the impulse to ask Miss Graves if she'd tried raspberry leaf tea.

Dr. Stewart leaned toward the patient. "I need to take your pulse. Would you please remove your gloves?" When she complied, he lifted her wrist and rested two fingers at the base of her thumb, his other hand holding his watch. After a minute, he closed the timepiece. "A little rapid, but nothing abnormal."

He palpated the glands in her neck. "No swelling." Stepping back, he studied her face.

"How long have you been ill?"

"A few weeks."

"Any other symptoms?"

"No . . . well, I'm tired, but that's because I'm sick."

He leaned against the table. "Is there any possibility you might be expecting a child?"

Her face grew whiter, then flushed scarlet. "Yes," she said, her voice nearly inaudible. "I was hoping you'd say it was something else."

"A baby's certainly better than a disease. I believe the druggist carries Hoofmann's German Bitters. That should help with your nausea. Tell him I sent you." Compassion softened his features. "You'll need to tell the father."

"He's gone. Went north looking for work. I don't know where."

"Your parents, then."

"I dassn't. They'd kill me." Tears rolled over her cheeks.

"I doubt that, Miss Graves," Dr. Stewart said in a gentle voice. "I suggest you talk to them." He turned to Rosemary. "There'll be no charge for this visit. You may see the patient out." He entered his private office and closed the connecting door behind him.

Jolene covered her face with her hands. "What am I going to do?" She choked the words through her sobs.

Rosemary put an arm around the girl's shoulders. "Come with me. I have some ginger water in my carryall. It might help settle your stomach." She kept her voice low, mindful of the doctor's prohibition against her "potions."

She settled Jolene on the sofa and poured ginger water into a cup. "Sip this slowly," she said, then perched next to her. "You can't hide this from your parents."

"Yes, I can."

"They're sure to notice as time passes."

"I don't live with them. I share a room in town with two other girls." Fresh tears slid from her eyes. "But I can't work. I can't pay my part of the rent."

Rosemary threw a glance at Dr. Stewart's closed door. "I can show you how to brew a tea that may help you. That way you won't have to spend money on patent medicine. Can you come to my house this evening, say around half past five?"

Jolene's woebegone features brightened. "Oh, thank you, miss. I know I could think better what to do if I wasn't so sick all the time."

Her heart constricted at the hope in the girl's eyes. Helping her with the nausea would be simple compared to what faced Jolene in the months ahead.

5

*R*osemary bustled around the kitchen, building up the fire, heating water in a kettle, all the while trotting back and forth to the sitting room to keep an eye on the clock. She'd given Jolene clear directions to her house. It was the only one on this block to have a four-foot-high picket fence surrounding the yard, so it shouldn't be difficult to find. As the minutes ticked toward six, she went to the front window and peered along the deserted boardwalk. Perhaps the girl had second thoughts about trusting her.

Water sputtered on the stovetop, drawing her back to the kitchen. She slid the kettle to one side. If Jolene didn't arrive in the next few minutes, she'd return the jar of dried raspberry leaves to the pantry and fetch the remainder of last night's soup from the springhouse.

In the quiet, she heard Bodie gnawing on the bone Jacob had given him. Every now and then his tail thumped the floor. When a knock sounded, he looked up and gave a halfhearted "woof."

"Some watchdog you are. Seduced by a bone." She strode to the entryway and opened the door. "Jolene. I was afraid you weren't coming."

41

The young woman stepped inside, then peeked over her shoulder. "Someone was standing by your gate watching the house. He left when he saw me on the sidewalk." She spoke in a shaky whisper.

Fear prickled the hair on Rosemary's arms. She leaned past Jolene and surveyed the empty street, then slammed the door. "What did he look like?" Her pulse hammered in her throat. The note. Footprints. Now this.

"Hard to tell, miss. I only saw the side of his face under his hat. Might've been old—he walked kind of bent."

Rosemary sucked in a deep breath. Her worries weren't Jolene's problems. "Perhaps it was a coincidence." She moved toward the kitchen. "Maybe he merely paused to rest for a moment."

"Maybe." Doubt in her voice, Jolene followed her.

When they entered the warm room, Rosemary drew a chair away from the table. "Please sit. I'm going to show you how to brew raspberry leaf tea. I'm quite sure it will help settle your stomach."

"I can't believe you'd do this for me. You're an angel straight from God."

"No. I'm a nurse. It's a blessing for me to be able to help you."

Jolene clasped her hands under her chin. "I've been praying. You're the answer to my prayers, and that's the end of it."

Rosemary patted the girl's shoulder, then placed the jar of dried leaves on the table next to a teapot. While she measured, she explained how much to use and how long to steep the tea. "Be sure to drink it warm. A little honey won't hurt if you like sweetness." She set the lid on the pot. "When it's ready, you can try a cup."

Bodie padded out from behind the stove and laid his chin on Jolene's lap. Her eyes widened. "He looks like the dog we have at home." She put a tentative hand on his head, rubbing his ear with her thumb.

"Where is home?" Rosemary asked, her voice soft. She hoped she didn't sound prying.

Jolene pressed back in her chair. Dark circles around her eyes accented her gaunt features. "Between here and Hartfield. My folks have a farm. They wanted me to stay and work the fields along with my brothers, but I had hopes for better things. I came here and found me a job helping make hats." She dropped her gaze to the top of Bodie's head. "I should've stayed home. None of this would have happened."

Rosemary thought of the decisions she'd made that brought her to the place where she found herself today. If she hadn't volunteered as a nurse for the Union, her parents might acknowledge her existence. She'd probably still be living in St. Louis. Instead, here she was struggling for independence in Noble Springs.

She dusted her hands together. "No sense playing what-might-have-been. Let's see what we can do about your situation today."

"The doctor was my last hope. Anything would be better than the fix I'm in." She turned anxious eyes on Rosemary. "I do piecework for Miss Lytle, but when I'm too sick I don't earn anything. The girls I live with said they want me to move out so they can find someone else."

Rosemary poured the tea and pushed the cup toward Jolene. "Try this. If it helps as much as I think it will, you could be able to return to your sewing tomorrow. Surely the other girls will give you more time if they see you can do your job."

"They might." She sipped the tea, made a face, and reached for the jar of honey next to the teapot.

"Start your day with this tea, then try some dry toast." She studied the girl's peaked face, wishing she could do more to help.

Cassie slipped into Dr. Stewart's office midmorning the following Monday. She hastened to Rosemary's desk, her taffeta skirt rustling. "Mother's at the mercantile. She sent me over for her tonic. You said you'd have it today."

"I do." After casting an anxious glance at the doctor's closed door, Rosemary reached into her carryall and removed the valerian tincture. She thrust the paper-wrapped vial into Cassie's hands. "After this, you'll have to come to my house, either in the evening or on the weekend. Dr. Stewart doesn't want—"

The door to his private office opened. "Miss Haddon, isn't it? Paying another social call?" His gaze shifted to the package in her hand.

Rosemary closed her eyes, wishing Cassie would tuck the tincture out of sight.

Cassie looked confused. "You don't want people to come to see Miss Saxon? I do apologize. I had no idea."

He cocked his head in her direction. "Miss Saxon is free to visit with callers anytime she's not occupied with her duties. However, keep in mind only one of us is a physician, and it's not Miss Saxon."

Rosemary folded her arms across her chest. "I've had no opportunity to let my friend know that you're concerned about my herbal remedies." She turned to Cassie. "The doctor is afraid I'll poison somebody and he'll be blamed."

"Miss Saxon. I didn't say that." Dr. Stewart's face reddened. "Don't put words in my mouth."

"Well, words to that effect." She turned her back on him

and faced a wide-eyed Cassie. "After this, can you visit me at home?"

"Yes. Of course. Soon, I hope." She inched toward the door. "Good day, Doctor."

He tugged at the hem of his coat. "Good day to you."

Elijah watched through the window as Miss Haddon hurried west along the street. What must she think of him? Squabbling with the nurse as though they were children. He should have known better than to hire the woman. It wasn't as if her prickly nature came as a surprise.

Miss Saxon spoke from behind her desk. "I promised I'd have that tincture ready for her. I'm sorry you were upset. She won't bother you again."

He flopped on the sofa and gave her a hard look. "She's not the one who's upsetting me. You are. I'm trying to build a practice in this town and I can't have people thinking I'm unsociable."

"Well, you certainly didn't sound sociable toward Miss Haddon." Two spots of red glowed on her cheeks. Her round hazel eyes sparked.

He gripped his thighs, fighting for calm. All his life he'd been accused of being too easygoing. This woman could raise his hackles with a single sentence. "I don't want you prescribing for my patients. Otherwise, I don't care if half the town troops in here to call on you."

"That's not likely to happen," she said. "I can count on my fingers the number of people who want to associate with me." She sounded wistful.

The glimpse at her vulnerability touched him. He softened his voice. "I assumed you had many childhood friends here in Noble Springs."

"No. I came here from St. Louis a year ago in March to join my brother. He passed through the area while he was in the Army and thought this would be a good place to settle." A wry smile lifted a corner of her mouth. "Once word got around that I'd been a nurse, many of the proper women in town believed my morals had to be in question. I'm hoping to disabuse them."

"Most nurses returned to their families after the war. Why didn't you?"

Her lips thinned. "I had no home to return to." Her expression told him not to ask any more questions.

He stood, gazing at her with new respect. If her home had been destroyed, small wonder she needed to survive on her own. A question pricked at the back of his mind. No major battles had been fought in St. Louis—what happened to her family?

Bodie greeted Rosemary with licks and wiggles when she arrived home that evening. She locked the front door behind her, then sank to her knees and hugged his soft fur. "I missed you too."

Dr. Stewart's question had pricked a scab over the wound that opened during her conversation with Jolene. A wound she hoped had healed. The war had ended, but not for her mother. Amanda Saxon's Carolina roots influenced her every action, and when her brother was killed at Gettysburg, she'd turned on Curt and Rosemary as though their Union affiliations made them personally responsible. The never-ending echo of her parents' door slamming behind her rang in Rosemary's ears.

Her eyes stung with unshed tears as she rose to her feet. If only there were some way . . . Rosemary shook her head. She'd tried more than once, only to be rebuffed. She had Curt, and now Faith. The three of them would form their own family.

The dog nosed her hand.

"You need to go outside, Bodie. You've been in since noontime."

He wagged his tail and ran to the back door. Smiling at his anticipation, she unlocked the door and followed him down the steps into her small yard. Rain clouds scudded overhead, but the sun pushed through from the horizon, propelling shadow arrows from the picket fence across the winter-stunted grass.

Rosemary strolled to the door of her greenhouse and slipped inside. An earthy fragrance rose from terra-cotta pots lined on shelves along three interior walls. In the southwestern corner, a large pot held her sprawling mint plant. Herb and flower sprouts nodded from their soil beds on two narrow tables in the center of the space. Another few weeks and she'd be able to transplant most of the starts outside.

Through the wavy glass panes spaced along the sides of the wooden structure, she saw Bodie sniffing along the gravel path that led to the front of the house. Suddenly his body stiffened. He growled. Taking one slow step after another, he stalked forward along the walkway.

Her hand at her throat, Rosemary grabbed a shovel and stepped out of the greenhouse. If the person who'd left the message on her porch thought he was going to scare her, he had a surprise coming. She raised the shovel and held it at her shoulder like a club.

Bodie disappeared around the corner.

She listened but heard no footsteps on the gravel. The dog must have frightened away whoever it was, unless he was biding his time until she appeared. Rosemary marched to the front of the house, her grip tight on the handle.

"Miss Rosemary? What are you doing?" Jolene stood inside the gate. Bodie leaned against her leg, his feathery tail waving.

Rosemary lowered her makeshift weapon, feeling foolish. "When Bodie growled, I thought—well, never mind. Please, follow me. We'll have to go in the back way. The front door is locked." She hoped the fading light concealed her flushed face. After replacing the shovel in the greenhouse, she led the way into the kitchen.

"I hope you don't mind me coming unexpected." Jolene's anxious eyes sought hers. Her pale face looked thinner than it had the previous week. She swayed and caught herself on the edge of the table.

Alarmed, Rosemary slid a chair behind her. "Of course I don't mind." She sat, facing her visitor. "It doesn't look like you're feeling any better. Have you been drinking the tea?"

"Some. It doesn't help, miss. I'm still sick most of the time. I only worked one day last week." She leaned forward. "Do you have anything else I could try?"

"Sadly, no. I wish I did."

Jolene wilted. "Guess that's it, then. My roommates told me I couldn't live there without paying. Miss Lytle gave me the name of a place in Ohio that takes girls like me." She shook her head. "I don't even have enough money to pay for a shared room. How will I get to Ohio?"

"I don't know about Ohio, but for now you can stay with me. I have an extra bedroom upstairs." The words escaped her lips before she had time to think.

"Oh, miss, I couldn't."

"Of course you could." Rosemary waved her hand toward the sitting room. "It's lonely here since my brother married. I'd appreciate the company." She ignored the voice in her head that screamed, "What are you doing? You can barely feed yourself!"

Tears welled up under Jolene's lashes. "I don't know what to say." She pushed to her feet. "I'll go get my things."

Rosemary placed a steadying hand on the girl's arm. "Not tonight. You need rest. Tomorrow I'll ask my brother to help you." She bit her lip, wondering what Curt's reaction would be to her decision. She had the uncomfortable feeling he wouldn't be happy.

6

The following day, Rosemary left Dr. Stewart's office at noon and hurried to Lindberg's Mercantile. Faith greeted her with a hug.

"I'm so glad to see you. Mornings are lonely without you and Bodie to keep me company."

"We still have Sundays at church and after, but I agree. It's not the same." Rosemary walked to the woodstove and held her hands toward the warmth.

Faith glanced out the window before joining her. "Where's Bodie?"

"He's staying home with . . . my guest. That's why I came." She swallowed. "Would you please ask Curt to stop by Dr. Stewart's office this afternoon? I kind of promised he'd help her move her things."

Faith settled into one of the chairs beside the stove and patted the other one for Rosemary. "I'll ask him when he gets here after school. Now, are you going to tell me what this is about?"

"A girl came to see Dr. Stewart last week, complaining of nausea." She smiled to herself, remembering his kindness to Jolene. "After he checked her for symptoms and found nothing amiss, he asked her if she might be with child."

Faith raised a questioning eyebrow.

Rosemary nodded affirmation. After explaining Jolene's circumstances, she said, "I invited her to stay with me." She held up a hand. "Before you say anything, I know it will be difficult. But I couldn't just stand by. What if she's wrong about her mother and father? They might miss her and want her home."

"And if they don't?" Faith's sympathetic gaze rested on her. "You of all people should know that parents can be . . . unreasonable. Yours didn't attend our wedding when I married Curt."

"We never should have sent the letter." Sorrow rolled through her at the memory of Faith's hurt and Curt's anger when her parents ignored their invitation.

"Their lack of response wasn't your fault."

"I should've known better." She shook her head to dispel regrets. "But this is different. I won't know what Jolene's family is like unless I take a chance and talk to them." She stood, eyeing the clock on the wall behind the cash drawer. "It's time to get back."

Faith slid an arm around her waist. "You wouldn't be Rosemary if you didn't care about people. Just don't get hurt."

As Rosemary covered the block and a half between the mercantile and the doctor's office, Faith's parting words spun through her mind. Her friend worried too much. She had no intention of putting herself in a situation where she could be hurt.

When she turned onto Commerce Street, she noticed Dr. Stewart bundled in an overcoat, standing beside his buggy. A man on horseback waited next to the hitching rail.

Dr. Stewart strode toward her. "Mr. Haggerty needs us." He nodded toward the rider.

"His wife's time has come and she's asking for a doctor."

Rosemary thought of Curt and Jolene, both expecting to see her in a few hours. She wished she had some way to let them know she'd likely be gone all afternoon and possibly longer. The waiting man's horse pawed the ground. From the looks of Mr. Haggerty, if he were standing on the street he'd be pawing the ground too. She sent him a reassuring smile.

"I'll get my things." She dashed into the office and retrieved her carryall, then hurried outside.

Dr. Stewart helped her into the buggy. They took off at a trot after Mr. Haggerty, following him south across the railroad tracks and out of town. She shivered as cool air penetrated her shawl.

The doctor reached behind him, lifting a folded blanket from the rear seat. "Put this over you."

"Thank you." Grateful for the extra layer, she settled the blanket over her shoulders and tucked her arms underneath. She'd been waiting for an opportunity to show Dr. Stewart her skills as a nurse. If only the moment had arrived on a different day. She hoped Curt wouldn't be upset when he arrived at the office and found the "Doctor is Out" card hanging on the door.

Dr. Stewart held the reins in both hands while urging the horse at a fast clip along the country road. Bare trees on hillsides stretched finger-like branches toward the cloudy sky.

He turned his head toward her, face creased in a smile. "Haggerty insisted I bring you along. His wife's never had a doctor at a birthing before, so she's skittish about a man helping her. Don't know what I'd have done if it was the middle of the night."

"I'll assist in every way possible." She kept her tone respectful, but inside she wanted to whoop with joy. Maybe now he'd see her as more than someone to wash bandages and keep records. She ignored the inner voice that reminded her she'd never assisted at a birth.

Ahead of them, Mr. Haggerty rounded a bend in the road, then galloped up a rutted track toward a small frame house perched atop a rise. As they rolled past a run-down farm to follow him along the track, Rosemary recognized the property as belonging to Mr. Bingham, Cassie's stepfather.

For a moment, she gazed over her shoulder at the two men sitting in the shade of the vine-draped porch. No wonder the place looked neglected. Mr. Bingham and his manservant should be out caring for the property instead of lolling about in rocking chairs.

She made a "tsk" sound with her tongue. "My friend Miss Haddon lives there."

"A strange setting for such a well-turned-out young lady."

"I agree."

The farm passed out of sight behind a grove of trees. When the doctor stopped his buggy in front of the frame house, Mr. Haggerty swung off his mount and took the reins from his hands. "Just go on in. I'll take care of your horse."

Red gingham curtains hung over the front window in the tidy room. A kettle steamed on the stovetop. Two young girls sat side by side on a bench next to a table, shoulders touching. The older one appeared to be around four years old. Their wide blue eyes fixed on Rosemary. "Did you come to make Mama well?"

"I'll help the doctor make her well." She smoothed the little girl's hair. "Why don't you go see if your papa needs you?"

They scrambled out of the room, their faded calico dresses fluttering at the backs of their stocking-covered legs.

A groan issued from behind a curtain pulled over a doorway. "In here." The woman's voice sounded more like a gasp than speech.

Dr. Stewart gestured for Rosemary to precede him. When she stepped into the room, a sweating blonde woman gave her a tremulous smile and held out a hand. "Thank the Lord. I've been so afraid. Never had this much . . ." She closed her eyes and moaned. "Baby's been coming for hours."

Rosemary took her hand. "Dr. Stewart knows what to do. Don't worry." She hoped she sounded calmer than she felt.

He turned to Mrs. Haggerty. "I need to examine you. Miss Saxon will be right here helping me."

Mrs. Haggerty clutched Rosemary's hand with a bone-bending grip. "Go on, Doctor. Long's I've got someone to hold on to, I'm ready."

Rosemary cradled the squalling baby boy next to a basin of warm water and stroked his pink body clean with a square of toweling. A lighted lamp hanging from a rafter burnished the blond fuzz covering the top of his head. "You're a handsome one," she whispered, grateful the birth had gone well. Her fears that she wouldn't know what to do had evaporated while she followed Dr. Stewart's calm instructions.

After tucking the infant into a soft flannel gown, she wrapped him snugly in a blanket and cuddled him close to her chest. "Let's go back to your mama."

She placed Mrs. Haggerty's new son in her arms and stepped away from the bed. A lamp glowed on a bureau across the room. Dr. Stewart dropped his forceps into a leather satchel, then unrolled his sleeves and fastened the cuffs at his wrists.

"You need to rest for a few days, Mrs. Haggerty. Is there a neighbor who could look after you?"

She settled her newborn son at her breast. "No. There's two ladies at Mr. Bingham's now, but they're about as useless as can be. Swan around doing fancy work and reading books. That old man who looks after the place isn't likely to be much help, either." She shifted her shoulders. "I'll be fine. My husband can cook a fair bit. You tell him to come in now, would you?"

Rosemary followed Dr. Stewart as he strode to the door and swung it open, allowing lamplight to flow onto the porch. The two little girls sat on the top step, bundled into coats against the chill of the evening. Mr. Haggerty sat in a rocking chair behind his daughters.

He sprang to his feet when he saw Dr. Stewart. "Is Carlene all right?"

"She's doing well. You have a healthy son."

"I'm grateful to you, Doc, and you too, Mrs. Stewart."

Rosemary hoped the dim light hid her embarrassment. "Dr. Stewart and I are not—"

"Miss Saxon and I are not married." The doctor cleared his throat. "Miss Saxon is a nurse, employed in my practice."

Mr. Haggerty stared at the two of them. "Well, if that don't beat all. I heard about you, miss, but never figured I'd end up with you in my house. No one told me you worked for the new doc. When he said he was waiting for his nurse, I thought he meant—"

"Papa?" One of the little girls tugged at his trouser leg. "Can we see Mama now?"

"Go on in. I'll be there directly."

They scurried through the door. When they were out of sight, he fumbled in his pocket and brought out a small leather purse. "Here's ten dollars." He handed two gold coins to Dr. Stewart. "Don't have to pay extra for the . . . nurse, do I?"

"Same fee. I'll compensate Miss Saxon."

Mr. Haggerty shook the doctor's hand, tipped a nod at

Rosemary, then dashed inside. As soon as he left, Dr. Stewart took Rosemary's arm and helped her into the buggy. "I apologize for the lateness of the hour. I'll take you straight home."

"Thank you." She held her hands in front of her face and blew on her fingers to warm them. For the first time in several hours, she thought of her brother. By now, Curt would have gone home. She hoped he'd stop by in the morning so she could explain her absence.

While the doctor lit the carriage lamp, she wrapped the blanket around her shoulders, praying none of the local gossips would notice her late arrival.

The buggy bounced when he climbed inside and settled his weight on the seat. Yellow light from the lamp splashed the road and a half moon bowled shadows across the track. After guiding the horse down the rutted hillside, the doctor relaxed against the back of the seat.

"You've never assisted at a birth before, have you?" He tilted his head toward her when he asked the question. His tone was conversational.

Rosemary couldn't see his features well enough to determine whether or not he was upset. "This is the first time. That particular issue didn't arise while I was at Jefferson Barracks." Amusement filled her voice.

He snorted a laugh. "I imagine not. Not your everyday soldier's complaint."

As much as she appreciated his good-humored response, she regretted making light of a serious question. "Please forgive my flippancy. You had a reason for asking. Did I do something wrong?" She held her breath.

"On the contrary. You followed instructions perfectly. I'm grateful for your assistance."

Dr. Stewart seldom handed out compliments. Relieved, she murmured, "Thank you."

As they traveled the distance to town, Rosemary peeked at the doctor's profile from time to time. The moonlight erased the tired lines that so often crouched at the corners of his eyes. For the moment the young physician she remembered rode beside her.

A scene from a twenty-bed ward at Jefferson Barracks entered her mind. The night had been late, like this one. She'd leaned over one side of a bed holding a towel while Dr. Stewart administered laudanum to a soldier whose coughing threatened to reopen the stitches in his side. The expression on the doctor's face showed his own agony at the man's suffering. She'd observed that same expression when he assisted Mrs. Haggerty through the birth of her son.

"This isn't the first time we've treated a patient late at night," she said, then covered her mouth. Perhaps he wouldn't welcome the reminder. Her brother spoke little of his wartime experiences.

Dr. Stewart didn't respond until several seconds had passed. "Why do you say that? Of course it is." He guided the horse right onto King's Highway.

"I mean at Jefferson—"

He jerked on the reins. The buggy jolted to a halt in front of the house next to Rosemary's. "There's a light in your window. Didn't you say you live alone?" Alarm spiked through his voice. "Someone's inside. Wait here."

Jolene. She grabbed his arm to stop him from jumping out of the buggy. "I have a guest. She must have left a lamp burning for me."

"How can you be sure?" He shook her hand loose and coaxed the horse forward to the hitching post outside her gate. "I'll see you to the door."

"That's not necessary."

"I insist. I want to be certain you're safe." He helped her from the buggy and kept a firm grip on her elbow as they walked to the porch.

The pressure of his hand sent a crack through the professional wall between them. Warmth coursed along her arm. Could it be he saw her as more than a nurse who worked in his office? She faced him when they reached the steps. "Good night."

He leaned toward her. She lifted her face, wondering what he'd do next.

The door swung open. Jolene stepped onto the porch holding the lamp. "I've been worried sick. Your brother came here looking for you hours ago."

Dr. Stewart swung toward Jolene, then stared at Rosemary. "*She's* your guest? What possessed you? We can't be involved in our patients' lives."

"There's no 'we' to it, Doctor. I am the one involved." She stalked past him, tucked her arm under Jolene's, and banged the door behind them.

Elijah traveled the additional distance to his home in a daze, stunned at finding Jolene Graves in Miss Saxon's house. Visions of his physician father seared his memory. His father had started with the best of intentions, trying to help the needy, but instead had taken a dishonorable path. Elijah had promised himself he'd never succumb to the same temptations, yet his nurse's actions were too familiar for comfort. Not here. Not now. Not ever.

He stabled his horse, scooping extra grain into the feed trough. After hanging the bridle, he brought the carriage lamp from the barn and climbed the back steps to his house. A cold kitchen greeted him. Too weary to bother with a fire, he slumped onto a chair. Without revealing his father's shameful actions, he had to find a way to tell Miss Saxon she couldn't continue to house Miss Graves.

Depression weighted his bones. His steps dragged as he walked through the spacious dining and sitting rooms of his home, removing and discarding his jacket over the back of an armchair. His vest followed, landing on a writing table under the bay window. He grasped the newel post at the foot of the

59

stairs and rested his forehead on its smooth oak surface. A solid night's sleep would restore his good humor—at least on the face he presented to the world.

The following morning, Elijah strode toward West & Riley's for breakfast. He needed something more substantial than his usual oatmeal to fortify himself for his planned confrontation with Miss Saxon.

Thaddeus Cooper overtook him a few feet from the restaurant's door. "Want company with your eggs?"

He tacked a cheerful expression on his face. "Sounds good. I haven't seen you in a while."

The sheriff tugged at the corner of his moustache. "Been courting Amy Dunsmuir." His lean face reddened. "She's the widow gal who looks after old Judge Lindberg. Pretty little thing."

The two men entered the restaurant and took places at one of the long tables. Plates and tableware were set before each unoccupied chair. Once they were seated, a serving girl approached with a steaming pot and poured coffee into their cups. Another patron passed a platter heaped with fried eggs and bacon. A bowl of biscuits followed.

Elijah forked the food onto his plate with a contented sigh. If this didn't cheer him up, nothing would. Around a mouthful, he asked, "Is that the same Lindberg who owns the mercantile?"

"Yup. Guess he still owns it. The judge's mind isn't quite as keen as it used to be. That's why Amy looks after him." He swigged his coffee. "Faith Saxon, his granddaughter, manages the business. She's the one I warned you about. Her and Miss Rosemary are quite a pair."

Elijah considered the sheriff's remarks as he chewed a strip of bacon. Small towns had histories that took an outsider like himself a long time to decipher. Nothing like Chicago, where he'd lived before the war. There, no one expected to know everyone who had lost a family member in the conflict, or why one neighbor didn't speak to another. Between Miss Saxon and Thaddeus, he was beginning to understand the community he'd chosen for his practice.

He slid his chair away from the table. "Time I left for the office." His mood deflated at the prospect of speaking to Miss Saxon about her guest. He enjoyed the moments they spent together with patients, yet every time they had a disagreement she retreated behind a revetment as unyielding as any he'd seen on a battlefield. He shook his head. No help for it—she'd crossed a line he never thought he'd have to defend.

"Good seeing you, Doc." Thaddeus reached for the platter and helped himself to more eggs.

"Always a pleasure." The words were rote, but he meant them. After the camaraderie of the Army medical service, he found his spare time in Noble Springs to be lonely. Maybe one of these Sundays he'd visit the church across the street from his house.

"Rosemary! Someone's trying to get in your door." Jolene's shrill warning sliced through the early morning stillness.

Rosemary glanced down at Bodie, who dozed behind the cookstove. "Must be my brother. He stops by most mornings. Otherwise the dog would bark."

She hurried to the entry and slid the bolt. Jolene scurried partway up the stairs and then paused, watching.

"Where were you?" Curt said as soon as she opened the door.

"Good morning to you too. Want to come in, or would you rather stand on the porch and hector me?"

"Sorry." He stepped inside and bent to kiss her cheek, then glanced up the stairs at Jolene. "Did Miss Graves tell you I was here last night?"

"She did. Come where it's warm and I'll tell you where I was." Rosemary spoke over her shoulder as she led the way to the kitchen. When Curt took a chair, she sat at the table opposite him. "Dr. Stewart asked me to assist at a birth out in the country. There wasn't time to let Faith know I'd be gone." She leaned forward and rested her hand on his. "I apologize. I knew you'd be worried."

"I just don't like the idea of you being here alone. Anything could have happened."

"As you see, I'm not alone right now." Rosemary folded her arms over her chest.

"Faith said you'd like me to bring Miss Graves's things over here."

"Yes, please."

He lowered his voice. "She also said you plan to visit the girl's parents." Frowning, he shook his head. "We can't get *our* mother to talk to us. Why do you think you can influence Miss Graves's family?"

"I have to try. She needs help beyond what outsiders can provide." She stood and moved to the oven, wrapped her hand in her apron, and lifted a pan of golden brown biscuits to the stovetop. With a spatula, she scooped three onto a plate and placed them in front of Curt. "Put some honey on these. It will sweeten your disposition."

He split open a biscuit and drizzled honey on the cut surface. Around a mouthful, he said, "Meals are another thing. How can you feed an additional person?"

Rosemary felt a laugh bubble up inside. "Ask me next month. Right now she's too sick to eat much."

He sent her an exasperated look. "This isn't a joke."

"I know. I love you for your concern, but I'm a grown woman. Please let me make my own decisions."

After seeing Curt to the door when he left for the academy, Rosemary sagged against the frame. Somehow she'd believed he would support her decision to help Jolene. Neighbors and friends had reached out to them once their parents shut them out. She was merely repeating the kindness. After a moment, she straightened her shoulders. No matter what he thought, she'd done the right thing.

Wind gusts billowed Rosemary's cloak as she walked the short distance between her home and the doctor's office. From habit, she glanced at the hedge growing along the side of her neighbor's property, looking for Bodie. He'd always accompanied her when she helped Faith at the mercantile. She missed him. Maybe today she'd ask the doctor if he would allow her to bring the dog to work with her.

Out of the corner of her eye, she noticed movement in the neighbor's yard. When she stopped to take a closer look, whoever it was appeared to duck behind the house. Her heart fluttered in her throat. Would Jolene remember to keep the back door locked? She turned, ready to dash home with a reminder, then realized she was being silly. Anyone could be walking between the houses. It was none of her business. She gave herself a mental shake and strode toward Dr. Stewart's door.

"Miss Saxon." The doctor emerged from his private office the moment she entered. "I'd like a word with you."

From the sound of his voice, whatever he had to say wasn't good. Remembering his reaction to Jolene's presence in her home the previous evening, she braced for battle. If he thought he could dictate her private life, he'd better think again.

She hung her cloak on a hook and faced him. "Yes, Doctor?"

"It's about Miss Graves."

She lifted her chin, determined not to make the conversation easy for him. "What about her?"

He grasped the front of his coat, tugging it downward. His face reddened. "You can't continue to shelter her. How do you think it would look if word got out that she'd been my patient?"

Her jaw dropped. "Why should that matter? I'll shelter whomever I want. It's my home, not yours."

"You're an exasperating woman." He took a step closer. "It matters because your actions with my patients affect my reputation. People will believe you're acting under my direction."

"You'd have me turn her out on the street?"

"Just find another place for her to live."

"If she had another place, she'd already be there."

He narrowed his eyes. "I can't allow you to take in an unmarried girl who's with child."

"That's the most unreasonable statement I've ever heard. She's already in my home, and she's not leaving." She thought about telling him her intention to visit Jolene's family. Then anger burned through her. He was completely wrong. He didn't deserve an explanation.

"I'm not asking you. As your employer, I'm telling you."

Rosemary turned and lifted her cloak from the hook.

"Then you're no longer my employer. Good day, Doctor."

8

*R*osemary stalked toward home, her anger cooling. What had she done? Curt warned her to keep her temper. Now she'd cost herself the job she so desperately needed.

She drew in a deep breath and held it while she tried to think what to do next. Buggies and riders on horseback passed by on the street. Sheriff Cooper entered the barbershop on the corner. A small boy darted past, schoolbooks swinging from a strap. Everyone had someplace to go—everyone but her.

Without any conscious plan, her feet carried her to West & Riley's. She needed a few extra things now that she was cooking for two people. In spite of what she'd said to Curt, Jolene had begun eating small amounts.

She'd spend what she had on food and then tomorrow collect what Dr. Stewart owed her for helping with Mrs. Haggerty's baby. Her mind skittered away from another confrontation with him. She'd worry later.

Entering the grocery store, her mouth watered at the combined aromas of coffee and fried bacon wafting from the restaurant portion of the building.

Jacob West strode toward her, a smile lighting his attractive face. "What a fine way to start my day. Has the doctor changed his hours?"

"No." She swallowed. "I've changed mine, you might say."

He cocked his head. "How so?"

After Dr. Stewart's harshness, Jacob's friendly interest was a balm to her spirit. "We had a . . . disagreement. I don't work for him anymore." She dropped her gaze, focusing on a crack between the wooden floorboards.

"He was a fool if he sent you away. I hear nothing but good about your help in his practice."

A smile quivered on her lips. "Really?"

"All the time." He reached into a glass jar on the countertop and handed her a peppermint. "This'll make a bad day look better. Now, what can I get for you?"

"Just a few things. Two pounds of rice, a pound of oatmeal, and some baking powder."

"Would your dog like a ham hock? The butcher brought more than I can use." His eyes crinkled at the corners. "I'd be happy if you'd take it off my hands."

"Jacob—"

He lifted a hand to stop her. "It's the least I can do for my favorite nurse."

In spite of her embarrassment, she chuckled. "How many nurses do you know?"

"One. But she's special."

Rosemary left the grocery with the image of Jacob's face before her. The Lord must have guided her feet to the store, knowing how much she needed a kind word. Fortified by the encouragement, she turned west on High Street toward Lindberg's Mercantile.

Faith needed to know what happened, but Rosemary quailed at telling her. She'd been so proud of finding a way to support herself and now she was right back where she'd been before. Barely enough money to feed herself, let alone Jolene.

Clouds blurred the sky, blotting out the feeble rays of the sun. She drew her cloak tighter against the gusting wind. She'd endured storms before—she would do it again.

She turned onto King's Highway, passed the newspaper office, and slipped inside the mercantile. Faith glanced up from an open ledger at the sound of the bell over the door. Her eyes widened when she saw Rosemary.

"This is a lovely surprise." She closed the book with a snap and darted around the counter for a hug. "Did the doctor send you here for supplies? Paper? Ink?"

"No." The enormity of the morning's happenings engulfed her. Her eyes stung. "I came to say . . ." She cleared her throat. "I told Dr. Stewart I wouldn't work for him any longer."

"What? Come, sit." Faith took her hand and led her to the chairs near the stove. "Please tell me. Was he unkind to you?"

Rosemary dropped her grocery-filled carryall next to a chair and sank down. "He said he couldn't allow me to shelter Jolene. He *told* me she'd have to go." Remembering the scene, her anger boiled afresh. "Can you imagine? He said it reflected on him, of all things."

Faith leaned back, a bewildered expression on her face. "How absolutely odd. I must say, I'm surprised. He seems such an affable soul. In fact, for a doctor, he's quite friendly."

"Yes." She remembered the conversations they'd had in his office. He enjoyed learning about the townspeople and often went out of his way to chat with patients. His reaction to Jolene's presence in her home left her baffled. She rubbed the back of her neck. "I remember him from when I first started at the Barracks. No matter how bad the injury to one of our soldiers, he remained calm."

"You didn't tell us you knew him." Faith's voice squeaked with astonishment. "Did he recognize you?"

"No. I was only there for a month or so before he was sent to a battlefield depot." She glanced at her sister-in-law, feeling a flush creep up her neck. "I must confess I hoped he'd remember me."

"No wonder you wanted to work for him." Faith sent her a knowing look. "He's very attractive."

"Doesn't matter now, does it? I've got bigger things to worry about." Rosemary stood. "I need to go home, but I'm afraid if I tell Jolene what happened, she'll blame herself. The poor girl is frantic with fear already."

Mr. Slocum entered the store and meandered over to them. "Miss Rosemary. Thought you was working for the new doc."

"Was. Not anymore."

"You coming back here again?"

"I'll give it some thought." She leaned over and kissed Faith's cheek. "Don't worry. I'll be fine."

Drops of rain spat at the boardwalk as she strode home. There had to be a way to explain today's events to Jolene without upsetting her. Rosemary wished she knew what it was.

"I'll leave right now." Jolene jumped up from the settee.

Rosemary blocked her path, arms extended. "You're not leaving. I want you here."

"You lost your job because of me." Tears streaked the girl's face.

"No, I lost my temper. I cost myself my employment. I should have tried to explain things to him." She dropped onto one of the chairs in front of the window and blew out a weary breath. Not having the job was bad enough. Explaining the particulars to everyone was worse.

Bodie padded over and poked his nose under her arm. She reached down and scratched his silky ears. "Good boy," she murmured.

Jolene settled back onto the settee, sniffling. "Say what you want. It's my fault. If I left, would he hire you back?"

"I wouldn't work for him under those circumstances. My life is my concern—not his."

"Maybe Miss Lytle would give me piecework again. I'm feeling some better now." Her large brown eyes reflected a sheen of tears. "I don't want to be a burden."

"You're not." Rosemary crossed to the settee. Bending over, she hugged the girl's thin shoulders. "I've already thought of something we can do together."

By the time Curt arrived that afternoon with Jolene's possessions, Rosemary had changed from the drab clothing she wore in the doctor's office into her pleated moss green outfit. Her skirt swished over the floorboards as she hurried to answer the door.

"You're very prompt. No students kept late today?"

He blinked. "You didn't tell me you'd be home. I expected Miss Graves would let me in."

"She's upstairs, in your old room." She pointed at a battered trunk next to him. "Could you carry this up for us, please?"

He hefted Jolene's belongings onto the entry floor, then tucked his thumb under Rosemary's chin. "I'm always happy to see you, but why are you here? It's only four o'clock."

After already explaining her actions to three people, Rosemary abbreviated her answer to her brother. "Dr. Stewart told me I couldn't have Jolene here. I disagreed. Faith can give you the details."

Curt brought his heels together and saluted. "Yes, ma'am."

Rosemary led the way up the stairs and tapped on Jolene's door. "My brother brought your trunk," she called.

In a moment, the girl stood facing them wrapped in Rosemary's striped blue dressing gown. Her hair hung down behind her in a long braid. "I must have fallen asleep." When she noticed Curt standing in the hallway, she ducked to one side, cheeks crimson. "I thank you. Just leave it, please. I'll unpack directly." Backing away, she closed the door.

Pity clutched Rosemary's heart. From the girl's swollen eyes, she knew she'd been crying. The sooner she got her busy on a new enterprise, the sooner Jolene would feel useful.

The following morning, Rosemary woke with a sense of dread nagging at her. She'd promised herself she'd collect her share of the Haggertys' payment today, but the thought of facing Dr. Stewart was enough to remove all joy from the morning.

She shoved her feet into wool slippers and threw her wrapper over her shoulders. No sense delaying what had to be done. As soon as she opened the door, Bodie rose from his post, stretching. His body heat seeped from the floorboards to the soles of her feet.

"You're supposed to sleep in the kitchen, not outside my room," she said to him, secretly pleased at the thought of him keeping watch over her.

Bodie wagged his tail and ran down the stairs toward the back door.

She stepped onto the porch after him, shivering in the early morning chill. He circled the yard with his nose to the ground. After a minute, he disappeared inside the green-house.

Half-awake, it took Rosemary a moment to realize the door stood open. Her senses jangled. Although it was late March, the previous night had been chilly. Her tender plants might not survive the cold. She sped down the steps and along the path to the small outbuilding.

Stepping through the entrance, she scrutinized the tidy tables. The mint plant appeared unaffected by the drop in temperature. Rosemary inspected each of the pots containing infant sprouts while Bodie nosed about the corners of the window-lined enclosure. On some of the stems, new leaves curled downward in the chill air. She shook her head. Nothing to do now but wait to see if they recovered.

She took a final look around, trying to remember when she'd last watered. Surely the door had been latched upon returning to the house. But perhaps the distraction of Jolene's arrival had made her careless.

"Rosemary?" The girl's high-pitched voice warbled from the porch steps. "Where are you?"

Bodie's ears perked up when he heard Jolene. He bounded across the yard and stopped at her feet, wagging his tail.

Rosemary ducked through the opening and fastened the door behind her. "I found the greenhouse open and went to check." She rubbed her forehead as she crossed the yard. "I don't understand how I could have been so forgetful."

"Maybe the door blew open. The wind howled last night." She shuddered. "I don't like that noise. Sounds like ghosts."

Rosemary slipped an arm around the girl's shoulders. "There's no such thing as ghosts. Besides, this house is stout. We won't blow away."

She locked the back door, grateful for the heat radiating from the cookstove.

"I got the fire going," Jolene said. "The kettle's on for tea. I think after a cup and a bite of toast I'll be able to help you." Her pale skin belied her brave words.

Rosemary glanced at the corner of the worktable where she'd left a block of lard and a can of lye. "We'll start this afternoon. Drink your tea and rest for a bit." She blew out a long breath. "First, I'm going to see Dr. Stewart."

Dr. Stewart met Rosemary when she entered the waiting area. "Good. You changed your mind. I hoped you would." He strode toward her, a broad smile on his face. "I'm willing to give you a little time to find a home for Miss Graves. Perhaps a week?"

She wondered why he hadn't noticed she was wearing her gray silk dress and spoon bonnet rather than her normal work attire of plain calico. "Miss Graves's situation need not concern you further. I came to collect my share of the payment from Mr. Haggerty."

His eyebrows shot upward. "You're not coming back?"

"No." She kept her voice steady, but her throat tightened. Spending the days with him had been educational as well as pleasurable. If Jacob were correct, she'd gained the respect of some of the townspeople in the process. She prayed their favorable regard wouldn't disappear along with her employment.

"Miss Saxon . . ." He held out a hand toward her, then dropped it. "How about two weeks?"

The pleading in his deep brown eyes unnerved her. He looked like a boy—quite a tall, burly boy, but a boy nonetheless. She straightened her shoulders, determined not to weaken. "Miss Graves will remain with me as long as necessary. Now, I'd appreciate my wages, if you please."

"Of course." He strode to his office and took a small envelope from his desktop. "Here's your share from Mr. Haggerty. I set it aside last evening." He placed the sum in her hand, but held on to an edge of the envelope. "You're sure?"

"I am." She kept her tone brisk and dropped the money in her handbag, hoping her uncertainty didn't show on her face. The next stop would be the mercantile for a talk with Faith. She'd find another way to remain independent. She had to.

9

*R*osemary stood on her back porch, wearing an apron and wrapped in a shawl. She held a wooden spoon over a large glass bowl half-filled with water. "Be careful. Pour slowly," she said to Jolene.

"I know. I did this for my ma all the time. Just never had store-boughten lye—we always made soap from stove ash." Holding the container close to the surface of the water, she poured the concentrated lye while Rosemary stirred.

As the mixture dissolved, the sides of the bowl warmed. Rosemary wrinkled her nose as she set the water aside to cool. "Let's go in. The lard should be melted by now."

Once in the kitchen, she removed the pot from the stove and carried it outside, placing it on a bench next to the glass bowl. When the liquefied fat cooled, they'd be ready to combine ingredients for her special shaving soap.

Jolene sank into a chair and sniffled. "I miss my ma. Wish I'd never left home."

Understanding pierced Rosemary's heart. "It's the little memories that pain us the most, isn't it? I remember my mother teaching me about herbs and plants. She loved growing things."

"Oh, I'm sorry!" Jolene's eyes filled with compassion. "I didn't know your ma had passed."

"She hasn't." At least, not that she knew.

"But you said—"

Rosemary replaced her shawl over her shoulders. "I need to check the lard. We can't let it get cold." She escaped out the door, berating herself for letting memories run away with her. Her own mother might be unreachable, but surely Jolene's would welcome her daughter back. The next time she saw Curt she'd ask to borrow his buggy.

Jolene trailed her onto the porch, carrying a second glass container. She cast a curious glance at her before raising the pot and pouring the cooled lard into the empty bowl.

Grateful for her help, and her silence, Rosemary lifted the lye mixture. "Ready?" This time she poured while Jolene stirred. When the spoon left traces in the white compound, she uncorked a vial of sassafras oil and tipped in two teaspoonfuls, then placed a square wooden box on the bench. A sweet licorice aroma rose when Jolene poured the soap into the mold.

"Now what?" she asked. "Ma always made soft soap, nothing fancy like this."

"We'll let this cure for a few days, then cut it into circles to fit shaving mugs."

Rosemary lifted the box and carried it indoors, remembering with a pang the elegant scented soaps her mother made as gifts. She wondered whether she'd approve of Rosemary's intention to sell one of her recipes as a shaving compound.

She pictured a shelf in the mercantile filled with soaps, herbal teas, and tinctures. In no time, she'd compensate for the loss of income from Dr. Stewart.

On Sunday, Rosemary tucked her arm under Jolene's as they walked to the end of the block and crossed the street to the church. Reverend French stood at the top of the stone steps greeting his flock while the bell pealed from the steeple atop the square brick building. When they approached, he descended to the lawn and bowed in their direction.

"Miss Rosemary. Always a pleasure." His thick eyebrows raised in inquiry. "Who is your guest today?"

She introduced Jolene and smiled through the reverend's welcoming words. She'd never known anyone with such an ability to put people at ease. She sensed the tension leaving Jolene's body.

A younger man, his face a duplicate of Reverend French's, stepped next to them. His empty left sleeve was pinned up at the elbow. The reverend took his good arm. "Miss Graves, this is my son Galen. He teaches at the academy with Miss Rosemary's brother."

Galen's eyes brightened. "Happy to know you, Miss Graves. Will you be visiting our area for very long?"

Jolene's face flamed. "I . . . I'm not sure." She turned a frantic gaze on Rosemary. "Shouldn't we go in?"

Rosemary squeezed her arm. "Certainly."

Once inside, she scanned the pews. "There they are." She nodded her head in the direction of her brother and Faith, sitting next to Judge Lindberg.

When Faith noticed them, she patted an empty space on the seat beside her. After a whispered introduction between the judge and Jolene, Rosemary settled next to her sister-in-law.

At the front of the sanctuary, Clarissa French, the reverend's wife, stroked the keys of a piano. The hymn "Holy, Holy, Holy" rose over the sound of worshipers' footsteps entering the building.

Faith poked Rosemary in the side. "Look," she whispered, pointing discreetly at a pew in front of them where Sheriff Cooper sat with Amy Dunsmuir. Although she couldn't see the child over the couple's shoulders, Rosemary knew Amy held her young daughter on her lap. Faith leaned close to Rosemary's ear. "He's at the house nearly every night. Amy seems happy with him, but needless to say, Curt's not thrilled."

"As long as the sheriff has stopped trying to arrest him, he can relax." They smiled at each other, remembering their campaign to clear Curt's name after a robbery at the mercantile.

A husky man with curly hair walked past, apparently seeking an empty seat. Rosemary sucked in a breath. "Do you know who that is?"

Faith nodded. "The doctor. I've never seen him here before."

They watched while he entered a pew close to the front. "Wonders will never cease," Rosemary said. "Maybe he'll—"

Reverend French faced the congregation and motioned for everyone to stand while his wife played the introduction to "My Faith Looks Up to Thee." Out of the corner of her eye, Rosemary watched Dr. Stewart fumble through a hymnbook seeking the song. Her heart gave an unexpected twist. If she were standing beside him, she'd show him the place. She blinked, surprised at the direction her thoughts had taken.

Jolene's hand on her arm broke her reverie. "Sometimes Ma and Pa took us to church in Hartfield. I'm glad you brought me here today," she said in a soft voice.

"So am I." She'd done the right thing in God's eyes. That's all that mattered.

When Clarissa left the piano, Reverend French stepped to the pulpit and opened his Bible. "Our text today is from the Epistle of James, second chapter, sixteenth verse. Here James is speaking of caring for the needs of others. 'And one of you say unto them, Depart in peace, be ye warmed and filled; notwithstanding ye give them not those things which are needful to the body; what doth it profit?'"

Rosemary nodded as he read the verse. The subject matter had to be more than a coincidence. She hoped Dr. Stewart was listening.

Elijah hunched over what had been Miss Saxon's desk, grumbling to himself as he made entries in the ledger. Her pages contained tidy figures and dates, with patients' names included. Each sheet was totaled at the bottom. He raked his fingers through his hair. If there was anything more tedious than record keeping, he didn't know what it could be. Two weeks without her help, and already he'd fallen behind.

The outside door opened and a man entered, rain dripping from his oilskin coat. "Mornin', Doc." His gaze darted around the room. "Where's that pretty nurse? I come to show you both how good my burn healed. Used that comfrey root she told me about—and the ointment you gave me, o'course."

After a moment's pause, Elijah recognized him as Mr. Eldridge, the patient who'd injured himself when he threw kerosene on a fire. "Miss Saxon has gone on to other pursuits," he said, using the response he'd perfected after answering the same question almost daily since she left. He rose and met the man near the door. "But I'd like to take a look at your arm."

Mr. Eldridge draped his coat over a hook, rolled up his sleeve, and held his bare arm toward Elijah. The new skin looked pinker than the surrounding tissue. In all other respects, he'd healed without a scar. "Looks good, don't it? Tell Miss Saxon my wife made a poultice of some of the root, like she said."

Elijah shook his head. "You used the Hansen's Ointment too, didn't you? I suspect that had the greater effect."

"Maybe." He looked doubtful. "Stung something fierce, so I pretty much stuck to the comfrey root."

Knowing better than to argue with a patient, he patted the man's arm. "Glad you're healed. Be careful with kerosene, now."

"Don't have to tell me. Say, do you know where I'd find Miss Saxon? The wife sent her some wild grape jelly." He shoved his arms into his coat sleeves and then drew a stubby jar from one pocket. "Figgered she deserved some thanks."

"I believe she's at Lindberg's Mercantile most mornings. The store's across from the courthouse on King's Highway." As he spoke, Miss Saxon's earnest face floated in front of his eyes. He'd thought himself charitable when he hired her, but now that it was too late, he recognized her value. The fact that she was attractive had nothing to do with his sense of regret. Nothing at all.

"Thanks, Doc." Mr. Eldridge clapped his hat on and stepped out into the sodden morning.

Elijah watched him walk north toward King's Highway. Miss Saxon told him she had few friends in Noble Springs. He wondered whether she knew how many people missed her once she left his practice.

He walked to her desk and slammed the ledger closed.

Rosemary tilted her head and surveyed the row of shaving soaps displayed at the front of a shelf near the door of the mercantile. Each blue calico-wrapped disk was tied at the top with green ribbon. On a shelf below she'd arranged fabric bundles of herbal teas, with names like "Calm After-noons," "Blissful Sleep," and "Memory Enhancer" written on attached tags.

Faith stepped up behind her. "Everything looks so pretty. Like little flowers in my store."

"You're looking at pieces of an old skirt I used to gar-den in. It made the supreme sacrifice." She sighed. "Now if only customers would buy something, the effort would be worthwhile."

"Except for the man who brought you the jelly, no one seems to be venturing out in this rainstorm. Even the wood-stove regulars stayed home this morning."

"I'm not talking about today." Rosemary folded her arms over her waist and stood next to the stove. "I've only sold fifty cents' worth this past week."

"Give it time—"

The bell over the door jangled and Cassie Haddon and her mother pushed into the store, shaking water from their wet umbrellas.

"There you are!" Cassie's mother marched up to Rosemary. "We've been all over town looking for you. That waif you've got at your house said you were spending time here again. And of course we found *that* out after we'd already called at the doctor's office and didn't see you there." She paused to draw a breath.

"I didn't know you were coming to call, Mrs. Bingham, or I would have made it a point to stay home. What can I do for you?" She hadn't seen the woman in several months. With concern, she noted that she'd lost much of her ample flesh, and hollows surrounded her eyes. If it weren't for her un-naturally bright red hair, Rosemary wouldn't have known her.

Cassie stepped forward and took her mother's arm. "We hoped you'd have some of your valerian tincture made up."

Mrs. Bingham shook her arm free. "I can talk for myself, thank you." She eyed the shelves containing bundles of tea and shaving soaps. "You're selling your remedies here now?"

"Not everything. I prepare tinctures and cures as need arises." Rosemary reached behind the herb teas and selected a vial containing the restorative she sought. "This is all the valerian I have right now. My supply of the herb is running low until the plants start their growth cycle again."

"This will do nicely." She turned to her daughter. "Cassie, look outside to see if Mr. Bingham has come for us yet."

"He's waiting in the buggy, Mother."

A haunted look crossed the woman's face. "Oh, dear." She shoved the vial into her handbag and thrust a coin at Rosemary. "Thank you." Seizing her umbrella, she dashed for the door.

"Next time I'll come directly to the mercantile," Cassie said, addressing both Faith and Rosemary. Her tone was apologetic. "I'll try to stay long enough to visit."

"Cassie!"

"I'm coming." The door banged behind them.

Faith and Rosemary stood together, watching the women scramble into the carriage, unassisted by Mr. Bingham. The whip snapped over the horse's back and they rolled out of sight.

"That poor woman got more than she bargained for when she married that man," Faith said.

"Indeed. She'd have been better off staying with her family in St. Louis, and so would Cassie." She fingered the disks of soap she had concocted with Jolene's help, her mind skipping to her guest's well-being. "Jolene would be better off with her family too. Her morning sickness has eased, but she's overcome with melancholia. She pines for her mother."

"Rosemary, we've talked about this. You're setting yourself up for disappointment."

She stared out at the curtain of drizzle obscuring the courthouse lawn. "Just because I don't know what will happen is no excuse for not trying."

On Saturday morning, Curt stood in Rosemary's sitting room, arms folded over his chest. "You're not going by yourself. It isn't safe."

"Then come with me."

He'd opened his mouth to reply when Jolene drifted into the room. "Where are you going?" Judging from her listless tone, the answer didn't matter one way or another.

Rosemary glanced at her brother and gave her head a tiny shake. "Just on an errand in the country. We'll be back before supper. Bodie will be here with you."

Curt's face turned thunderous. "I didn't say—"

"I'll get my bonnet." Rosemary patted his arm and hurried upstairs.

Once they were headed east toward Hartfield, she leaned against the seat back and blew out a relieved breath. Until he'd helped her into the buggy, she hadn't been sure Curt would agree to take her to meet Jolene's parents.

He sent her a sideways look. "Just so you know, I only agreed because you'll need someone to pick you up when they throw you off the property."

Her palms moistened. In spite of her brave words, she knew from experience the risk involved. "Jolene is miserable. I refuse to believe her mother will behave like ours did."

"We recovered."

"Did we?"

Curt didn't respond. The horse's hooves plopped along the road, making a sucking sound when they lifted out of the mud. Pale sunshine lit redbuds and flowering dogwoods scattered across the countryside. After they'd passed several farms, he asked, "How will you know which one belongs to Miss Graves's family?"

"She told me they had a small log house with only two windows, apple trees inside a rail fence, and chickens running about."

Property after property rolled by, but none fit Jolene's description. The sun angled past noon and began its descent toward the horizon. A new worry needled at Rosemary. "Do you suppose she fabricated a story? We must be more than halfway to Hartfield."

"We've come this far. We'll go until we see the jailhouse at the edge of town." He snapped the reins over the horse's back.

The buggy rounded a bend and Rosemary drew a sharp breath. "There's a log house." She sat up straighter. "Those must be apple trees—they just aren't in bloom yet." Her heartbeat increased. It was one thing to think about meeting Jolene's family but quite another to carry out her plan.

"Here goes." Curt guided the horse through an opening in the fence and stopped next to a square garden patch.

When he jumped down to tie the reins to a rail, a dog appeared in the open doorway. The growling animal stood with legs braced as though daring them to come nearer.

She swallowed a knot of fear. This dog did resemble Bodie,

as Jolene had said, down to the sable patch on one side of his face. She hoped he also possessed Bodie's sociable nature.

A tiny woman emerged from the cabin. She wore an apron over her butternut-brown dress. Her dark hair was parted along the middle and drawn back into a bun the size of a fist. Not moving from the stoop, she rested one hand on top of the dog's head. "You folks lost?"

Rosemary scrambled from the buggy and approached the woman, all her senses jangling. This was the point where she could be ordered from the property. "I'm Miss Rosemary Saxon, and this is my brother, Curt Saxon. We're seeking the Graves family." She strove to prevent her voice from trembling. "Have we come to the right farm?"

"You have. I'm Mrs. Graves." The color drained from her face. "Has something happened to my Jolene? I knew no good would come of her traipsing off to live in town. What is it? You can tell me."

"Perhaps we'd be more comfortable inside."

"Tell me right here." She gripped her elbows with work-reddened hands. "The mister's up at the woodlot cutting trees. The boys are with him. Whatever it is, I want to know before they come back."

Rosemary took a step closer, longing to put an arm around Jolene's mother, but afraid the dog would misinterpret her actions. "Your daughter is unharmed. She's staying with me in Noble Springs."

Mrs. Graves stood rigid. "Why? What happened to her fine job?"

"She's not able to work right now." Rosemary drew a deep breath before continuing. "Jolene's . . . with child."

The mother wailed and clapped her hands to her mouth. "Oh, great heavens, no! Not my baby girl." She sagged against the door frame.

Rosemary dashed to her side, heedless of the rumble coming from the dog's throat. "Please. Let me help you inside. You need to sit for a moment."

A bulky cookstove sat close to one wall in the main room. Against the opposite wall, a ladder led upward to a loft, which presumably held a sleeping area. Mrs. Graves tottered toward a cloth-covered table set with tin plates and surrounded by several chairs. She slumped onto one of them.

After a few moments she looked up, a puzzled expression on her face. "How d'you know Jolene? She never mentioned you."

"She came to see Dr. Stewart. I was his nurse."

"His nurse. Never heard of such a thing," Mrs. Graves said in a scoffing tone. She stood and eyed the doorway. "How do I know you're telling the truth about my girl?"

Rosemary spread her hands, palms open. "Jolene needs you. Why would I lie to you, ma'am?"

"I don't know! You're lying about being a nurse. Ain't no lady nurses." Her sharp gaze took in Curt, who waited on the stoop. "You two just git on back where you come from. If you know Jolene—and that's a mighty big if—tell her to come home and talk to me herself."

"She's afraid to."

"Afraid of her own ma? Now I know you're lying."

Curt crossed the threshold and moved to Rosemary's side. "Let's go," he said in an undertone.

She took his arm. As they passed Mrs. Graves, she paused, fighting to control her disappointment. "I'm sorry to have been the bearer of bad tidings. I'll deliver your message to Jolene."

The woman turned her head away.

Rosemary sat on the buggy seat, her spine starched into immobility. Once they were out of sight of the Graves's farm, she slumped against the seat back and turned to Curt. "I don't know which feels worse, being ordered off the property or being called a liar."

"I tried to tell you."

"I know, but 'I told you so' is no help right now. What will I do about Jolene?"

He opened his mouth and closed it again. Grateful he'd refrained from whatever blunt remark hovered on the tip of his tongue, she waited while he formed a reply.

After a long moment, he said, "I'm more concerned about you. How are you managing without your salary from the doctor?"

"I'm getting by."

"That girl's been with you almost three weeks. Shouldn't she be over the worst of her sickness? Maybe she can get her job back. Buy her own groceries."

"I don't see how. She can't hide her condition much longer, and you know how people are." Tension tightened the muscles across her shoulders. She pinched the pleats in her skirt and tugged at a loose thread until it snapped. "I thought I was doing the right thing by visiting Mrs. Graves."

"Perhaps you did."

She studied him, wondering whether he was serious. "How?"

"The woman said her daughter should come home and give her the news in person." He shifted the reins to his left hand and patted her arm with his right. "I'm willing to take her if she wants to go."

Relief trembled through her limbs. "You're a blessing."

"That's what Faith says."

The savory fragrance of chicken cooking greeted Rosemary when she entered the house. Bodie frolicked over to her, a bone clamped between his teeth. Chicken and a fresh bone for the dog? Faith must have stopped by after she closed the mercantile for the day. She shook her head. She'd refused offers of help, but apparently Faith waited until she knew Rosemary was away, then brought the food.

After hanging her shawl and bonnet next to the front door, she headed for the kitchen. "Jolene?"

The girl appeared in the entrance, wiping her hands on an apron. "I hope you don't mind. I put the hen on to stew for our supper." Apprehension tightened her features. "Guess I could have put it in the springhouse. Maybe you don't like boiled chicken."

"I'm not fussy about food. But I'm certainly curious. When did my sister-in-law bring us the chicken?"

"Wasn't Mrs. Saxon. The grocer done it. Said it was too old and tough for his customers, and wanted you to take it off his hands. It's been stewing all—" She stopped and studied Rosemary's face. The brightness in her eyes dimmed. "Did I do wrong?"

"Not at all. I'll thank Jacob the next time I see him." Much as she appreciated his kindness, a tiny coil of embarrassment wound through her at being the object of charity.

She lifted the lid from the kettle and sniffed. "Smells delicious. You're a good cook."

"My ma taught me." Jolene blinked and looked at her hands. "She taught me lots of things. Wish I'd listened."

Rosemary drew a chair away from the table. "It's not too late." She patted the seat next to her. "Let me tell you where we were this afternoon."

Jolene's eyes widened while she listened to the account of the visit to the Graves's farm. When Rosemary concluded by

88

telling her of Curt's offer to take her to see her parents, she shook her head. "I can't do it. I won't. My little mama—even if she says she wants to see me, it'll be too hurtful to have me about the place in my condition. And my pa . . ." She buried her face in her hands and sobbed. "I didn't want them to know."

Leaning forward, Rosemary patted the girl's shoulder. "Believe me, I understand how you feel. But she did say she wanted you to tell her—"

"She probably didn't believe you, is all. She sure don't want to hear about me getting myself in trouble."

Rosemary leaned back and stared unseeing at the herbs hanging from the beams. A sense of defeat weighted her shoulders. She might know what was best for Jolene, but she couldn't force her to go see her parents. With a heavy sigh, she studied the stubborn set of the girl's jaw.

"Will you at least think about it? Curt will take you whenever you want to go."

"Tell him I'm obliged, but something else is bound to turn up. I'm not going out there."

After church, Rosemary strode toward Jacob West's. She knew the restaurant would be open on Sunday to feed men from the rooming house. Bodie wandered behind her, stopping to sniff every other bush, then scampering to catch up.

Jacob had used the excuse of needing to share an oversupply of food once too often. Last night's chicken had been tender and meaty, certainly something he'd have been able to serve his patrons. She hoped she could express her gratitude and at the same time discourage future charity.

After instructing Bodie to wait outside, she pushed open the door of the restaurant. Ignoring the stares of the men at the tables, she surveyed the room. Jacob was nowhere in sight. Upset with herself, she turned to leave. She should have waited until Monday and talked to him in the grocery. There'd be fewer curious eyes.

"Miss Saxon?" Dr. Stewart stepped up behind her, carrying his coat over one arm. "This is a pleasant surprise. I would have expected you'd be enjoying Sunday dinner with your family." His gaze swept over the room filled with men. "This isn't a fitting place for a lady."

She felt a flush color her cheeks. "I wanted to have a word with Mr. West, but I see he's not here."

"He generally leaves the Sunday meal to Mrs. Fielder, the cook. She's standing over there if you wish to speak with her." He nodded his head in the direction of the kitchen.

"No, thank you. I'll return tomorrow." She took a sidestep toward the door. She'd planned a conversation with Jacob, not an encounter with Dr. Stewart. If she'd known he'd be at the restaurant, she'd never have come.

He donned his jacket. "I was just leaving. May I escort you home?"

"I wouldn't want to take you out of your way. My brother and his wife are expecting me. They live across town." She wished he wouldn't look at her with those mesmerizing brown eyes.

"Better yet. It's a fine day for a walk." Cupping his hand under her elbow, he steered her from the building. "Which direction?"

"To the left. It's nearly five blocks. Truly, you needn't trouble yourself."

"It's no trouble. I've missed our conversations."

So had she, but she didn't want to admit as much to him.

A mild breeze feathered the silk taffeta bow securing her bonnet over her hair. Meringue clouds dotted the sky, their puffed outlines spinning shadows over the boardwalk. After they passed several storefronts, Bodie trotted around them and ran ahead to the lawn in front of the courthouse.

Dr. Stewart glanced at him, then at Rosemary. "I thought that dog would chew my leg off when I visited your home."

"His name's Bodie. I found him as a stray and we adopted each other. He's harmless unless he believes I'm being threatened."

Smiling, the doctor moved a half step away from her side while continuing to keep his hand on her elbow. "I'll be careful." He cleared his throat. "Is Miss Graves still staying with you?"

She suspected more than casual interest in his question. Stopping in mid-stride, she faced him. "Yes. Why?"

"Your situation has been on my mind." He ran a finger under his high collar. "What do you propose to do when her time comes?"

She resumed walking. "I don't see where that's any concern of yours." Her brisk tone matched her stride.

"You're right. It's not." He bit off the words.

For a moment Rosemary was tempted to share her worries. She didn't have the least idea what she'd do if the visit continued through the birth of the child. An extended stay had never occurred to her.

She cocked her head, studying the firm set of his jaw. How nice it would be to have him as an ally instead of an opponent.

11

acob's face lifted in a smile when Rosemary stepped into West & Riley's on Monday morning. "Miss Rosemary. Welcome. I trust you were able to make use of that scrawny hen."

He looked so pleased she hated to dampen his spirits. "The chicken was delicious and far from scrawny." She glanced around to be sure there were no other customers in the grocery store, then stepped closer before continuing. "I thank you, but please, let this be the last time."

He spread his hands. "I don't sell flowers, so I give you food. It's the same thing. I'm a single man and you're an unmarried lady. How else will I capture your interest?"

She took a step back, her mind reeling. She'd never mastered the coquettish ways of some of the young women she knew. How was she expected to respond?

Jacob filled the silence. "I hope you're not offended." A flush darkened his skin. "I don't know how to talk to ladies when I'm not filling their grocery orders."

"No, I'm not offended. Just surprised. I had no idea."

"The next thing to do is ask you to go for a buggy ride

with me next Sunday. Will you?" He rolled a pencil back and forth on the counter, looking as uncomfortable as she felt.

She gulped. "Yes, thank you. That would be fine." Her voice came out as a strangled squeak. Jacob West, of all people. She couldn't wait to tell Faith.

His features relaxed. "Good. I will come for you at two."

"I'll be ready. And Jacob, please, no more chickens."

After leaving the grocery, Rosemary strolled along High Street until she reached the square. Several brown thrashers flitted in and out of the shrubbery next to the stone courthouse as she passed. Their songs echoed her lighthearted mood.

Humming to herself, she stepped off the boardwalk and crossed the street to the mercantile. Faith waved at her through the window.

"You look cheerful this morning," she said when Rosemary entered.

"The most amazing thing just happened. Jacob West invited me to go for a buggy ride Sunday afternoon."

"The only amazing thing is that he hasn't asked you sooner. Every time I'm in his store he inquires after you."

Rosemary moved behind the counter and dropped an apron over her moss green skirt. "He's probably just lonely, although I'm surprised some of the younger girls in town haven't set their caps for him."

"Maybe he doesn't want someone young and silly." Faith reached over and squeezed Rosemary's hand. "You don't realize how attractive you are."

"Piffle. Sometimes I feel like those soaps sitting on the shelf. Attractive doesn't mean much if no one wants them." She tweaked a bow tying the blue calico wrapper around a sassafras-scented disk.

"Dr. Stewart escorted you to our house yesterday. Now

Mr. West invites you for a buggy ride. That doesn't sound like you're sitting on a shelf."

"The doctor and I were barely on speaking terms when we parted." Her lightheartedness evaporated at the memory. If only he weren't so unreasonable on the subject of Jolene.

"Things aren't always what they seem. Look how long Curt and I took to cross the barriers we'd erected between ourselves." Faith's cheeks bloomed pink. "I never expected to be this happy. Someday it will be your turn."

"Perhaps." But with Jacob West? She doubted it.

To change the subject, Rosemary pointed to a display of cookware stacked in the window. "Why don't we arrange your caster sets in place of the pots and skillets?" She removed a bolt of chrome yellow chintz from the fabric area and held it up. "We can drape this underneath. The effect will be quite eye-catching."

Faith snickered. "Good idea. None of my customers seem interested in wearing a garment quite so bright. That bolt's been on the shelf so long the edges have faded."

Rosemary put the cloth aside and reached for a three-legged skillet on the shelf beneath the window. As she drew the heavy cast iron piece toward her, she noticed Mr. Bingham's wagon stopping in front of the store. "Cassie's here!" She left the window display and joined Faith. "I hope she can stay long enough to visit this time."

"So do I. She's almost a prisoner on that farm."

They watched Cassie fight to prevent her wide skirts from flying up when she climbed down from the wagon. Her mother remained on the seat, dabbing at her eyes with a handkerchief. Mr. Bingham plodded to the endgate as Cassie fled through the door of the mercantile.

"He's sending me away," she said between sobs. "Says he can't afford to feed both of us. He expects me to find a job and give him the money I earn. I told him I wouldn't do it. He paid no attention." She spun around and stared out at the street. "He has Mother so browbeaten that she won't utter a word against him."

Rosemary held out her arms and Cassie ran to her. "I knew you'd help me. I've never worked anywhere. We always had servants. Tell him."

While they watched, her stepfather hoisted a dome-topped trunk onto one shoulder, then turned and deposited it on the boardwalk.

Rosemary's heart drummed. Perhaps Mr. Bingham might listen to her. She wouldn't know if she didn't try. Keeping an arm around the young woman's shoulder, she guided her to Faith's side.

"I'll talk to him for you." She had no idea what she'd say, but with firm steps she marched out to the sour-faced man.

He faced her, thumbs tucked around his suspenders. His belly strained the fabric of his collarless chambray shirt. "If that shiftless girl sent you out here, you can just turn around and go back inside. I don't need no one poking their nose into my business."

She shot a glance at Cassie's mother. The woman avoided her eyes.

Rosemary said the first thing that popped into her mind. "Mr. Bingham. This is wrong. You know Cassie has been gently reared. You can't turn her out."

"Who are you to tell me I'm wrong?" His ruddy complexion turned purple. He cocked his head. "You ain't Judge Lindberg's granddaughter, are you?"

"No, sir. I'm Miss Saxon. Faith Lindberg married my brother."

He took a step toward her, squinting. "You're the one who fools with them roots and berries. Thinks you can cure folks."

"We're talking about Cassie, not me." She wrinkled her nose as his pungent breath assailed her nostrils. "You can't do this to her. She's been sheltered all her life."

"Not no more, she ain't. Children is obliged to help out. Sooner she gets that straight, the better off she'll be."

A man and a woman passing by in a buggy turned to stare when they heard Mr. Bingham's strident voice. He glared at them, then left Rosemary standing beside the trunk and clambered onto the wagon seat. Cassie's mother slumped forward when he flicked the reins over the horse's back. Rosemary thought she heard sobs.

"He's leaving me here!" Cassie burst through the door. She took a few running steps in the direction of the departing wagon, then stopped. Dust stirred up by the horse's hooves rolled over her.

Horrified, Rosemary watched the Binghams' wagon disappear around a corner.

Cassie stumbled to the front of the mercantile and collapsed onto a bench. "I never thought he'd do this," she said, more to herself than to Rosemary. "What's going to happen to my mother?"

"Has he . . . lifted his hand against her?" Rosemary felt herself flush when she asked the question. She had no right to venture into such private territory. Her question was inappropriate, even for a family member.

"No. He's a tyrant who strikes with words." Cassie's jaw tightened. "He claims he loves her, but he's made her life a nightmare. I wish he was dead."

"You don't mean that."

She pointed to the trunk sitting on the boardwalk. "He abandoned me here. Why would I have charitable feelings toward him?"

"You're upset—understandably so." Rosemary took Cassie's

hand and drew her to her feet. "Come inside. We need to decide what to do next."

On Sunday, Rosemary left the church with Jolene and Cassie at her side. Townsfolk dressed in their best go-to-meeting clothes clustered in small groups scattered over the lawn. Conversations hummed like bees over the gathering. As she descended the steps, Rosemary noticed Clarissa French hurrying in her direction.

"May I speak to you for a moment?"

If she were to be ready when Jacob called for her, she needed to go right home. Clarissa was one of the kindest women she knew, but she loved long conversations—usually about herself.

Rosemary swallowed. "Certainly."

"May we speak in confidence?" Clarissa darted a glance at Rosemary's companions.

Jolene's cheeks reddened with embarrassment while Cassie nodded and stepped back.

"I won't be long, if you don't mind going on ahead."

When they walked away, the reverend's wife said, "I pray they weren't offended. My concerns have nothing to do with either of them. I need your help."

"You have only to ask. After everything your husband did for my brother—including recommending him for the teaching position—I'm in your debt."

Clarissa waved her words aside. "We're grateful to the Lord that everything turned out so well. But this is a personal matter." She stepped nearer and spoke close to Rosemary's ear. "I understand you mix curative teas. I didn't see what I need on your shelf at the mercantile and wondered whether you might prepare something special for me."

"I'll be happy to, if at all possible. What is your complaint?"

"Ever since Galen came home without—well, the way he is, I've suffered the most terrible headaches. I pray for relief, but nothing changes." Shamefaced, she lowered her voice even further. "I fear I must lack faith."

Rosemary rested a hand on the woman's plump arm. "The Lord often uses ordinary people when he answers our prayers. Feverfew tea helped my brother during his difficulties after the war. I'll bring some to you later this afternoon."

Tears glittered in Clarissa's eyes. "I don't want to impose."

"Nonsense. Our homes are barely a block apart."

"You're a blessing. Thank you." She turned and made her way to her husband's side, greeting members of the congregation as she crossed the lawn.

Out of the corner of her eye, Rosemary glimpsed Dr. Stewart observing her. She lifted her chin. Her potions, as he called them, were no longer any of his concern. With brisk steps, she left the churchyard and strode across the street.

Jolene called to her from the porch as soon as she closed the gate in the fence surrounding her yard. "I want to go home. The sooner the better."

*R*osemary forced herself to remain calm in light of Jolene's obvious distress. Leaning against the porch railing, she asked, "Did Cassie say something to upset you?"

Jolene shook her head. "She treats me fine. It's Galen French. He said he wants to come courting. Did his ma tell you?" She made a sound partway between a laugh and a sob. "He thinks I'm a lady. I can't let him find out different. I want to go home."

Taken aback, Rosemary surveyed the young woman's face. Since the morning sickness had subsided, her cheeks had taken on a rosy tint. With her walnut-brown hair and golden eyes, she'd draw the interest of any man. Right now those eyes held a frantic expression.

"At supper this evening we'll ask my brother if he can take you."

"Can you come too? Ma and Pa won't light into me so bad in front of strangers."

"I'd be happy to accompany you." She rested her hand on Jolene's shoulder. The thought of seeing Jolene reconciled with her parents lifted her heart. It would be her turn to say "I told you so" to Curt.

Rosemary sighed, wondering how she'd managed to commit every free minute of what should have been a restful day. When she entered the house, Bodie bounded over to her, his tail whisking back and forth. "Oh, mercy, I forgot about your walk." She glanced at the clock in the sitting room, then dashed upstairs to change from her gray leather slippers to sturdy boots. If she hurried, she and Bodie could circle the block and return before two.

She left the house, walking east along the residential section of King's Highway. When she reached the corner, she came to an abrupt halt at the sight of Dr. Stewart entering a two-story brick house across the street. Astonished, she realized she'd worked with him for a month and not known he lived four doors away.

"Come on, Bodie. Hurry." Averting her head, she turned south.

Elijah leaned forward, hands resting on his writing table, and gazed out his bay window. Miss Saxon's dog frisked in front of her as she walked in the direction of the railroad tracks. Over the past week he'd observed her friend Miss Haddon accompanying her home from Lindberg's Mercantile in the evenings. Then this morning, both Miss Haddon and Miss Graves attended church with her. Taking in strays seemed to be a penchant of hers.

He settled in an armchair next to the window and opened a copy of the *New York Medical Journal*. After flipping past several pages without reading a word, he dropped the periodical on the table. A walk would help him focus. He stood to don his jacket when a closed carriage stopped out front drew his attention.

Torn, he glanced at Miss Saxon's retreating back. Whoever his caller might be, the person had thwarted his opportunity to pretend an accidental encounter with his former nurse.

Elijah stepped away from the window, but not before he caught a glimpse of the carriage's occupant. His scalp prickled. He could refuse to answer the door, but what if the man had seen him through the glass? Knowing him, he'd stand on the porch and pound on the wooden panels all afternoon.

With a sense of doom, he strode to the entryway and opened the door.

"Father. This is more than a surprise. You should have written ahead."

Dr. Carlisle Stewart glared at him from beneath bushy eyebrows. "Aren't you going to invite me in?" His voice wheezed.

Elijah stepped aside. "Of course." The elder Dr. Stewart's well-tailored garments concealed his bulk, but years of prosperity had left their mark. Though they were the same height, he outweighed his son by at least fifty pounds. His sanguine complexion resembled the burgundy he liked to consume.

He handed his hat and coat to Elijah, then sank into one of the armchairs in the sitting room, leaning back to accommodate his belly. He cast a disdainful glance at his surroundings. "So this is where you've been hiding. You could do better."

"I like it here." Elijah gritted his teeth and seated himself facing his father. "You didn't come all the way from Chicago to criticize my house, did you?"

"I didn't come to criticize you at all. I'm here to ask for your help."

He braced himself. His father saved that jovial tone for coaxing patients to allow him to perform painful procedures.

"You don't need my help with anything. Your practice has made you rich. The woman you married after Mother died is young and beautiful. What could you want from me?"

"I want you to return to Chicago as my partner." He fumbled in his breast pocket and removed a handkerchief. After blotting his forehead, he balled the linen cloth in his fist. "You could carry on after I'm gone—inherit my patients and my bank accounts."

"Your wife will expect the bank accounts, and I don't want any part of your practice. I've said so more than once."

"My wife left me last winter for younger pastures. Apparently she grew tired of waiting for me to die." He surveyed the room. "What do you have against a successful business? Did you take a vow of poverty?"

"I earn enough to get by."

For a moment, his father's face sagged. Downward lines fanned from the corners of his eyes. Before compassion had a chance to grow in Elijah's breast, the lines hardened into their accustomed steely ridges. "You're my only child. If a man can't depend on his own family, who does he have?" He pushed himself to his feet and lumbered to the door.

His conscience pricked, Elijah trailed after him. "Please, spend the night before leaving for Chicago."

"Not going to Chicago. I'm returning the carriage to a colleague in Hartfield and taking the train north in the morning."

How typical of the man. He'd never travel just to visit him—he made the trip to see a colleague. Elijah was an afterthought, as always.

Carlisle Stewart swiveled to face his son. "My offer stands. When you get tired of beans and bacon as payment for your services, let me know." He crossed the porch and strode toward the street.

Elijah gripped the door frame, trying to ignore the guilt

102

that threatened to send him running after the carriage. Was he being manipulated? Or did his father truly need him? At any rate, he'd never stomach his father's covert dealings with wealthy clients. Until that changed, he'd remain in Noble Springs.

As he stepped inside, an open buggy rolled past. Jacob West held the reins and Miss Saxon sat on the seat beside him. He banged the door shut. All he needed now was to find rats in the attic to make this a perfect day.

Rosemary tightened her hold on her hat as Jacob urged the team into a trot along King's Highway. The redbuds had faded since her visit to the Graves's farm earlier in the month, but the dogwoods were at their peak. The countryside wore a cloak of spring green. "This is my favorite time of year. I like all the flowers."

"I like having more customers. People come to town when the weather's better." He kept his eyes on the narrow road.

She searched for something else to say that would draw him into conversation. For a moment she wished she'd paid more attention when her mother attempted to teach her social graces.

Jacob broke the silence. "A wagon's coming." He slowed the horses and guided them onto a grassy verge. Once they stopped, he met her eyes. "I'm glad you agreed to come out with me this afternoon. I hope we can become better acquainted."

In their dealings at the grocery, she'd never taken time to pay attention to him as a man. With his darker skin and black moustache, he reminded her of illustrations in *The Arabian Nights*. Gray hair flecked his temples. Her heart stirred at the yearning written across his handsome face. Yet as hard as she tried, she felt nothing more for him than friendship.

"You're very kind. I always enjoy the opportunity to visit the country."

The oncoming wagon pulled even with them. Over Jacob's shoulder, she glanced at the couple on the seat and gasped. Without a doubt, the tiny woman in the sunbonnet was Jolene's mother. The rangy man with the lined face who held the reins must be her father. Once the two reached Noble Springs, inquiries would tell them where she lived. A pulse pounded in Rosemary's temple. She wanted to be at home to provide moral support before Jolene's parents found her.

"Jacob . . ." She hesitated. To ask him to take her home now would be an affront after what he'd said.

He looked at her, waiting.

The Graves's wagon rolled out of sight around a bend.

"I must ask you to take me back." She pointed at the dust trail that lingered over the road. "I fear that wagon is headed for my house."

He raised his eyebrows. "You were expecting them when you accepted my invitation?"

"No, certainly not. I believe they are the parents of one of my guests—Miss Graves. She may fare better during their visit if I'm present."

"She's in danger, then?" Puzzlement clouded his voice. "Miss Haddon is with her, is she not?"

"Miss Haddon is indisposed this afternoon." Rosemary clenched her gloved hands together in frustration. If she could, she'd take the reins and drive the buggy herself. She took a deep breath and released it slowly. "It's a private matter. Please, if we turn around now, I'll be most grateful."

"As you wish." He clicked his tongue and steered the team west onto the road. "Since our time together today is so brief, would you accompany me again next Sunday?"

She realized she was leaning forward, silently urging the

horses to greater speed. She relaxed against the seat and nodded. "That would be very pleasant. Thank you."

One more Sunday wouldn't hurt and would relieve her of the guilt she felt over ruining his afternoon. Now if he would only stir the team to a faster clip. Her stomach knotted at the thought of Jolene facing her parents by herself.

13

$\mathcal{R}$osemary shushed Bodie's barking and opened the door, thankful to have reached home before Mr. and Mrs. Graves discovered where she lived.

Jolene waited out of sight in the kitchen.

"So, you're the one who's got my daughter." The tanned man on the porch bunched his hat brim in his fist. He wore a faded blue shirt with sturdy denim trousers held up on his narrow frame by suspenders. Gray stubble bristled from his cheeks.

"That's her," Mrs. Graves said. She peered up at Rosemary from beneath the coal scuttle rim of her bonnet. "I didn't tell him about . . . what you said . . . until this morning. He thought maybe you wasn't lying after all. Told him we shouldn't come, but he didn't pay me no mind."

"Come in, please." Rosemary stepped aside to allow Jolene's parents into the cramped entry. She gestured toward the sitting room. Now that she faced them, she didn't know what to say next.

Mr. Graves preceded his wife into the room, then stood awkwardly staring around him. "Where's my girl?"

"She'll be here in a minute. First, I'd like to help you understand what happened to her."

He snorted. "I've got four young'uns. Don't need you to tell me what happened."

Rosemary's face heated. "That's not what I meant." She turned to Mrs. Graves, who had sunk onto one of the chairs beneath the window. "Just so you understand. She misses you and wants to come home, if you'll have her."

Tears rolled down the woman's cheeks. "It's not up to me. Her pa's the head of the house."

"I'm asking you again." Mr. Graves swatted his trouser leg with his hat. "Where's my girl?"

Rosemary shrank away from the anger in his voice. She couldn't allow Jolene to face her father in this state, nor could she keep her away. Cringing at the scene she envisioned, she moved toward the kitchen. "I'll see if I can find her."

"She ain't lost. Just git her in here."

Perspiration prickled her skin. *Please, Lord, calm our hearts.* If her interference brought Jolene further pain, she'd never forgive herself.

Jolene huddled next to the back door, her hand resting on the top of Bodie's head. "I can't face Pa," she whispered. "I'll go hide in the greenhouse and you tell him I'm gone."

"I won't tell a falsehood." She took the girl's arm, keeping her voice low. "I'll be right beside you. The only way to get through this is to plunge straight in. Whatever happens, the Lord already knows about it. He's with you."

Jolene twisted her hands together. "I . . . I just can't do it."

"Yes, you can. I'll stay right beside you." Rosemary felt quivers vibrate through the girl's body. She tugged gently on Jolene's arm.

When they entered the sitting room, her father stared at her as though she were an insect he'd discovered in his apple trees. Her mother started to stand, but subsided upon a hard glare from her husband.

Heart pounding, Rosemary faced Mr. Graves. "Please don't shut your daughter out. She needs you, and her mother. To turn her away would be—"

"She can talk for herself." He folded his arms over his chest.

Jolene disengaged her arm from Rosemary's and stepped in front of her father. "I'm so sorry, Pa." Her voice shook. "I met this boy. He said he wanted to marry me, soon as he had some money saved. He talked awful sweet. I thought he loved me, so I . . ." A sob escaped her throat.

Mrs. Graves made a moaning sound. Her husband silenced her with a glance.

Using her knuckles to swipe away tears, Jolene tilted her head so her gaze locked with her father's. "Miss Rosemary must've told you he's gone. He never knew about . . . my condition."

Her father's jaw worked, as if he were fighting to swallow something he couldn't quite get down. "Never thought I'd see the day a daughter of mine . . ."

Her face crumpled. "I just want to come home. Please, Pa."

Sadness washed the anger from his face. Tears crept through the stubble on his cheeks as he opened his arms and gathered her to him. His chin rested on top of her head. "My baby girl."

Jolene's mother flew across the room. "Praise God."

"Don't carry on so," he said, his voice gruff. "She's our flesh and blood. We got to do right by her."

Blinking back tears, Rosemary looked away. Seeing Jolene reunite with her family left her aching for reunion with her own parents.

Elijah woke with Miss Saxon on his mind. Her presence with Jacob West the previous afternoon had taunted his dreams. Miss Graves and her predicament notwithstanding, he would stop at Miss Saxon's house first thing and ask her to—

No, he'd tell her—

He dragged his fingers through his tousled hair and swung his legs to the floor. Miss Saxon wasn't likely to care what he said after his uncharitable behavior. After dressing in a new white shirt and his best black trousers and jacket, Elijah faced the mirror over his washstand and studied his appearance. Jacob West's image floated in front of his eyes. He could understand why some ladies might find him attractive, but he was much too old for Miss Saxon. Furthermore, they had nothing in common. With her keen mind and caring nature, she'd be better suited for, say, a doctor.

He turned from the glass with a rueful chuckle. First he needed to convince her to return to her job in his practice, and if he didn't hurry, she'd be on her way to the mercantile.

Within minutes, Elijah stood on Miss Saxon's porch, hearing Bodie bark on the other side of the door. The latch clicked.

"Dr. Stewart." Hand covering the lace at her throat, she stared at him. "A gentleman never calls this early. Is something amiss?"

Her glossy hair shone in the morning light. In contrast to the drab calico she wore in his office, she was attired in a green skirt and bodice that caused her dark-lashed eyes to resemble forest pools. He fought the impulse to smooth a wayward curl away from her temple.

Thankful she couldn't read his thoughts, he straightened and used his most professional tone. "I find myself at a loss without your capable presence. The accounts are in disarray."

"Did you stop by to tell me of your difficulties, or are you asking me to come to work for you again?" A teasing gleam lit her eyes.

"I'm asking you."

Her voice turned chilly. "Do you still claim the right to dictate what I do in my own home?"

What an exasperating woman. She should know he wouldn't have asked if he still harbored any reservations. "I wouldn't think of trying to dictate to you." His jaw tightened. "Miss Graves, or anyone else, can stay with you as long as you want. Now, do you wish to return to my employ, or not?"

Bodie nosed past her skirts and sniffed at Elijah's trouser leg, his tail wagging. The patch around his left eye made the dog look like he was winking at him. Rosemary's expression softened as she reached down to rub the animal's fur.

"Bodie's used to accompanying me to the mercantile. He doesn't like being separated all day. I'm sure you'll have no objections if he stays with me in your office."

He raised an eyebrow. "Are you bargaining?"

She turned her hazel eyes on him. "Not at all. Just establishing our terms." A smile lit her face. "We'll be there shortly."

"I'll be expecting you." He left the porch with the distinct feeling he'd been bested in a contest of wills.

When the doctor departed, Rosemary closed the door and breathed a prayer of thanksgiving. The offer of employment couldn't have been more timely. The thrice-yearly payment from the trust fund her grandparents provided wouldn't arrive until the end of the month, and she was beginning to feel like Old Mother Hubbard.

Humming, she hurried up to her room to change into her calico dress. Cassie met her at the top of the stairs. "Are you ready to leave?"

"Yes, but not for the mercantile. Dr. Stewart just asked me to return to his employ."

"And you're happy? Didn't you say he was stubborn and unreasonable?"

"He is. But I'm going to try to overlook his faults." She rested her hand on Cassie's forearm. "If he fully accepts me in his practice, maybe the townsfolk will overcome their prejudice against female nurses. I pray that will be the case."

"I still don't understand why you want to be a nurse." Cassie wrinkled her nose. "All that messiness—blood and heaven knows what."

Rosemary settled on the top step and patted the place beside her for Cassie. "I need to support myself. Nursing is what I know. Before the war came, the thought of caring for the injured never occurred to me. My family relied on my mother's herbal medicines and we were rarely ill. But then . . ." She closed her eyes at the memory. "Men were brought from battlefields to St. Louis. Hospital wagons passed me when I walked along the street. Sometimes I heard the men moaning as they jounced over the cobblestones."

She faced Cassie. "After the first few months, I couldn't bear it any longer. I had to help, so I went to Jefferson Barracks and offered my services. Then after the war ended, I found myself with a skill I wasn't expected to use."

"But surely you could find a husband to take care of you." Cassie folded her smooth, white hands together in her lap.

Rosemary bit her tongue to keep from asking, "Like your mother did?" Instead, she shook her head. "Marriage is a dream. I'm twenty-seven. Pretty girls like you are the ones the few remaining bachelors want." She patted Cassie's shoulder and stood. "I need to change my dress. Dr. Stewart is expecting me."

Cassie scrambled to her feet. "Do you think Faith will let me come to the mercantile in your place?" Her lower lip trembled. "It's my only hope of seeing my mother—that is, if Mr. Bingham allows her to come to town."

"Faith would welcome you, especially considering your circumstances. Please tell her I'll stop by this evening for a visit." She wondered whether Cassie would be of any help at the store. Her main skill so far seemed to be looking decorative.

Rosemary opened the door to her room. "As soon as I'm dressed, we can walk as far as the corner together."

Bodie bounded off the porch, his tail telegraphing his delight at being allowed to accompany his mistress. Rosemary followed him down the steps and then stopped short, staring in horror at her garden. Tidy rows of seedlings had been uprooted and trampled into the dirt. Outraged, she jerked off her gloves, dropping to her knees on the brick pathway. "My plants! Who could have done this?"

Bending over the flattened earth, she lifted a diminutive lavender start. Its roots dangled, limp and broken. She flung the destroyed herb at the fence. "I spent hours on Saturday in my garden, and now look. Is anything left?" She raked through the ruins of her work with her fingers, lifting one shoot after another and setting aside those whose roots appeared intact.

Cassie dithered next to the gate. "This is dreadful. What are you going to do?" She clutched her embroidered handbag close to her chest like a shield. "You can't just drop everything to—"

"Yes, I can. These plants won't live if their roots are exposed all day." Rosemary stood and squared her shoulders. "I've spent too much time and money on my herbs to let them die."

"But the doctor—"

"He'll have to understand. I'll be there as soon as possible." She slid her gaze over Cassie's wide-skirted taffeta dress, knowing there would be no point in asking for her help. "Would you please stop at Dr. Stewart's office on your way to the mercantile? Tell him I've been delayed."

After Cassie hurried away, Rosemary placed her gloves and carryall on the porch and marched to the greenhouse for a trowel and watering can.

Sun leaked through a filter of fragmented clouds as she dug one circular hole after another and tucked undamaged plants back into the soil. She was thankful to note the furry leaves of her second-year mullein growing next to the fence hadn't been disturbed, probably because the plant looked like a weed. Bodie stretched out on the top step watching her work.

"Some watchdog you are," she said. "Why didn't you bark when this happened?"

He thumped his tail.

She walked over and rubbed his neck, then returned to sorting, planting, and discarding. An empty bucket served to collect seedlings whose roots had been destroyed. By the time she finished her task, the sun floated above the clouds and warmed her back. Past noon. Dr. Stewart would probably order her to turn around and go home the moment she arrived.

Rosemary wiped her hands on the towel she'd used as a kneeling pad and then flexed her stiff shoulders. After resting for a moment, she'd go inside to wash and pin up the hair that had come loose at the nape of her neck. Then she'd face the doctor.

"Miss Saxon. Are you hurt?" His voice boomed through the quiet. The gate squeaked on its hinges and with brisk strides he stood beside her. He extended his hand. "Are you able to rise?"

"Of course I am." She reached up with earth-stained fingers and permitted his strong grasp to draw her to her feet.

"I was concerned when you didn't arrive. Evidently you decided you'd rather work outside than in my office."

"Didn't Miss Haddon give you my message?"

"I haven't seen her this morning, but I've been busy with patients most of the time."

She massaged her temple, not caring that she was probably leaving smudges on her face. "I asked her to stop on the way to the mercantile." She blew out an exasperated breath and pointed at her freshly bedded herbs. "This was an emergency. Someone trampled my garden—either during the night or early this morning. I had to try to save all I could."

He folded his arms and studied her.

She held her breath.

His gaze moved from her face to the replanted area. "You prepare your . . . remedies from these herbs?"

"Some of them. Others are kept in my greenhouse, and I've ordered a few roots from back east. Not many, though. Too expensive."

"Then you should notify Sheriff Cooper. Whoever did this trespassed on your property—that's illegal. You could collect damages."

Rosemary gave a derisive snort. "Sheriff Cooper is a far cry from the Pinkertons. I'd have to lead him by the hand and personally point out the miscreant."

"I doubt that. As it happens, I've spent time with Thaddeus and find him to be a reasonable fellow. I'll mention to him what happened here."

"Please don't. There's nothing he can do." She saw no need to inform him that her distrust of Sheriff Cooper began with the man's unfounded harassment of her brother. The story might be old news, but the wounds caused to her family had yet to heal. She lifted the bucket containing ruined plants. "If you'll excuse me . . ."

"Certainly." A genial smile replaced the puzzled expression on his face. "Likely you'll require a few minutes to freshen up. I'll expect you by one o'clock." He directed his attention to the porch. "Bring your dog."

14

*R*osemary arrived promptly at one and flipped through the pile of receipts Dr. Stewart had shoved into the center drawer of her desk. When he told her his accounts were in disarray, he hadn't exaggerated. Still, things could have been worse. He'd noted the date on each item. Once she put the receipts in order, posting them to the ledger wouldn't take long. Then she'd be ready to help with patients.

Bodie sniffed in circles around the reception area. After a thorough inspection, he collapsed at Rosemary's feet.

"Good boy. You stay right there and be quiet."

She glanced at the closed door to the examination room. Bodie's behavior would be tested when the patient emerged. In spite of her earlier bravado, she knew Dr. Stewart wouldn't let the dog remain if he proved hostile to strangers.

The latch clicked and the doctor stepped into the room, followed by an older man whose face resembled the grooved bark on a bitternut hickory tree. He clutched a square brown bottle in his right hand. The man's eyes widened when he saw her. "What's a woman doing here?"

Bodie growled low in his throat. She clutched the scruff of his neck and gaped at the stranger.

116

Dr. Stewart stepped between them. "Miss Saxon is my nurse. Don't worry, she'll keep your visit confidential."

"Miss Saxon, is it?" He studied her face for a long moment. "Know all about you. Wondered what you looked like." After slapping a stained brown slouch hat over his white hair, he compressed his lips and limped to the door.

Once he left, Rosemary released her grip on Bodie's neck. "Who was *that*?"

"Name's Abraham Grice."

"Have you treated him before?"

"First time. He's a strange one. Most of my patients have taken the sight of a female nurse more calmly." He handed her a crumpled bank note with a receipt. "Enter his complaint as gout, please."

She took comfort from the "please," hoping his kindly tone meant he wasn't upset about her dog's reaction to the patient.

"I'm sorry Bodie growled. I really believed he'd behave himself. He never bothered customers when I had him with me at the mercantile."

"I don't blame him for growling. The man sounded hostile. Your dog thought you needed protecting." Dr. Stewart leaned against the wall, a sympathetic expression on his face. "What a way to welcome you back. Mr. Grice notwithstanding, I'm glad you're here." His face flushed. "I mean, the paperwork is in need of some organization."

"I noticed." She hid a smile as he ducked into his private office. Once in a while his starch and bluster façade cracked and the young doctor she remembered broke through.

The following Sunday, Rosemary bent over her garden while she waited for Jacob to arrive, wishing she'd never agreed to a second buggy ride. It wasn't fair to encourage him. Spotting a yellowed geranium toppled on the ground, she reached for the dead plant, taking care not to drag her blue and gray wool skirt through the soil. Only one casualty over the week. Better than she'd hoped. At the sound of horses' hooves, she turned and saw Jacob stop his buggy next to the hitching post. She waved a polite greeting.

He jumped down and wrapped the reins through the loop at the top of the post. "Tending your flowers, I see." In contrast to the garb he wore at work—shirtsleeves and dark blue trousers, covered by an apron—today he was dressed in an iron-gray suit. Its careful tailoring flattered his stocky build, while the white collar on his shirt accented his dusky skin and black moustache. If he'd dressed to impress her, he'd succeeded. Perhaps this would be a pleasant afternoon after all.

"I'm afraid this one's past help," she said, displaying the floppy geranium clasped in her left hand. She opened the gate and smiled up at him. "Please come in. I'll be ready to leave as soon as I fetch my shawl."

When they entered the sitting room, Cassie lifted her gaze from her needlework. "Mr. West. How nice to see you." She gave him a polite smile and then turned back to her tatting.

He bowed in her direction. "And you as well, Miss Haddon." His tone was courteous, but his attention remained on Rosemary as she lifted her gray fringed shawl from the back of a chair and handed it to him. As soon as he draped the soft wool over her shoulders, he took her elbow and guided her to the door.

Rosemary paused and turned to Cassie. "Would you please check on Bodie after a while? He's on the back porch sunning himself."

"Of course." Cassie sighed. Her lower lip trembled the tiniest bit.

"Miss Haddon seemed to be in low spirits," Jacob said as they walked toward the buggy.

"She worries about her mother. And of course, she's at loose ends. Mr. Bingham ordered her to find employment, but she has no particular skills. I can't imagine him turning her out like that."

After helping her onto the tufted leather seat, he lifted the reins and clucked at the horse, then they rolled west on King's Highway. "Will Miss Haddon continue to stay with you?"

Rosemary considered her answer for a long moment before replying. Although providing for Cassie's healthy appetite put a strain on her finances, she didn't want to give Jacob the idea she'd welcome further help with groceries. She looked up at him and found his intent gaze upon her.

"Cassie may stay as long as she wishes." Rosemary lifted her lips in a half smile. "'Woe to him that is alone when he falleth; for he hath not another to help him up.' I'm just making sure she's not alone."

"Your generosity is one of your many admirable qualities."

"You're too kind," she murmured, her cheeks warm.

"Not at all." He guided the horse around the courthouse square and west onto High Street. They passed the livery stable and then the two-story brick home where Faith and Curt lived with Judge Lindberg. Soon residences gave way to thick vegetation interrupted by rocky outcroppings and gurgling streams.

Rosemary broke the silence that had fallen between them. "Pioneer Lake should be lovely today. I haven't been there yet this spring."

"No doubt it is. We'll see it from the road. There's something just beyond that I'd like to show you."

With another person, she'd have felt uneasy traveling so far from town, but Jacob's solid presence reassured her. She never heard of him crossing the lines of propriety. At the moment, he looked so pleased with himself that her curiosity stirred.

"What are we going to see?"

"Be patient. We're almost there."

The road wound above the shores of Pioneer Lake, then led up a long hill. Jacob turned the horses onto a less-used track and followed a stream that gurgled over flat rocks.

Uneasy, Rosemary gazed around at the oak trees pressing in on each side of the buggy. The lake lay somewhere below, hidden by the forest. Her confidence in Jacob's integrity wavered. She scooted as far away as the buggy seat permitted.

Jacob kept his attention on the horse as they made their way over the rough terrain. In a few minutes they reached the top of the hill where a small pond gleamed yellow and green in the filtered light that slipped through the leaves. He pulled up on the reins.

"Here it is. What do you think?"

She remained pressed against the side of the buggy. She should never have allowed him to take her this far from the main road. Her mind filled with whispered stories she'd heard of women who'd been ruined because they were too trusting.

"What do I think of what?" she asked, her tone wary.

He waved his arm in a broad sweep, taking in the clearing where they'd stopped. "This piece of land. The owner came in last week and wants to sell. I told him I wanted another opinion before I made a commitment—your opinion, to be exact."

Her eyes widened. "We hardly know each other. Shouldn't you ask someone else?"

"Who?" He remained on his side of the seat, making no attempt to move closer.

Some of the tension left her shoulders. He'd brought her

here to see the land, not to compromise her honor. In a few minutes, they'd no doubt turn around and leave.

"How about your partner, Mr. Riley?"

Jacob threw back his head and guffawed. "Colin Riley lives in Boston," he said when he regained control. "What does he care if I build a house up here?"

Heat flooded her face. "I didn't know. I always assumed he stayed in a back room somewhere, balancing your accounts." As she said the words, she realized how ridiculous she sounded. "I'm sorry. I've been reading too many novels by Mr. Dickens."

"Colin loaned me a stake to open my store." He chuckled again. "Back when I was in my twenties he hired me and taught me the grocery trade. When I wanted to come west, he offered to help. His name's on the business because without him I'd still be . . ." He dropped his gaze. "Well, I'd still be in Boston."

He reached across the seat and clasped her gloved hand. "Forgive me for laughing. I didn't mean to hurt your feelings."

"Apology accepted." She slipped her hand free. "But my mistake aside, why would you want my opinion?"

"You're a sensible lady. If I build a house here, it will be because I've chosen a wife and plan to start a family. Do you think this land is suitable?"

She surveyed the grassy flat, which curved downward toward the west. Thick oak and hickory trees grew on all sides. In the distance, water gurgled over rocks. When she raised her eyes, she caught him watching her. Not wanting to give him false hope, she chose her words with care. "It's lovely. Any girl would be happy in such a spot."

"I feared you'd think this was too far from town. Don't ladies like to pay calls on one another and such?"

"Some do, certainly. However, not everyone is involved in a

social circle." She dared a teasing smile in his direction. "This road does run both ways, does it not? I presume your wife would be able to visit Noble Springs whenever necessary."

A fleeting thought about Cassie's mother darted through her head. Mrs. Bingham's visits to Noble Springs had diminished over the months of her marriage. Rosemary's mind rested on the woman's situation for a brief second, then she caught herself. She shouldn't be worrying about Cassie's life now, of all times. She turned her full attention back to Jacob.

He captured her gaze with his intense brown eyes. "I wouldn't deny my wife anything she wanted, be it in Noble Springs or St. Louis."

Rosemary's heart gave a little flutter at the message behind his words. She hoped he didn't mean her. Time to change the subject. One and a half buggy rides didn't constitute a courtship. She glanced at the western side of the clearing, noting the sun angling behind the hill. "Perhaps we should start home. The afternoon is fading."

He nodded and shook the reins over the horse's back, guiding the buggy in a half-circle until they faced downhill. "So it is. I need to check on the restaurant's receipts for the day." He grinned at her. "Since I don't have Mr. Riley stashed in a back room, the accounts are part of my duties."

She chuckled, enjoying his rare flash of humor.

The buggy jolted into motion down the rugged track, rocking like a boat on a choppy lake. The horse's iron shoes rang when its hooves struck against rocks jutting up in wagon ruts. Rosemary kept her feet jammed against the floor so she wouldn't bounce into Jacob's side. When they reached the turn to the more-traveled road, the buggy gave an additional lurch and settled sideways against a chokecherry.

She banged her shoulder on the side of the buggy when

Jacob jerked the reins to prevent the horse from dragging them forward. He turned anxious eyes on her. "Are you hurt?"

"Not at all. Startled? Very." She straightened on the tilted seat and peered over the side. "What happened?"

He didn't answer until he'd set the brake and jumped to the ground. "The back wheel must've run off into a hole. I'll line up some rocks and roll us out of here." He tied the reins to a branch, then removed his jacket and placed it on the seat. When he rolled up his shirtsleeves, she had a clear view of the dark hair that covered his muscular forearms.

Rosemary's eyebrows shot up at the sight. He looked strong enough to lift the buggy with her still in it.

His next observation dashed her hopes of such a quick resolution to their dilemma. "Wheel's broken. Must've got stuck between two rocks." He leaned against the side of the buggy and removed his hat, wiping his forehead with a handkerchief. "Can't be repaired. Got to get a new one." Leafy shadows cast by the setting sun speckled his white shirt.

"What . . . what are we going to do?" She pushed the words past the fright that clutched her throat.

"Only one thing we can do." He strode to his horse and began unfastening the harness. When the animal was free of the shafts, he led it next to the carriage and held out his hand to her. "We'll ride Jackson to town."

We? She stared at the animal, her heart drumming. Jackson's broad chestnut back gleamed in the fading sunlight. "I've been afraid to ride since I was thrown as a girl." Her voice shook. She hated herself for having to admit weakness. "I can drive a buggy, but ride? No. Besides, he doesn't even have a saddle."

Keeping one hand on the reins, Jacob clenched the other into a ball and gave her an impatient look. "We don't have a choice. It'll be dark soon. There's a lap robe behind the seat—we'll use that for a saddle blanket. Just hang tight to his mane. I won't let you fall."

She didn't know which would be worse. Being that close to Jacob, or riding on an animal that stood as high as the top of her head. Rosemary took a deep breath. She'd been frightened before, and the Lord had seen her through. He was with her now.

She lifted her chin. "All right. I'm ready when you are."

"Good." He handed her the reins. "Hold him while I put the blanket over his back."

Within moments, he placed his hands around her waist and swung her from the buggy to the horse. "You'll be safer if you straddle him," he said when she tried to sit sideways.

Her face burned. Ladies rode sidesaddle. Cringing, she swung a leg over Jackson's back and gripped his mane with tight fists. The animal's hide prickled through the fabric of her petticoats.

Jacob settled behind her. One strong arm encircled her waist, while the other held the reins and guided the horse south toward town. She sat stiffly, trying for as little contact as possible between her back and Jacob's chest. Embarrassment swept over her in waves.

He leaned forward. "Relax. You'll be more comfortable if you move with the horse's gait rather than bouncing up and down with every step." His breath was warm next to her ear.

She drew a deep breath. Puzzled, she sniffed again. Bacon. Up close, Jacob smelled like bacon. With all the time he spent in the restaurant kitchen, cooking odors must have settled in his hair. Rosemary felt a smile cross her lips. How could she distrust a man who smelled like breakfast?

Twilight had settled over Noble Springs by the time they passed Judge Lindberg's house. Rosemary kept her head lowered, hoping no one would recognize her. If they could travel to her front door without encountering a familiar face, she'd be grateful. They turned right at Courthouse Square, then left on King's Highway. Rosemary sighed with relief. One more block and she'd be home.

With an abrupt motion, Jacob jerked on the reins. "Looks like you have company." He pointed at a horse and buggy tied to the hitching post.

Dr. Stewart stood next to the fence, a stunned expression on his face.

15

lijah fought the urge to step forward when Jacob placed his hands on Miss Saxon's waist. With a swift motion, the grocer swung her to the ground. She kept her head averted while she fluffed her skirts where they bore the outline of her legs. Elijah could almost feel the heat of her embarrassment from where he stood.

He set his jaw. How she chose to spend her afternoons was her own business. But to ride through town tandem, and bareback to boot, was an astonishing act of either bravery or foolhardiness.

Jacob placed his hat over his chest. "Miss Saxon, this isn't the way I planned our day. Once the buggy is repaired, I hope you'll come with me for another ride."

"Certainly. The mishap was not your fault at all." She kept her eyes on the grocer.

Elijah thought he detected a note of warmth in her voice. He cleared his throat. "Pardon the intrusion. I came by to see if Miss Saxon would accompany me to treat a patient." He turned to Jacob. "That is, unless you object."

"Of course not, Doc. I know you have to go where you're

needed. Anyway, Miss Saxon has to answer for herself. She's not my possession." He nodded at her. "I'll see you soon."

"Yes." She kept her back to Elijah and waited until Jacob mounted his horse and rode in the direction of his store. Once he was out of sight, she turned around. If the light were better, Elijah would have sworn her cheeks were scarlet.

"Shall we go?" She strode toward his buggy. "You can tell me about the patient while we ride." Her tone was crisp and professional.

He raised an eyebrow at the change in her demeanor. Apparently she felt she owed him no explanation. In truth, she didn't. But it would be comforting—no, enlightening—to learn why she and the grocer came to be out riding bareback on a Sunday evening.

He took her arm and helped her onto the seat. After a few moments of uneasy silence, during which he unhitched the horse and started west on King's Highway, he said, "I've never seen a woman in skirts astride a horse before. And to ride without a saddle. I didn't realize you were an equestrienne." His voice missed the casual tone he'd hoped for and struck a waspish note.

She spun around and glared at him. "Do you believe I chose to travel home in that manner? And if I did, what business is it of yours?"

He noticed a glitter of tears hovering beneath her lashes before she turned away. He massaged his jaw, wishing he'd had the good sense to keep his mouth shut. Miss Saxon had been right when she said her actions were none of his business. Now he'd not only made her angry, he'd hurt her feelings. He darted a glance in her direction, but she kept her back to him.

"Miss Saxon."

"What?" She didn't look up.

"I apologize. I'm glad you're coming with me. I need your help." He drew in a breath and waited for her response.

Frogs and crickets filled the silence, pausing when the buggy grew close, then tuning up again when they rolled past.

After a long moment, she shifted on the seat and stared straight ahead, her chin in the air. "Very well. My help is what you pay me for. Please tell me about the patient."

He exhaled with relief. At least she was speaking to him. "His name is Benny Harper. He's four years old. According to his father, he was playing with a scythe and cut his hand open. I know you had plenty of experience caring for knife wounds during the conflict."

"Indeed I did." He saw her shudder.

A memory teased at him, but he couldn't bring it into focus. He shook his head. Later. When he had more time to think, he'd try to dredge the thought to the surface.

He guided the buggy north past the academy and on out into the country. One by one, early stars appeared on the cobalt canvas overhead. If it weren't for the boy needing help, Elijah would have been content to ride on into the evening with Miss Saxon beside him. He dismissed the fancy. After the way he spoke to her earlier, why would she want to spend more time with him than necessary?

"We should almost be there. Mr. Harper said he'd meet us at the road."

She leaned forward and peered into the growing darkness. "Why didn't he bring the child to town instead of wasting time by riding in and asking you to come to their house?"

"They have a new baby. His mother wouldn't leave, and wouldn't let her husband take the boy without her."

Upon rounding the next bend, he noticed a light flickering on his left. "That must be Mr. Harper." He followed their guide up a narrow lane to a low-slung cabin planted at the edge of a plowed field. After grabbing his bag, he reached up to help Miss Saxon descend.

She brushed his hand away. "You go ahead. I'll be right behind you."

Rosemary watched Dr. Stewart jog to the cabin and disappear inside. She sighed as she climbed down from the buggy. If only he, rather than Jacob, were the man showing an interest in her. She stifled a snort. The doctor's only interest seemed to be in monitoring her behavior, and she already had a brother. She didn't need another one.

A stab of guilt pierced her conscience at the sound of the child's cries. How shameful to be thinking about herself when a little boy was injured.

Mr. Harper approached with the lantern. "Come this way, ma'am. We got Benny set under the lamp so's the doc can see good." He held the light low to illuminate where to step on the rocky ground.

The metallic smell of blood was the first thing Rosemary noticed once she entered the cabin. Drops darkened the wooden floor, stained the tabletop where the boy lay, and soaked through the rag tied around the boy's right hand.

She checked the room but didn't see Mrs. Harper. If the woman wouldn't allow her husband to take Benny to town, shouldn't she be here with him? Rosemary dropped her shawl over a chair and crossed to the table.

Dr. Stewart's eyes met hers. "Please take the laudanum from my bag and give him five drops."

At his words, Mr. Harper turned to a shelf, removed a cup, and added water from a barrel near the door. "Stuff tastes terrible. This'll help him get it down."

She squeezed the drops into the cup, using a syringe with a

rubber bulb on one end, then bent over their patient. "Please sit up and open your mouth, Benny."

Apparently surprised to be asked to do more than howl, he complied. She held the cup to his lips while he swallowed the medicine.

His face contorted. Before he had an opportunity to spit out the mixture, his father put a second cup to his lips and the boy gulped clear water.

"Thank you," the doctor said. "Now we'll wait a few minutes, then examine the wound." He turned to Rosemary. "Try to keep him still if you would, please."

While they waited, he addressed Mr. Harper. "You got any whiskey? I need some towels too."

"Right here." He took a brown bottle from a cupboard and passed it across the tabletop, then disappeared into an adjoining room and returned with folded toweling.

Dr. Stewart removed a rolled-up piece of buckskin containing sutures from his bag and threaded one of the needles with silk. He placed the supplies to one side.

As Benny relaxed, Rosemary brushed sweaty blond hair from his forehead and murmured, "Dr. Stewart will fix you in no time. I'm going to hold you now. Be as brave as you can be." She placed her hands on the child's shoulders, feeling his body tremble through his homespun shirt.

"Ready?" Dr. Stewart asked.

She nodded.

He unwrapped the bloodstained rag, rested the injured hand on a towel, and poured whiskey into the wound. She wrinkled her nose as the strong odor of spirits spread over the room.

Benny tried to jerk his hand away, but she pinned his arm to the table. Mr. Harper joined them, holding the boy's feet still.

Working quickly, the doctor pressed the edges of the cut together and drove the first suture through the skin.

Rosemary felt perspiration dampen her forehead when the boy screeched. They should have given him more of the laudanum. "Just a couple more jabs and he'll be finished," she whispered in his ear. She swallowed and increased her pressure on his upper arms as the needle pressed through his flesh a second time. Scenes from the Army hospital flickered through her thoughts. The screams, the sweating bodies. She banished them to the place where her nightmares lived, and slammed the door. "All we can do is help the patient in front of us," a doctor once told her. She followed the advice and focused on the boy.

In minutes, Dr. Stewart tied a fourth suture and blotted blood from the palm of Benny's hand. The child's wails subsided. Rosemary helped him to sit again and slipped an arm around his shoulders. "You were very brave."

He hiccupped, his chest in spasms from crying. "Mama?"

A pale young woman dashed from the other room and wrapped him in her arms. She looked at Rosemary. "Thank you. I purely can't abide the sight of blood. I'm so glad the doc brought a woman to help. I believe it eased things for Benny, having you here."

"I hope so. Poor little fellow." Rosemary rolled her shoulders to relax the muscles after her firm grip on the woman's son. "If you make a poultice of comfrey root and put it on the cut, he will heal faster."

She felt the doctor's eyes on her and looked up to see his brows knit together in a frown.

Once they were out of sight of the Harpers' cabin, Dr. Stewart slapped his hand against his thigh.

Rosemary jumped when she heard the pop.

"Miss Saxon." He hissed her name through clenched teeth. "I will not have you prescribing for my patients. We've been over this before."

"A poultice isn't the same thing as a tincture." She folded her arms over her chest and glared at him, although she knew he couldn't see her expression in the dark.

"That's not my point."

"I beg your pardon. I thought it was."

"Have you stopped to think what would happen if Benny's wound becomes corrupted? Who will be blamed? Certainly not you." He snapped the reins over the horse's back. The animal jerked forward, picking up speed.

"Why do you persist in thinking everything I do reflects on you? Comfrey won't cause corruption. To my knowledge, a poultice never has."

He tipped his head forward and blew out a long breath. "We could bicker all night." His voice sounded tired. "Let's accept that we'll never agree and let it go at that."

A lump rose in her throat at the finality in his words.

Lamplight shone from the front window when Dr. Stewart stopped his buggy in front of Rosemary's house. "It appears your guests waited up for you."

After enduring his silence during the ride to town, she felt relieved that he'd decided to speak. However, this wasn't the best time to inform him she only had one guest. Their jousting match over the comfrey reminded her of the disagreement over Jolene. She'd mention the girl's return to her family another time, when he wasn't so irritable.

Taking his proffered hand, she descended from the carriage.

"A light in the window is a welcome sight at this hour. Better than entering a dark house."

"Quite so." He guided her through the gate and onto the porch. "Good night, Miss Saxon." In the dimness, she noticed weary shadows under his eyes. Dark stubble lined his cheeks.

"Good night." She opened the door and stood on the threshold until he drove away. Regret at her sharp words pricked her conscience. Tomorrow she'd be pleasant, no matter what he said to her.

When she closed the door, Bodie charged down the stairs, tail wagging. Cassie followed, holding her dressing gown above her slippered feet.

"What happened? Why were you and Mr. West out so late? I've been frantic with worry."

"Dr. Stewart was waiting at the gate when Jacob brought me home. He had an injured child to tend to and wanted my help." Rosemary slid an arm around the other woman's waist. "I'm sorry you worried. I should have stopped in and told you."

Cassie cupped a hand over her mouth while she took several deep breaths. "I hope I'm not presuming. You're almost like a sister to me. First after the train derailed, and now with Mr. Bingham . . ." She faced her. "I never had a sister—or a brother, for that matter—and I just know sisters act like you do."

Rosemary hugged the words to her heart. "You're not presuming. I wish we'd met under more pleasant circumstances. Your mother—"

"We'd have been better off if she'd never married that man."

She thought of her success with Jolene's parents. "Maybe there's something I can do to help. Sometimes people surprise you."

Dr. Stewart swiveled around in his chair when Rosemary entered the office the following day. "Good morning." His tone lacked its customary amiability.

Determined to be pleasant, she gave him her brightest smile as she untied her bonnet. "It's a fine day, isn't it?"

"I suppose." He turned back to the book he'd been reading.

She winced. Her hasty words last evening had caused more damage than she realized. "Dr. Stewart, I—"

"Receipts need to be posted. And would you see to it that the soiled bandages in that pail over there are laundered?" He pointed to a covered bucket in the corner next to the stove. "In fact, why don't you take them to your house right now, before the office smells of corruption."

"Certainly." She matched her tone to his. If he wanted to give orders, she'd obey. Anything to restore an easy relationship. After settling her bonnet back on her head, she grabbed the bucket's handle, snapped her fingers to summon Bodie from under her desk, and marched out.

Once Rosemary left the office behind, her steps dragged. Last night the doctor had said they needed to accept that they'd never agree, but she never dreamed he'd retreat behind an impersonal wall. She felt a traitorous sting behind her eyelids. No. She would not cry. She'd go home, leave the bandages on the back porch, and keep a civil tongue in her head in the future.

After completing her errand, she left her yard and covered the distance to the doctor's office with brisk steps. When she turned the corner onto Commerce Street, a slate gray mare tied to the hitching rail caught her attention. The blaze on its face reminded her of Galen French's horse, but at this hour he'd be teaching at the academy. Curious as to who might be in the waiting room, she popped through the door, then stopped short.

16

*R*everend French's son perched on the sofa, dressed for a day in the classroom. Galen wore his walnut-brown coat buttoned over a white shirt with a high collar. As always, his left sleeve was pinned up above his elbow.

"Miss Saxon. Thank the Lord." He jumped to his feet, a frantic expression on his face.

His intensity drove her back a step. "Why aren't you at the academy? Does the doctor know you're here?"

Dr. Stewart swung open the unlatched door to his private office. "He asked to see you." He cocked an eyebrow. "I trust he's not expecting one of your remedies."

Heat flared in her cheeks, and she swallowed a biting retort. "I assure you—"

"I'm here for information, not healing." Galen turned desperate eyes on her. "Where is Miss Graves? I didn't see her in church yesterday. When I called at your home earlier, fearing she was ill, Miss Haddon said she left eight days ago."

"She's gone?" Dr. Stewart planted himself next to Galen. "Why didn't you tell me?"

Facing the two men, she had the sensation of standing in front of tall trees. She took another step away and craned her neck to look up at Galen. "She went home. Her parents came for her."

"But I planned to see her again. Where do her parents live?"

What could she say? His expression pleaded, but Jolene would be devastated if he appeared at her door.

Dr. Stewart tipped his head in her direction. "I'd like to hear this too."

Galen shot him a hard look. "She's already spoken for."

The doctor's mouth dropped open. "Are you—?"

"Certainly not." Rosemary glared at him, then turned to meet Galen's astonished eyes.

"Am I what?"

"Never mind. The doctor has you confused with some-one else." Her mind raced to find words to answer Galen's question about Jolene's whereabouts. She wouldn't lie, but couldn't tell him the whole truth, either. "I believe Miss Graves's family has a farm somewhere east of here." She held her breath, hoping he wouldn't press further.

"She left without saying good-bye." He cupped his right hand over his stump. "It's my arm, isn't it? Please be honest."

"Not at all. She never said a word to me about your . . . injury." Rosemary reached out to comfort him, then let her hand drop. She knew how self-conscious her brother felt about the wound that left his neck scarred. She could only imagine Galen's adjustment to postwar life.

"Then why?" Galen's voice echoed his bewilderment.

Dr. Stewart cleared his throat, apparently ready to join the discussion.

Rosemary silenced him with a glance. "Galen, Miss Graves had her reasons, but believe me, your missing arm was not among them. She held you in extremely high regard."

He backed toward the entrance. "I'll find her, if it's the last thing I ever do."

Elijah waited until the door closed before facing Miss Saxon. "All this time you've led me to believe you were harboring Miss Graves in your house. You knew I was concerned. Why didn't you say she went home?"

"Why should I have? You didn't care what happened to her, as long as your reputation wasn't affected." She stood before him, hands on hips, a pink flush on her cheeks. Bodie sprawled at her feet, his head turning from one to the other as they spoke.

The truth in her words stung. He'd tried so hard not to emulate his father that he'd lost sight of his own reasons for becoming a physician. He opened his mouth to defend his actions, then closed it. She'd be appalled. Best keep his family secrets to himself.

He dropped his gaze. "Unfortunately, you're right. I regret my behavior."

Before she could respond, he strode to his private office and closed the door. After flopping into his chair, he leaned his elbows on the desk and rested his head on his hands. "Lord, help me to make things right with Miss Graves." He kept his voice low.

The clock on the wall next to the window ticked in the silence. Through the closed door, he heard Miss Saxon walk to her desk and slide her chair over the wooden floor. He closed his eyes again. "And please help me get back in Miss Saxon's good graces."

Crossing his arms over his chest, he leaned back and stared out the small window at the brick exterior of the law office across the alley. The blank wall offered no direction to his jumbled thoughts.

Young Galen's tormented expression haunted him. Miss

Graves's falsehood regarding her child's father was a noble gesture, but the poor man deserved to know where the woman who carried his child could be found. As the pastor's son, surely he'd do the right thing in spite of the inevitable gossip. Once the two of them were married, all would be well.

Elijah straightened his shoulders and grabbed his hat from its resting place atop the skeleton in the corner. On his way out, he stopped in front of Miss Saxon's desk. "I have a call to make. I'll be back by one. You may take dinner early if you like."

"Thank you. Perhaps I will." Her tone was respectful, but cool. She turned her attention back to the open ledger.

Feeling the chill of her response, he left the office, eager to complete his mission. She'd be pleased to see Galen and Miss Graves reconciled. Perhaps his efforts would restore his relationship with Miss Saxon, as well.

Early morning clouds had dispersed, revealing a brilliant blue sky. Whistling, he strode along King's Highway toward Courthouse Square, passing the barber, a boot maker, and a dress shop before crossing the street to the block that contained Lindberg's Mercantile. Miss Haddon stood gazing out the front window of the store. He tipped his hat to her, marveling again at Miss Saxon's proclivity for taking in strays.

He turned the next corner and pushed open the door of the jailhouse.

"Thaddeus, I have a favor to ask."

After Dr. Stewart left, Rosemary sprang to her feet. His absence gave her a perfect opportunity to dust and sweep his private office, as well as the examining room. She collected the necessary supplies from a cupboard and began her task in the doctor's office.

In contrast to his often rumpled appearance, he kept his books and papers arranged in tidy stacks. She dusted the bookcase, gritted her teeth and brushed dust from the skeleton, then tackled the desktop. A book lay open facedown. Her eyes widened when she read the title—*A Compendium of Herbal Medicines*. The same volume she had at home.

She darted a glance at the door. It wouldn't do for him to remember he'd forgotten something and return while she was—admit it—snooping on his desk. She flipped the book over to see what he'd been studying. "Comfrey: Description, Cultivation, Parts Used Medicinally."

An alarm bell rang in her head. It wasn't enough that he forbade her to offer remedies to his patients, now he was arming himself to overrule her recommendations. Well, let him study all he wanted. He'd not find errors in her judgment.

She returned the *Compendium* to his desk, careful to position the book as she'd found it, then returned to cleaning. Her mind raced. She had until one o'clock—time enough to walk to the mercantile and share her concerns with Faith.

As soon as she swept the last bit of dust out the door, she whistled for Bodie and the two of them hurried toward the center of town.

Rosemary paced between the fabric display and the storeroom in the mercantile. Thankfully, Faith and Cassie were alone so she could share her concerns.

"Why do you think he's reading Mrs. Kilbourne's book? Is he planning to report me to the county medical society?"

Faith leaned over a counter displaying watches and ladies' brooches. "How can he? Your suggestion to Mr. Eldridge helped him heal."

"Dr. Stewart would debate that."

Cassie rose from one of the chairs beside the stove. Her polished chintz dress rustled as she stepped next to Rosemary and patted her forearm. "Why don't you ask him why he's reading the book?"

"I can't let him know I was poking around on his desk. You've seen him when he's upset."

"He's bound to notice that the room's been cleaned." Cassie turned to Faith. "Don't you agree?"

"Men don't notice things like that. Curt certainly doesn't. I think Rosemary's right. She can't come out and ask." Faith placed her forefinger against her lips and stared at the floor for a moment, then turned her head in Rosemary's direction. "Maybe he's sincerely interested. Have you considered that possibility?"

Rosemary snorted. "Not for a moment. You should have heard him last night. His mind is closed tighter than a snapping turtle's jaws."

"Apparently not," Cassie said. "I think—" Her mouth dropped open and she pivoted toward the door. "My mother's here! Driving the buggy by herself." She dashed out to the hitching rail, where Mrs. Bingham struggled to secure the horse. A passing freight wagon caused the animal to jerk its head sideways.

"Hold still!" Cassie's mother snapped. She sounded near tears as she tied the reins.

"Where's Mr. Bingham?" Cassie's high-pitched question carried through the open door.

"He took sick a few days ago. His man is sitting with him, but I don't know how much good that old buzzard can do." She leaned on her daughter as they entered the mercantile. When she spotted Rosemary, she straightened.

"Here you are. Don't you ever stay in one place? I've been to your house and the doctor's office looking for you."

Rosemary forced a polite smile. "Shall I send Dr. Stewart to your home? He'll be in the office soon."

"No. Mr. Bingham doesn't trust doctors." The woman's red hair framed her ashy complexion. "I want one of your tinctures."

"What are your husband's symptoms?"

"He says his stomach is jumping. Everything he eats comes back up." She sucked in a ragged breath. "I'm so worried." She looked at Cassie. "I know he's a harsh man, but I need him."

Rosemary had never heard the woman apologize before. She glanced in Cassie's direction to gauge her response.

Cassie's lips thinned. "You don't *need* him, Mother. Look what he's done by sending me away. We were fine before, just the two of us."

"We lived on your uncle's charity." Her mother scowled. "I'm not here to discuss family matters. Miss Saxon, will you help or not?"

"Ginger tea should settle his stomach." Rosemary went to the shelf holding her soaps and teas. She selected a blue cloth-wrapped bundle that had a paper tag tied on with a green ribbon. "This is dried ginger root. Boil some for ten minutes and give him a cupful between bouts. You should see results within a day."

Cassie's mother dug into her handbag. "Ten cents is rather dear for a bag of roots."

"I'm not forcing you to buy them. You're welcome to find another remedy."

The woman's glare could have blistered paint. She slapped a coin on the counter. "This better work." Her expression softened when she looked at Cassie. "I wish I could stay longer, but I don't dare."

"I know." Cassie kissed her cheek. "I miss you," she whispered.

Tears swam in Rosemary's eyes. As brusque as Mrs. Bingham seemed, she loved her daughter.

A longing for her own mother shuddered through her. She drew a deep breath and forced her thoughts to her questions about Dr. Stewart. Faith and Cassie both suggested he might be interested in her herbal remedies. Maybe he was. It wouldn't hurt to ask.

Dr. Stewart returned after the dinner hour. He gave Rosemary a broad smile when he greeted her and then strode into his office. After dropping his hat on top of the skeleton's head, he settled in his chair and opened the book resting on his desk.

Taking courage from his cheerful expression, she stepped to his doorway. "I notice you're reading Mrs. Kilbourne's *Compendium*." She strove to keep her voice neutral. "Are you finding her information helpful?"

"You know this book?"

"I have a copy at home. My mother gave it to me when I turned twenty-one."

He leaned back in his chair and regarded her with a puzzled expression. "A strange gift. Perhaps a ring or a brooch would have been more appropriate for such an occasion."

"At the time, her expectation was I'd follow in her footsteps and help people with her herbal remedies."

"And then the war came?"

"Yes." She flinched when she realized she'd revealed her age, something a lady never did.

He rested his hand on the open pages. "I'm only reading this out of curiosity. These little treatments are interesting, but I'm far from convinced of their effectiveness."

She bristled. "I've seen them succeed where doctors fail."

"Miss Saxon—" He raked his fingers through his hair,

making the curls stand on end. "For once, can we still the debate? When I've finished reading Mrs. Kilbourne's theories, I'll make up my own mind. Then we'll talk more." He used the same voice he reserved for calming agitated patients.

"I'll look forward to the discussion." She hid a pleased smile. Their relaxed conversations had come to mean more to her than she liked to admit.

*B*roken clouds scattered a mosaic of sunlight over the boardwalk as Rosemary set off for Sunday supper at Faith's home. Much to her disappointment, the week had passed without Dr. Stewart mentioning the *Compendium* again. She shook her head to dislodge him from her mind. She wouldn't allow his opinion, or lack of it, to spoil time with her family.

Bodie frisked around her legs as they walked. She smiled down at him. "You enjoy Sunday supper as much as I do, don't you?"

He woofed and disappeared under a lilac bush that frothed with lavender blooms. Rosemary slowed her pace to savor the fragrance. Lilacs always blossomed in time for her mother's birthday at the end of April. With a pang, she pictured a bowl of the flowers gracing a table in her home.

A moment later, the dog burst forth in pursuit of a gray and white cat. Fur bristling, the feline darted across the street and under the porch of the brick house Faith and Curt shared with Judge Lindberg and Amy.

Her jaw tightened when she recognized Sheriff Cooper's chestnut gelding tethered to the hitching post in front of the house. She wouldn't have come if she'd known he'd be there. One day she'd have to forgive him for his misguided persecution of her brother. She knew that. But not today.

Faith opened the door at her knock. "Welcome. Grandpa's been looking forward to your visit." She glanced down as Bodie scampered past them into the parlor on her left. "Good. You brought the dog."

"He's anticipating a plate of table scraps." She chuckled.

"Cassie couldn't join us?" Faith spoke over her shoulder while leading the way to the parlor.

"She sends her regrets. She's fretting about her mother. Mr. Bingham still isn't well."

"The poor girl. Wish we could think of a way to improve her situation."

"I wrote him a letter. I'm hoping he'll respond favorably once he recovers."

When Judge Lindberg saw Rosemary, he pushed himself up from his green wing chair and crossed the room, his cane tapping the polished wood floor.

"Always a pleasure, Miss Rosemary." He bowed over her hand.

"And you, Judge." She smiled at his courtly manner. He greeted her in the same fashion even when he saw her more than once a day. She suspected he forgot she'd visited, so each occasion was fresh in his mind. What a blessing Faith had Amy to stay with him while she operated the family business.

Sheriff Cooper unfolded his rangy form from the sofa. "Good afternoon, Miss Saxon." His sandy hair appeared freshly barbered, and he'd waxed his drooping moustache so that it formed a straight line along his upper lip.

"Sheriff. This is a surprise." She took a chair as far across the room from him as possible.

"Thaddeus here is courting our Amy," the judge said. "He's getting to be a regular fixture at suppertime."

To Rosemary's amazement, the sheriff blushed. "Amy's a fine woman, and a good cook to boot."

Faith spoke from the doorway. "Our good cook has supper ready. Please come and eat."

Curt stood at the head of the table in the dining room, slicing a crusty baked ham. He waved a greeting at Rosemary with the carving knife and then resumed his task.

Amy's fourteen-month-old daughter, Sophia, toddled in Rosemary's direction. "Romie, Romie!"

She swooped the child up and kissed her button nose. After hugging Amy, she took a seat next to Judge Lindberg, her mouth watering at the fragrance of the savory baked ham. A parade of side dishes, including sweet potatoes mashed and baked with a pecan crust, beets swimming in vinegar sauce, and a platter heaped with golden biscuits, moved from hand to hand along the table. She suspected Curt and Faith made sure she had a sumptuous meal once a week to balance out her own simple fare.

Between bites, Rosemary's gaze traveled between the sheriff and Amy, then to her brother. Judging from their easy conversation, Curt appeared to bear the sheriff no ill will. She wondered how he'd managed to forgive the man who'd treated him like a criminal after the mercantile was robbed the previous year.

The grudge she bore the lawman threatened to choke her. She crossed her knife and fork over her half-finished meal and stared at the napkin in her lap. *Lord, please take away my anger.*

After clearing the supper plates, Amy served slices of Dolly Varden cake. As soon as she returned to her seat, Sheriff Cooper cleared his throat. "Miss Amy and me have news.

Come July, we're fixing to have the preacher marry us. Right here in the parlor, just like Curt and Faith was."

Amy lowered her lashes. A pink flush bloomed on her heart-shaped face.

Stunned, Rosemary paused in mid-bite of the jam-filled dessert. She remained silent through the wave of congratulations. Amy said yes to the sheriff?

The beaming girl met Rosemary's eyes. "Would you put flowers around the room for us? You made everything look so pretty when Faith married your brother."

The sheriff placed one of his broad hands on Amy's shoulder and leaned toward Rosemary. "You don't have to. I know you don't care for me much." His tense expression reminded her of a little boy facing punishment.

She focused her attention on Amy's hopeful face. "I'd be happy to. My garden should be in full bloom by then."

Faith rose from her seat at the foot of the table and smiled at Amy. "Why don't you and Thaddeus enjoy a stroll together? Rosemary and I will look after Sophia."

While Curt and Judge Lindberg played chess at the dining room table, Sophia sat on a braided rug nearby, playing with carved wooden animals. Dishtowel in hand, Rosemary watched them from the kitchen doorway, her mind circling the image of Amy married to Sheriff Cooper. She turned to Faith. "He's at least a dozen years her senior. Do you think she'll be happy?"

"She's come to love him. He treats her like she's made of spun sugar, and he's very fond of Sophia." Faith shook dishwater from her hands and dried them on a corner of her apron. "The marriage will be a blessing to all three of them."

Rosemary lowered her voice. "I certainly hope so. Amy was shattered when Joel was killed. She deserves to be happy."

"You're allowing your dislike of Thaddeus to influence you."

"He's Thaddeus now?" Irritation spiked her tone.

Faith placed her hand on Rosemary's shoulder. "Let it go. Please. For your sake."

"How did Curt—?"

"You'll have to talk to him. I think Reverend French helped somehow."

"Did I hear my name taken in vain?" Curt stepped inside the kitchen. He slid one arm around Faith's waist and kissed the top of her head. "Did you ask her?"

Rosemary looked up at her brother. "Ask me what?"

"Amy will be living in Thaddeus's home when they're married. We're hoping you'd move in with us and take her place as companion for Faith's granddad."

Companion for Faith's granddad. Curt's words echoed as Rosemary strode along the boardwalk toward her home across town. How could she refuse? Judge Lindberg's mind had been failing for some time. He was most content among familiar surroundings.

Between managing the mercantile and caring for her grandfather, Faith had been near the end of her endurance before Amy's return to Noble Springs following her husband's death last year. Now, with Amy's departure, Faith had nowhere else to turn for help.

Rosemary's boots thudded with every new thought that assailed her. If she responded to Curt's request, she couldn't keep her house. She'd have to abandon her herb garden. And what would happen to Cassie?

148

She kicked at a pebble on the walkway. She didn't want to lose her independence or give up nursing. What had begun as her best option for earning her own way had grown into a source of pride as she'd come to see her job as a profession. There was no reason a woman couldn't care for the sick as well as a man did—maybe better.

No doubt Faith and Curt needed her. Then a vision of Mrs. Haggerty's gratitude for having Rosemary's help with the delivery of her baby crossed her mind, followed by one of Benny's mother thanking her for caring for her injured son. They had needed her too.

She paid scant attention to the buggies that rolled past, until one pulled abreast and stopped.

"Miss Rosemary?" Jacob raised his hat. "I'd be happy to take you wherever you're going."

Startled from her reverie, she hesitated a moment before replying. In truth, she'd rather be alone to struggle with her decision. But the weight of her carryall packed with leftovers dragged at her arm, and Jacob's kind face beckoned.

"Thank you. A ride home would be nice."

After helping her into the buggy, he stowed the carryall behind the seat. Bodie followed them as Jacob turned right at Courthouse Square. He slowed the horse when they rounded the corner onto King's Highway.

"Would you like to accompany me to Hartfield next Sunday? I need to see a farmer about supplying me with eggs." His eyes met hers. "You might be interested in learning how the business is run."

She had little interest in the operation of the grocery, but perhaps . . . "Could we stop along the way so I can call on a friend of mine? I won't stay long."

"Be glad to." He stopped the buggy in front of her house. "See you next Sunday."

She sighed as he drove away. As attractive as he was, he wasn't the one who stirred her heart. *Admit it. Dr. Stewart is another reason you don't want to leave nursing.*

That evening, Rosemary and Cassie sat across the kitchen table from one another, each holding a cup of chamomile tea. When Rosemary explained her brother's request, Cassie's eyes grew wide, but she didn't utter a word. The oil lamp overhead tinted the steam rising from their cups into a golden mist that swirled upward and disappeared.

"I want to do the right thing—by both of you. I never dreamed I'd be faced with such a choice." Rosemary's teacup clinked when she placed it in the saucer. "I know they wouldn't have asked if there were another solution."

"There may be other unmarried ladies in town who could help." Cassie's voice wavered. "The war left many of us with no prospects."

"True enough. But Judge Lindberg's mind is no longer clear. I doubt he'd take kindly to a stranger."

Cassie fiddled with the hem on the tablecloth for a moment, then took a deep breath and met Rosemary's gaze. "I'm not a stranger. Perhaps he'd tolerate my company. Then you wouldn't have to leave your house and your garden—and your employment."

Rosemary studied her, taking in her pale hands with their smooth nails, her fashionable rose chintz dress, and her auburn hair arranged in the latest style. No one looked less like a domestic than her guest.

"There's more to do than keep him company." She gentled her voice. "Amy prepares the noon meal and keeps the house tidy."

Cassie's eager expression faded. "I can't prepare meals. I

never learned how. We always had help—even horrible Mr. Bingham has a servant." She lifted her chin. "If they would hire a cook, I could do everything else. Keep him company, read to him, play chess. Whatever he might need." She leaned across the table and clasped Rosemary's hand. "Please. You've done so much for me. I want to repay you somehow."

Rosemary carried their empty cups to the washbasin. A flicker of hope sparked through her quandary. Now all that remained was to convince her brother and Faith.

osemary shivered and drew her sunburst-patterned quilt tight around her shoulders. Rain ticked against the bedroom window, and gusts of wind rattled the panes. What had seemed like a simple solution earlier that evening now sounded improbable in the hours after midnight. Even if Curt and Faith agreed to have Cassie stay with Faith's grandfather, they were bound to balk at the idea of hiring a cook.

Lord, your Word says to cast my cares on you, so please take this one and show me what to do. Once she shifted her burden, her eyes drifted shut. Amy's wedding wouldn't take place until July, so she had over two months to make a decision. She sighed and snuggled farther under the quilt.

A strong blast of wind screamed around the corner of the house, followed by a crash and the sound of shattering glass. Bodie burst into a fury of barking. Rosemary leaped to her feet and grabbed her flannel wrapper, then groped for a match to light the candle next to her bed.

When she flung open the door, the dog bounded to the top of the stairs and continued to bark. He looked over his shoulder, inviting her to follow him.

Cassie stood in the entrance to her room with one hand at her throat. "What happened?"

"That's what I'm going to find out." She clutched the candleholder and followed Bodie down the stairs, through the sitting room, and into the kitchen. Everything appeared undamaged. If there were no broken windows, then where—

Rosemary froze. Her greenhouse.

Hands quivering, she hurried to the pantry and took a lantern from the shelf. She touched the candle flame to the wick, then settled the chimney in place.

Cassie trailed her into the kitchen. "Surely you're not going out in that storm."

"I'll only go as far as the greenhouse. I have to know what happened."

"Maybe a tree branch—"

"We don't have any trees back there." Rosemary lifted the lantern. When she opened the door, the dog bolted into the darkness. "Bodie! Come back."

He ignored her and raced toward the front of the house. Thankful he couldn't escape the fence, she stepped into the pelting rain. In moments, damp chill penetrated her wrapper. Pebbles on the walkway pressed into the soles of her felt slippers.

When she reached the greenhouse, she held the light high. Instead of reflecting off the panes in the door, the lantern beam shone through into the interior. Jagged edges in the frame showed where glass had been.

She took one step inside. Shards glittered on the earthen floor. A quick survey of the area showed a pot overturned and a fist-sized stone on the ground next to broken pieces of terra cotta. The scene told her all she needed to know.

Swaying from shock, she put out a hand and steadied herself against the wall. She took several deep breaths and waited until she felt calm enough to return to the house.

Come daylight, wearing boots to protect her feet from glass, she'd clean up the damage. For now, she wanted the safety of her warm kitchen.

Shivering, she marched along the pebbled walk with rain trickling down her spine. Cassie stood in the doorway, holding a blue-and-white-striped blanket in her outstretched hand. She took the lantern.

"I built up the fire in the stove. Wrap yourself in this." She dropped the blanket over Rosemary's shoulders.

"Bless you." She let her soaked wrapper fall to the floor and kicked off her wet slippers. "Where's Bodie?"

"I thought he was with you."

"He must be on the front porch, waiting for me to let him in." Rosemary clutched the blanket around her with one hand and carried the lantern in the other while she hurried through the sitting room. Cassie stepped around her and opened the door.

Bodie wasn't on the porch.

Alarmed, Rosemary whistled the two notes that always brought him running. No response. "Bodie!"

The only reply was the sound of rain drumming on the porch roof.

"Where could he be? He can't get out of the yard." She descended the steps in her bare feet, holding the lantern in front of her. Halfway to the fence, her breath stopped.

The gate stood open.

Rosemary set her jaw in a hard line. First thing in the morning she'd find her dog, then repair her greenhouse. Whoever was responsible for this would soon learn they weren't going to scare her away.

After spending the remainder of a sleepless night listening for Bodie's bark, she rose at daybreak. A glance out the window told her the rain had stopped. Water puddled in low spots behind the house. The greenhouse door stood open, as she'd left it. Maybe the dog had sheltered in there.

She threw on her warmest dress and laced her boots.

Mud from last night's rainstorm sprayed from the wheels of Elijah's buggy as he traveled east toward Noble Springs Academy. He grinned to himself at the thought of the message he planned to deliver.

He bounded up the half-dozen granite steps in front of the largest of three brick buildings on campus. A rangy man with gray hair like sheep's wool approached him with his right arm extended. "You're Dr. Stewart. I've noticed you at church lately." He pumped Elijah's hand. "I'm Malcolm Robbinette, the principal here. What brings you to our school? No one sick, I hope."

"Nothing like that. I'd like to speak with one of your instructors—Galen French."

"Fine young man. Touchy about that missing arm, but he'll adjust." Mr. Robbinette pointed east. "You'll find him in the next building. He teaches classic literature to the older students."

"Thank you." Elijah had his hand on the door handle when the principal spoke again. "Been hearing good things about you from our mathematics instructor, Curt Saxon. According to his sister, you're a skilled physician."

Warmth bloomed inside his chest. Miss Saxon approved of his methods. High praise, considering the number of physicians she would have assisted at Jefferson Barracks.

"Happy to hear that. She's a fine nurse." Prickly, but a fine nurse nevertheless.

"She'll be an excellent wife for some fortunate man." A bland smile rested on Mr. Robbinette's lips.

"No doubt." Elijah pictured Jacob West, his hand tucked under Miss Saxon's elbow as he escorted her to his buggy. The warmth inside chilled.

He followed a brick pathway next to the carriage drive toward a square building with chimneys towering at each corner of the roof. Granite steps, like the ones next door, led to a recessed entry. Signs attached to the walls of the center hallway identified the subject taught within. Gothic script spelled out "Classic Literature" outside the second door on the right.

Galen French stopped in the act of unloading books from a satchel onto his desk. "Dr. Stewart. Is one of my students ill?"

"I came to see you—with good news."

"Good news would be welcome." Galen sank onto a chair and rubbed his forehead. "Heaven knows I've had little enough lately." Sunlight angled through a window and sketched pinched lines around his mouth.

The lines stretched into a face-lifting smile when Elijah delivered his message.

"How'd you find out?" Galen sprang to his feet. "I've tried everything I know."

"Sheriff Cooper told me. He asked around."

The morning shone with rain-washed freshness when he left the school a few minutes later. Galen's effusive thanks echoed in his ears.

Elijah couldn't stop smiling, thankful he'd been able to atone for his earlier treatment of Miss Graves.

When Elijah opened his office door a half hour later and saw Miss Saxon's haggard face, his high spirits crashed. Purple shadows rimmed her tear-bright eyes.

He whipped off his hat and flung it on the sofa as he strode to her desk. "Ro—Miss Saxon. You're upset. What's happened?" Without waiting for her reply, he added, "I shouldn't have left you alone. If someone has come in here and hurt you, I'll—"

"No one's been here." Her voice trembled. "It's Bodie. He's missing." Tears brimmed and spilled over. "He's never run away. I'm afraid something bad happened to him." She groped in her pocket and removed a handkerchief, dabbing at her cheeks. "I'm sorry. I know he's just a dog, but I love him."

He remembered the plump black mongrel that had been his constant companion when he was a boy. When Inky died, he'd been inconsolable. Without thinking, he stepped around the desk and clasped her shoulder. "Tell me."

Her weight settled against him as she fought for control. He resisted the impulse to drop to her side and gather her in a comforting embrace. Instead, after a moment he let his hand fall, then perched on the edge of her desk. "How long has he been missing?"

"Since last night's storm." She told him about the open gate and the damage to her greenhouse. "I found this when I cleaned up the broken glass this morning." She handed him a wrinkled piece of brown paper.

You bin warned about them witchs brews. There won't be no next time.

Anger seared through his body when he read the scrawled lines. "By heavens, Miss Saxon. You've got to tell the sheriff."

"What can he do?" She drew a shuddering breath. "I just want Bodie back—unhurt."

"I'll help you look for him." The words were out before he could stop them.

She gazed at him, a startled expression in her eyes. "I couldn't ask you to do that."

"You didn't ask. I offered." He retrieved his hat from the sofa. "Shall we go?"

"You can't just close the office."

"Miss Saxon. We're wasting time."

Rosemary stood with Dr. Stewart in front of her house. He pointed at the muddy street. "There are dog tracks here. Did you see them?"

"I did. But they've been trampled by horses on the road. You can't tell where they lead."

He took her elbow. "We'll do this scientifically. Search each yard and alley on your block, then go on to the next one."

"I already searched my block before I left for your office."

"Good. Then we'll start across the street. You call his name and I'll look under shrubbery and porches. Maybe he was spooked by the storm."

He kept a firm grip on her arm as they stepped over water-filled ruts to the other side of King's Highway. They looked and called in front of each residence, stopped in to ask at the post office, then doubled back through the alley that ran between houses and the rear of West & Riley's. The aroma of frying bacon drifted from the screen door of the restaurant's kitchen. The scent reminded her of Jacob. Rosemary picked up her pace, heading for the front entrance.

"Where are you going?"

"To ask Jacob if he's seen Bodie."

Dr. Stewart tipped his head to one side. "Don't you think he'd have brought the dog to you if he found him?" His tone held an edge.

She slowed. "You're right."

The screen door squeaked open. "Miss Rosemary? I thought I heard voices out here." As if she'd conjured him, Jacob stood on the threshold, an apron wrapped around his middle. He nodded at Dr. Stewart.

"The doctor is helping me look . . ." She swallowed the fear that rose in her throat. "We're looking for Bodie. He's been missing since last night."

Jacob crossed the alley and faced her, concern shining from his eyes. "Your dog. I'm sorry. Can I help?"

"Would you . . . would you please tell your customers he's missing?"

"Let them know there'll be a reward if he's found." Dr. Stewart hovered close enough to her shoulder that she felt warmth radiate from his body.

"Good. I'll match whatever you put up." Jacob dropped a half bow in their direction and returned to the kitchen.

osemary left the church the following Sunday with her mind in rebellion against Reverend French's sermon. He'd chosen a verse from the First Epistle General of Peter—*Casting all your care upon him; for he careth for you.*

She held her Bible tight against her chest as she walked home through the balmy May morning with Cassie at her side. "I cast all my care on the Lord the night Bodie disappeared, and look where it got me."

Cassie gave her arm a comforting pat. "You're always telling me the Lord takes his own time to answer prayers. Bodie could still come back. It's only been a week."

"A week." Her steps lagged. "We've posted handbills in every store. By now, someone would have seen him." She blinked back tears. "He's gone."

"Are you still planning to ride to Hartfield with Mr. West this afternoon?"

Rosemary forced a smile, recognizing Cassie's effort to change the subject. "Yes. I hope to pay a call on Jolene on the way."

Two buggies rolled past, throwing up a cloud of dust in their wake. Cassie waved a gloved hand in front of her face. "If it's not mud, it's dust. I don't know which is worse."

"The mud. Definitely. Bodie always—" She gulped. "He loved to get dirty."

At the sound of footsteps behind them, she turned to see Dr. Stewart hurrying in their direction. He tipped his hat. "Good afternoon, ladies. Miss Saxon, I hoped for a chance to talk to you after services."

Excitement pulsed through her. "Do you have news of Bodie?"

He lowered his voice. "No." Apparently he noticed her crestfallen expression. "I'm sorry."

"Then why—?"

"I paid a call on the Harper family yesterday to see how little Benny is faring."

She recalled the doctor's objection to her suggesting comfrey root to the boy's mother, and prayed there had been no complications in his recovery. "Is . . . is he well?"

"Indeed. His hand is healing perfectly."

"I'm so glad. Thank you for telling me." She half-turned, ready to continue toward her home.

"One more moment, please."

"Of course, Doctor. What is it?"

"I wondered . . ." He harrumphed. "Would you have time this afternoon to show me how you prepare a comfrey poultice?" The eagerness in his deep brown eyes sent tingles down to her fingertips.

Rosemary fought disappointment. "I'd be pleased to show you, but unfortunately I have an engagement this afternoon. Perhaps another day?"

"Would tomorrow evening do?"

"That would be lovely. Miss Haddon and I will be at home."

After he strode away, Cassie turned to her. "This is the first time I've seen you smile since Bodie disappeared."

"I've hoped he—" She bit her lip. "Imagine. He asked about comfrey."

"I told you he might be interested. He wouldn't have been reading that book otherwise."

"You could be right." She clasped Cassie's hand. "I hope so."

Rosemary had no sooner changed from her Sunday dress into her blue plaid skirt and a white lace-trimmed bodice when she heard Jacob's knock. She gathered her shawl and bonnet and hurried to answer the door, wishing it were Dr. Stewart instead of Jacob on the porch.

"You're very prompt."

"Years of minding a business will do that to you." He took her shawl and settled the fluffy wool wrap over her shoulders, hands lingering a moment before releasing her. "I don't see your dog. He's still missing?" His voice softened with concern.

She looked down, willing herself not to cry. "Yes. I fear I'll never see him again."

"Perhaps a new puppy would help? One of my customer's dogs just had a litter."

"No. Thank you. Not now." Not ever.

"I understand." He took her arm and escorted her to his buggy.

The previous Sunday she'd been too preoccupied with Curt and Faith's suggestion to notice the bright new wheels. Red spokes contrasted smartly with the ebony body of the carriage. From the appearance of the polished exterior, Jacob had spent extra time preparing for their afternoon together.

She shot a glance at Dr. Stewart's home as they traveled east, wondering how he was spending his Sunday. She knew he'd struck up a friendship with Sheriff Cooper, but now that the sheriff and Amy were engaged, she doubted the two men spent much time together.

Stop it, she told herself. Just because he asked about comfrey, there was no reason to let her thoughts run away. The doctor's private life was none of her business.

A gust of wind tugged at her pancake hat. She grabbed at the ribbons to keep the flat headgear from blowing away.

"Shall I stop and raise the cover?"

"No, thank you." She folded her hands in her lap, wishing she could think of something more to say than yes or no.

He flexed his shoulders, letting the reins hang slack between his fingers. "Have you given any more thought to the property I showed you?"

"I'm afraid . . . what with Bodie . . . I haven't . . ."

"Maybe one day you'd like to see it again." He shook the reins and guided them around a bend in the narrow road. A man mounted on a dark gray horse barreled toward them.

The tendons in Jacob's wrists stood out with his efforts to direct the carriage out of harm's way. They lurched over uneven ground and stopped beside a downed tree covered with woodbine.

The rider blew past them, leaving a billow of dust in his wake.

"Blasted fool." Jacob flicked the reins to turn his gelding back to the road. "Nothing's important enough to risk a fine animal like that. He could break a leg."

She swept dust from her skirt. "At least your new wheels are intact."

"I'm happy you noticed. Cletus Wylie built them in his wagon shop. Did a fine job."

"He's one of Faith's customers at the mercantile. I remember him."

He gave her a nod of approval. "That's good you recall customer's names. It's useful when running a business. I know you'll be interested in my meeting with Mr. Kreskey—he's been supplying the grocery with eggs for several months now."

"Hmm." Try as she might, she couldn't think of anything more to say about eggs or Mr. Kreskey. She shifted on the seat and peered into the growth along the roadside.

"Are you looking for your dog?"

"Always."

"Let me know when you decide you want another one. I'll get you a pup."

She'd already told him no. Didn't he listen? "I—"

Jolene's cabin came into sight. Rosemary tapped Jacob's arm. "Could we please stop here a moment or two? I want to call on Miss Graves."

"Certainly." He guided the carriage through the opening in the rail fence and rolled past the apple trees, now covered in bright green foliage. Before he could help her down, Jolene burst out the door of the small cabin. The rounded shape of her belly showed beneath the full apron she wore.

"How could you? I told you I didn't want to see Galen French." Her voice shook.

Rosemary climbed down and crossed the dirt yard to the front stoop. "That's not Galen. He's Jacob West."

"I know that." Jolene stamped her foot. "Galen was here not twenty minutes ago. He said Dr. Stewart told him where to find me. You must've told the doctor." She placed her hands over her abdomen, tears streaking her cheeks. "He saw me . . . like this." She gulped. "I thought I could trust you."

Rosemary remembered the rider who'd passed them on their way from town. Galen. She took Jolene's hand. "He came to the office one day looking for you, but I didn't tell the doctor anything."

"Then how——?"

"I don't know, but I intend to find out."

The next morning, Rosemary stormed into Dr. Stewart's waiting room and banged the door behind her. He jumped to his feet, eyes wide.

"Miss Saxon. What on earth . . . ?" He rested his right hand on the door jamb of his private office.

"Did you tell Galen French where to find Miss Graves?"

A smile broke across his face. "Yes. I knew I had to do something to make amends to both of you for the way I treated her."

Her legs turned to rubber. She slumped on the sofa and stared at him, mouth agape. "What does Galen have to do with your treatment of Miss Graves? She was almost hysterical when I saw her yesterday. He's the last person she wanted to see."

"She can't protect him forever. I know he'll take responsibility for his actions if she gives him the chance."

"You believe *he's* the father of her child?" Her voice rose in disbelief.

"Of course. It's obvious."

Rosemary bent her head and covered her face with her hands. She didn't know whether to laugh or burst into tears. Poor Jolene.

She heard the doctor's footsteps as he crossed the floor. When she looked up, he stood in front of her, his clean-shaven face pale. "You mean Galen isn't . . . ?"

"No. They met at church after she came to live with me. He's the reason she left. He expressed a desire to court her, having no idea of her condition."

He flopped on the sofa next to her. "I was so sure."

She scooted to one end and pinned him with her gaze. "The poor girl couldn't bear for him to know what she'd done. She'd rather face her parents than have him find out. Now, thanks to you—"

"I'll make things right somehow."

"I think you've done enough." She stalked to her desk. "Patients should be in soon. Mondays are busy."

The doctor stood and tugged at his collar. "Call me when I'm needed." He entered his office. The door closed with a sharp click.

Rosemary sat at her desk and stared at the wall separating her from Dr. Stewart. The stricken look on his face hovered before her eyes. How could he have made such a mistake? And why didn't he talk to her about Jolene before he carried out his plan? She laced her fingers at the back of her neck to loosen tight muscles. She'd have to do all she could to repair the harm done to Jolene. At the moment, she couldn't think where to begin.

When the outside door opened, it took her a moment to recognize their patient. Mr. Grisbee, one of the woodstove regulars from the mercantile, shuffled in. He removed his hat, giving her a wide smile.

"Miss Rosemary. Pleasure to see you. Me and Jesse miss you down to the store."

"I miss you too, Mr. Grisbee." She rose and met him in the center of the room. "Mornings are quiet without your checker game going on."

He made a sound between a snort and a chuckle, then lapsed into a fit of coughing. Rosemary took his arm and helped him to a seat on the sofa. "I'll tell the doctor you're here. In the meantime, would you like a cup of water?"

He nodded, still choking.

She tapped on Dr. Stewart's door, then dashed to her desk

and poured ginger water into a cup. He took a sip, then another. After taking a deep breath, he set the cup on the floor next to his feet. "Appreciate it. That helped." The flush on his cheeks glowed through his unkempt gray whiskers.

When Dr. Stewart stepped from the examining room, Rosemary turned to him. "This is Mr. Grisbee. He sounds like he may have a bronchial—" She snapped her lips closed at his warning glance.

"Right this way, sir." Dr. Stewart placed his hand on the older man's shoulder and guided him to the examining table, then closed the door behind the two of them.

As Rosemary collected their patient's empty cup on her way to her desk, her mind raced through her stock of cures for bronchial disease. A mullein infusion would be the thing to try, but she'd have to meet Mr. Grisbee away from Dr. Stewart's presence. Two confrontations in one day would be too many. She busied herself with patients' records until the doctor emerged from the room.

He handed a bottle to the older man. "Here's some Ayer's Cherry Pectoral syrup. Try this for your cough, and drink plenty of hot tea."

Mr. Grisbee pocketed the remedy without looking at it. "Can't abide tea."

The corner of Dr. Stewart's mouth twitched. "Hot water, then."

"That's worse."

"Peppermint tea is rather pleasant, Mr. Grisbee," Rosemary said. "Faith has some leaves at the mercantile. I can stop in after five and explain the brewing." She didn't add she'd also bring mullein with her.

"All right, Miss Rosemary." He plopped his hat on and shuffled to the door. "See you after five." Coughing, he left the office.

The doctor folded his arms across his middle. "You're prescribing again."

For some reason, he didn't appear angry. He looked almost . . . amused.

"Mint tea isn't a prescription. People drink it all the time."

"If you say so." Shaking his head, he returned to his office. This time he didn't close the door.

At the end of the day, Rosemary gathered her things and prepared to leave.

"Miss Saxon?"

She turned, hoping he didn't want her to stay later. She had enough time to keep her appointment with Mr. Grisbee. Then she hoped to pay an additional call before sunset, if the doctor didn't give her more to do.

"Am I still welcome to visit you this evening? You were to show me how to prepare a comfrey poultice."

Her hand flew to her lips. "Oh! I completely forgot. The incident with Miss Graves—"

At the mention of the young woman's name, his face reddened. "Can we set that aside for the time being? I'm asking about tonight."

"Something has come up." She didn't add that the "something" had to do with Jolene and Galen. "If you're willing, tomorrow evening would be suitable."

Relief flooded his features, followed by a shy smile. "Tomorrow evening. I look forward to it."

The doctor remained in her thoughts long after she completed her visit to the mercantile. She loved the creases that formed in the wake of his smile, like ripples on a pond. Day-dreaming, she reached the corner in front of the barbershop and paused to let Bodie catch up to her.

Reality jolted her back to the moment. She cupped her hand over her mouth to prevent a sob from escaping. Her dog wouldn't be running after her, now or ever.

The last traces of sunlight cast a beacon between the shadows on the road ahead. Squaring her shoulders, she marched the final block to the Frenches' house. She couldn't do anything more about Bodie, but she could attempt to help Jolene.

Clarissa answered her knock. Her face wore a harried expression, which smoothed when she saw Rosemary. "How good to see you." The reverend's wife stood in their spacious entryway. The polished wood floor behind her shone in lamplight spreading from twin sconces on either side of a mirrored hall tree stand. "I must tell you, the tea you brought helps ever so much with my headaches. I wonder, though, the next time you drop by, could you bring some more?" She glanced over her shoulder and lowered her voice. "Just when I think Galen is adjusting, something agitates him. Then yesterday—"

"Yesterday is why I came to talk to you and Reverend French." Rosemary wondered whether Clarissa could hear her heart thudding in her chest. "Is he home?"

"Oh goodness, I've left you standing on the porch while I chatter away. Please, come in. I'll fetch Ethan." She led her into the sitting room and patted a high-backed chair upholstered in flowered fabric. "You'll be comfortable here. Would you like some refreshment?"

She felt perspiration tickle at her hairline. "Thank you, no. What I have to say shouldn't take long."

"My gracious. Now I'm curious." Clarissa bustled from the room. Within moments, she returned with her husband.

After he greeted Rosemary, he sat next to his wife on a set-tee. A frown creased the bushy eyebrows above his gray eyes. "You're concerned about something that happened yesterday? How can I help?"

Now that she faced Galen's parents, she didn't know where to begin. She closed her eyes for a moment to gather courage.

"I'm sure you remember Miss Graves, the young woman who stayed with me for several weeks."

The two of them nodded in unison.

"Apparently she caught your son's fancy. He asked to court her."

At this, Clarissa beamed. "Thank the Lord. I've prayed he'd settle down with a nice girl."

"It's not that simple." Rosemary hesitated, aware she was treading on shaky ground. "Miss Graves is expecting a child. The father left before she knew of her condition. When Galen showed an interest in her, she fled to her parents, not wanting him to learn that she wasn't . . . pure." She leaned forward. "She cares enough for your son that she didn't want him to find her. Unfortunately, yesterday—"

Reverend French sprang to his feet and finished Rosemary's sentence. "Galen found her."

She nodded. "Would you please explain the circumstances to him? Whether or not he decides to pursue a friendship with Miss Graves, he deserves to know."

The reverend and his wife exchanged an agonized look. "I'd tell him if I knew where he was," Reverend French said. His voice choked. "He didn't come home last night. No one's seen him."

After leaving the Frenches' house, Rosemary covered the distance to her home feeling like she'd been trampled by a team of horses. Galen missing. Although his parents said he'd disappeared on other occasions since returning from the war, she felt in some way responsible for yesterday's events. If she weren't working in the doctor's office, Galen would never have gone there to ask about Jolene. Then Dr. Stewart wouldn't have interfered.

He meant no harm, a little voice inside said. *He must have a good heart.*

He does, she told the little voice. *He cares about his patients—even to the extent of worrying that I'll harm them with my herbs.*

Rosemary crossed the street and passed his house, noticing the windows were dark. He was probably at Jacob's restaurant for supper. If she weren't so tired, she'd bake a small treat for him before he called on her tomorrow evening.

She climbed the stairs to her porch, her steps dragging. Tea would have to do.

Cassie opened the door before she could reach for the latch.

"When you left the mercantile, I thought you'd go straight home. Where were you?"

"I paid a visit to Reverend French and his wife." She hung her shawl and bonnet next to the door and sniffed the air. "Do I smell food?"

"I put last evening's pea soup on to warm." Cassie lifted one shoulder in a tiny shrug. "I may not know how to cook, but I can heat the stove."

"I'm grateful. Today has been . . . trying. After supper, I'm going straight to bed."

"Didn't you say Dr. Stewart was expected this evening? I tidied the sitting room."

The loose cushions on the settee had been fluffed and scattered reading material stacked in the bookshelf. The basket holding Cassie's tatting rested beside one of the chairs.

Rosemary gave her a one-armed hug. "Bless you. I asked him to wait until tomorrow. I'm sure the room will still look lovely."

She wondered whether she should tell the doctor about Galen. Probably not. No telling what he'd do.

Rosemary woke from a fitful sleep at the sound of someone pounding on the front door. She clutched her nightdress at her throat. What if the person who'd damaged her greenhouse and her plants had returned? Unlikely he'd knock, but—

The pounding continued. She pulled on her wrapper, lit a candle, and stepped into the hallway. Cassie stood at the top of the stairs, a small revolver in her hand. The light bounced off the pearl handle.

"Good heavens, Cassie. Put that away."

She shook her head. "My father taught me to use this when the war started. Mother has one too. There were soldiers at our door more than once, coming to take our food and valuables."

"Rebels?"

"From both sides." She linked her arm with Rosemary's. "Let's go see who's there. Could be your brother. Maybe something happened to Judge Lindberg and they want your help."

"It isn't Curt. He'd call my name rather than scare us to death."

She led the way down the steps. When they reached the entry, Cassie clicked the hammer back and stepped to one side, allowing her the first glimpse of their visitor when Rosemary opened the door.

"I wish you'd put that away," Rosemary whispered.

"No."

Lord, please protect us. She slid the bolt away and inched the door open a crack.

A black boot shoved the opening wide. Dr. Stewart stood on the porch, a limp bundle of fur in his arms.

Rosemary's muscles went slack. The candle fell to the floor, leaving them in near darkness. She held both hands toward the doctor's burden. "Bodie?"

"I'm sure it's him." Silver moonlight silhouetted his frame as he stepped inside.

Rosemary moaned and lifted the dog from his arms. Trembling, Bodie licked her chin. She sank to the floor and buried her face in his muddy fur. "Thank you, Lord. Thank you." The hammer snapped closed on the revolver. She looked up as Cassie slipped the weapon into a pocket in her wrapper, then moved to the sitting room and lit the lamp. Dim yellow light traced the outline of ribs and hip bones on Bodie's emaciated body. A frayed rope dangled from his neck.

With gentle hands, Dr. Stewart helped Rosemary to her feet. "Would you please carry him to a table so I can examine him?"

Clutching her dog close to her chest, she led the way to the kitchen. Cassie followed with the lamp and placed it on a shelf where the light would reach them.

When Rosemary laid Bodie on the worktable, he thumped his tail against the wood. Tears slipped from her eyes. "Where did you find him?"

"South of town several miles. The Haggertys' girls were sick, and Mr. Haggerty came to fetch me. I spotted Bodie in a ditch next to the road on my way home. It's providential we had a moon tonight or I'd never have seen him."

She fingered the rope. "And this?"

"Looks like someone kept him tied up and he chewed his way free."

"Who would do such a thing?"

"Wish I knew. I'd have him horsewhipped." He rested his hand on her shoulder. "Let's clean this mud off so I can see if he's hurt anywhere."

"Of course." She took a dishpan from a shelf under the window and held it under the tap on a reservoir beside the stove. "Thankfully, the water's still warm." After setting the filled basin to one side, she dashed into the pantry, returning with a cake of soap and an armful of towels.

When the doctor reached for one of the towels, she shook her head. "Let me."

He stepped to one side while she dipped the cotton flannel into the basin. Starting at the dog's neck, she used gentle strokes to swab the clotted dirt from his fur. "You'll be fine. Dr. Stewart will help you," she whispered. The dog's trusting eyes didn't leave her face while she worked.

Elijah watched as Rosemary bathed her dog. She paid no heed to the fact that she wore nightclothes, with her black hair twined in a thick braid hanging almost to her waist. Something about her intent expression stirred a memory.

He saw himself standing at the entrance to one of the wards in the Post Hospital at Jefferson Barracks. An incoming soldier lay sprawled on a cot, a bowl of water and a cake of soap resting on a low table beside him. A nurse leaned over the man and washed blood and grime from his upper body so Elijah could treat the wound in the man's side. While she worked, the nurse murmured encouragement to the soldier, who didn't take his eyes from her.

The picture in his mind sharpened. When Rosemary raised her head to look at him, her image sliced through the curtain he'd placed over his wartime years. *She's the same nurse.* Without further thought, he touched her damp hand where it rested on Bodie's side. "I remember you. From the Barracks. You were there during the first month of my medical service."

A small smile flitted across her lips. "Yes. I recognized you the first time I called at your office."

"Why haven't you said anything?"

"Clearly, you didn't know who I was. It would have been forward of me." She moved to one side. "We can reminisce later. Please, examine my dog."

He ran his hands along the animal's sides and down over its abdomen, then lifted each of its legs in turn, manipulating the joints. Resting his fingers on Bodie's chest, he felt for the heartbeat. Steady and strong. When he finished, the dog struggled to stand.

"Careful, boy, you don't want to fall off the table." He placed a restraining hand on the dog's back and turned to Rosemary. "Fortunately, I find no visible injuries. He needs some warm food and plenty of water. Don't feed him too much at once."

Cassie struck a match on the stovetop to light the candle

she held. "There's a tad bit of soup left from supper. I'll fetch it from the springhouse."

Elijah looked around, surprised. He'd forgotten she was in the room. "Good. If you have any eggs, give him one."

Cassie sent Rosemary a mischievous smile. "We have plenty of eggs right now."

Pink crept over Rosemary's face. "Indeed we do. Please take a bowl with you and bring several."

After Cassie left the room, Elijah cupped his hands under Bodie's belly and stood him on the floor. "After he eats, he'll no doubt sleep for quite a while. Why don't you spend tomorrow at home with him? I know you'll want to watch his progress."

"Thank you." She knelt beside her chair and Bodie wobbled over to her, tail waving. "I'm beyond grateful for your help tonight. To have him back . . ." She dipped her head for a moment, apparently fighting for control. "His return is an answer to prayer."

He shoved his hands in his pockets, suddenly embarrassed by the intimacy of the small room and Miss Saxon's dishabille. "Must have been. Why else would he have been in that spot when I rode past?" He inched toward the doorway. "I should go."

She glanced down at her mud-stained wrapper, crimson staining her already pink cheeks. "Of course." When she rose, she folded her arms over her chest. "I'll see you out."

"No need. Best if you stay with Bodie." He retrieved his jacket from the back of a chair. "If I may, I'll stop by tomorrow to see how he's doing—and maybe you'll teach me how to make a comfrey poultice."

"I'd be happy to."

The light in her eyes buoyed his steps as he crossed the street to his house. Finding Bodie had answered more than one prayer.

21

*I*n the midst of a meandering afternoon stroll around the backyard with Bodie, a horse's snort and a harness jangle caught Rosemary's attention. The dog lifted his head, growling, but didn't leave her side.

"Good boy. Stay with me." Heart thumping, she slipped into her greenhouse. Dr. Stewart wasn't due until evening. If the person who broke the window had returned, he'd have an unpleasant surprise. She hefted a hoe, then decided she needed a stouter weapon. Her hand closed around a mattock hanging from two parallel pegs on a wall. Swinging the ax-like tool, she strode the path to the front of her house.

Mrs. Bingham paused in the act of tying her horse and buggy to the hitching post next to the boardwalk. "My land. You'd think you were under attack."

"I have been. More than once." She walked to the fence, leaned her weapon against a picket, and opened the gate. "If you're here for Cassie, I'm afraid she's at the mercantile."

"I'll visit Cassie before I return to the farm." Her visitor huffed. "You're the person I came to see. I went to the doctor's office first, but as usual, you were somewhere else." The peacock feathers on her black and white straw hat bobbed as she spoke. Her carelessly arranged orange-red curls bunched at the back of her neck, trapped under the fringed shawl she wore over her brown poplin dress.

Rosemary rested her hand on the gate. "Please, come in. I'll prepare tea." She led the way to the front door.

Bodie stuck to her side as if tethered to her leg. A lengthy overnight rest and several small meals had restored some of his strength, but when outdoors he trembled at unfamiliar sounds and movement.

Mrs. Bingham followed them into the sitting room. She spread her skirts and lowered herself onto one of the chairs in front of the window. "No need to bother with tea. This isn't a social call."

After choosing a spot on the settee, Rosemary faced her. "Then how may I help you?"

The woman drew a folded paper from her handbag. "You sent this letter to Mr. Bingham?"

Rosemary nodded.

"Fortunately, I intercepted it before he could read your message."

Disappointment weighted her shoulders. "I merely requested that he allow your daughter back into your home. To send her away as he did was most unkind. Indeed, cruel. But since you read my letter, you know I didn't use those words to him."

"Mr. Bingham's farmhouse is not *my* home. His servant controls the management of the household." She picked at the beaded fringe on her handbag, then raised shamed eyes to Rosemary. "I'm not allowed to replace any of the broken-down furnishings, nor do I choose our food—particularly I have no say whatsoever over the food. That manservant prepares meat that's so old it's green." She shuddered. "I won't partake of such victuals and neither would Cassie.

Mr. Bingham says I coddle her—that's really his reason for sending her away."

She leaned forward. "Make no mistake, I miss my daughter sorely. I'm grateful you took her in. But your letter will only cause him to fly into a rage. In his weakened state, I fear the consequences."

Rosemary stood. "He's still in a weakened state? I gave you the ginger root two weeks ago." She massaged her forehead. "Ginger is the best cure I know, but perhaps a mint tea? After you brew the tea, have him eat the leaves, as well."

"The fault isn't with the ginger. That old servant distrusts me. When he's in the house, I'm not allowed in the kitchen. So I can only brew the tea when he's occupied outdoors." She lifted her chin, as though defying Rosemary to pity her. "I made my bed. Now I have to lie in it."

Rosemary took a step in her direction. "I'm so—"

"Please. My purpose this morning was to tell you not to send any more letters. Mr. Bingham won't read them." She rose and swept to the entrance, then paused, her hand on the latch. "Why do you do this, Miss Saxon? Involve yourself in other people's lives? Is your own so perfect?"

After Cassie's mother left, Rosemary leaned against the closed door. A dozen responses to Mrs. Bingham's questions filled her mind. At a deep level she knew the truth. Her own life was far from perfect. If she could restore a parent with a child, she could experience secondhand the reconciliation she longed for with her own mother.

That evening, Rosemary stole glances at Cassie during their supper of beans and bacon. No wonder the girl was such a hearty eater. She would be, too, if she'd had to subsist on spoiled meat or not eat at all.

Cassie caught her looking, and smiled. "Mother visited the mercantile today. We had a lovely few minutes together before she had to leave."

Rosemary pushed a square of bacon to one side of her plate to give to Bodie, wondering as she did so whether she should mention seeing Mrs. Bingham. "She came to town to see you?"

"Yes. I was surprised that she drove all that way to spend such a short time. Evidently Mr. Bingham is still sick, so she's allowed to take the buggy—just not for long." She patted her lips with her napkin and sighed. "I feel like I'm in limbo, living in your house day after day. Maybe Mr. Bingham was right about one thing—I need to seek a permanent arrangement. Have you spoken to Faith yet?"

"When I lost Bodie . . ." She reached beneath her chair and stroked his head. "Nothing else seemed important. I will speak to her soon, I promise." Her doubts surged back. Cassie as a caretaker? She slid her chair away from the table and carried her plate to the washbasin. The decision was Faith's, not hers.

Cassie stood to one side, watching while Rosemary cleared the table. "Dr. Stewart will be here this evening?"

"In an hour." Rosemary stilled a flutter in her throat. As far as she knew, he wasn't courting any of the young women in Noble Springs. She hoped his memory of their shared time at Jefferson Barracks might draw them closer. Then, if he would only accept her herbal remedies, who knew where things might lead?

She swished the plates through the dishpan and stacked them for Cassie to dry. With time to spare before the doctor's arrival, she entered the pantry and retrieved several carrot-like stalks of dried comfrey root. After putting a kettle of water on to heat and lowering a lamp over the worktable, she joined Cassie in the sitting room.

The girl glanced up from her tatting. "You're fluttering around like a little bird. It's not like you."

"It's necessary that he sees how competent I am with my remedies. I don't want to look foolish."

Cassie rested her thread and shuttle in her lap. A smile curled the corners of her mouth. "I suspect he cares more about spending time with you than he does about comfrey."

"He spends every weekday with me in his office."

"That's different, and you know it. The lady doth protest too much, methinks." With a grin, Cassie resumed tatting a half-finished lace collar.

Bodie stirred at Rosemary's feet and uttered a low growl. Within a moment, they heard a knock.

When she answered the door, Dr. Stewart beamed down at her. "You're looking rested. A day at home agreed with you." As soon as he stepped into the entry, he crouched in front of Bodie and rubbed his fur. "How you doing, boy?"

Bodie answered the question with a wag of his tail.

Rosemary moved to one side so the doctor could enter the sitting room. "He's so much better. Thank you again for bringing him home."

"You're more than welcome. I like happy outcomes."

Did she imagine it, or did his voice send a more intimate message?

After he greeted Cassie, Rosemary led the way to the kitchen, talking to overcome the drumming of her heart.

"I've laid out everything we need to make a comfrey poultice. If it were a bit later in the spring, I'd have leaves ready instead of roots. Either one will work. Of course you already know how to make a poultice with mustard, I'm sure. So this will be simple." She paused next to the worktable to catch her breath.

"I'm looking forward to our lesson." Lamplight brightened

his curly hair, highlighting the few strands of gray at his temples. A faint scent of something spicy wafted from his freshly shaved face. He removed his jacket, dropping it over the back of a chair, and rolled up his shirtsleeves. "So this is comfrey?" He lifted the bundle in his broad hand and rubbed the knobby roots.

"Indeed." She drew a cutting board close and picked up a knife. "After I chop them, I'll place the bits into this bowl and cover them with hot water."

He nodded, his eyes following her movements as she minced the roots. "Then what?"

"Wait for the water to cool, strain out the mush, and mix in a bit of flour or cornmeal to hold it together. After that, the process is the same as preparing any other poultice." She met his attentive gaze, wishing there were more to the procedure so she could keep him with her longer. "I told you it was simple."

"Too simple. I'd hoped—"

She thought she detected a look of disappointment in his eyes. What if he were no more eager for the evening to end than she was? She glanced at the kettle steaming on the stove. It wouldn't hurt to ask.

"Would you like to stay for a cup of tea?"

His face creased into the smile she loved to see. "Make it mint."

The following afternoon, Rosemary remembered her promise to Cassie. Dr. Stewart hadn't returned from a house call, so she locked the office door at five and walked the block and a half to Lindberg's Mercantile. Bodie trotted at her side, tethered by a leash to prevent him from running off.

When they entered the store, Faith dashed from behind a

counter and swooped down beside the dog. "We missed you, little fellow." She rubbed his neck under his new leather collar. Settling back on her heels, she tipped her head up to look at Rosemary. "He seems healthy, if a bit skinny."

"As big as he is, it's all I can do not to cuddle him on my lap when we're at home." Rosemary chuckled. "I know it's past closing time. I hoped I'd catch you before you left."

"I was just going to roll down the shades. Curt's coming by in a few minutes. We'll walk home together." Once the windows were covered, she pointed at the chairs grouped around the stove. "It's a joy to see you both. Come tell me the reason for your visit."

"As if I needed one." Rosemary squeezed her friend's hand, then took a seat. "I mentioned to Cassie your need for help after Amy's marriage, and she offered to stay with your grandfather." She sent Faith a wry smile. "With one caveat. You'll have to hire a cook."

"Oh, mercy." Her forehead wrinkled. "Are you sure you're not interested?"

She sidestepped the question. "I promised Cassie I'd tell you of her offer. She'd benefit from having a purpose, but the decision is up to you and Curt."

"I'll talk to him tonight. Hiring a cook. I don't see how we could afford one."

Rosemary nodded. Faith's response was what she'd feared. Amy looked after Judge Lindberg in exchange for room and board for herself and her daughter, so the situation benefited both families without any extra cost to Faith and Curt.

"You have plenty of time. The wedding's not for weeks." She bit her lower lip, feeling guilty for not agreeing to help as soon as she was asked.

As if she'd read her mind, Faith patted Rosemary's arm. "I

know you want to be on your own. We'll think about Cassie. She's a dear person, but . . ."

"I know." She shifted in her seat. "I do have other news." She felt excitement bubble to the surface. "Guess who came to my house last night to learn how to make a comfrey poultice?"

"Dr. Stewart?"

"The very same. He stayed and drank tea until—"

The bell over the door jangled as Curt walked in. "My two favorite ladies." He bent to kiss Faith, then squeezed Rosemary's shoulder before flopping into an empty chair. He ran his fingers through his straight brown hair, tucking long strands behind his ears. "What a day. Malcolm Robbinette has me teaching classic literature as well as mathematics. All I know about the classics you could put in those little pancake hats you ladies wear, and still have room for a dozen eggs."

Rosemary smiled at her brother's imagery, then her eyes widened when she comprehended the importance of what he'd said. "Galen French hasn't returned?"

At church the following Sunday, Rosemary noticed tired lines etched across Reverend French's brow when he entered the sanctuary. Clarissa's hymn selections tended toward the minor key—"Praise to the Lord, the Almighty" was followed by "Come Thou Fount of Every Blessing." A natural soprano, Rosemary struggled to bring her voice down to follow the notes as Clarissa played.

She couldn't fault them. Galen had yet to return. According to Curt, in the past the Frenches' son had never stayed away for so long a time. She glanced across the center aisle at Dr. Stewart. If only he hadn't become involved . . .

Then she bowed her head and focused on her clasped hands. She shouldn't blame him for something she'd started. *Lord, you know where Galen is. Please deliver him to his family.*

Reverend French used the first two verses of Psalm 123 as the theme for his sermon. When he spoke of lifting his eyes toward heaven and waiting on the Lord's mercy, he aimed his words at the faithfulness of those in the congregation who had waited for a loved one to return from the war. Rosemary suspected he used the verses to encourage himself as he and Clarissa waited once again for Galen's return.

Dr. Stewart joined Rosemary as she left the sanctuary after the close of the service. A soft breeze swirled the scent of lilacs and fresh-cut grass around them. He moved close to her side as they descended the steps.

"Would you like to accompany me on a house call in the country this afternoon? We can combine medicine with pleasure, and stop somewhere afterward for a light picnic. I'll have the cook at West & Riley's wrap sandwiches and cookies." The eager expression in his eyes sent a pang through her.

"I wish I could." She dared to place her hand on his arm, wishing she'd never agreed to another Sunday afternoon with Jacob. The time had come to discourage him. If only she could think how to do it without losing his friendship. "Unfortunately, this afternoon is already promised."

At the doctor's downcast look, she stopped near the edge of the lawn. Her hand remained on his arm. She couldn't let him walk away believing she didn't want to spend time with him. "Maybe next Saturday? Or Sunday? I'd be pleased to prepare the food." She held her breath.

His winning smile spread over his face. "Saturday. Rain or shine. Would late morning suit you?"

"Absolutely." She wrapped her arms around her middle and gave herself a squeeze. Late morning would suit her just fine. As he strolled away, her mind raced ahead to what she might prepare, given her limited budget.

Cassie joined her at that moment. Eyes sparkling, she clasped Rosemary's hand. "I just talked to your brother and Faith. They're considering my offer to spend days with Judge Lindberg. Faith said they had a few details to consider first."

"What good news." Rosemary felt sure the details involved making a decision to hire a cook. She glanced at Dr. Stewart's retreating back. If a cook were found, she wouldn't have to worry about leaving her position in the doctor's office—and the opportunity to spend time with him daily.

"How long should I wait before I ask them again?" Animation brightened Cassie's face.

"A few more days, at least." She turned her steps toward home. "Let's take Bodie for a walk and enjoy a bit of this fine afternoon before Jacob arrives."

"You're going for a buggy ride with him again today?"

"This will be the last time. It's not fair to give him false hope."

Cassie's eyes rounded with surprise. "He's awfully nice. I thought you liked him."

"I do—just not enough."

After Jacob settled Rosemary on the buggy seat, he paused before slapping the reins over the horse's back. "Last week we went to Hartfield at my suggestion. Today it's your turn. Where would you like to go?" He spoke as though Sunday afternoons together were a regular event.

Rosemary twisted her gloved fingers around the satin cord on her handbag. From his trimmed hair to his polished boots, she knew he'd spent extra time preparing for their afternoon together. She couldn't hurt his feelings by telling him at the outset what she'd rehearsed before he arrived. Where should she suggest they go? Certainly not to the property he wanted to buy north of Pioneer Lake.

She raised her eyes to meet his. "I'd like to call on Miss Graves again." She swallowed, praying they'd be welcome.

Doubt flickered across his face. "Are you sure you want to? She acted angry when we were there last week."

"She'd just had a shock. I'm sure things have settled down by now."

"For your sake, I hope you're right." He guided the horse toward the eastern end of town. "If I spent as much time worrying over my customers as you do the doctor's patients, I'd never get any sleep."

Her temper sparked. "It's not the same thing at all. Miss Graves isn't the doctor's patient. I'm concerned for her as a friend. Heaven knows, she needs one."

"No need to bark at me. If you want to help her, go ahead." He raised an eyebrow and gave her a half smile. "Whatever the reason, let's enjoy our ride. These spring days will be over soon. When summer gets here, we'll be seeking shade."

She had to tell him that when summer arrived they wouldn't be spending time together. She drew a fortifying breath. "Jacob—"

"I see them too." He pointed the buggy whip at a flock of wild turkeys in a clearing beside the road. The toms were strutting, their iridescent plumage glowing in the sunlight. "Those birds are overrunning our county. I'm going to send a couple of fellows out here tomorrow to bag a few for the restaurant. I'll make sure you get one of them."

"Jacob—"

"I know you don't want charity. This is different. They're free for the taking."

Rosemary heaved a sigh and rolled her eyes upward. She'd talk to him on the way home from Jolene's. Right now he was so focused on the turkey population she doubted he'd pay attention to a word she said.

When he turned the buggy through the opening in the fence at the Graves's farm, their dog bounded up to the wagon, barking. She noticed several men working in the garden plot near the cabin.

Mrs. Graves appeared in the open doorway. Shading her eyes with her hand, she peered up at them. "Miss Saxon."

Rosemary held her breath. Would she be asked to leave?

The tiny woman snapped her fingers to shush the dog, then smiled at the two of them. "I'll tell Jolene you're here. You and your beau come on in for a cool drink."

"He's not—"

"Thank you, ma'am. We appreciate the offer." Jacob hopped to the ground and offered his hand to Rosemary, then kept his hand on her elbow as they followed the woman into the cabin.

Jolene dashed toward her. "Thank you so much! I just know you had something to do with him coming back."

Jacob stepped to one side to allow the two of them to embrace. Even in the dim light, Rosemary noted the glow on the girl's face. The baby's father must have returned. She sent up a silent prayer of thanks that Jolene's situation had been resolved.

"I wish I could take credit, but I don't even know who he is. The Lord brought him here, I didn't."

Jolene chuckled and squeezed Rosemary's wrist. "Of course you know him. You took me to church the day we met."

"You don't mean Galen French?" Stunned, Rosemary glanced between Jolene and her mother.

Mrs. Graves nodded. "Thought you knew. He come back last Sunday eve. Told us he cared for our girl." She waved a hand at the chairs next to the table. "You two sit. I'll fetch some water while Jolene tells you what he said."

While the older woman busied herself with glasses and a dipper, her daughter slid into a chair beside Rosemary. "He told Ma and Pa he had feelings for me." She cupped her hands around her abdomen, blushing. "Said he didn't care what happened before."

"But why is he still here? His parents are very worried."

Jolene covered her mouth with her fingertips. "Oh, gracious. I thought they knew about me."

Mrs. Graves placed tumblers of water in front of Rosemary and Jacob. "He should be coming in with Pa and the boys any minute. You can tell him about his parents." A smile crossed her lips. "He told us he'd stay and work for her, like Jacob in the Bible story did for his Rachel. We figured he's a man grown, he can make his own decisions. Course we wouldn't have kept him for seven years." She chuckled.

The warmth in the small cabin felt oppressive. Mrs. Graves expected *her* to talk to Galen? Rosemary extracted a handkerchief from her handbag and dabbed perspiration from her temples. The last thing she wanted to do was interfere any further in their lives.

At the sound of men's voices outside the cabin, Rosemary stood and approached the doorway. Better to speak to Galen in private than to embarrass him in front of Jolene's family.

Mr. Graves entered first. He swept his hat off when he recognized her.

"Miss Saxon. Never expected to see you again."

"Mr. West kindly brought me out to visit your daughter. Now that I'm here, I'd like to have a word with Galen, then we'll be on our way." She gripped her handkerchief in one hand.

Galen French waited on the stoop behind Jolene's father, the empty left sleeve of his chambray shirt knotted at the wrist. He lifted his chin when Rosemary spoke.

"I know what you have to say, and I don't want to hear it." He crossed the room and rested his hand on Jolene's shoulder. "Soon as we can, I want to marry her. I don't care a bit about people's opinions."

"Could we step outside for a moment?"

"No, thank you." He leaned against the tabletop behind

191

Jolene's chair, eyes narrowed. "Whatever it is, you can have your say right here."

Exasperated, Rosemary thrust her hands on her hips. "I'm more than happy for you and Jolene. I couldn't have dreamed of a better outcome for her."

"Then what—?"

"Your parents, Galen. You're putting them through a terrible ordeal. They deserve to know where you are, and that you're well."

Shamefaced, he met Rosemary's gaze. "You're right, of course. I was so happy being here, I didn't think."

He and Jolene exchanged a glance. Tears glittered in her eyes.

"What if your folks tell you they won't give us their blessing?"

Rosemary took a deep breath when Jacob guided the horse onto the road to Noble Springs. The air smelled of damp earth and new growth, a welcome relief from the stuffy cabin with its lingering aroma of greasy salt pork.

Her words to Galen echoed in her mind. She thought of her own parents. Didn't they deserve as much from her? Her stomach tightened. No, they didn't. Not after the way they treated her and Curt. *But if ye forgive not men their trespasses, neither will your Father forgive your trespasses.* She tightened her jaw. Her situation was different. They didn't want her forgiveness. They'd made it clear they didn't want her.

Jacob's voice cut into the silence. "Never expected to find young French at that farm. Folks've been talking all week about where he got to."

"I need to tell his parents as soon as we get back to town."

"We shouldn't say anything. Better they hear the news from him."

"If I can ease their worries, I must do so. They don't deserve to suffer an extra minute wondering what became of their son. Wouldn't you want to know if you were a parent?"

"I'm not a parent, yet." He cut a smile in her direction.

Warmth crept up Rosemary's neck at the clear message in his eyes. Now. Tell him now. She cleared her throat.

Jacob fished in his pocket and handed her a paper-wrapped lozenge. "You must be thirsty. This'll help 'til we get to town."

"Thank you." She tipped her head back and sighed. Whatever she thought of him as a suitor, he was a kind man through and through. She didn't want to hurt him with her words. She'd wait a few days and talk to him in a different setting, like the grocery.

When the buggy rolled into town, he turned on Third Street and stopped in front of the parsonage.

Surprised, Rosemary faced him. "So you agree with me—they need to be told."

He tied the reins to a hitching post and helped her down. "Women know more about such matters. Do what you think best. I'll stay out here."

Nerves twitching, she crossed the path to the Frenches' door and knocked.

Late Friday afternoon, Rosemary gathered her courage, along with her grocery list, and headed for West & Riley's. Her palms moistened at the thought of seeing Jacob. She'd postponed the encounter all week, and now her need for supplies forced the issue. Maybe she should buy her groceries, then tell him. Or would it be better to get right to the point?

She rubbed her temple. No matter what she said, his feelings were bound to be hurt.

When she entered the grocery, the scent of roasted turkey wafted from the restaurant side of the building, reminding her of the young bird one of Jacob's helpers had delivered to her house during the week. Another kindness for which he deserved thanks. She fought the temptation to turn around and flee.

"Miss Saxon."

Rosemary jumped when she heard her name.

Clarissa French bustled across the oiled wood floor, a woven basket hanging from one arm. "I want to thank you for sending Galen back to us." She took Rosemary's arm and led her toward a quiet corner. "He seems quite determined to marry that young woman. We know nothing about her, except for her . . . condition. We've always taught him not to pass judgment on others, but I never dreamed he'd take the lesson this far. What if people think he's responsible?" Her cheeks flamed.

"He's doing what's right for him and Jolene. From what I saw, I don't think he gives a fig for what people think." Rosemary placed her hand over Clarissa's. "We can't predict who we'll fall in love with, can we?"

"But she's a stranger."

"She's a good girl who made a bad mistake. Why don't you ask Galen to take you to her parents' farm for a visit? I'm sure he'd be delighted, and so would they."

"Of course. I'll do that." Clarissa offered a shaky smile. "Please don't tell anyone I spoke to you about this. I feel like a hypocrite to have such feelings about another person. My husband would be appalled."

Rosemary patted the woman's hand. "I wouldn't dream of saying anything. Besides, once you see Galen and Jolene together, I believe your doubts will vanish."

"What are you ladies whispering about back here? No complaints about my merchandise, I hope." Jacob stood behind them, wrapped in an almost-white apron.

"No complaints at all, Mr. West. Miss Saxon and I were just passing the time of day." Clarissa nodded at him, then turned to Rosemary. "Thank you . . . for everything." The flowers on her hat bobbed as she left the store.

"What can I get for my favorite customer this afternoon?" Jacob moved closer to her side.

Rosemary's heartbeat picked up speed. She glanced around the store, hoping for another distraction, but at the moment she was the only patron. She unfolded her list, although she had the contents memorized. "Ah, a pound of sugar, a bag of Dundee's baking powder, and a lemon."

"That's all?"

"Curt will bring the wagon next week so I can get heavier items."

"I'd be happy to deliver anything you need." He plucked a lemon from a basket and placed the yellow fruit on a counter before reaching onto a shelf behind him for the baking powder.

"I appreciate the offer, but Curt doesn't mind."

"I don't mind either, Miss Saxon. You should know that by now." He placed the sugar next to her other two items, then leaned over the counter. "If you leave your order with me, I'll bring it Sunday afternoon."

"About Sunday—" She drew a deep breath. "It's not fair for me to spend Sundays with you when I don't—"

He held up his hand, palm out. "Why don't you let me decide what's fair? Perhaps I've been too hasty. For the next few weeks, let's go back to simply being friends."

Her resolve melted at the hopeful look in his eyes. If she thought she'd never see him again, he'd be easy to dismiss.

But West & Riley's was the only grocery in Noble Springs. "Friendship is exactly what I had in mind." She laid two dimes on the counter and gathered her purchases into her carryall. "Thank you, Jacob."

As she walked toward home, she tried not to think about his forlorn expression when she left the grocery. Surely as the weeks passed with no encouragement from her, his interest was bound to wane.

Bodie capered around her feet when Rosemary entered the front door. She stooped and hugged him, enjoying the doggie smell of his clean fur. "Are you ready for your walk? Just let me put these things in the kitchen."

He raced ahead into the next room, where Cassie sat in front of the window, her fingers busy with her tatting shuttle. She smiled up at Rosemary. "Did you talk to Jacob when you went to the grocery?"

She grimaced. "In a way. We're going back to being friends only."

"Well, that's what you wanted, isn't it?"

"'For a few weeks' is what he said."

"Maybe by then he'll meet someone else."

"I hope so."

Cassie pointed the tatting shuttle at Rosemary's carryall. "Is that lemon and sugar?"

"Yes. As soon as I take Bodie for his walk, I'll bake the bread." A thrill of anticipation shot through her at the thought of her picnic tomorrow with the doctor. She prayed he'd enjoy the food she prepared.

After depositing her purchases on the kitchen table, Rosemary fastened Bodie's leash to his collar and set out. The setting sun quivered above the horizon, sending streaks of gold and coral across the sky. She paused a moment to gaze with satisfaction on her flourishing garden. Since the broken glass in her greenhouse, there'd been no further damage to her property.

Her feeling of safety wilted when she recalled that the incidents had come at two- or three-week intervals. Time for another one. She closed the gate behind her with a firm click. *No more. Please, Lord.*

As she approached the corner across from Dr. Stewart's home, a closed carriage passed by and stopped in front of his house. The driver dismounted to assist a well-dressed woman to the boardwalk.

Rosemary squinted to determine who she might be, but only had a glimpse of the caller's profile before the woman straightened her cloak over her flounced skirt and strode to the door.

24

lijah stood at his kitchen window, watching daylight
fade while chewing a bite of his sliced cheese and
pumpernickel sandwich. The coarse bread scratched at this
throat when he swallowed. Next time he visited the bakery,
he'd buy a white loaf.

A teapot steeped to his left. The faint aroma of mint rose
from the spout, reminding him of Miss Saxon. When he saw
her tomorrow, he planned to ask if she could spare more of
her mint leaves. He'd come to look forward to the fragrant
brew at the end of a tiring day.

He lifted his cup and took a gulp to wash the food down,
then bit off another chunk of his supper. A sharp rapping
from the brass knocker on his front door startled him into
dropping his sandwich. Still chewing, he marched to the entry
hall, paused to swallow, then opened the door.

"Dr. Stewart?"

He nodded.

"Might I come in?"

The woman on the porch wore an outfit he suspected few
of the ladies in Noble Springs could afford. Her fur-trimmed
cloak and silky-looking skirt testified to a city background.

"Of course." He stepped aside, brushing crumbs from

the front of his vest. As she passed, he detected the scent of lavender trailing in her wake.

She faced him as soon as he closed the door. "I'm Mrs. Arnold Colfax. A friend recommended you."

Although her bonnet concealed much of her hair, he noticed gray strands at her temples. A sharp line was drawn between her brows, as if by a careless artist. "Mrs. Colfax. If you have a medical condition, I'm sure you'd be more comfortable calling at my office. I have a female nurse in attendance during the week."

"This visit doesn't concern a medical problem—at least not directly." She glanced into the next room. "May I sit?"

He moved a side chair from the far wall and held it while she arranged her hoops. Once she was settled, he seated himself facing her. "You said a friend recommended me, yet you don't have a medical problem. How may I be of help?"

"My friend . . . knows your father."

Elijah tensed. "And?"

"Your father helped her through a trying situation. I'm sure you know what I'm referring to."

He did know. All too well. "My father's practice has nothing in common with mine. Why did you come all the way from Chicago to Noble Springs?"

"I don't live in Chicago. My husband and I reside in St. Louis, where my friend and her new family came to live shortly before that dreadful war. Somehow she learned that Dr. Carlisle Stewart's son had a medical office here." She leaned forward in her chair, knotting her lace-gloved fingers together. "There must be girls in trouble in this town, just as there were up north. Dr. Stewart, I'm desperate for a child. We'll pay whatever you ask to obtain one."

Elijah choked on the bile that rose in his throat. Was there no place far enough away to escape his father's legacy?

"As I said, my father's practice—and his practices—have nothing to do with me. Many children were orphaned during the conflict. I believe there are societies in St. Louis to shelter them. Perhaps if you—"

"I don't want some little urchin off the streets. A child of ours would stand to inherit my husband's business. As such, he'd need to be trained properly from infancy."

Revulsion shuddered over him. His father made a handsome living from women like Mrs. Colfax. He rose and held out his hand. "May I assist you to the door? You'll want to be on your way before it grows dark."

She jutted her chin in the air. "I need no assistance." She brushed past him, hoops swaying. "You've just turned down a goodly sum. To what purpose? Evidently you learned nothing from your father."

He reached around her and opened the door. "On the contrary. I learned all I needed to know about his way of life. Good evening, Mrs. Colfax."

Once she left, he walked to the polished oak staircase and dropped onto the second step, shoulders hunched. He knew only one way to overcome his father's reputation. He'd start tomorrow.

Questions about the woman she'd seen outside Dr. Stewart's house the previous evening nagged at Rosemary's mind while she packed their picnic lunch on Saturday. Patients came to him at all hours—she knew that—but this person's gait seemed remarkably brisk for someone with an urgent need for a doctor. If she'd really been ill, she'd have sent her driver to the door.

Rosemary massaged the back of her neck. Perhaps the caller was his mother, or an aunt. A cautionary tingle vibrated in her chest. Despite spending time together at his office, she had little knowledge of his private life. What if he already had a lady friend and had asked Rosemary on a picnic out of courtesy?

She gave herself a mental shake. Such speculation led nowhere. When they were alone, she'd ask him about his caller. Simple as that. After tucking a bowl of chopped turkey salad into her picnic basket, she placed a loaf of lemon-thyme bread on top of a folded tablecloth. First the food, then conversation.

Bodie pressed next to her legs, his eyes never leaving the basket.

She stroked his ears. "If the doctor invites you, you can come with us. Otherwise, Cassie will keep you company."

Cassie spoke from the kitchen doorway. "He misses you when you're gone. I'm a poor substitute."

"He's been more clingy since his rescue. I'm glad you're here with him." She smiled. "And with me." She walked past Cassie and deposited the basket in the sitting room next to a quilt, so she'd be ready when the doctor arrived.

Bodie sped around her at the sound of footsteps on the porch. He skidded to a stop at the entrance, tail fanning the air. Rosemary hurried to the door and opened it at the doctor's knock.

"How'd you know it was me?" His voice teased. He bent over and rubbed the top of Bodie's head, then gazed up at her, a slow smile spreading across his face. "That green dress is much prettier than the one you wear to the office." He flushed. "Not that there's anything wrong with the other one. It's just . . . you look pretty this morning."

"Thank you." She hid a smile at his discomfiture. One thing for certain, he wasn't a lady-killer. He charmed her when he wasn't being stuffy Dr. Stewart. "Would you mind if we took Bodie with us? He'll be no trouble."

"I was going to suggest that myself." He nodded thanks at Cassie when she handed him the picnic basket and quilt, then stepped to one side so Rosemary and the dog could precede him to his buggy.

Once they were seated, with Bodie curled on the floor between them, Dr. Stewart turned west on King's Highway. A few cloud ribbons swam beneath the morning sun. Since it was Saturday, the wide street was filled with buggies and wagons as outlying farmers and their wives came to market.

Rosemary waved when they passed Lindberg's Mercantile. She knew Faith might be watching from the window to see them ride past.

Dr. Stewart glanced over at her. "I've looked forward to this picnic all week." He chuckled. "I know we're together every day in the office, but work is different than pleasure." He directed the horse around Courthouse Square.

"Much different. I've waited for this day too." She pressed her lips together. She sounded too eager. "That is, I always enjoy visiting Pioneer Lake and seldom have the opportunity."

"Perhaps we can correct that." His words carried a promise.

The image of the woman she'd seen in front of his house the previous night loomed in her mind. Had he made promises to her too?

After tying the horse to a young hackberry tree on the south side of the lake, the doctor helped Rosemary from the buggy. The touch of his hand on hers felt gentle, intimate. He pointed to a shady spot overlooking the jewel-like water. "That should be a good place to enjoy our meal, don't you think?"

"It would be perfect, Doctor."

He touched her shoulders with his fingertips. "Elijah, please. We're not in the office. And may I call you Rosemary?"

She nodded, feeling warmth spread over her face. They'd been close to one another physically any number of times, but he'd been right when he said work was different than pleasure. She was near enough now to reach up and touch his curly hair if she wanted to. And she did want to.

At that moment, Bodie dashed past them in pursuit of a blue heron at the water's edge. Thankful to have her thoughts interrupted, Rosemary took a step away from Elijah and clasped her hands behind her back.

He gave her a lingering look, then returned to the buggy for the food. Once they'd spread the quilt in the freckled shade cast by the tree, she opened the basket and filled their plates, along with a small bowl for the dog.

Elijah leaned against the gray bark of the hackberry while he ate. His eyes widened when he took a bite of the bread. "I've never tasted anything like this. I recognize lemon, but what's the other flavor?"

"Thyme. It's one of the herbs I grow."

"Delicious. Best bread I've ever tasted."

She did a quick mental inventory of her pantry. "I'd be pleased to bake another loaf and bring it to you on Monday if you like."

"Can't think of anything I'd like more." He rested his plate in his lap. "I wish we'd done this sooner. And not just for the food. The more I remember of you at the Barracks, the more remarkable you are in my estimation." He rubbed his neck. "Guess this is the long way around to asking if you'd allow me to court you."

Joy washed over her. The sight of him relaxed against the tree, his shirtsleeves rolled up and his hair tousled, left her breathless. Then an unwelcome image intruded.

His forehead wrinkled. "You're hesitating. I'd hoped you felt the same."

"I do," she whispered. She set her plate to one side and drew a ragged breath.

"Something's bothering you. What is it?"

"Last evening at the time I took Bodie for a walk, I saw a woman going to your door." She squirmed at the stunned look that crossed his face. "Was she . . .?" Rosemary dug her fingernails into her palms. "Is she a lady friend?"

He seized her hands, holding them in a firm grip. "No! Rosemary, I'm sorry. To think you spent last night believing the worst of me." His grip tightened. "If we're going to have a future, you need to know about my background." He drew her close to his side, then told her of his father's practice in Chicago. "When I decided to come here, I believed myself free of his reputation. The woman who came last night wanted me to obtain a baby for her."

Rosemary gasped and covered her mouth with her hand.

"I refused." He bowed his head and tugged at his collar, then turned agonized eyes on her. "This whole thing . . . that's why I sent Miss Graves away. My father helped unmarried girls, then sold their babies. With the girls' consent, of course. He paid them a small sum, then pocketed a large profit from the new parents."

She pulled back and knelt in front of him. "You're not your father."

"I know that now. I promise I'll help Miss Graves in any way I can when her time comes." One corner of his mouth lifted in a half smile. "From what you tell me, she may be Mrs. French before then."

"So it would seem." She stood, extending her hands. "I'll put our plates away, then let's take a walk along the water's edge. It's a beautiful day."

A cool breeze had sprung up by the time Elijah and Rosemary left Pioneer Lake. The morning's thin clouds had coagulated into rolling gray lumps that threatened rain. She shivered and slid closer to Elijah's side for warmth, wishing she'd remembered to bring a shawl.

He clasped her hand. "Would you like to slip my coat over your shoulders?"

"It's not that far. I'll be fine."

When they turned onto King's Highway, Bodie sat up and draped his paws over the dashboard, eyeing a dilapidated vehicle in front of Rosemary's house.

She cocked her head. "That looks like Mr. Bingham's wagon. I wonder if Cassie's mother has come to visit her."

"One way to find out." Once he tied his horse to a post behind the wagon, Elijah reached up and swung her to the ground, holding her waist for an extra moment before retrieving the picnic basket. She glided toward the front porch, feeling happier than she could ever remember.

The door flew open. Cassie stood in the entrance dressed in a traveling cloak and carrying a carpetbag. "Thank goodness you're here. I was afraid I wouldn't get to say good-bye."

Mrs. Bingham appeared beside her. The threatening sky intensified harsh lines on her face. "Elmer Bingham's dead. The train for St. Louis is due in half an hour, and we'll be on it."

25

*R*osemary hastened toward Cassie and her mother. "Mrs. Bingham. I'm so sorry to hear of your loss. When did he pass?"

"In the early hours of this morning. I stayed long enough to prepare his body while his manservant built a coffin. Then I came straight here to fetch Cassie."

"But his funeral—" She took a second look at Cassie's mother. The woman wore a magenta cloak over a royal blue poplin dress. No black.

"His man will bury Mr. Bingham next to his parents in the plot behind the house. There'll be no service." She took her daughter's arm. "He's getting back what he put into life, Miss Saxon. No more and no less. Please don't involve yourself further."

The wind gusted, carrying scattered drops of rain. Rosemary felt Elijah's hands settling his coat over her shoulders. His voice rumbled behind her.

"If you leave your husband's horse and wagon in town, she will be involved. It's common knowledge that your daughter is staying in Miss Saxon's house. With your consent, I'll drive you to the station, then deliver the wagon to his farm."

"As you wish, but hurry. I don't want to miss the train."
Mrs. Bingham propelled Cassie down the path to the waiting
conveyance, her cloak billowing in the wind.

After Elijah helped the three women into the wagon, he
took the reins and sent the horse trotting toward the depot.
When he stopped in front of the station, Rosemary heard the
tracks hum with the approach of a train. Within moments,
the engine came in sight. Gray smoke trailed over the cars.

Cassie's mother sprang to her feet. "Just in time."

As soon as Elijah helped her to the ground, she dashed to
purchase their tickets. He lifted a trunk from the back of the
wagon and deposited it on an empty baggage cart.

Cassie dropped the carpetbag she carried and threw her
arms around Rosemary. Tears streaked her cheeks. "I . . . I
don't want to leave you. Not like this." She put her lips close
to Rosemary's ear. "It's my fault. I wished him dead," she
whispered. Her shoulders shook with sobs. "The Lord knows
I didn't mean it—doesn't he?"

Rosemary took a step away and clasped Cassie's upper
arms. "Of course he knows. You're not to blame. Whatever
took your mother's husband had nothing to do with you.
Remember that."

Gulping back sobs, the girl nodded.

Mrs. Bingham descended upon them, waving two paste-
board tickets. "Come, Cassie." She faced Rosemary. "We'll
let you know as soon as we have a fixed address. You can have
my daughter's trunk sent."

Raindrops splattered as the two women boarded a passenger car. She should be happy to have her house to herself
again, but all she felt was sorrow. Cassie'd been right when
she said they were like sisters.

"You'll miss her." Elijah tucked his hand under her elbow
and guided her toward the wagon.

"The house will feel empty." The bell clanged when the train built up enough steam to leave the station. She stopped to watch until the last car was a tiny speck on the tracks. Shivering, she pulled his coat tight around her, then noticed his wet shirt.

"How thoughtless of me! You're getting soaked. As soon as you leave me at my door, promise you'll stop at home for dry clothing before you return the wagon."

He flashed his beautiful smile. "It's been a long time since a lady fussed over me. I like it."

She settled near him on the wagon seat. Truth be told, she liked having someone to fuss over. Not merely someone. Elijah.

Once he'd kept his promise and changed into dry clothes and an oiled canvas greatcoat, Elijah drove Bingham's wagon through the rain toward the sheriff's office. The earlier busyness on the streets had all but ceased. Heavy clouds obscured the setting sun, leaving the front of the stone jailhouse in deep shadow.

Thaddeus Cooper looked up when Elijah entered. "What brings you out on such a miserable evening? Looking for a supper companion?" He dropped the book he'd been reading on top of his desk and tilted his chair against the wall.

"Later, maybe. I need to take Elmer Bingham's horse and wagon to his farm. Hoped you'd follow me out so I can get back to town."

"Glad to. But why isn't Bingham driving his own wagon?"

"He's dead."

Thaddeus's chair thudded to the floor. "First I've heard of it."

Elijah repeated what Mrs. Bingham had told them when

208

he and Rosemary returned from their picnic. "They took the train to St. Louis a half hour ago. Miss Saxon and I drove them to the station."

His friend grinned at him. "Miss Saxon, eh? You're a brave soul." He stood, smoothing the ends of his drooping moustache.

"She's a caring lady and a pretty one." Elijah shot him a cool glance.

Thaddeus harrumphed. "No doubt. My Amy sets quite a store by her. Myself, I keep out of her way." He grabbed a broad-brimmed hat and canvas coat from pegs on the wall. "If we're going, we'd best get started."

The two wagons traveled in tandem through town and along the rutted road leading south. Rain dripped from Elijah's hat brim, chilling his neck with occasional stray drops. Mr. Bingham's horse plodded through puddles with its head down. When they reached the lane that Elijah remembered as belonging to Cassie's stepfather, the animal turned left with no urging on his part.

Thaddeus followed close behind.

Elijah drew back on the reins when the farmhouse came in view. After a moment, a man dressed in muddy clothing stepped from behind the building, carrying a shovel. He pushed his hat off his forehead and stared.

"Doc. What're you doin' with our wagon?" In the dusk, he blended in with his shadowed surroundings.

With a start, Elijah recognized Abraham Grice, the patient he'd recently treated for gout. He must be the manservant Mrs. Bingham mentioned. "I told your mistress I'd return this to you. She and her daughter are on their way to St. Louis, as I'm sure you know."

"Don't know nothing of the sort. She don't tell me where she's going, and I don't ask—and she ain't my mistress."

"Well. In any case, here's the wagon. Your horse probably needs to be grained." Elijah hopped down and held out the reins.

Mr. Grice dropped the shovel and snatched the leather straps so fast they squeaked when they slid through Elijah's gloves. "Who's in that other wagon?"

"Thaddeus Cooper. He's taking me home."

The older man tugged his hat lower on his forehead and half-turned toward a tilted structure that probably served as a barn. "Be on your way, then. I ain't stopping you."

Rosemary awakened early Sunday morning, her heart torn between excitement over her new relationship with Elijah and sorrow at Cassie's abrupt departure. She'd have much to tell Faith after church.

Wishing she had something new to wear, she dressed in her gray silk and took extra pains arranging her thick hair into a coiled braid covered by an emerald-colored hairnet. Perhaps Elijah would escort her home. She hoped so.

While she prepared a simple breakfast, Bodie nosed around the house, first upstairs, then down. Rosemary felt sure he was looking for Cassie. By now the girl and her mother would have arrived in St. Louis.

From what she could recall, the two of them had lived with a member of Cassie's father's family after they lost their home—and her father—during the war. Since they were returning with no notice, she prayed his relatives would take them in again. Cassie had been bounced around enough.

She left Bodie with the promise of an afternoon walk and directed her steps toward the square brick church a block away. When she reached the corner of Third Street, Elijah dashed up to her.

"Saw you from the front window." He tipped a half bow. "May I escort you to services this morning?" His black coat and gray trousers appeared freshly brushed. A tidy black bow tie rested at the point where his collar fastened. Although she couldn't see his hair beneath his hat, she felt sure he'd combed his curls into submission.

"Of course you may." Her heart gave a little jump at his nearness. She extended the crook of her arm and he clasped her elbow.

They reached the churchyard as the steeple bell tolled its final note. When they hurried inside, Rosemary noticed Faith had left room for her on the pew she shared with her grandfather and Curt.

Rosemary glanced up at Elijah, questioning him with her gaze.

He nodded, and the two of them squeezed into the space. Faith turned to her. "Looks like yesterday afternoon turned out well," she whispered.

Rosemary smiled, then noticed Faith's eyes bore signs of recent tears. She opened her mouth to ask why, but before she could speak, Clarissa French played the introductory notes to "O Day of Rest and Gladness" and the congregation stood to sing.

She half listened while Reverend French preached a message on forgiveness, her attention focused more on Elijah's presence next to her. His clean, soapy fragrance mingled with the wool of his jacket. How amazing to be sitting side by side during worship. *Thank you, Lord.*

Her buoyant spirits dropped back to earth when she noticed Faith touch a handkerchief to her eyes. She darted a concerned glance at her friend. Normally she followed every word of the sermon, but this morning she wished the reverend would finish early. Something drastic must have happened.

Perhaps she'd learned of Cassie's departure, but would that news leave her so upset? Rosemary doubted it.

The moment Reverend French dismissed the congregation, she seized Faith's arm. "What's wrong?"

Faith squeezed her lips together and shook her head. "I'll tell you when we're outside."

Conversations buzzed among the departing worshipers. Elijah lowered his voice to be heard beneath the general hubbub. "Would you excuse me for a moment? I'd like to have a word with Thaddeus."

Sheriff Cooper stood nearby, holding Sophia's chubby hand. Amy gazed at the two of them with happiness written over her face. For a moment, Rosemary's heart softened toward the sheriff. No doubt he'd make Amy a fine husband. But still . . . how could she forget how he'd hounded her brother?

"Certainly. I'll wait for you on the lawn," she said in response to Elijah's request, before hastening to catch up with Faith.

She found her near Curt's buggy. "Can we stroll around the churchyard for a moment? I'd like to know why you're unhappy this morning." She slipped an arm around her friend.

Faith sniffled. "Yes, let's." Skirting past groups of chattering parishioners, they followed a brick pathway toward the rear of the building. When they reached the curtained shade of a willow tree growing at the edge of the burial ground, Faith stopped.

"I try to leave my troubles at home, but this morning . . ." She sniffled again. "This morning my monthly courses began. Again." Fresh tears brimmed in her eyes. "I want a child so much. We've been married for seven months! What's wrong with me?"

Rosemary hugged her close. "Nothing's wrong with you.

God has his own timing." She took a step back, pondering a thought. "Of course, if you drink a little raspberry leaf tea with your breakfast, it couldn't hurt."

Faith's expression brightened. "Do you have the leaves?"

"As it happens, I do. I'll bring some with me when I come to supper this afternoon."

"Would you like to ask the doctor to join us?" She raised an eyebrow in a coquettish arch. Her voice teased.

"Not just yet. I want to wait until I'm . . . sure."

"Of him? Or yourself?"

"Both."

When Elijah opened the door to the examination room and beckoned to her, Rosemary paused in writing ledger entries.

"I need your help, Miss Saxon."

"I'll be right there, Doctor." She smiled to herself at their office formality. After a week, the novelty of calling each other by their first names in private hadn't yet worn off.

Her smile faded the moment she stepped into the room. The sickly sweet stench of infection assailed her nostrils, sending her thoughts reeling back to Jefferson Barracks. She wondered if Elijah had the same reaction. One day soon she'd ask him.

A middle-aged man sat on the edge of the examining table in his undershirt and trousers, cradling his right hand with his left. A fleshy portion of his palm was blackened and swollen to twice its normal size. Below the table, a bucket held the soiled bandages he'd worn when he entered the office.

Elijah met her gaze. "You know what I must do. Twenty drops of laudanum."

She nodded and reached inside a cabinet for a bottle of

the opiate. After pouring water from a jar into a tin cup, she counted out the drops, watching as the drug swirled and dissolved.

Elijah turned to his patient. "Mr. Ormond, Miss Saxon will give you some laudanum. As soon as you feel drowsy, I'll cut away the dead flesh."

Mr. Ormond reached for the cup and gulped the opiate, then stretched out on the table with his right arm at his side. "Go ahead. Get it over with."

"Not so fast. Give the drug time to work."

While they waited, Rosemary passed several folded towels to Elijah and then threaded a suture needle. She stepped around the table and took Mr. Ormond's left hand. "Look at me instead of the doctor. It won't hurt so much if you can't see what he's doing."

"You're prettier too," he murmured. His eyelids drooped.

She nodded at Elijah, and he took a scalpel from a tray. Mr. Ormond gripped her hand as the doctor worked at removing layers of corrupted tissue. When he finished, bright red blood pulsed from the wound onto a towel beneath the patient's forearm.

"Going to sew this closed now." He dropped the scalpel on the tray, wiped his hands on one of the towels, then lifted the suture needle. With quick motions, he stitched the skin together over the man's injury.

Mr. Ormond's grip on Rosemary's hand relaxed when Elijah wrapped a bandage around his wrist and across his palm.

"That wasn't so bad, Doc. Hurt worse when I cut m'self in the first place."

"You almost waited too long to see me. A few more days and you might have lost your hand to gangrene." He assisted the man to a sitting position. "Put on a fresh dressing every day and don't use that arm more than necessary." Elijah grinned at Rosemary. "A comfrey poultice wouldn't hurt, either."

On Saturday afternoon, Rosemary arranged two chairs on the front porch and placed a triangular wicker table between them. Once she gave Elijah a tour of her greenhouse, she'd offer him some of the lemon-thyme bread she'd baked last evening. The prospect of a pleasant visit in the shade should appeal to him on such a warm day.

She bit her lip when she thought of the cost of the ingredients—lemon, sugar, and wheat flour—luxuries she could ill afford. Then the image of his expression when he first tasted the bread erased the pricking of her conscience. She'd eat plain food during the week to make up for her indulgence.

Bodie watched her from his rug in front of the door. When she had the furniture arranged to her satisfaction, she bent over to rub his fur. "We should go indoors. We look like we're waiting to pounce the moment Elijah comes to the gate."

The dog wagged his tail and followed her into the house. Rosemary dashed upstairs to tidy the stray curls that the humidity had coaxed from her coiled braids, then hurried to the kitchen to slice the bread. After covering the fragrant treat with a napkin, she dropped a handful of mint leaves into her white porcelain teapot. When Elijah arrived, she'd put the kettle on to boil.

The clock in the sitting room chimed twice. She paced to the front window and peered out at the street, expecting to see him. Instead, Jacob stood on the boardwalk, tying his horse to the hitching post.

Startled, Rosemary took a step away from the window. Why would he leave the store on the busiest day of the week?

And why in midday? Sure that some disaster must have occurred, she greeted him from the porch before he reached the front steps.

"My goodness, this is a surprise. Has something happened in town?"

"In a manner of speaking." He folded his arms at his waist. "I overheard some disturbing talk in the restaurant at dinner."

Glancing over his shoulder, she saw Elijah cross the street and come their way. She tipped her head in his direction. "Dr. Stewart will be here in a moment. Whatever it is, he may need to hear it too."

A frown crossed Jacob's face, but when he turned he offered a bland smile as the doctor opened the gate. "Good afternoon. How fortunate you happened to pass by."

"Yes. Very." Elijah raised his eyebrows. "Don't often see you away from the grocery on a Saturday."

"I overheard something unsettling awhile ago and felt Miss Rosemary should know about it."

Elijah stepped around him to stand next to Rosemary. "Tell us, please."

"There's talk going around that Miss Rosemary had something to do with Mr. Bingham's death. Rumor is one of her remedies poisoned him."

She gasped. "Dear Lord, no!"

"That's nonsense." Elijah's voice boomed. "Who's responsible for this?"

Jacob shook his head. "I heard the whispers at noon. Whoever is spreading the story claims her cures are to blame."

"But I never . . ." Heat washed over her. The ginger tea. She blew out a long breath. Fortunately she hadn't given Mrs. Bingham enough of the chopped roots to cause illness.

She lifted her chin, ignoring the anger that pounded in her heart. Her herbs brought health, never harm. "The next time you hear anything, please ask who's behind the accusations. I'll deal with them."

Elijah rested a cautioning hand on her arm. "I'm not sure that's wise. A woman alone . . . We need to get Thaddeus to help."

"You know what I think of him." Her voice faltered. She sounded like a stubborn child, refusing help with a task too large for her.

"Doc's right, Miss Rosemary. If I hear more, I'll take the news to the sheriff."

She surveyed the two men, different in appearance but alike in their concern. "You're both very kind to worry about me. If you think it's best to talk to Sheriff Cooper, please do." In the meantime, she'd proceed on her own.

Jacob touched his hat brim. "I'd best get back to work." He faced her, concern in his eyes. "Take care. You need anything, let me know."

"I will. Thank you." Grateful for his friendship, she watched him stride to his horse. She probably should have asked him to stay for tea. Her gaze traveled to Elijah. No. She didn't want to share their time together.

Once the grocer was out of sight, Elijah laced his fingers through hers. "I *am* worried about you. The person who's spreading this calumny must be unbalanced. Not to mention this kind of gossip can be serious in a small town like ours."

She led him up the stairs and into the shade of the porch roof, warmth from his strong grasp radiating through her. Despite her brave stand, she couldn't subdue a web of fear. Rumors were like the stench that blew from a stockyard— impossible to ignore. She'd come too far to lose what respect she'd gained.

To conceal her apprehension, she focused on his last few

words. "We're not a small town. Noble Springs is the county seat."

"Don't change the subject. You're here by yourself now—"

"With Bodie. He's a good watchdog."

"I grant you that. But a dog can only do so much. You'd be safer with your brother and his wife for a few weeks, until this blows over."

She tugged her hand free and folded her arms. "No rumor is going to drive me from my home."

Shaking his head, he dropped onto one of the chairs she'd arranged on the porch. "Has anyone ever told you that you're an obstinate woman?" His eyes crinkled with amusement.

"Only my brother . . . and my parents." She tried for a smile but felt her lips quiver at the thought of her parents.

"Sit a moment, Rosemary. I'm sorry to have distressed you. How long have your parents been gone?"

The affection in his eyes threatened to undo her. He'd trusted her with his father's unsavory history—shouldn't she match his trust with her own? She perched on the edge of the other chair.

"My parents aren't gone, in the sense you mean. They're still in St. Louis, as far as Curt and I know. In their eyes, we committed an unforgiveable sin by supporting the Union cause."

He leaned toward her, resting his forearms on his thighs. "The war's been over for two years. Perhaps they've softened."

"If they have, we haven't heard of it." She brushed tears from the corners of her eyes with her fingertip. "Mama's from South Carolina. When her brother was killed fighting for the Confederacy at Gettysburg, she turned her back on us completely."

"What about your father?"

"Papa does what Mama says."

"So here you are, and here I am, both of us in Noble Springs." He took her hand. "I don't believe in coincidence, do you?"

She leaned back in the chair. At her age, she'd never expected to find someone to love. And to think she'd seen him as an opponent. A tiny smile lifted her lips. "There are no coincidences in God's providence."

*L*ate that afternoon, Rosemary stood inside her picket fence and watched as Elijah walked toward his home. He carried the remainder of the lemon bread in one hand. He didn't realize it, but he carried her heart with him, as well.

He turned to wave before crossing the street. She lifted her hand in reply, then hurried inside for her bonnet. She had time for an important errand before supper.

With Bodie straining at his leash, she covered the blocks to Courthouse Square in a few minutes' time. A glance through the mercantile's windows showed her that Faith was occupied with customers. She'd stop on her way back.

Spears of sunlight lanced over the jailhouse roof when she crossed Court Street. Blinking into the brightness, she drew a deep breath and put her hand on the cool iron latch of the sheriff's door. *But if ye forgive not men their trespasses, neither will your Father forgive your trespasses.*

"Yes, Lord," she murmured. The time had come. She'd be foolish to reject Sheriff Cooper's help because of an old resentment. If Curt, who'd been injured far more than she had, could forgive, she could too.

When she pushed open the thick wooden door, the odor

of stagnant air, stale food, and neglected slop pails assailed her. The sheriff sat at his desk to the right of the barred door that barricaded the stairs to the basement where prisoners were held. He glanced up, then straightened in his chair, astonishment written over his face.

"Miss Saxon?" He stood. "You're the last person I expected to see in here."

"No doubt." She snapped her fingers at Bodie and pointed to a spot where he was to stay, then crossed the room with her right hand extended. "I've come to apologize for my rudeness over these past many months. I've been uncivil and un-Christian. Please forgive me." Her pulse hammered in her throat. She hadn't stopped to consider what she'd do if he refused.

Sheriff Cooper stepped around his desk and gripped her hand. "Consider yourself forgiven." He grinned down at her. "My Amy will be pleased."

Relieved, she returned his smile. "So am I."

He gestured to an empty chair against the wall. "Sit a moment. You'll scarcely credit this, but you've been on my mind this afternoon."

"Whatever for?" She sat, angling the hard wooden chair so she could keep an eye on Bodie and pay attention to the sheriff at the same time.

"Heard some talk today that didn't set well with me. Seems someone's claiming you gave Elmer Bingham something that caused his death."

Her shoulders sagged. The gossip had spread faster than she expected. "The only thing I ever sent for Mr. Bingham was some ginger root to help nausea. His wife asked for my help." She held his gaze. "Ginger tea is perfectly safe, even for children."

The sheriff held up a hand to stop her. "Just so you know,

I don't believe the rumors. He wasn't young, and never was too spry. Likely he just up and died, particularly if you say he'd been puking."

"So how can I stop the talk? You know better than most how difficult it's been for me to settle in here."

"So it has, and I'm real sorry for my part in causing trouble for you and your brother. Told him so too." He leaned back in his chair. "You got any idea who might hold a grudge against you?"

"None whatsoever. But someone's come on my property a few times . . . and there have been a couple of threats."

His brown eyes darkened. "Threats?"

She told him about the two messages, the broken window, the uprooted plants. "Except for the first note, I thought possibly some young rascals were behind the damage—you know, playing pranks. But then when Bodie disappeared and I found that second message in the greenhouse, well, I couldn't pretend anymore."

"And you didn't come to me?" He tugged at the ends of his moustache. "Guess you wouldn't, seeing as how I treated you."

"Elijah—" Heat rose in her cheeks. "That is, Dr. Stewart urged me to. I let my stubbornness get in my way. Now this happens." She swallowed. "I'm worried."

Having a conversation with the man she'd avoided for months left her with a sense of unreality. But then, being accused of causing Mr. Bingham's death was even more un-real. Thankful she had obeyed the inner prompting to ask the sheriff's forgiveness, she leaned forward. "What should I do now?"

"Not a thing. I got ways of stopping rumors. Somewhere in town there's a coward that's got nothing better to do than harass a defenseless lady, and I mean to find him." He rum-maged around on his desk for a blank sheet of paper, then dipped a pen in an inkwell. "When did that first message show up?"

Thankful for the sheriff's promise that he'd keep a closer watch over her section of town, Rosemary directed her steps toward the mercantile. If Faith hadn't yet heard the gossip, she wanted to be the one to tell her.

As soon as she stepped into the store, she could see by the way everyone looked at her that stories about Mr. Bingham's death had already circulated through the community. She held her breath as Mr. Grisbee shuffled toward her.

"Hold your head up, Miss Rosemary. Ain't no one in here believes a word of what we're hearing."

His faded blue eyes shimmered through the sheen of her tears. "Thank you." She patted his gnarled hand.

At the counter, Mrs. Wylie, one of Faith's steady customers, turned from her purchase to face Rosemary. She lifted a blue cloth-wrapped bundle. "I recommend your teas to all my friends. Don't you worry about what a few folks are saying. Personally, I think someone's jealous of you. Maybe one of those grannies who lives out in the hills."

"You're very kind, Mrs. Wylie. Thank you." Some of the tension left her shoulders. At least she had a few supporters in Noble Springs.

When the older woman left with her packages, Faith hurried to Rosemary's side. "Would you feel safer staying at our house?"

"I feel more threatened at the prospect of having people turn against me than I do by any one person. Hiding in your house won't change that." She kissed Faith's cheek. "But I appreciate your offer."

Mr. Grisbee dragged an extra chair over to the woodstove.

"Bring the dog over here and set a minute. Saw you come from over by the courthouse. You didn't go to the sheriff, did you?"

"I did." Rosemary settled in the offered seat.

Faith's eyes widened. "You talked to Thaddeus?"

"I made peace with him. My apology was long overdue—and I need his help. I don't understand how anyone could feel threatened enough by my simple remedies to go to this length to discredit me."

"You're the one who's threatened." Faith placed her hands on her hips. "With Cassie gone, this is the perfect time for you to move to our house. Amy will be married in six weeks' time. You know we need you."

Rosemary breathed a sigh. "Anything can happen in six weeks. Right now I'm so stunned by these rumors I can't think clearly. I want to stay where I am for now."

"This whole thing's bound to blow over, Miss Rosemary." Mr. Grisbee touched her arm. "You got more friends than you know."

She left the mercantile for the walk home bolstered by his words. Who'd believe what a few men said over their noon meal? Her steps lightened.

As she approached the barbershop, Bodie pressed close to her leg and whined. Two men leaned against a wall beneath the red-and-white-striped pole. From their scruffy beards to their straggly hair, they needed the services offered inside.

She averted her eyes and picked up her pace. As she passed, she heard one of them say, "That her?"

A deeper voice responded with a snicker. "She's the one. If'n she offers you somethin' to drink, you'd best not take it."

Rosemary arrived at work early on Monday morning. She'd been awake since daylight worrying that Elijah's practice would suffer because of her presence in his office, but when she arrived she found a young man waiting, a leather pouch tucked under one arm. The door to the examining room was closed, so she knew the doctor had someone inside as well.

Breathing a sigh of relief, she unfastened Bodie's leash. He trotted to his rug beneath her desk and flopped on his side.

She turned to their patient. "Does Dr. Stewart know you're here?"

"No, miss. He was busy when I came in." He dug inside his bag and produced a buff-colored envelope. "If you'll give this to him, I'll be on my way."

She held out her hand for the missive, then noticed the words "Western Union Telegraph Company" printed across the paper. Her heart gave a little flip. A telegram seldom represented good news.

"I'll see that he gets the message."

"Thank you." He touched the brim of his cap, then hurried on his way.

She busied herself at her desk until Elijah stepped into the reception area. He had his hand on the patient's shoulder. "Mr. Ormond wanted to show me how he's healing. I think it's the comfrey." He winked at her.

"I'm glad to hear you're doing well." Rosemary smiled at the older man.

"Didn't used to hold much with medicos, but you and the doc here make a good pair. Wanted to thank you again for saving my hand." He stepped closer to the desk and lowered his voice. "Heard some gossip about you down at West's, but I told the feller he was talking through his hat."

Rosemary straightened. "Told who?" She and Elijah exchanged a glance.

"Don't know his name. Some old bird who comes in there

from time to time. Hope he thinks twice before he opens his mouth again."

Elijah patted the man's back. "I appreciate you speaking up for Miss Saxon. She's a dedicated nurse who'd never harm anyone."

She warmed at his praise. After Mr. Ormond left, Elijah turned to her, beaming.

"I'm happy to see you today—and every day, for that matter."

"I'm happy to see you too." Her gaze fell on the envelope resting on her desk. Reluctant to break the mood, she said, "A telegram was delivered for you while you were with your patient."

His smile faded as he plucked the missive from her hand. "Might as well get it over with. Can't be anything good." He ran his forefinger under the flap, removed a small sheet of paper, and scanned the contents. After a moment he looked up. "It's from my father. He's calling me back to Chicago. He's dying." His voice sounded bleak.

"Oh, gracious. Is there any family with him now?"

"I'm an only child." He slumped on the sofa, his head resting on his fingertips.

In the silence that followed, Rosemary crossed the floor and sank onto the sofa beside him.

"When will you leave?"

On Tuesday, Rosemary stood next to Elijah in front of the depot while he waited for the eleven o'clock train. He kept one hand on her elbow and held a paper-wrapped package in the other. His valise rested at his feet.

She'd taken pains with her hair and dress, choosing to wear her moss green paisley skirt and matching bodice because she knew he liked the color on her. She missed him already. Striving to hide her feelings, she asked, "Are you certain there's nothing more I can do for you while you're away?"

"The ledgers are current, we posted a notice on the door . . ." He pressed her arm against his side. "And you baked a loaf of your delicious bread for my journey. I'd say I'm well taken care of." Releasing his hold on her arm, he reached into his jacket and withdrew an envelope, which he gave to her. "I calculated what your share of the coming week's income might be."

Tears stung her eyes. "You didn't have to do that."

"My family issues shouldn't affect your well-being." He spoke over the rumble of the approaching train.

She tucked the heavy envelope into her handbag, already planning to purchase more wheat flour and a lemon as soon as he returned. A cloud of steam rolled toward them as the engine came to a stop in front of the depot. She swallowed and pasted a cheerful expression on her face. "Well, here you go. I'll be praying for your father—and you."

He bent toward her and lifted her chin with his thumb. His mouth settled on hers in a gentle kiss. For a moment she lost herself in the wonder of his soft lips, then she took a step away. "Elijah . . ."

He cupped her cheek with his hand, his dark gaze searching her face. "I'll miss you. I hope you feel the same about me."

"I do," she whispered. "Come back quickly."

Elijah boarded a passenger car and took an empty seat on the left side of the coach. Rosemary stood on the platform with her hands clasped together. Of all the unfortunate times to be leaving, when she needed support against the gossip that he knew circulated in spite of his and Thaddeus's efforts. He'd never met anyone like her. She had to be at least a foot shorter than he was, yet she stood her ground against rumors with the same ferocity Bodie demonstrated when guarding her door.

The bell on the engine clanged and the train jerked into motion. He waved at her for as long as she remained in sight, then leaned against the back of the wooden seat and closed his eyes. He'd write to her prior to returning, so he'd have the pleasure of seeing her face the first thing upon arriving home in Noble Springs.

His thoughts traveled ahead of the rails to Chicago, a city he hadn't visited since his mother died. And now his father was mortally ill. Elijah's mind traced a path over possible diagnoses. He knew his parent liked spirits. Perhaps his liver was failing. Or his heart. He'd certainly had difficulty breathing when he visited in April.

Elijah straightened on the seat and stared out the window. Hills cloaked in spring green marched over the landscape on both sides of the car, giving him the impression he was traveling through a verdant corridor on his way to—what? Chicago, with its crowded streets and refuse-filled river.

The following afternoon, he stepped off the train from St. Louis into the hubbub of Chicago's Great Central railway station. He held tight to his valise while keeping a wary eye out for pickpockets in the mass of passengers coming and going from the trains. When he emerged onto Lake Street, several open cabs were lined along the walkway awaiting passengers. He strode toward the first one.

"You looking for a good hotel?" the driver asked.

"No, thank you. If you'd take me to Indiana Street, near State, I'd appreciate it."

The man jumped down from the carriage and surveyed Elijah. "That'll cost you. It's a fair distance to them fancy neighborhoods."

"I grew up here. I know how far it is." He dug in his pocket and handed over a coin. "You'll get the rest when we arrive."

Once he seated himself behind the driver, the man flicked the reins over his dusty roan horse and guided them away from the station. After an absence of several years, Elijah had forgotten how imposing the sight of city blocks crowded with five- and six-story buildings appeared. Nothing like Noble Springs, with its three-story courthouse being the tallest edifice in town.

When the spire of the Presbyterian church loomed ahead, he leaned forward. "One more corner and we're there. The gray two-story on the right." Would his father be bedridden? Had he engaged nursing care? Elijah prayed he wasn't too late.

The Italianate mansion looked as he remembered it—gray

clapboards, arched windows trimmed in white, and a cupola overlooking a park across the street.

The cabbie jumped down and swung the valise to the ground. Elijah paid the remainder of the fare, squared his shoulders, and marched up the brick walkway to the portico over the main entry.

A thin woman wearing a black dress covered by a long apron opened the door at his knock. Her dour expression was less than welcoming.

"You must be the son. You've arrived at a poor time."

"I came as quickly as I could."

She moved to one side so he could enter. "I'm Mrs. Simmons, the housekeeper. If you'll wait in the parlor, the doctor will be with you shortly."

"He doesn't need to rise if he's unwell. I'll go up to see him."

She gave him a peculiar look. "Wait in the parlor. Please. You can leave your bag here." She indicated a point next to a tall crockery umbrella stand.

"Very well." He dropped his valise and glanced around the marble-tiled foyer, noting the elaborate draperies that shadowed potted palms standing at the corners. His mother had preferred sunlight to gloom. The changes must have been wrought by the young woman his father married, and who had now departed. Through open double doors on his right he spied a fire burning on the parlor grate.

He passed in front of the sweeping staircase that led to the upper floor, then entered the adjoining room, making his way around a shawl-draped table to sit in a red plush wing chair beside the fire. The woman disappeared through a passageway that led to the kitchen.

Minutes passed, marked by the ticking of an ornate case clock standing against an interior wall. Elijah stood and paced. If his father were resting in the master suite upstairs, why would he want to meet his son in the parlor? Elijah could climb stairs far more easily than a sick man could descend.

He pushed aside a thick brocade drapery and gazed out a side window to see if his mother's flower garden remained. By tilting his head to the right, he saw her prized rosebushes in bloom against the fence. The familiar sight comforted him.

"Welcome home," his father's voice boomed.

Elijah whirled to see the older man lumber across the room, both arms extended. His thick hair was combed into a wave that crested over his forehead. A smile creased his ruddy complexion. He looked . . . healthy.

"You said you were dying," Elijah blurted.

His father clapped him on the back. "Couldn't think of any other way to get you here. Never felt better." He drew a couple of shallow breaths. "Sorry to keep you waiting. Had some papers to sign for my attorney. His messenger will be here shortly."

Elijah narrowed his eyes. "What's so important that you took me from my patients?" He dropped into a chair, arms folded across his chest. "Whatever you have to say could have been said in a letter, I'm sure." Anger tinged his words.

"A letter couldn't spell out all you're missing by staying in that sorry little town. When was the last time you saw a play? Or attended a concert? Or made a good living, for that matter?"

"How many times must I tell you I'm content where I am, with what I have?"

The elder Dr. Stewart settled in a chair opposite Elijah, shifting his weight to accommodate his girth. His face assumed a sorrowful expression. "What's wrong with wanting to spend time with my only son? Will you at least stay the week?"

Elijah stared at the Persian rug at his feet, thinking of Rosemary in Noble Springs, thankful she had her brother to lean on in his absence. Torn between filial loyalty and anger at being manipulated, he glared at his father. "One week. No longer. And not one word from you about taking over your practice."

On the second Saturday following Elijah's departure, Rosemary entered the mercantile and led Bodie to his blanket next to the stove. After unfastening his leash, she took an apron from her carryall and wrapped it around her waist.

Faith peeked out of the storeroom. The burlap curtain over the opening framed her fair skin and blue eyes. "I thought I heard you come in. It's like old times, having your help with customers."

"I appreciate you giving me something to do. I've been at loose ends since Elijah left."

Her friend grinned at her. "I'd wager you can tell me down to the hour and minute just how long he's been gone." Then she sobered. "You look worried."

"He hasn't written. Not that he said he would, but I expected to hear something by now. He's been gone longer than he planned."

"If his father passed, he's been busy with arrangements. And if not, you know how much time it takes to care for an invalid."

"You're right." She dusted her hands together, then placed her carryall on a counter and reached inside. "Here's some raspberry leaf tea, in case you're running low."

Faith blushed. "Thank you." She slipped the bundle into the pocket of her apron.

Rosemary unpacked the rest of the soaps and teas that she'd brought for Faith's shelves, piling them in front of her.

"I'm happy to see you made more soap. Word is spreading about how good it is." Faith arranged the cloth-wrapped rounds on the shelf near the door. "Unfortunately, we haven't had much call for your teas since . . ." She cleared her throat. "Well, I'm sure sales will pick up soon."

Rosemary scooped up the bundles and replaced them in her carryall. "Then I'll take these to West & Riley's. The men who eat in the restaurant appear to be the ones who won't let the rumors die. If Jacob sells my teas in the grocery, that should stop the talk."

"I thought you and Jacob—"

"We agreed to be friends." She squeezed Faith's arm. "Just like you and me."

"It's not the same thing, and you know it."

They both turned as the bell over the door jingled. Clarissa French bustled into the mercantile, her round face wearing a pinched expression. She glanced over the room. "Good. You're here by yourselves. I came to invite you to a wedding."

"Galen and Jolene?" Rosemary hastened across the floor to the older woman's side.

Clarissa nodded. "Tomorrow after services." She drew a handkerchief from her sleeve and dabbed at the corners of her eyes. "The haste is unseemly. I just know people will think Galen is responsible for the girl's condition."

"They'll admire him, whether or not they know her story. He's a good man. You should be proud." She smiled to herself at the way the Lord had turned Jolene's mourning into dancing.

"I'm trying. But this isn't the way I pictured our son's marriage. I wanted him to meet a nice girl, have an engagement party, invite all our friends to the wedding. Not a hidden ceremony in our sitting room, with no one there but her family and you girls—and Curt, of course."

Rosemary patted the woman's arm. "You said some time ago that you prayed he'd settle down. This is an answer to your prayer."

"I know you mean well, but you can't understand a mother's heart. I had such dreams for my son, but he's chosen a path I have trouble accepting. Someday, when you have children, you'll know what I'm saying." Her shoulders slumped. "We'll expect you at three tomorrow. Please don't say a word to your customers."

Rosemary and Faith stared at each other for a long moment after she left.

"Poor Jolene," Faith said. "I never would have expected Clarissa to feel as she does."

Rosemary pressed her hand against an ache in her chest. "She's right. We don't understand a mother's heart."

Until now, she'd never considered that her choices had destroyed her own mother's dreams.

29

The following afternoon, Rosemary tapped on the Frenches' door two hours before the ceremony. She held a basket of cut daisies in one hand.

After a moment, Reverend French responded to her knock. "Miss Rosemary. Come in. We weren't expecting you this early—but you're always welcome, of course."

"I'll only be a moment." She held up the basket. "I brought some decorations for your mantelpiece. Clarissa seemed so distraught yesterday that I wanted to help make this event special for her. If you'll permit me, I'll arrange these, then return in time for the ceremony."

His eyes brightened. "She'll be pleased to see them. She's been in a state ever since Galen told us his plans." He led the way, still talking. "Mind you, I'm delighted at this turn of events. I'm sure Miss Jolene will make him a fine wife."

In the center of the sitting room, a half-dozen straight-back chairs had been arranged to face the fireplace. Reverend French swept several framed miniatures from the mantelpiece into his hands and carried them to a sideboard behind the dining table. "Now you should have plenty of space for your flowers."

"Thank you." She lifted the garland she'd woven at home and spread it across the velvet-draped surface. Sunlight streaming through tall windows along the right side of the room cast a glow over the white petals. "Lovely. Now all we need is the bride and groom."

"Galen is upstairs, and Miss Jolene and her parents will be here soon." He turned to Rosemary, his expression serious. "I can't thank you enough for your kindness. These flowers will raise Clarissa's spirits more than you know."

Her heart lifted at his obvious love for his wife. Maybe someday she and Elijah . . .

She shook her head. *Don't get ahead of yourself. He's made no promises.*

At three, when Rosemary returned to the Frenches' home in the company of Faith and Curt, Clarissa greeted them at the door and ushered them to the sitting room. The first thing Rosemary noticed was a fluted cake adorned with white icing resting in the center of the dining table. A punch bowl and cups waited on the sideboard.

The second thing she noticed was Jacob, who occupied a chair next to Jolene's father. Her surprise must have shown on her face, because Mrs. Graves rose from her chair and scurried to Rosemary's side. "We invited your young man to join us," she said in a low voice. "I knew you'd be pleased."

"He's not—" She swallowed the rest of the sentence at the sight of Mrs. Graves's crestfallen expression. Later, she'd explain that she and Jacob were not courting.

"Did I do wrong?" Jolene's mother pressed her fingers over her lips.

"Not at all. He was kind enough to bring me to your house. He deserves to see the happy ending." She sighed, wishing

Elijah weren't so far away in Chicago. In his own fashion, he'd done as much to bring Jolene and Galen together as she had.

From his place in front of the hearth, Reverend French cleared his throat. "If you'd all take your seats, we'll begin."

Jacob stood and rested his hand on the back of an empty chair to his left. "Miss Rosemary?"

Once she was settled, with Faith and Curt in the two seats next to her, Jacob leaned close and whispered in her ear. "Mrs. Graves wanted to surprise you, or I'd have fetched you here in my buggy."

"It certainly was a surprise. Why did you let her believe we were—"

Faith poked her arm and nodded toward the rear of the sitting room, where Galen guided Jolene from the entryway to stand in front of his father. Her flushed cheeks matched the wine-colored shawl draped over her gray-checked dress.

Rosemary took a quick look around for Clarissa. She sat on a high-backed slipper chair against a side wall, hands clasped in her lap, head bowed. As her husband read the words of the ceremony, she lifted her chin and arranged her face in a stiff smile.

Lord, help her to see what a blessing Jolene will be to her son.

Reverend French's face shone with pleasure while the young couple repeated their vows. Resting his hands on their shoulders, he said, "What therefore God hath joined together, let not man put asunder."

Rosemary blinked back tears as Galen turned to Jolene and placed a kiss on her forehead. When the newly married couple turned to face their guests, Mrs. Graves was the first person to reach her daughter's side. "It was a fine wedding."

She seized Jolene's hand and tugged her toward Rosemary.

"Me and Mr. Graves can't thank you enough for all you done for her. And now . . ." She waved her hand in Galen's direction. "We got us a fine son-in-law to boot."

"I do thank you. For everything." Jolene's voice trembled.

"This was the Lord's doing, not mine. I wish you every happiness."

"Going to be your turn next, I reckon," Mrs. Graves said. She arched an eyebrow toward Jacob, who stood nearby.

"Mr. West and I are friends. That's all."

Jacob's moustache lifted when he smiled. "Let's say we're discussing terms and haven't reached an agreement."

Rosemary wanted to stamp her foot in frustration. Jacob had promised they'd be friends. There were no terms to discuss.

The morning after the wedding, Rosemary walked along Second Street toward West & Riley's, her carryall packed with bundles of herb teas. Jacob could think what he would of his prospects with her. They were friends, and friends they'd remain.

She pushed open the door to the grocery and was instantly surrounded by the aroma of breakfast swirling from the adjoining restaurant. Bacon, fried potatoes, biscuits . . . her mouth watered. The click of utensils and the rumble of male conversation reached her ears.

"Miss Rosemary." Jacob strode toward her, his eyes bright. "Two days in a row. What can I get you this morning?"

She reached into her carryall and set a blue cloth-wrapped bundle on the counter. Its tag read "Blissful Sleep." She drew out another, labeled "Calm Afternoons."

He studied her with a puzzled expression. "You're bringing me remedies?"

"I was wondering, would you be so kind as to sell my herb teas in your store?" She held her breath and waited for his response.

"Why? Doesn't your sister-in-law have these in the mercantile?"

"I want you to have them here." She gestured toward the restaurant side of the building. "Those men in there are the ones spreading talk that somehow one of my herbal cures caused Mr. Bingham's death. You know that. If you put my teas on your shelves, it will be a testimony to their safety."

He folded his arms over his apron and stared at the blue bundles on his counter. Then he lifted his gaze to a shelf on his left, where one-pound packages of roasted coffee were displayed.

He took a step toward the wall and pushed the coffee to one side. "There's room here. How many can you supply?"

"Oh, Jacob. Thank you!" She handed him her carryall. "Here's a dozen. The varieties are named on the labels."

As he stacked the bundles on the shelf, a patron from the restaurant walked through the archway between the two businesses, stopping close to Jacob. His dingy brown hat rode low on his forehead. Suspenders buttoned over a faded blue shirt held up a pair of homespun trousers rolled at the hem. His gaze bounced between Rosemary and the cloth-wrapped teas.

"You that woman with the potions? Heard you poisoned old Bingham."

She glared at him, feeling anger radiating from her in waves. "And who'd you hear that from?"

"Dunno." He smirked at her. "Someone eatin' here this mornin' mebbe said somethin'."

"Only the Lord knows what happened to Mr. Bingham." She planted her hands on her hips. "I had nothing to do with his death. You tell that to the next man who 'mebbe' says something."

"Whoo-ee. You're a feisty little thing."

Jacob spun around and stalked over to him. "Move along. I don't want to see you in here again." He grabbed the man's shoulder and turned him toward the door.

Mumbling curses, the patron slouched out to the board-walk.

Rosemary's heart threatened to pound its way out of her chest. She sagged against the counter and drew in a slow breath.

Jacob faced her. "Are you all right? Your face is red."

"I don't doubt it." She gave a shaky laugh. "I can't remember ever being so angry. It wasn't just him, it's everybody. Why are people so quick to point a finger when there's not a grain of proof?"

He shook his head. "It's the way of the world, Miss Rosemary. From now on, I'll spend more time next door during meals. Maybe I can nose out who started these lies." He lifted one of the bundles of tea and cradled it in his cupped palm like a baby bird. "In the meantime, you'd best make up more of these. I'm going to sell them to everyone who comes in."

She laid her hand on his arm. "You're a good man, Jacob. I'm blessed to have your friendship."

"Same here." His light tone matched his grin.

She removed her hand and pretended she hadn't seen the caring in the depths of his eyes.

Rosemary fought to control her trembling limbs when she left the store, knowing her body was reacting to the intense anger she'd felt at Jacob's customer. She took a deep breath of the humid morning air and released it slowly. When she returned home, she'd brew a cup of chamomile tea, but first she'd stop at the post office. Perhaps today she'd hear from Elijah.

She climbed the two steps leading to a small white clapboard building across the street from the parsonage.

The postmaster looked up when she entered. "Miss Saxon. This is your lucky day." He flicked through a tray of mail on the table in front of him, and held out a cream-colored envelope. "This what you've been waiting for?"

Her name was scrawled across the front in Elijah's bold penmanship.

"Indeed it is. Thank you, Mr. Lyons." She tucked the letter into her carryall and hurried toward home, the earlier confrontation almost forgotten in her joy at hearing from Elijah.

Bodie raced toward her when she burst through the front door. She waved the letter at him. "Word from Elijah. Let's hope he's on his way."

The dog panted happy agreement and followed her into the sitting room. Using her forefinger, she tore open the envelope flap and removed a single sheet of paper.

Chicago, Illinois, June 5, 1867

Miss Rosemary,

I expected to be back in Noble Springs by this time, but my father had other plans. To begin with, he is not ill, nor dying. It was a ruse to bring me here.

He asked that I spend a week with him, which is now stretching into two. I'm weary of dinner parties, musical shows, and all the trappings of city life. This morning I informed him that I'm taking the train south on the 13th, Thursday. I believe I've fulfilled my obligation where he's concerned.

I'm eager to see your face and to tell you all that

*transpired here. If possible, would you be at the station
when the train arrives from St. Louis on Friday?*

> *With sincere affection,*
> *Elijah*

Rosemary held the letter close to her chest. Friday. She
breathed a sigh of relief. As each day of his absence had
passed, her worries grew greater that an established practice
in the city would lure him away. But no. In four days he'd be
home.

30

E lijah paused at the entrance to the dining room to adjust his jacket. His father turned from the laden sideboard. A frown curdled his forehead.

"We've been waiting for you." He gestured at an empty chair on the right of the head of the table. "Please seat yourself. I'll tell Mrs. Simmons to begin serving."

From the chair next to his, Miss Adele Mason smiled a greeting. This evening she wore a ruffled dress of shiny green fabric trimmed with darker green velvet. Her blonde hair was piled on top of her head in an impossible crown of curls. Elijah suppressed a groan. In the two weeks he'd spent in Chicago, his father had managed to invite Miss Mason and her brother, Dr. Lowell Mason, to every dinner party and play they attended. Now, on his last night here, he would have to endure her tedious chatter when he would have preferred a quiet supper alone.

"Miss Mason." He nodded at her as he took his seat. "How nice to see you again."

"Oh, and I feel the same about you, Dr. Stewart! I feared you'd have gone back to your little village by now, but your dear father said you aren't leaving until tomorrow. So we have one more evening together." She fluttered her fan over her exposed neck and shoulders.

Her brother leaned across the table. "We're assuming you are returning to your village. Have you changed your mind?" His ratlike eyes glittered in the gas lights from the chandelier.

"You'll be happy to hear I have not."

Miss Mason pouted. "He may be happy. I'm crushed."

Elijah's father took his chair at the head of the table. "The evening's young. Elijah may yet change his mind. I've ordered all his favorite dishes for tonight's meal."

As if on cue, Mrs. Simmons entered from the kitchen carrying a tureen. One by one she filled their bowls with pea soup for the first course, then whisked through the swinging door and returned with a platter of cold boiled salmon covered with white sauce.

Elijah paid no attention to the food in front of him. "I have a special reason for wanting to go home. I'm courting a lady. I hope she'll agree to become my wife." He rested a meaningful gaze on Miss Mason.

She flushed. "I hope you've chosen carefully. As a doctor, you need a wife who will properly manage your household. What would a backwoods girl know about social niceties?"

"You've picked out a wife? What's her name?" His father's soup spoon clattered onto his plate. "What do you know about her? You've been here for two weeks without saying a word—are you ashamed of your bride-to-be?"

"Not in the least." He glared at him. "I didn't believe my life in Noble Springs was of any interest to you."

Miss Mason tapped his arm with her fan. "I'm certainly interested. Please tell us about the lucky lady."

"Her name's Rosemary Saxon. She's from St. Louis, so she's far from being a backwoods girl. In fact, she was a nurse at Jefferson Barracks when I was posted there during the war. Now she serves as a nurse in my office."

"A nurse, of all things." Miss Mason gave a mock shudder, then swept him with a coquettish glance. "You should aim a little higher. Consider your future. I'm sure you'll change your mind about returning to Chicago."

"Nothing will persuade me to live here."

"Don't be so sure." She fluttered her eyelashes at him.

Elijah ignored her and lifted his fork, signaling that the conversation had come to an end.

Mrs. Simmons returned to remove the soup bowls and the salmon, replacing them with a platter containing roasted spring chicken surrounded by browned vegetables. While they enjoyed the main course, Lowell Mason and Elijah's father kept up a steady conversation about their medical practices. The chicken was followed by a dessert of individual molds of chocolate blancmange.

When Elijah finished his last swallow of the custard-like treat, he drew a breath and returned his spoon to the plate. "A delicious send-off, Father. I thank you."

His father leaned against the back of his armchair, hands resting on his abdomen. "Doesn't have to be a send-off. You could eat like this every night if you'd get over being stubborn and join me in my practice." He glanced at Miss Mason. "Please excuse us if we talk business in your presence."

She waved her hand in a dismissive gesture. "Think nothing of it, Doctor. I'm accustomed to hearing my brother ramble on." She gave Elijah a demure smile. "I'd be delighted to introduce you to Chicago society should you decide to stay."

Rosemary's earnest face swam in his vision. Tomorrow he'd be on his way back to her and to his "village," as his father persisted in calling Noble Springs. He couldn't wait to leave the smothering atmosphere of his father's luxurious home. Everywhere he looked he was reminded of the means his parent had used to purchase the opulent furnishings and abundant meals.

Elijah folded his napkin and laid it next to his empty dessert plate. "I have my ticket. I'm leaving on tomorrow's train." His gaze swept the three people at the table. "After all that I saw during the war, I have no desire to live as you do, Father. A quiet life suits me."

Miss Mason rested her hand on Elijah's forearm. "Please, don't be hasty. Chicago has so much to offer." Her tone implied she'd be part of the city's offerings.

"I warn you, I won't ask again," his father said. "Dr. Mason has already agreed to join me. I'd hoped the two of you would work together, but if not, I can easily find someone who won't disdain a comfortable life."

Elijah pushed his chair back on the thick carpet and stood. "So be it. I've ordered a cab to take me to the station early tomorrow." He gave a formal bow in Miss Mason's direction. "Thank you for your pleasant company during my stay."

Turning to his father, he said, "You're welcome to visit whenever you wish. My spare room is always ready."

He left the dining room and took the stairs to the second floor two at a time. Another day and a half and he'd be in Noble Springs, where Rosemary waited. His Chicago stay would be no more than a memory.

Rosemary stood outside the station before noon on Friday. Bodie sniffed around the platform as far as his leash would allow him to roam, then returned to sit at her side. When the smoke of the oncoming engine showed on the horizon, she smoothed her paisley skirt and tucked stray wisps of hair into the net covering her coiled braids.

In a few short minutes, the train whooshed to a stop, bell clanging. The stationmaster sprinted along the platform, pushing a cart toward the baggage car. Through the windows, Rosemary saw passengers standing and gathering their possessions, but she couldn't discern whether Elijah was among them. What if he'd decided to remain in Chicago? After all, he'd written the letter nine days ago. Plenty of time to have a change of heart.

A family of four descended to the platform, followed by two cigar-smoking salesmen carrying sample cases. An elderly couple was assisted down by the conductor. Rosemary had taken a step closer to the passenger car to better see inside when Elijah appeared in the opening between cars. He leaped to the ground and sprinted toward her.

"Rosemary! I've thought of nothing but you since I left Noble Springs." He clasped her hands in his. "Thank you for meeting me. I hoped you'd be here."

His strong grip sent a current of heat through her. "When I didn't see you at first, I was afraid you'd decided not to return."

"Nothing could keep me away." He tucked her arm close to his side, then bent over and touched his lips to her forehead. "Excuse me a moment while I collect my valise, then I'd be pleased if you'd walk with me. I'm eager to get home and rest. You can tell me everything that's happened since I left."

"I'll be glad to, if you tell me about Chicago. Your father wasn't ill?"

His jaw tightened. "Not any more than he was the last time I saw him. You'll be happy to know he's planning to bring another doctor into his practice. I closed that door permanently."

She smiled, relieved. "Did you leave on good terms?"

"As much as it depended on me, yes."

Once he had his baggage in hand, they strolled north toward King's Highway. Rosemary tried to remember all of the news that occurred during his absence. Jolene's wedding, her own visit to Sheriff Cooper, her decision to sell her teas in the grocery. Unless she imagined it, he narrowed his eyes when she mentioned Jacob's defense of her on Monday.

Before she knew it, they'd reached the corner and turned right toward their respective homes. When she glanced down the block, something fluttering from her gate caught her attention. She tugged at Elijah's arm and pointed.

"What could that be?"

"One way to find out." He quickened his stride.

Bodie tugged at the leash, apparently thinking Elijah wanted to run. Rosemary jerked him back to her side and picked up her own pace. When she reached her fence, Elijah had dropped his valise and gripped a sheet of paper, which he tried to hide behind his back.

"What is it?"

"Nothing."

She held out her hand. "If it were truly nothing, you wouldn't hide it. Please, let me see."

"Rosemary—"

She moved closer and took the paper from him. Puzzled, she glanced over a handbill advertising a public sale of farm animals and implements. Directions to a farm southeast of Noble Springs were printed near the top.

"What is this?"

"Look on the other side."

Large black letters marched lengthwise over the page.

WITCH.

Rosemary paced from her kitchen to the front door and back again. Her eyes stung. After nearly a year and a half in Noble Springs, she still wasn't accepted—not as a nurse, and not as an herbalist. Her mother had spent much of her life growing and dispensing herbs, and no one had ever called her a witch.

She kicked at a footstool. "I won't let this stop me. I believe in what I do. I won't quit." Her voice sounded hollow in the small house.

For a moment, she regretted sending Elijah on his way when he'd offered to sit on the porch with her until she felt calm. As if there were a way to feel calm with rumors and name-calling pounding at her.

The paper Elijah had torn from her gate lay on the dining table. She studied the jagged letters for a moment, then folded the edges over, hiding the ugly word. Bodie watched her from his rug in the kitchen.

"I'm going to see Sheriff Cooper." She put the message in her pocket and knelt next to her dog, rubbing the fur at his neck. "You're staying here. I won't be gone long."

After closing the gate behind her, she stood on tiptoe and leaned over to fasten the bolt Curt installed following the greenhouse incident. Doing so made her chuckle in spite of her worries. If she, as short as she was, could reach the bolt, anyone could.

She passed the barbershop and stole a glance inside. Somewhere in town lurked the person behind the harassment. Sheriff Cooper would find him if she didn't discover him first.

A few men on horseback rode by and stirred up dust, but for the most part the streets were quiet as the community dozed in the afternoon sun. Rosemary drew a deep breath before opening the door of the jailhouse. Her doubts about the sheriff's effectiveness warred with her need for his help.

"Miss Saxon." Sheriff Cooper stood. "What brings you here? Not more trouble, I hope." He rubbed his badge with his thumb.

She handed him the folded sheet of paper. "Someone put this on my gate this morning while I was at the depot."

He grinned at her. "Miss Faith told Amy that the doc was due back today. You met the train, eh?"

"I did."

He continued to smile, as though waiting for her to tell him more.

"Read what it says, please." She gestured toward the message.

"'Witch.'" His eyes widened. "That's a serious accusation. Could lead to trouble." He crushed the paper in his hand and tossed it on his desk. "Sit down, please. D'you have any idea who might have written this?"

"No more than I had with the notes I brought you earlier."

"Anyone particular bothering you?"

"I can't go anywhere now without someone muttering behind my back." She told him about the man she'd encountered in the grocery when she took the teas to Jacob. "But no one person in particular, no."

He tipped his chair back against the wall and tugged at a corner of his moustache. "Blast it all. Here I'd been hoping things had quieted down." He huffed out a breath. "Can you tell me who all you've given your cures to? Anyone with a special complaint?"

She shook her head. "I'll bring you the names of those I remember, but I have no idea who bought my herbs at the mercantile. Could be any number of people. Tinctures and teas have been for sale there since March."

"Gotta be a way to figure this out. I've heard the gossip going around, but anyone could have written this." He flicked the crumpled paper with his finger.

"That's what concerns me. I'll have the names I know for you tomorrow. Maybe Faith can provide a few more."

His chair thudded to the floor and he stood. "Don't you worry none. We'll get to the bottom of this."

When she left his office, all she could think of was pouring her fears out to Faith. Having the sheriff tell her not to worry was a concern in itself, considering how long it took him to solve the mystery of the robbery at the mercantile.

osemary shot a quick glance around for hostile faces before slipping into the mercantile. The chairs next to the checkerboard were empty, as she'd expected this late in the afternoon. Faith tossed her a wave and then returned her attention to a customer who apparently couldn't decide between two oil lamps.

At the rear of the store, a man dressed in a jacket and tie surveyed the shotgun display. Aside from Faith's brief acknowledgment, no one paid attention to her. She moved to a glass-enclosed counter that held doorknobs and lock sets. Sturdier locks for both of her doors would have to be installed. She'd see if Curt was free tomorrow . . . or maybe Elijah would be willing to help her. It wouldn't hurt to ask.

After the woman at the counter left with her parcel, Faith joined Rosemary. "Did the doctor's train arrive on time?"

"Yes, thankfully." For a moment she'd forgotten that her trip to the station had precipitated her visit to the sheriff.

"So why aren't the two of you spending the afternoon together?" Faith's voice teased.

Rosemary leaned close to her friend's ear. "Something

happened today." She whispered where the message was found and what the paper said.

At Faith's shocked expression, she continued. "Someone had to have been near my house in order to tack that to the gate in the short time I was away."

"How frightening! Please go pack your things. Curt will come for you as soon as school is dismissed."

She shook her head. "With new locks and Bodie there, I'll be perfectly safe. Besides, no one's ever tried to get into the house."

"Yet."

Bending over the display of locks, Rosemary pointed at a square metal box with a heavy key attached. "If I have these on my doors, even you won't worry."

"Why don't you stop being so stubborn and let us look after you? I'm still hoping you'll agree to live with us after Amy and Thaddeus are married. That's only a month from now."

"There must be someone else who'd be willing. As fond as I am of your grandfather, you know I want to stay where I am."

"Even now?"

The man looking at shotguns turned his head toward them. "Mrs. Saxon, I'd like to see that Perkins you have on the rack."

"I'll be right there." She laid her hand on Rosemary's arm. "Please wait."

Bustling over to the wall, she lifted the double-barreled weapon from its grooved holder and handed it to the shopper. After he rubbed the stock, sighted along the front bead, and opened the breech, he grunted and returned the shotgun to her. "Handsome firearm. Little too rich for my means, though."

The bell over the door jingled as he departed.

Faith rejoined Rosemary, shaking her head. "That shotgun's going to get worn out with men looking at it. Someone was in here the other day, an odd little man. Practically drooled on the barrels, but ended up not buying that or anything else." She frowned as she related the incident. "I was glad the woodstove regulars were here at the time. The fellow gave me an uneasy feeling."

Rosemary glanced around the deserted store. "Would you like me to wait here with you until you close?"

"Not unless you come home with me afterwards."

She shook her head and pointed at the locks. "With these I'll be as secure as if I were in one of Sheriff Cooper's cells."

The cases of her new steel lock sets clanked together as Rosemary walked home from West & Riley's with a lemon and a package of sugar riding at the top of her carryall. She'd bake a loaf of bread this evening, then tomorrow invite Elijah to help her with the installation.

The afternoon had grown so still that even the birds were silent. Bruised clouds piled overhead, their edges fiery in the setting sun. She quickened her pace. Hoofbeats sounded behind her and in a moment Sheriff Cooper reined his horse to a halt in front of the post office.

"Miss Saxon. We'd best get you home. Storm's brewing." He slid from the saddle and tied the animal to a hitching post. "Soon as I ask Mr. Lyons if there's a new crop of wanted posters, I'll see you to your door."

"My house is just on the next street. I thank you, but that's not necessary."

"I believe it is." He gazed down at her, his mouth set in a half smile. "You don't have your dog with you, so you get me instead." He pointed at the door. "After you."

Lifting her chin, she preceded him inside, chafing at his overprotectiveness. She stood to one side while Mr. Lyons gave him several handbills.

"Here's something for you, Miss Saxon," the postmaster said, holding out a square envelope. "Two letters in one week. You're keeping me busy."

She smiled to indicate she appreciated his little joke. "That's two more than I've had in the past month. Thank you." She glanced at the sender's name written on the back flap. *Haddon. St. Louis.*

Word from Cassie. Pleasant news would be welcome after the events of the afternoon. She tucked the missive into her carryall, eager to learn what her friend had to say.

Sheriff Cooper held the door open for her. "I'll ride alongside until you get home."

"Thank you." Resigned to his presence, she resumed her pace. The clop of the animal's hooves mimicked the sound of her heels on the boardwalk. She hated to admit it, but she appreciated the feeling of security she gained from the sturdy chestnut gelding and its tall rider.

At her gate, he reined in his horse and leaned over the saddle. "Soon's you get inside, I'll be on my way."

"You're very kind." After unfastening the bolt, she locked the gate behind her, then turned to wave when she reached her porch.

The sheriff tipped his hat before riding into the gathering dusk. A flash of lightning forked across the sky as she closed her door. The windows rattled with an explosion of thunder.

She hurried into the kitchen and lit the lamp over the table. With Bodie trembling at her feet after each rumble of thunder, she tore open the envelope from Cassie and drew out a thin sheet of paper. Her friend's tiny script covered both sides of the page.

Dear Rosemary,

Mother and I are again staying with my uncle, my father's brother, here in St. Louis. I fear we're not the most welcome of guests, as they are already crowded with his numerous family members. However, Mother says 'family is family,' and he dare not turn us away.

After several paragraphs describing her uncle's home and his children, Cassie continued,

While I am once more relishing my mother's companionship, I must admit to feeling awkward about our circumstances. My uncle's wife is decidedly chilly toward us.

Enough complaining. My purpose in writing, other than to say thank you again for giving me shelter in your home, is to ask that you would arrange to have my trunk sent as soon as is convenient. Enclosed you will find a draft for the expense of shipping. Please address the trunk in care of my uncle, Rudolph Haddon, at the location printed at the end of this letter. The stationmaster in St. Louis will arrange for delivery. Thank you in advance for your trouble.

I miss you terribly. If time permits, I would love to have a letter from you. Or better yet, dare I suggest a visit?

> *Affectionately, your friend,*
> *Cassie*

Rosemary dropped onto a chair and reread the missive. How like Cassie to suggest a visit—she'd never known the necessity of steady employment. Rosemary wasn't free to travel on a whim, nor did she have any desire to return to St. Louis.

When Rosemary looked outside on Saturday morning, mist hung like steam over the ground. Puddles glittered in the golden sunrise. In spite of her claims of fearlessness, her heartbeat increased as she slipped into a work dress and boots to check her yard for intruders. With the noise of the storm last night, a person could have torn her gate off its hinges and she wouldn't have heard a sound.

Bodie waited while she descended the stairs, his tail beating the air, then barged outside as soon as she opened the kitchen door. The sweet fragrance of moist earth and greenery greeted her when she stepped onto the back porch. She leaned against the railing to savor the early coolness. Soon enough the sun would be high, and June would deliver another sticky, oven-like day.

Bodie sniffed in circles along the fence line, then sped around the house. Rosemary hurried off the porch to follow after him. Losing him once was enough.

When she reached the front yard, she stopped. Bodie stood at the fence in a half crouch, his tail extended like that of a hunting dog, his fur ridged along his spine.

"What is it, boy? What do you smell?" She moved toward him with slow steps. Nothing appeared disturbed. No footprints. The gate was closed.

She planted her hands on her hips. "That's enough. Let's go in." Bending over, she tucked her hand under his collar and pulled him away from the pickets. Then she saw what he'd sensed.

The gate was closed but unbolted.

Rosemary pounded up the back steps and slammed the door behind her. As soon as she breakfasted and changed clothes, she'd call on Elijah to ask him to install her locks.

She shook off a worry that he'd think her request was presumptuous. After all, more than once he'd expressed concern about her welfare. She'd give him the opportunity to show her he meant what he said.

After feeding Bodie, she prepared a hasty meal of toasted cornbread and jasmine tea, which she ate while staring out the kitchen window. Her hands shook when she lifted her teacup.

An hour later, Rosemary stood on Elijah's porch and knocked. She held a towel-wrapped loaf of lemon-thyme bread on a plate in her left hand. Quick footsteps sounded from inside. His face brightened when he opened the door and saw her. He wore a loose tan shirt and the type of trousers she remembered her father wearing when he planned to relax at home.

"What a perfect way to start my day. I was afraid the knock would be a patient calling me out."

"I am calling you out, in a way. I came to ask for your help."

"Anything. Name it."

"Yesterday after we parted, I purchased sturdier locks for my doors."

"Very wise."

"Would you be willing to install them for me?" Smiling, she held the plate of bread in front of her. "Here's payment in advance."

His fingers brushed hers as he took the offering, sending a tingle along her arms. "Spending time with you is payment enough, but I thank you. You know how much I enjoy your bread." He took a step backward and put the plate on a table next to the open door. "Excuse me while I get my tools."

In moments, he returned, swinging a canvas satchel in one hand. "When I've finished, would you like to go for a buggy ride? Maybe to Pioneer Lake?" He tucked his free hand under her arm as they descended his porch steps. "I feel we have a lot of catching up to do after my long absence."

"I'd love to." The fear she'd felt earlier that morning drowned in a wave of pleasure. Once her new locks were in place, what difference would it make if someone opened her gate? She'd be safe inside.

Nevertheless, once they reached her fence she stopped and leaned forward to check the bolt. Closed. A pulse pounded in her temple and she realized she'd been holding her breath.

"What's wrong?" Elijah reached past her and pushed the bolt free. "You're pale all of a sudden."

"I . . . it's nothing."

He dropped the tool bag on the walk and put his hands on her shoulders, turning her to face him with gentle movements. "When I said that to you yesterday, you didn't believe me. Now it's my turn."

Apprehensive about his reaction, she lifted her head and looked into the depths of his brown eyes. "This morning I came out early to see if there'd been any damage to my plants from the rainstorm."

"They look fine to me."

"Thankfully, they were undamaged. But my gate . . . the bolt was open although the gate was closed."

"You sure you didn't forget?"

She glared at him. "Quite sure."

His hands tightened on her shoulders. "Then someone sent you a message. You're not safe here, strong locks or not."

"I was afraid you'd think that. But I don't agree. The person who's doing this is more interested in harassment than harming me. Consider all the time I spend walking around town. There's more risk there than in being inside my house."

Looking exasperated, he removed his hat and ran his fingers

through his hair. "If the Lord made a woman more stubborn than you, I've never met her."

"I'm glad to hear that." She grinned at him. "Now, will you please install those locks? I'll pack some food for us while you work."

A gentle breeze rippled the waters of Pioneer Lake when Rosemary and Elijah arrived. Several couples and families were scattered about on the grassy area, while children played and splashed along the shoreline.

Elijah stopped the buggy near the hackberry tree where they'd had their first picnic. He helped her down, then removed a sheet of oiled canvas from behind the seat and spread it over the ground. "There. This will give us a dry place to sit." He held out his arm. "Would you like to walk a bit first?"

Nodding her agreement, she lifted her skirts above the wet grass. "Let's go watch the children." She hugged her happiness to herself when she took his hand and felt the strength of his firm grip. The day couldn't be more perfect.

As they moved down the slight slope, Elijah released her hand and slipped his arm around her waist. "I thought about our last visit to Pioneer Lake the whole time I was in Chicago. Our courtship barely got started before I had to leave."

She leaned against his side. "I thought of you too. Often."

He tugged her closer. "I know you feel I'm overstepping myself when I press you to be careful. I want to protect you." His voice grew husky. "I'd like to have you this close to me every day."

She stopped and stared up at him, her eyes wide. "Are you asking . . . ?"

"Let's say I'm asking permission to ask. I saw too many soldiers get their hearts broken by hasty engagements that didn't last." He put his arms around her, drawing her to his chest. "I love you, Rosemary. I've never felt this way before." His voice vibrated against her ear. "A doctor's life is not an easy one. I want you to be certain before you say anything."

She relaxed in his arms for a moment, struggling against the impulse to shout, "Yes!" before he properly asked the question. When she drew back, she saw the brightness of tears standing in his eyes.

"If you want me to wait before I answer you, I will." She stood on tiptoe and settled a soft kiss against his cheek. "But not for long."

The following Friday morning, Rosemary stepped onto her porch holding Bodie's leash. Sheriff Cooper waited astride his horse at the hitching post, as he'd done every day for the past week.

She had learned that protests were futile, so she smiled at him as she opened her gate. "Good morning, Sheriff. Another lovely day, isn't it?"

"Going to be a hot one."

She leaned over the gate and fastened the bolt, then turned west toward Elijah's office. The horse snorted and sidestepped when she passed close to his nose. She shied out of the way, her fear of the large animal prickling her skin.

The sheriff chuckled. "He ain't going to bite you."

"I hope not." Embarrassed, she picked up her pace. A steady *clop, clop* on the dusty street told her that her escort was following a step or two back. When she reached the office, she paused before entering.

"Thank you, Sheriff. Have a pleasant day."

"Hope it's quiet." He tipped his hat. "See you this evening."

Shaking her head at his persistence, she pushed open the

door and unhooked Bodie's leash. He trotted across the room, settling on his rug beneath her desk.

Elijah left his private office as soon as he saw her and strode across the floor to take her in his arms. "I wait for this moment every morning." He planted a kiss on her forehead. "If it weren't for early patients, I'd walk you over here myself, but Thaddeus offered to step in."

"I must confess to feeling comforted by his presence." She smiled up at him. "But yours would certainly be welcome."

The doorknob rattled, and they sprang apart. She scooted behind her desk as the first patient of the day entered. She recognized Mrs. Fielder, the cook at West & Riley's. Elijah had pointed her out on the day in April when she'd stopped in the restaurant seeking Jacob.

The woman wore an unadorned gray dress, with a straw bonnet tied under her double chin. She held her left arm close to her ample waist.

"Mrs. Fielder. How may I help you?" Elijah crossed the room, stopping a few feet in front of her.

"Burned myself right bad with bacon fat. Hurts something fierce." She held out her hand, palm up.

Rosemary could see the extent of the burn from where she sat. Blisters covered the woman's fingertips. Her crimson palm telegraphed pain.

Elijah turned to her. "Would you please assist me, Miss Saxon?"

She rose and opened the door of the examining room. "Mrs. Fielder, I'll wait in here with you while Dr. Stewart looks at your injury."

"You're the one folks are talking about, aren't you?"

Rosemary's smile died. "Yes." She jutted her chin in the air. "If you'd prefer me to keep my distance, please say so."

"Just curious, is all. I don't believe a speck of what I overheard. Mr. Bingham was getting up in years. No surprise to me that he passed." She tipped her head in Elijah's direction, pinning him with a stern glare. "Don't take too long. I got a dinner to cook."

A smile tugged at his lips. "Yes, ma'am." Once inside, he studied the wounds left by the hot grease. He touched each blister with his fingertip, then sighed. "You'd better get one of your daughters to take over for the next few days."

"Can't do that. I need the money I get from Mr. West. My daughters have husbands. I don't."

He shook his head. "If you break open the skin, you could get an infection. I'll give you a beeswax balm for the pain, but you mustn't use that hand."

The woman sniffled. "That all you can do?"

Rosemary cleared her throat and mouthed "comfrey" at Elijah.

"Miss Saxon here can make a comfrey poultice for you. It may help you heal faster." He turned to Rosemary, smiling. "Would you mind taking the time to do that now? You could deliver the poultice to the restaurant when you're finished."

Hope spread over the woman's face as she looked at Rosemary. "You'd do that for me? I'd be purely grateful."

"I'll be glad to. The process takes about an hour."

"That'll give me time to go get one of my daughters to help me and be back at work in time to get the chops a-fryin'." She shot a defiant glance at Elijah. "I can still use my right hand."

Rosemary retrieved Bodie's leash from a peg near the door, bending in front of her desk to fasten the leather strap to his collar. He licked her nose while she fumbled with the buckle. Holding the leash in one hand, she joined Mrs. Fielder. The woman chattered all the way to the corner of King's Highway, then headed west, and Rosemary turned toward home.

Comfrey grew in one corner of her front yard. By now the plant should be mature enough so that she wouldn't need to use dried roots. As soon as she changed her dress, she'd harvest a basketful of the broad, hairy leaves.

She smiled with pleasure at the prospect of spending a bit of time in her garden on such a glorious morning. Imagine. Elijah had recommended comfrey to a patient—again.

Bodie wandered around the kitchen, his toenails clicking on the wooden floor, while Rosemary waited for the stove to heat. Humming to herself, she dumped crushed comfrey leaves into a pan and added a few spoons of water. Once the mixture came to a boil, she'd spread a portion on a clean rag and take the poultice to Mrs. Fielder.

When Bodie whined to go out, she hurried to the back entrance with light steps. "Good boy." She rubbed the fur at the scruff of his neck, then opened the door. He bolted down the steps as soon as he was free.

The pan on the stove made bubbling sounds as the green paste came to a boil, and she turned to stir her project. The wet leaves smelled like the rotting compost heap behind her greenhouse. Wrinkling her nose, she pulled the pot off the stove. Clean pieces of cloth waited on her worktable. She swung around and placed the mixture on a trivet, then scooped a spoonful onto one of the strips of muslin.

A piercing howl, followed by cries of an animal in distress, broke into the silent kitchen. *Bodie*. Rosemary dropped the spoon and raced for the door.

She tore down the back steps, her gaze sweeping across the yard for a sign of her dog. His cries had stopped.

"Bodie!"

Movement inside the greenhouse caught her attention.

Questions spun through her mind as she raced toward the building. Had he stepped on an overlooked piece of broken glass? But how would he get through a closed door? Her second question was answered when she saw the door standing ajar. Bodie—she was sure it was Bodie—whimpered from inside.

She flung the door wide open, then stopped dead. A shadowy form crouched against the rear wall with his back to her. He held Bodie with one arm around the dog's neck. When the dog struggled, the man tightened his hold.

She glanced toward the house next door. On Sunday, her neighbors had left for Hartfield to visit their grandchildren. No one would hear if she screamed for help.

With a swift motion, Rosemary grabbed the mattock from the wall and held it like a club as she stepped around a potting table. One more table stood between her and the intruder.

"Release my dog. Now. Or I'll bring this down on your skull." She kept her voice low and steady.

He turned his head slightly, his face obscured under the floppy brim of a grimy hat. "You ain't got the gumption." His voice rasped as if he were the one with an arm around his neck. "Git away from me and I'll let the mutt go."

"I'm not moving. You're trapped in here. Sheriff Cooper will be passing by any moment."

"Ha. You're lying."

She moved a step toward the next table. Her heartbeat threatened to choke her. "You're the one. You wrote those messages and damaged my property."

"So? What'll you do? Cast a spell on me?" He cackled.

Bodie's breath wheezed as he fought the man's grip.

She took another step between the two tables. "Let him go. You can leave. I won't stop you." She gripped the handle of the mattock.

In one blurred motion, he dropped Bodie and shoved the potting table over against her side. Plants crashed to the floor and she fell with them, dropping the mattock as she went down. She felt a blinding pain in her midsection, then nothing.

The side of Rosemary's face felt wet. Bleeding. She was bleeding. Fighting for breath, she touched her cheek and then brought her hand in front of her eyes. Her fingers were clean.

She heard whining next to her ear. A warm tongue lapped her face.

"Bodie. Praise God." Her voice emerged in a croak. She rolled onto her back, gasping at the pain when she attempted to sit. Falling back on the earthen floor, she drew shallow breaths as she turned her head to each side to survey the surrounding damage.

The potting table that had knocked her to the ground lay to her left. Broken pots rested beside her body. When she ran her hands down her skirt, dirt grated against her palms. Her midriff throbbed.

Bodie poked his nose under her arm and licked her chin. Rosemary made another effort to sit, this time succeeding. The mattock she'd used to threaten the intruder pressed against her hip. She pushed the makeshift weapon to one side, then gingerly prodded her ribs. *Please, Lord, let nothing be broken.*

When her thoughts cleared, she remembered she'd been preparing a poultice for Mrs. Fielder when she heard her dog's distress cries. How much time had passed? A few minutes? An hour? A glance out of one of the windows showed the sun high overhead.

Reaching up, she grasped the edge of the remaining upright table and dragged herself to her feet, then doubled over, clutching her middle. Bodie pressed himself against her skirt like a burr when she stumbled into the house.

The comfrey poultice lay on the table where she'd left it. The edges had dried to a cracked green paste. After collapsing onto a chair, Rosemary reached down and ran her hands over the dog's body, feeling for wounds. She patted his head with relief upon finding nothing amiss.

"Go drink some water. Then we'll decide what to do next," she said in a whispery voice.

Bodie wagged his tail and ran to his water dish.

In spite of her discomfort, she chuckled to herself at her one-way conversation with the dog. If anyone overheard her, they'd think she'd injured her head instead of her ribs.

Without leaving the chair, she folded the poultice into a rectangle, covering the dry edges with a fresh strip of muslin. If she refreshed the surface with water, the comfrey would still be effective. Then all she'd have to do would be to somehow get herself back to the office to tell Elijah what happened. He could deliver the poultice.

She took a shallow breath and pushed herself to her feet. She must have moaned, because Bodie stopping drinking and ran to her.

"I'm fine. Just getting the kettle and a plate."

With one hand clutching her middle, she placed the poultice in a pie pan and dribbled warm water over the muslin covering. As she turned to replace the kettle on the stove,

Bodie's fur rose. Growling, he stalked to the front of the house, reaching the entrance just as someone pounded on the door frame.

"Rosemary!"

When she heard Elijah's shout, she tried to call out, but couldn't draw enough breath to produce more than a squeak. He hammered at the door again, harder this time. "Are you there?" His voice carried an edge of panic.

She crossed the sitting room as quickly as she could.

Once she'd unfastened the lock, he barreled inside and wrapped his arms around her. "What happened? You've been away for more than two hours."

She pulled back from his embrace, wincing at the pain. "Someone . . . was in the greenhouse. I fell."

His eyes widened as he surveyed her. From his shocked expression, she knew she must look worse overall than merely the stains she could see on her skirt. He reached into the breast pocket of his jacket and withdrew a handkerchief. With tender strokes, he brushed the folded linen over her cheeks, then showed her grains of dirt clinging to the white surface.

"You fell inside the greenhouse?"

"Yes." She failed in an attempt to straighten her shoulders.

Elijah slipped one arm around her waist to support her while he guided her to the settee. Once she was seated, he drew a chair close and stroked her forehead. His brow creased.

"Where are you hurt?"

"Here." She placed her hand above her abdomen. "I can't draw a full breath."

He leaned close in order to hear her. She yearned to reach up and cup her hand over the back of his head. Instead, she gripped her fingers together in her lap.

"I should examine your ribs."

Her cheeks heated. "We're alone here. It wouldn't be proper."

"You're a nurse. You know the complications that can arise from a broken rib." He stood and paced. "If I fetch your sister-in-law, will you allow an examination?"

"We may have to wait until she closes the store."

He dropped back on the chair. "So be it."

"Will you take Mrs. Fielder's poultice too? It's on the kitchen table."

"Yes, nurse." He shook his head in mock despair. "Now, tell me everything you saw. Then I'll go to the mercantile—and the restaurant."

Halting between phrases, she told him about hearing Bodie yelp, then whine, and discovering her dog strangling under an intruder's grip. She concluded by saying, "When the man pushed the table over, I think I fell on the mattock."

Elijah shook his head. "You went after him armed with nothing but a garden tool? How could you be so reckless? He might easily have overpowered you."

"He was choking Bodie. I had to stop him. I'd do the same thing again."

"My fierce little Rosemary. I don't know what I'd do if I lost you."

"You won't lose me."

Within minutes after the clock chimed five, Faith bustled through Rosemary's front door and hurried into the sitting room.

Elijah stood when she entered. "Mrs. Saxon. Thank you for coming."

She smiled at him. "I'd have been here sooner, but I didn't have anyone to watch the store. The woodstove regulars went home early today." She plunked herself on the settee next to Rosemary. "Dr. Stewart's worried about you, and so am I. Let me help you into your shift so he can check your ribs. Can you climb the stairs to your room?"

"Mercy sakes, yes. After resting all afternoon, I feel better now."

Elijah cleared his throat. "I want to be sure. Call me when you're ready."

Faith took Rosemary's arm and headed for the staircase. "We won't be long."

Bodie scooted out from under the settee and raced ahead of them into the bedroom. Rosemary chuckled.

"He must think I'm going to sleep."

"You winced when you said that." Faith studied Rosemary's face when they reached the top of the stairs. "Dr. Stewart's afraid you may have a broken rib."

"I hope not." She pressed her hand over her midriff. Her face grew warm at the thought of Elijah touching her in such an intimate spot. Once they closed the bedroom door behind them, she met Faith's gaze. "I'm mortified beyond belief at having him examine me." She kept her voice low so he couldn't overhear. "I loosened my stays after he left to fetch you, and I'm sure nothing's broken."

"He won't rest until he knows for certain you're all right. You should have seen him when he came to the mercantile. The poor man was distraught."

Rosemary blew out a shallow breath. "Then let's get this over with." She unfastened the buttons on her bodice and, with Faith's help, slipped out of her rust-colored calico dress. Once she'd donned a fresh shift, she perched on the edge of the bed.

Bodie curled up at her feet, watching her with bright eyes. She leaned forward to smooth his fur, but bent only partway before pain at her waist sent her upright.

Faith raised an "I told you so" eyebrow, and opened the door. "Dr. Stewart, you may come upstairs now."

Within moments, he stood in the doorway clutching his medical bag. "You'll need to stretch out so I can feel your ribs." His face looked as red as Rosemary's felt.

She nodded and allowed Faith to swing her legs onto the quilt as she lay back. As soon as Elijah approached, she turned her head away and closed her eyes. His warm hands burned through her shift as he probed her ribs. For a moment, she let her thoughts drift into forbidden territory, then bit the inside of her lip to banish them. She hoped he wouldn't decide to take her pulse—he'd know how his touch affected her.

The warmth on her skin cooled as he stepped away from the bed. "Nothing's broken."

Her eyes flew open. She turned her head in his direction and said, "That's what I thought."

"But you bruised your diaphragm. You flinched when I pressed the area. You'll need a day or two of rest." Color rose in his face. "No tight . . . undergarments until you've recovered."

He backed toward the door. At that moment, Bodie sprang to his feet and raced past him down the stairs, barking.

"I hope that's Thaddeus." Elijah pivoted toward the hall.

Rosemary covered her chest with her arms. "The sheriff?"

"I asked him to come after I spoke to Mrs. Saxon." He followed Bodie down the stairs.

Rosemary struggled to sit, her curls tumbling over her shoulders. "Faith, would you please close the door? I need to get dressed."

Faith obeyed, then helped her into a sitting position on the edge of the bed. "We'll slip your dress back on and arrange your hair. The pins have come loose."

She lifted her hand and felt the back of her head. "There's

dirt in my hair. My word, I must look dreadful." She felt herself flushing again. "I wish Elijah hadn't seen me like this."

"He's too concerned about you to notice how you look." Faith held up the calico dress. "Put this on, then if you'll sit in the chair, I'll brush your hair and braid it."

Rosemary buttoned her garment and moved to the slipper chair next to the window. She heard male voices below, and surmised Elijah and the sheriff were deciding what to do next. "Hurry, please. I don't want them making plans without asking me first."

"Thaddeus came to talk to you. I'm sure they'll wait as long as necessary." Faith took a comb from the top of a chest of drawers and removed tangles from Rosemary's hair, then brushed the curls smooth. With swift motions, she lifted three sections of hair and plaited them, then wound the braids together and pinned them in place. "Now you're presentable. Let's go see what he has to say."

Elijah and the sheriff stopped talking the moment Rosemary and Faith entered the sitting room. Rosemary eyed the two of them. From the guilty looks on their faces, she'd been the topic of their discussion.

She crossed to the settee and lowered herself to the upholstered seat. "Sheriff Cooper. I understand Dr. Stewart told you what happened this morning."

"Yup." He slapped his hat against his leg. "I reckon you surprised the feller. He wouldn't have figured on you coming home when you did. Good thing you wasn't hurt worse."

"I'm sure he's the same person who's been harassing me all along. I don't believe he intended to injure me."

The sheriff set his jaw in a rigid line. "With respect, miss, what you believe don't count for much right now. Fact is, you're injured. He trespassed, attacked your dog, and pitched a table at you. Each one's agin the law." He glanced at Elijah. "Want to show me this greenhouse?"

Rosemary placed her hands on the upholstered seat and pushed herself to her feet. "It's my greenhouse. I'll take you there."

"You should rest. There's no reason I can't show him where to look."

"There's one good reason. You weren't there when I surprised him." Rosemary leaned against one arm of the settee and summoned her most determined voice.

"Then let me help you." Elijah cupped his hand around her waist, raising a flush in her cheeks. Without her stays, she felt the pressure of each of his fingers through the fabric of her dress.

"Don't matter to me who comes, so long as we git a move on. Going to be dusk soon." Sheriff Cooper inclined his head toward Rosemary. "Front door or back?"

"The back is quicker." With Elijah's hand firmly against her side, she led the way through the sitting room and kitchen.

When she opened the rear door, Bodie shot past her. He scampered down the steps and raced for the greenhouse. Rosemary's skin prickled. Had the intruder returned? She craned her neck to peer through the windows as Bodie charged through the building's entrance.

The sheriff chuckled. "I reckon he knows where we're going, eh?" His long legs carried him along the path ahead of her.

With Elijah supporting her, she followed as quickly as she could, ignoring the pain that stabbed each time she drew a breath.

Sheriff Cooper stopped inside the door. When Rosemary caught up with him, he was studying the destruction left by the intruder's hasty flight. "Anything missing?" He poked at a shard of broken terra-cotta with the toe of his boot.

Her gaze traveled to her garden implements, then across the shelves along the walls. "Everything's here. Except for what got broken when he knocked the table over, I don't see further damage."

Bodie sniffed along the rear of the building, then pounced. Tail wagging, he brought a limp brown object to Rosemary and dropped it at her feet. She took an involuntary step away. At first glance, his offering resembled a dead rodent.

34

Elijah crouched beside Rosemary and retrieved Bodie's find from the earthen floor. "A hat." He turned the crushed felt object over and looked inside. "No name."

"That would be too easy." The sheriff snorted, then took the hat from Elijah's fingers. "Nothing special about this one. Half the men around here wear 'em."

Elijah heard Rosemary sigh as she leaned against a wall shelf. When he turned, her face had paled and she held her hand against her midriff.

He jumped to his feet. "This has been a shock. There's no need for you to remain out here. I'll help you back inside."

"But I—" Her hazel eyes appeared huge against her white skin. She swayed.

He caught her before she fell and scooped her into his arms. "Sheriff Cooper doesn't need your help—or mine, for that matter."

"Doc's right. You get some rest. Let me figure this out."

"I don't have much choice, do I?" She gave Elijah a weak smile and leaned her head against his chest.

His love for her threatened to overpower him. The moment

she recovered, he'd reopen the conversation about marriage. He felt certain he already knew her answer, but he wanted to hear it from her lips.

Faith dashed toward them when Elijah entered the kitchen. "What happened?"

He gave her a wry smile. "My patient overestimated her stamina." He strode to the next room and helped Rosemary recline on the settee, then bent and kissed her forehead. "I'm going to fetch my buggy and take Mrs. Saxon home. You and Bodie are going with her."

"No. I'm fine. Really."

Faith folded her arms and looked down at her. "You're not fine. I promise not to keep you a prisoner. As soon as your bruises heal, you're welcome to leave."

"Just for the weekend, then." Rosemary's eyes brightened. "While I'm there, Amy and I can decide on the flowers for her wedding."

Elijah's heart bumped when she said "wedding." He knew Thaddeus and the widow Dunsmuir planned to marry in July. Perhaps there'd be time to plan a double ceremony.

On Sunday morning, Elijah stopped his buggy in front of Judge Lindberg's house. After church, he'd promised to take Rosemary and her dog back home. He smiled to himself. As much as she'd chafed at staying with her family, he knew she benefited from the enforced rest. Once they were married, he'd insist on hiring a housekeeper. Not a cook, though. He enjoyed her unique recipes too much.

Rosemary's sister-in-law answered the door at his knock.

"Mrs. Saxon." He swept his hat from his head. "I'm here to escort Miss Rosemary to church."

She rested her hand on his arm. "Please. Call me Faith. I

have a feeling we're going to be seeing a great deal of each other in days to come." A mischievous sparkle lit her eyes.

"Faith it is." His hopes lifted higher. Rosemary must have shared her feelings for him.

Glancing over Faith's shoulder, he watched as Rosemary crossed the entryway, her steps light. She carried a shawl and wore the green dress he liked. He used all of his self-discipline to prevent himself from taking her in his arms. Instead he said, "You look fully recovered."

"Almost." She touched her hand to her waist. "I can breathe without pain." She tucked the hand under his elbow, then paused beside Faith. "I'll come for Bodie after church."

"He'll be fine in the back room until then. Don't worry." Faith hugged Rosemary. "We'll see you in a few minutes. Curt's hitching up the horse right now."

Elijah replaced his hat and cupped his hand around Rosemary's elbow while they walked to his buggy. He knew he was smiling too much but couldn't help it. He'd never seen a prettier Sunday morning. Or a prettier girl than Rosemary.

He leaned over and spoke in her ear. "How does a picnic at the lake this afternoon sound?"

"Lovely. But I don't have anything prepared."

"My turn this time. Mrs. Fielder promised to pack sandwiches and a dessert for us. After church, I'll pick up our food from the restaurant."

Elijah paused at the kitchen entrance to West & Riley's and peered through the screen. Mrs. Fielder had her back to him and was using a long fork to poke at something on the stove. The smoky aroma of boiled ham hovered in the air.

She turned in his direction when he entered. "Afternoon,

Doctor. Got your order right over here." She favored him with a teasing smile. "We fixed everything mighty special."

"Thank you. I'm sure you did." He wondered at the "we" and decided she meant herself and one of her daughters.

Leaving the fork resting on a plate beside the stove, she crossed to a worktable in the center of the kitchen and handed him a round woven basket.

He lifted a napkin covering the contents. A plate of sandwiches, a wide-mouth container of pickles, and a jar filled with sugar cookies met his gaze. "You've outdone yourself. What a feast."

Mrs. Fielder's cheeks pinked. "Your young lady should be pleased."

"I told her to make chicken sandwiches. I know Miss Rosemary favors them."

Startled, Elijah turned when he heard Jacob West's voice. The restaurant's owner stood in the doorway between the kitchen and the public area.

Jacob never spent time at the restaurant on Sundays. Masking his irritation at the man's proprietary tone, Elijah stepped toward him. "I didn't realize Mrs. Fielder had involved you in our plans."

"Why wouldn't she? You paid for the food. When she told me who it was for, I wanted to be sure she included Miss Rosemary's favorites." His lips curved with the suggestion of a smile. "Be sure to give her my regards."

Elijah drew a deep breath and released it slowly. He wouldn't ask how Jacob knew what Rosemary liked. In fact, judging from the flare of jealousy heating his veins, he knew the sooner he left the kitchen, the better. He grabbed the basket and strode to the door. "I'll pass your message along."

Someday. If he remembered. But not today.

Rosemary scooted close to Elijah on the buggy seat, her heart fluttering at his nearness. The idea of his planning a picnic for the two of them filled her with pleasure. He'd asked her to wait to give him her answer to his proposal, and she'd waited long enough. This afternoon would be the perfect time.

They passed Courthouse Square and turned west toward the edge of town, traveling past Ripley's Livery and a scattering of homes, including Judge Lindberg's. Once beyond the last house, the road narrowed. Chokecherries growing beside a stream displayed fruit, green now, but ripe with promise. Ferns and moss filled spaces between rocks at the water's edge.

She slipped her hand under Elijah's elbow. "I'm so glad you suggested visiting the lake today. It's a perfect afternoon."

He squeezed her hand against his side. "Indeed it is."

When the buggy rounded a corner, Pioneer Lake lay ahead on their left, gleaming with reflected blue from a clear sky. Elijah turned off the narrow road and followed a worn track partway around the lake, stopping beneath an umbrella-like weeping willow. After removing his jacket, he jumped to the ground and tied the horse to the trunk, then placed his hands on Rosemary's waist and helped her from the buggy. The tree's drooping branches formed a green curtain around them.

Rosemary drew in a breath. "It's beautiful here."

"I drove out yesterday to find just the right spot. I'm glad you're pleased." He turned her to face him and took her hands in his. The dappled light through the leaves washed him with splashes of gold. His expression softened when he looked at her.

"Ever since Friday . . ." He cleared his throat and began

again. "I hope you've had time to consider my proposal. I don't think I can wait any longer for your answer."

Happiness left her dizzy. She gripped his hands, feeling a flush spread over her cheeks. "I could have told you yes a week ago. I'd be honored to be your wife."

"My wife. I like the sound of that." He slipped his hands from hers and cupped her face between his palms. Bending his head, he placed a tender kiss on her lips.

Rosemary returned the kiss, her pulse pounding in her throat. Her mind spun. "Elijah . . ." She slid her arms around him and leaned against his chest. His shirt smelled like soap and clean linen, and something else. Elijah's own special scent.

He rested his chin on the top of her head. "I have one more thing to ask."

"What would that be?" She stepped away, gazing up into his eyes.

"Would you consider a double wedding with Thaddeus and Miss Amy?"

The thought of the sheriff's upcoming wedding sent a shock jolting through her. She pressed her fingers against her cheek. "Oh, no. When they marry, Curt and Faith are hoping I'll take Amy's place caring for Judge Lindberg. They want me to move in with them."

She paced toward the buggy. "No one said a thing when I stayed there this weekend, but I know they haven't found anyone else." She whirled. "What can we do?"

He joined her, shaking his head. "There's nothing we can do."

"What are you saying?" Her light heart turned to stone. She grabbed the side of the buggy for support.

He burst into laughter and kissed her forehead. "Thaddeus told me that Miss Amy has no plans to stop caring for the judge."

"Why didn't you tell me sooner?"

"I thought you knew. She'll spend her days with him, and return to Thaddeus's home in the evenings. That arrangement will work well for all concerned—including us." He dropped another kiss on the top of her head. "Now, what do you say to a double wedding?"

"I say yes."

At the edge of the water, a great blue heron squawked and rose into the air.

On Monday, Rosemary sat at her desk staring into space, ignoring the open ledger in front of her. Bodie snuffling on his blanket was the only sound in the room. Elijah had left early that morning for a house call north of town, leaving her free to daydream.

Three weeks until her wedding. Could she be ready? She'd go to the mercantile after work to share her news with Faith and select a dress pattern and fabric. She felt certain Amy would help her sew a gown. She sighed and leaned back in her chair. Imagine. A wedding gown. For her. She closed her eyes and smiled.

The door opened, jarring her back to the present. A blonde woman near Rosemary's age stood in the entrance. She wore a sweeping café au lait suit with a matching fringed shawl, topped by a narrow-brimmed hat sporting an ostrich plume. From the regal tilt of her chin to her narrow-toed boots, her appearance shouted wealth.

The woman's gaze swept the narrow reception room with barely concealed surprise.

"Is this Dr. Stewart's office?" To Rosemary's ears, accustomed to soft Missouri speech, the voice carried a flat Midwestern tang.

She clenched her fists in her lap. Another woman coming to see Elijah based on his father's reputation. Of all the days for him to be away.

"Dr. Stewart is out on a house call today. He may return by late afternoon. If you wish, I'll take your name and tell him your complaint."

Her gloved hand at her throat, the visitor chuckled. "I have no complaint—unless you count inattention. Please tell Elijah that Miss Adele Mason has come to see the town he prefers to Chicago. He will find me in the only suite provided by that dreadful hotel near the railroad tracks."

Apparently noticing Rosemary's stunned expression, Miss Mason continued. "I'm his fiancée, miss. Surely he's mentioned my name." She removed the glove on her left hand and spread her fingers to display a pearl ring on her fourth finger.

Rosemary felt the blood drain from her face. She gripped the edge of her desk for support as she rose.

"I don't believe you. *I'm* Elijah's fiancée. He would never deceive me."

"Then you don't know him very well, do you?" She tugged the ring from her finger and handed the gold circlet to Rosemary. "Look at the inscription."

Rosemary tilted the band sideways and saw, "*Always, ES,*" engraved on the inside. Her head swam. How could Elijah pretend he loved her when he already had a fiancée?

Miss Mason smirked. "Do you believe me now? This ring has been in the Stewart family for generations." She took the ring from Rosemary. "Now it's mine, to seal our betrothal."

She slid the ring back on her finger and looked with disdain around the reception area. "He's gone a bit far this time to get me to come after him. But what is the saying? Love covers a multitude of sins, and I shall forgive him again." She turned back to Rosemary and gave her a look of affected pity. "I must warn you, he will probably deny all of this to drag it out. I'm so sorry you were his pawn."

Tearing her gaze away from the gleaming pearl, Rosemary took a breath to subdue the pain that radiated through her chest. Heartbreak was more than a figure of speech. The agony she felt was real. She tightened her grip on the desk.

"As soon as the doctor returns, I'll give him your message." Her voice wavered. She remained standing until Miss Mason closed the door behind her, then she collapsed onto her chair.

Bodie whined and rested his head on her knee. "It's not possible," she whispered. Her tears splashed over his smooth fur.

By midafternoon, the wound to Rosemary's spirit had deepened to anguish. Elijah must think her a complete fool. How long was he planning to wait before telling her about Miss Mason? Or was Miss Mason the one to receive an unpleasant surprise?

It didn't matter. Nothing mattered. As soon as he returned to the office she'd give him the young woman's message, then add a message of her own.

At the sound of footsteps on the boardwalk, Bodie ran to the door, tail wagging.

"How are you, boy?" Elijah rubbed the dog's ears and then turned to Rosemary with a wide smile. "I missed you today. Of all the days to be out in the country for hours."

"My thoughts exactly." She moved to within three feet of

him, then stopped. His face wavered through the sheen of her tears. She held out a slip of paper. "I promised to give you this."

Concern crossed his features. "What's wrong?"

"Read it."

His complexion turned chalky as his gaze flicked over the written lines. "Miss Mason . . . she's here?"

"A surprise, is it?"

"Rosemary." He reached for her, but she stepped away.

With deliberate motions, she untied her apron, smoothed the folds, and tucked it into her carryall. Bending over, she clipped Bodie's leash to his collar.

"I trusted you, I believed you. We made wedding plans." Her voice caught on a sob. "You're welcome to Miss Mason. I . . . I'm leaving." She sidestepped him and stumbled toward the entrance. "Good-bye, Dr. Stewart."

"Rosemary, I'm as shocked as—"

She closed the door on his words.

Before she'd taken five steps, she heard the door open. Elijah overtook her and stopped her progress by resting his hand on her upper arm. "In that note—you wrote she was my fiancée. She's no such thing. I barely know the woman. She was a guest of my father's while I visited him."

Her sense of betrayal threatened to smother her. "I don't believe you. She showed me the ring you gave her, with your inscription inside the band. '*Always, ES.*' She was more than your father's guest."

"I didn't—"

Rosemary dashed a tear from her cheek. "How long were you planning to lead me along before you packed up and left for Chicago?"

"Please, listen to me."

"Just leave me alone."

She pulled away from his grasp. With Bodie tugging at the end of the leash, she hastened along the boardwalk toward King's Highway. Two blocks and she'd reach the mercantile. Her eyes stung with fresh tears, but she willed them away.

When she turned the corner at the barbershop, a group of men standing out front gestured toward her and snickered among themselves. She ignored them. No amount of mockery could be more humiliating than what she'd already endured today.

The bell over the door of the mercantile jingled when she entered. Faith stood at the rear of the store, unpacking lanterns from a wooden crate. She straightened when she saw Rosemary.

"My word. What brings you here before five?" She brushed wood shavings from her apron and met Rosemary next to the checkerboard. "How was your picnic yesterday? Did you tell Elijah you'd marry him?"

Her tightly bound tears burst free. She dropped her carryall and buried her face in her hands. "He already has . . . a fiancée," she gasped between sobs. "She came to the office."

"No. There must be a mistake. Elijah loves you." Faith wrapped her arm around Rosemary's shoulders. "Sit down and tell me what happened."

Rosemary obeyed, waiting until she had her sobs under control before speaking. She described Miss Mason, her expensive clothing and perfect coiffure.

"There's no mistake. She showed me her ring. It's a Stewart family heirloom. Elijah's initials are inside the band." Her voice shook. "She's at the hotel, expecting him right now." She drew a shuddering breath and dabbed at her eyes with a handkerchief. "In a suite, no less."

Faith rose and dashed to the front entrance. She rolled the curtains down, placing a "CLOSED" sign in the window.

Then she returned to Rosemary's side. "What are you going to do?"

"Take the morning train to St. Louis. Between Elijah's fiancée and everything else that's happened, I can't bear to remain here." She drew the dog to her side, hugging him close. "Will you keep Bodie for me while I'm gone? As soon as I find employment, I'll come back for him."

Faith's mouth dropped open. "St. Louis? Where will you stay? Surely you won't go to your parents'."

"I wish that were possible, but we know it's not." Regret tinged her voice. "Some time ago I received a letter from my former nursing supervisor at the Barracks. She invited me to visit. I pray she can also direct me to a hospital where I could work."

"There must be other jobs right here."

"I thought about that while I waited for Elijah—Dr. Stewart—to return this afternoon. I just don't want to be in the same town with him and his *fiancée*." She choked on the word.

"You're being too hasty."

"Too hasty? How would you feel if a woman came to you and said she and Curt . . ."

Faith blanched. "I'd be heartbroken."

"That's exactly how I feel." Rosemary pressed her hand to her aching chest.

"Things are bound to look better in a few days."

"They'll look better because I'll be in St. Louis."

"I don't want you to go." Faith's voice cracked. "I'll miss you so much. Curt will be devastated. So will Amy and Grandpa."

Rosemary stood on wobbly legs. "I'll return in time for the wedding. Please tell Amy I won't forget her flowers." Fresh tears threatened to spill. "Oh, Faith, just yesterday Elijah and I talked about our wedding. Now today those plans are ashes."

"The Lord must have something better for you." Her gaze softened with compassion. "I know this is no comfort right now."

"On the contrary, he's the one thing in life that never changes. He is my comfort."

Rosemary's steps dragged when she left the mercantile. Wagons and riders on horseback moved in both directions along the wide street. An errant puff of wind blew grit into her already swollen eyes, blinding her for a moment. Head bowed, she plucked a handkerchief from her sleeve and dabbed beneath her lashes.

A horse stopped next to the boardwalk. When her vision cleared, she recognized Sheriff Cooper's frowning visage.

"Why aren't you at Elijah's office? You know what happened the last time you left in the middle of the day."

She shook her head, struggling to find words. The sheriff and Elijah were friends. Were they both keeping Miss Mason a secret from her? She clenched her hands into fists, her nails digging into her palms.

"I'm leaving for St. Louis tomorrow. My association with Dr. Stewart has ended." To her relief, she sounded normal.

Sheriff Cooper reared back in the saddle with exaggerated surprise. "Well, if that don't beat all. Just like that? Why, the other day Elijah—" He stopped and stared at her. "You don't mean you're leaving for good?"

She nodded, not trusting her voice.

"Amy's all excited about the flowers you promised for our wedding."

"I'll keep my promise. Whatever happens in St. Louis, I'll be back for the ceremony."

He guided his horse away from the boardwalk. "I'll see you home, long as you're headed that way."

"Thank you." She faced east and continued to plod toward her door.

His horse clopped along the street beside her. With a detached sense of satisfaction, she noticed that the men in front of the barbershop disappeared inside the moment they saw the sheriff.

He leaned over the saddle horn when she reached her gate. "I been studying on everything that's happened to you—the messages and such. I think I got it figured out. Reckoned I better tell you, in case that's why you're running away."

"I am not running away." She frowned at him, pushing down the thought that running away was exactly what she was doing. "Who do you think it is?"

"Can't say just yet. Won't be long, though."

She huffed out a breath. "The sooner the better, Sheriff. Once I leave, he may find someone else to harass."

"If'n that happens, it'll make my job easier." He lifted his hat. "Evening, Miss Rosemary." Turning west, he rode toward the jailhouse.

She paused on the path to her front porch and unfastened Bodie's leash. He galloped up the steps and flopped down on the mat next to her door. Before following him, she surveyed her flourishing garden. Golden yarrow blooms brushed against stems of a coral climbing rose sprawled over one side of her fence. Spikes of lavender shot high over spreading purple geraniums. She swallowed a stab of regret at the prospect of leaving her months of careful work behind.

She assured herself her garden would be fine in her absence. Once she found a place to live in St. Louis, she'd put everything in pots and take the plants with her. She bit her lip, knowing few of them would survive.

Rosemary dropped spoonfuls of her precious jasmine mixture into her teapot, and poured boiling water over the dried tea leaves. The fragrance of summer flowers wafted from the steam. After a few minutes, she poured the light blend into a cup and sank onto a chair.

Later in the evening, she'd pack a valise with enough clothing to last at least a week. If she wore her green paisley skirt and bodice, and included an additional bodice, she should be able to get by without a trunk full of clothing. She took a sip of tea. The events of the past two days had left her groping through thick clouds of uncertainty.

Take therefore no thought for the morrow. That's what she'd do. One step at a time.

Cradling her teacup in one hand, she left the kitchen and went to a letter box she kept on a shelf in the sitting room. Alice Broadbent's most recent missive rested near the top. Rosemary remembered writing to her former nursing supervisor when she first met Elijah. She'd wanted to share her pleasure at meeting one of the doctors both women had known during the war.

What a difference from then until now. She hadn't known him as well as she thought she did.

The letter she held in her hand was filled with news about the opening of a home for disabled soldiers. Alice had invited her to visit and tour the facility should she ever return to St. Louis. Thus far, Rosemary hadn't replied, and now there wasn't time. She prayed she'd be welcome when she appeared at the woman's door tomorrow evening.

Movement outside prickled her senses. Not again. She stepped to the window and peeked through the curtain.

Elijah strode toward her porch.

She dropped Alice's letter and opened the door a crack. "Please, leave me alone."

"Not until you listen to me." His jaw tight, he gave her his haughty doctor look.

"Go talk to your fiancée."

"She's not—"

"I saw the ring." She choked back a sob. "Now go."

36

The next morning, Rosemary sat between Curt and Faith as they traveled toward the station. She appreciated that he drove past Second Street before turning south, so they wouldn't pass Elijah's office.

Another new beginning. When she came to Noble Springs, she'd had Curt. In St. Louis, she'd have Alice, and maybe Cassie, depending on Mrs. Bingham's current standing at her brother-in-law's. Rosemary tried not to think too far ahead. *Take therefore no thought for the morrow.*

Curt stopped the buggy in front of the station and then helped her and Faith to the ground. A team and wagon, along with another horse, were tied to the hitching rail.

"We'll wait here while you buy your ticket. Looks like you have plenty of time. I can't see the smoke yet."

She adjusted her green paisley shawl over her shoulders. "I shouldn't be long." Chin held high, she marched inside the boxlike station. An unoccupied wooden bench sat against the wall opposite the ticket counter. Sunlight streaked through the windows, highlighting the dusty plank floor. Save for the railway clerk, the room was empty. The wagon outside must belong to a teamster who waited up the street in the hotel.

The hotel. Her breath caught. Was Miss Mason there right now? Or was she spending time with Elijah at his office? She sucked in air and held it until her lungs ached. The train couldn't leave soon enough. Once she was in St. Louis, she'd be away from both of them.

"You wanting a ticket?" The clerk peered at her over round-rimmed glasses. He pushed them up on his nose. "One-way or round-trip?"

"Round-trip, please."

The train rocked from side to side as it rolled eastward toward St. Louis. The iron wheels seemed to mock her decision. "Running away. Running away. Running away."

Rosemary covered her ears. She was making a necessary change. Not running away at all.

She shifted on the seat, glancing around the car at her fellow passengers. Across the aisle, a gray-haired woman plied knitting needles around strands of brown wool. While she worked, a stocking took shape under her fingers. Her busy hands reminded Rosemary of Cassie and her tatting.

She patted her handbag, feeling the crisp sheet of paper inside. She'd copied Cassie's address next to Alice's, planning to visit her friend at the first opportunity. If Cassie had never left Noble Springs, perhaps her companionship would have made remaining in town tolerable.

Rosemary blew out a weary breath. No matter how often she considered her situation, she reached the same conclusion. She needed to leave.

The woman across the aisle tucked her knitting into a tapestry bag. Holding one of the supports that rose between seat backs and storage space overhead, she stood and peered over her spectacles at Rosemary.

"Excuse me, miss. Do you have any idea when we'll arrive in St. Louis?" Rays of wrinkles framed her kind blue eyes. A net covered a coil of braids at the back of her head. Something about her expression reminded Rosemary of times when her mother would join her while she sat reading in the library of her childhood home. They'd sit together and discuss whatever book Rosemary held in her hand. She blinked to dislodge the memory and turned to her questioner.

"We should be there soon." She pointed out the window at sunbeams sketching charcoal shadows over the landscape. "Before dark, the stationmaster in Noble Springs said."

"I'm so glad." The woman's cheeks rounded when she smiled. "I'm going to visit my daughter. I miss her since she moved to the city."

"I expect she misses you too." She knew the words were true of herself. In her situation, many girls would run home to their mothers. But she could not.

The woman reached over and patted her shoulder. "Thank you, dear." She returned to her seat, leaving Rosemary alone to stare out at lengthening shadows.

Within another thirty minutes, the train chugged into the Pacific Railroad depot. The wooden building glowed persimmon orange in what remained of the daylight. On the cobblestone streets, carts and covered vehicles awaited freight or passengers.

Rosemary descended to the platform carrying her valise. The distance from the downtown depot to the address Alice had given her was close enough that she could walk, but a glance around at several men loitering near the station sent her in the direction of a parked cab.

"Take you to a lodging house, missy? There's a clean place for ladies not far from here." The driver removed his cap, revealing close-cropped black curls. His eyebrows bristled in an almost-straight line across his forehead.

"Thank you, but I'm going to visit a friend." She consulted the paper she'd brought. "Her home is at the corner of Twelfth and Jardine streets."

"Have you there in a trice." He took her valise and plopped it on the floor of the cab, then offered his hand. "Up you go."

The carriage rattled over the cobblestones, past lamplighters illuminating the city for the night. She leaned back and watched the streets roll by until they turned on Twelfth and traveled toward Jardine. Here, the houses were closer together and modest in stature, some in need of paint or fence repair.

The driver stopped the carriage in front of the address she'd given him. The building had apparently been divided into two dwellings, since there were two front doors a few feet apart. Lights glowed from the windows on the left side.

After tying the horse to a hitching post, he again offered his hand and helped her down, then put her valise at her feet. "Want me to wait?" He cocked his head.

She looked at the dark windows on the right, surveyed the neighborhood, then turned her gaze to the cabdriver's questioning face. "Perhaps you'd better." She hoped the cost wouldn't be too high.

After mounting the steps, she turned to her left and rapped on the door. In a moment, a man responded, buttoning a wrinkled shirt over baggy gray trousers. His sandy hair appeared rumpled, as if she'd awakened him from a nap. Could he be Alice's brother or father? She squinted through the gloom, unable to decide how old he might be.

"If you're selling something, I don't want it." He started to close the door.

She motioned for him to wait. "Is this Miss Broadbent's home? I'm a friend from out of town."

He pointed at the darkened half of the building. "She ain't Miss Broadbent no more. Got married last Saturday. Her and her man went on one of them wedding trips. To Niagara Falls, up in New York, if you can credit that." He shook his head. "Lived here quiet-like for a couple of years. Now all of a sudden she's a traveler."

The collar on Rosemary's bodice suddenly felt too tight. She should never have counted on Alice as the answer to her difficulties—at least not without contacting her first.

She arranged her face in a polite smile. "Thank you for the information. I apologize for bothering you."

"Pretty lady like you ain't no bother." He opened the door wider. "Care to rest yourself before you leave?"

"I have a cab waiting. Good evening." She backed toward the edge of the porch, thanking the Lord she'd asked the driver to linger.

The driver met her at the foot of the stairs. "Your friend's not home?"

"No. She's traveling." Fatigue threatened to buckle her knees. She'd get a night's sleep, then consider her next step. "Would you please take me to the lodging house you mentioned?"

"Right away."

She handed him her valise and followed him to the street. He walked with a rolling gait, favoring his right leg.

"You're hurt. Did you sprain an ankle?"

He tossed her bag inside the carriage. "No, missy. I was in the cavalry during the war. My horse fell on me down at Sikeston. Busted my ankle all to—" He bit back whatever he'd been about to say. ". . . pieces. Time the doc got to me, I was lucky they didn't cut off my foot."

"I'm so sorry."

"Could be worse. I made it back. Lots of 'em didn't."

During the trip to the lodging house, she wondered if Elijah had been one of the surgeons at Sikeston, then chastised herself for allowing him to enter her mind. Gas lamps threw circles of flickering yellow flame over the corners as they retraced their path to the depot and traveled on south. Soon after the driver crossed Chouteau Avenue, he stopped the cab in front of a two-story house. Light glowed from several of the windows.

"Miz Kenyon will see to your comfort, missy." He stepped down from the driver's seat to help her to the boardwalk. "I'll carry your bag."

She smoothed her skirt as she walked along the brick pathway behind him, praying there'd be a room she could rent. After a long day's travel, she didn't think she could face a second disappointment.

A sign next to the door read KENYON'S LODGING FOR LADIES. A woman who must have been Mrs. Kenyon opened the door at the driver's knock.

"Joseph. How good to see you." A wide smile softened her angular face.

"You too, ma'am." He placed Rosemary's valise in front of the threshold. "This lady's in need of lodging."

The woman swung the door wider. "Fortunately, I have space right now. Please come in." Sconces on the walls brightened a spotless white apron tied over Mrs. Kenyon's dark blue calico dress.

Rosemary paused before entering to hand the driver the fare. "Thank you for watching over me."

"Glad to help." He tipped his cap and limped back to the cab.

Once in the entry hall, she dropped her bag and blew out a heavy sigh.

"I'm Mrs. Kenyon, but you probably guessed that." The landlady held out her hand, and Rosemary clasped warm fingers.

"I'm Miss Saxon. Rosemary." She glanced around the entry, noticing a wide flight of stairs to her left. A worn rug covered the center of the polished wood floor.

"Well, come on upstairs, Rosemary, and I'll show you your room." She lifted a lighted candle from a nearby table. "Then if you're hungry, we'll see what's left from supper."

Tears threatened at the kindness in her tone. "Thank you." She tried to keep her voice from wobbling.

A hallway divided the second floor into halves, with three doors on each side. Mrs. Kenyon stopped at the first doorway on the right. "This will be your room." She took a ring of keys from her apron pocket and fitted one of them into the lock.

A narrow bed, covered with a white spread, stood against a wall opposite the entrance. The washstand held a pitcher and bowl. White-painted hooks halfway up another wall lined one side of the space, and an upholstered slipper chair filled a corner.

Mrs. Kenyon crossed to the window, drawing ruffled curtains closed against the darkness outside. "I charge a dollar and a quarter per night. That includes breakfast and supper, of course. I hope you'll be comfortable here."

Rosemary reached into her handbag, trying to hide her dismay at the cost of the room. Holding up her hand, Mrs. Kenyon said, "No need to pay me now. I can see you're exhausted. Tomorrow morning will be fine." She paused at the doorway. "Can I bring you a tray from the kitchen?"

At that moment, the thought of food was more than Rosemary could bear. She wanted to crawl into bed and pull the blankets over her head.

"No, thank you. I'm afraid I'm not hungry." This time she knew her voice wavered.

37

*A*fter Mrs. Kenyon closed the door behind her, Rosemary drew a shuddering breath and sank onto the chair. Her body ached from the jostling of a day's travel, and her head throbbed with the decisions that lay before her. She'd hoped to spend two weeks with Alice and return to Noble Springs with only four days remaining before the wedding. That way she'd lessen the likelihood of seeing Elijah with Miss Mason.

One thing was certain—she needed to find employment soon. She had scarcely enough funds for more than a few nights in the lodging house. In the morning she'd start her search. St. Louis was a growing city. There were bound to be nursing jobs available.

Sounds of footsteps and women's voices woke her the next day. For a moment, she wondered where she was, then her memory flooded with images of Elijah, the railroad car, and Alice's neighbor. The voices in the hall must belong to other lodgers.

Her stomach grumbled with hunger. She hurried to dress, slipping a clean bodice over her chemise before covering her crinolines with her paisley skirt. Once her braids were arranged in a coiled chignon, she descended the stairs, following the sound of clinking china to the dining room.

Mrs. Kenyon stopped in the act of stacking soiled plates. "Good morning. I was afraid you were going to miss breakfast. My other guests have already left for the day." She pointed to covered dishes on the sideboard. "There's ham and gravy left. Maybe a biscuit or two. Please help yourself." She swished through a door that Rosemary assumed led to the kitchen.

She filled her plate, her mouth watering at the sight of gravy puddling around a ham slice. A good meal would fortify her for the day's activities.

The landlady returned with two cups of tea, and sat across the table while Rosemary ate.

"What brings you to St. Louis, Miss Saxon? Do you have family here?"

She let the second question pass. "I want to find a position as a nurse—the sooner the better. I hoped you'd be able to give me the names of doctors you might know."

"A nurse?" Her eyebrows climbed toward her hairline. "I wouldn't have any idea of a doctor who'd hire you. Surely there's something else you could do that's not so outlandish."

Rosemary swallowed a bite of ham. She'd fought for respect in Noble Springs. Apparently she'd have to begin the process again in St. Louis. "I spent the war years at Jefferson Barracks Hospital. I'm well qualified for nursing duties."

"That may be, but the Barracks is back to being an Army post now. One of my guests married a soldier from there." Mrs. Kenyon planted her elbow on the table, resting her chin in her hand. "There's other hospitals here. City Hospital's not far away, but that's for poor folks. Then there's that new place out west on Arsenal Road. It's got a mouthful of a name." She stared at the ceiling and recited, "National Home for Disabled Volunteer Soldiers." She chuckled. "Lord have mercy. Couldn't they have called it something shorter?"

"I've heard of the facility. A friend of mine from the Barracks mentioned it in a recent letter. She sounded quite enthusiastic."

"Maybe you could find a job there since you're used to caring for soldiers."

"I appreciate the suggestion, but the western end of Arsenal Road is too far from town. I don't know how I'd get there." She buttered half a biscuit. "I'll go to City Hospital. How close are you to a horsecar line?"

Rosemary stood in front of an iron fence surrounding a three-story brick building that filled half a city block. Stone steps rose to an arched entryway at the center of a row of windows on the main floor. Buggies clattered past on cobbled streets. She pushed away a brief longing for the quiet of Noble Springs. In time, she'd adjust to living in St. Louis again.

She touched her hat brim to be sure it rested squarely above her coiled braids. Keeping her shoulders straight, she marched up the steps and into the next chapter in her life. The familiar hospital odor of lye soap mingled with human suffering greeted her when she entered the austere reception area. An open corridor stretched ahead of her through an arched opening.

A middle-aged clerk seated at a desk near the corridor rose when he saw her. "We don't allow visitors in the morning, miss. You'll need to return after one."

"I haven't come as a visitor. May I please speak with the resident physician?"

"You mean Dr. Harding?"

"Yes." She kept her chin up and her voice steady.

The clerk surveyed her, one eyebrow raised. "I'll see if he's available. May I give him your name and the nature of your visit?"

"Miss Rosemary Saxon. I'm seeking employment."

"Ah." His expression softened. "This is a big hospital. He can probably find work for you. Please wait a moment." He bustled down the corridor.

Rosemary remembered Mrs. Kenyon's words that this institution was a charity hospital. Apparently the charity extended to providing jobs for those in need. She took a step after the clerk, intending to correct his assumption, but he turned a corner and disappeared from sight.

Floorboards creaked overhead, and she heard occasional bursts of voices from behind closed doors along the corridor. A man pushing a cart left one room and entered another. As the minutes ticked by, her anxiety rose. What if the doctor was too busy to be bothered by another petitioner?

"Miss Saxon?" An elderly man wearing a tidy brown jacket and trousers stepped toward her. He bowed in her direction. "I'm Dr. Harding. You're in need of a job?"

"Yes. Specifically, I'm seeking a position as a nurse." She held her breath, waiting for his response.

Dr. Harding glanced between her and the clerk, who stood nearby pretending not to listen.

"Please follow me. We'll be more comfortable in my office." He strode ahead of her and passed through an open door around the first corner in the corridor. The small book-lined room contained a worktable with chairs on both sides, framed diplomas on the walls, and a parlor stove in one corner.

He drew one of the chairs away from the table and held it until she was seated. Resting his slight form against the table, he tipped his head to one side and studied her. "So you want to be a nurse?"

"I am a nurse, Dr. Harding. I spent most of the war years at Jefferson Barracks."

A smile crossed his face. "Then I expect you know your way around a hospital ward."

"I do." She felt a surge of hope.

"We always need nurses here, but I prefer to hire men. They have families to support, and as a rule, don't run off to get married and have children."

She tightened her jaw. "I have no plans in that direction." Unbidden, a lump rose in her throat.

He paced to the window and stood looking out, his veined hands clasped behind his back. Several moments ticked by. Rosemary looked down at her green paisley skirt, wondering whether she should have packed her rust-colored calico to wear when applying for a nursing position. Perhaps she appeared too frivolous.

The silence lengthened. Sure that he was trying to find a way to discourage her, she fidgeted in the chair. When she returned to Mrs. Kenyon's, she'd consult a city directory for the names of physicians and go from one to another until she found someone who was willing to hire her. Her shoulders drooped at the prospect.

Dr. Harding faced her.

She braced herself for his rejection.

"Miss Saxon, I'll consider hiring you on a trial basis. If you can handle the duties, I'll make your employment permanent. How soon can you begin?"

"In around ten days." At his astonished expression, she hurried on. "I . . . I didn't expect such a quick response. I need time to . . ." Her voice trailed off. She needed time to adjust to the idea of living away from Elijah and Noble Springs, but that was none of Dr. Harding's concern. She cleared her throat. "Currently I have a home elsewhere. I'm sure I can be settled in St. Louis within that amount of time."

He flipped through a notebook on the table and ran his finger down a page. "Very well. This is only a trial, mind you. I'll expect you on the eighth of July." He dipped a pen in an inkwell and wrote her name next to the date.

Finding employment was one of the reasons she'd come to the city. She left the hospital wondering why she felt bereft.

When a horsecar stopped at the corner in front of the hospital, Rosemary paid the fare and climbed aboard with no destination in mind. She'd ride while she planned everything she needed to do in the next two weeks. First of all, she needed a permanent place to live. She'd ask Mrs. Kenyon for suggestions when she returned to the lodging house.

Beyond that, she had to pack her belongings in Noble Springs, along with as much of her garden as she could transport. She stared out the window of the car, overwhelmed at the idea of uprooting her plants, along with her life.

A longing for Faith's companionship surged through her. If only she were at home, she could walk to the mercantile and pour out her worries. She shook her head. Leaving Noble Springs meant beginning a new life. Might as well start now. She fished Cassie's address out of her handbag.

Street names rolled by as the tram traveled north through St. Louis. When the driver stopped at a corner, she walked forward with the address clutched in her fingers.

"Excuse me. Does this car go to Pratt Avenue?" She showed him the paper.

"Yes, ma'am. Toward the end of the line. I'll stop."

He flicked the reins over the horse's back and the car jolted forward, its metal wheels rolling smoothly over iron rails set in the cobblestones.

Rosemary's heart thudded when they passed a sign pointing toward Roubillard Street. Her parents' home lay in that direction. So close. She closed her eyes and didn't open them again until the driver stopped the tram.

"This here's Pratt Avenue, ma'am," he called over his shoulder.

She stood on the sidewalk and watched as the horsecar continued north, then looked at the row of narrow three-story brick homes. Cassie's uncle lived on a street not unlike that of her parents'—similar houses distinguished primarily by pocket-sized lawns and individual shrubbery choices. Relieved that the first address she noticed was close to Cassie's, she tucked her handbag close to her side and hurried down the block.

A tired-looking blonde woman answered Rosemary's knock. Two children peered around her skirts. "You're the laundress they said was coming?" Her tone carried disbelief.

"No, I'm afraid not." Rosemary held out her gloved hand. "I'm Rosemary Saxon, a friend of Cassie's from Noble Springs."

"Rosemary!" Cassie ran through the entry hall to stand next to the woman. "You came to see me! Aunt Eloise, this is the friend I stayed with before Mr. Bingham passed."

"Pleased, I'm sure." Eloise didn't smile. She stepped to one side. "Come in. Show her to the parlor, Cassie. I'll try to keep the children busy so you girls can have a nice visit." She plodded toward a door at the back of the hallway, one hand on each child's shoulder.

Cassie tucked her arm under Rosemary's. "Parlor's right here in front." She slid a pocket door open and stepped into an overfurnished room that smelled of dust and disuse. Scarves and shawls covered the tables, which in turn were strewn with bric-a-brac. The sofa was buried in plump satin pillows. Cassie waved her hand at the clutter and giggled. "The children are never allowed in here. You can see why."

"How many children does she have?"

"Six. I told you we were crowded." She swept the pillows to one side and patted a place for Rosemary to sit. "I never dreamed you'd come to see me, though. What a blessing."

Cassie's face shone with the same joy Rosemary felt at seeing a familiar face. "It's a blessing to me too. These past few days have been . . . trying, to say the least."

"Tell me, please. We'll have to talk fast, before Mother learns of your visit. I know she'll stop her incessant letter writing and want to join us."

"Letter writing?"

"She's hoping to find her brother. They were separated during the war. She thinks he will give us a better home than we have now." Cassie leaned against the back of the sofa, shaking her head. "Never mind my troubles. What brought you to St. Louis, if not to see me?"

Rosemary drew a deep breath while she gathered her thoughts, and then gave her friend a brief version of Elijah's deception and her subsequent decision to leave Noble Springs.

Cassie's eyes grew wide while she listened. "How dreadful! But I must say, I find Miss Mason's claim hard to believe, knowing how Dr. Stewart feels about you. He wore his heart on his sleeve."

"You didn't see her. She came all the way to Noble Springs after him. She's wearing his ring! His initials are inside. A Stewart family heirloom, she said." Her voice trembled as a fresh wave of grief filled her throat.

"I still don't believe it. Did you let him explain?"

"Well, no." Rosemary's doubts about her own actions boiled to the surface. She tamped them down.

By taking the job at the hospital, she'd made a commitment to leave Noble Springs. She met her friend's gaze.

"He obviously spent time with her when he was in Chicago. You should have seen his face when he read her message. Besides, she knew where—"

The pocket door slid open. "Miss Saxon. How surprising to see you here." Mrs. Bingham glided into the room wearing a fawn-colored day dress. Her hennaed hair was drawn back in a severe coil.

She placed her hand on her daughter's shoulder. "Cassie's been lonely since we arrived. Your visit is providential."

Her motherly affection assailed Rosemary's heart. She forced a smile. "You're kind to say so."

"And will you be long in St. Louis?"

She shook her head. "I have matters to tend to at home."

Cassie rose. "Indeed you do." She leveled a meaningful gaze at Rosemary. "Shall we take a stroll before you return to your lodgings?"

"You girls go ahead. I prefer to avoid the sun." Mrs. Bingham nodded to Rosemary. "Have a pleasant journey." She slipped from the room, leaving the door ajar.

"Poor Mother. The sooner she can find her brother, the happier she'll be." Cassie retrieved a parasol from a stand in the hallway. "Come. There's a park nearby with a goldfish pond."

As they meandered toward the park, Cassie chattered about her life in St. Louis, then turned the subject back to Elijah. "You said Miss Mason knew where Dr. Stewart's office was located. That doesn't mean much. You can find anyone in Noble Springs by asking at the grocery or the post office."

Rosemary chuckled. "True."

"So don't you think you should give him a chance to explain?"

"He tried, but I couldn't listen. I just wanted to hide from the hurt." She drew a deep breath and held it for a moment. "I know very little about his life before he came to Noble Springs. He and Miss Mason could have been childhood sweethearts. I must have been a pleasant diversion."

38

lijah paced the floor of his office. Without Rosemary and Bodie, the room felt deserted. He stopped pacing and stared out the window at the gathering dusk. He'd done everything wrong.

His decision to call on Miss Mason at the hotel was a mistake. He'd planned to be polite but firm, and send her on her way back to Chicago. Instead, she'd played the coquette and delayed their meeting. While he was at the hotel waiting to see her yesterday, Rosemary left town. Pain gripped his gut. She didn't tell him she was leaving.

Why should she? She believed him to be engaged to another woman. Now she was gone, and Miss Mason still refused to see him. He clutched his stomach as another pain seized him.

Supper and bed. Tomorrow he'd go back to the hotel. One way or another, he'd settle things with Miss Mason if it took all day.

Crickets chirped and fireflies swam through the moist night air as he walked toward West & Riley's for a meal. When he crossed at the corner of King's Highway, he glanced at Rosemary's house, hoping to see lights in the windows. Shadowed panes of glass stared back at him.

Another block and he entered the restaurant. Jacob West waved him to an empty seat at one of the long tables.

"Pork roast tonight. Beans on the side. Cornbread." His tone verged on hostile.

"Anything. I haven't eaten all day."

"I'll send Mrs. Fielder out with your plate." He walked away, leaving Elijah to stare at the red checked tablecloth and wish there was another restaurant in Noble Springs.

He heard spurs clink behind him. Thaddeus flopped into an adjoining chair. "You look lonely."

"I am lonely. Since word got out about Miss Mason being here, folks have treated me like I carry typhoid. You sure you want to keep me company?"

Thaddeus clapped him on the back. "I know you too well. Whatever game that woman's playing, she ain't your intended. Why haven't you told her so?"

"She won't see me. I can't get past that desk clerk at the hotel."

"You got to quit being polite, Doc."

A headache lurked behind his temples. He groaned and closed his eyes.

At noon the next day, Elijah locked his office and strode three blocks to the Lafayette Hotel. He'd allowed Miss Mason ample time to awaken and begin her day—doing what, he couldn't imagine.

The clerk in the hotel lobby leaned over the desk and gave him a knowing smile. "Here to see Miss Mason again, are you?"

Elijah set his jaw and glared until the man's smirk faded. "Please tell her I'm waiting."

"Sure thing, Doc. Good luck this time." His boots made little sound on the carpeted stairs. In a few moments, he returned. "She asks that you call later this afternoon."

"I don't care what she asks." He leaned over the desk. "What's the room number?"

"I can't tell you—"

"Of course you can. If she were ill, wouldn't you let me know where she was?"

"But she ain't sick."

Elijah laid his hand on the clerk's shoulder. His height and bulk dwarfed the skinny man. "Why don't we pretend she is? What's the number?"

"Two oh six. End of the hall." Sweat popped out on his forehead. "Her ladies' maid is with her. She's the one I been talking to."

"Thank you." He took the stairs two at a time, then rapped on Miss Mason's door.

"I told you, she's not receiving callers." A freckled girl stepped into the hall. Her eyes bulged when she saw Elijah. "Who are you?"

Elijah caught a whiff of cloying perfume before the maid closed the door. "I'm Dr. Stewart, the man your mistress has been toying with ever since you arrived." He reached for the latch.

"You can't—"

"I can and I will." He shoved the door open and left her standing in the hallway.

The room looked as if a snowstorm of garments had blown through. Dresses, crinolines, and stockings were draped over chairs and hung from the bedposts. Miss Mason sat upright on a chaise lounge beneath one of the windows. "Dr. Stewart!" She swung her slippered feet to the floor, smoothed wrinkles from her skirt, then crossed the room with deliberate steps.

"I hope you've enjoyed my little surprise. I knew once I came here that you'd remember the lovely times we had in Chicago and be eager to return." She placed her hand on his arm. "I'm quite certain your father would be delighted if we . . . merged our resources, you might say."

Elijah pulled free of her grasp. "Did he send you?"

"Absolutely not. I make my own decisions."

He folded his arms and glared down at her. "Then I suggest you *decide* to go back to Chicago on the next train. And take off that ring. I don't know where you got it, but I'm not your fiancé."

"We went everywhere together when you visited your father. I know we're suited for one another." Her pale blue eyes gleamed. "Lowell thinks that having your name added to the practice would be sure to increase the number of patients."

"I'm not interested in what your brother thinks."

"But . . . what will I tell Lowell?"

"Tell him whatever you like. Good-bye, Miss Mason."

He stalked through the doorway, nearly colliding with the maid. A shoe whizzed by his head and bounced off the opposite wall.

"You're missing your chance for a better life," Miss Mason shrieked after him.

He spun on his heel and glared at her. "Thanks to you, I've already missed my chance." His boots thudded as he stamped down the stairs.

After a restless night filled with disturbing dreams, Rosemary sat on the edge of her bed in Mrs. Kenyon's house. Thursday already. She should be on the train returning to Noble Springs, but she'd awakened knowing she couldn't leave without seeing her parents.

Had her actions contributed to their rejection? Perhaps if she'd been willing to listen to their feelings, rather than being so self-righteous, they might have reached a compromise.

The image of Cassie's mother with her hand on her daughter's shoulder flooded her mind and brought an ache to her heart, already sore with longing for Elijah. She glanced out the window. Over neighboring rooftops, the sky flamed with red and orange streaks—the Lord's promise of a new day.

If ye forgive not men their trespasses, neither will your Father forgive your trespasses.

She jumped to her feet. The first horsecar of the morning would be along soon. If she hurried, she'd reach the stop in time. Anticipation prickled her forearms. Even a glimpse of her parents would be better than nothing.

Mrs. Kenyon stopped her at the foot of the stairs. "You're leaving without breakfast?"

"There are some people I want to see before I go home." She inched around the landlady.

"It's barely daylight. No one pays calls at this hour."

Rosemary blew out a breath. Of course. Mrs. Kenyon was right. Breakfast, then she'd wait until midmorning before going to Roubillard Street. She chafed at the delay but turned her steps toward the dining room.

The driver stopped the horsecar. "We're at Roubillard Street, ma'am."

"Thank you." Nerves fluttering, Rosemary stepped off the tram. Locust trees lined the street, casting their lacy shade over the walk.

Her parents' home was four blocks west of the corner. Grateful that the trees deflected the morning sun, she walked past brick row houses similar to Cassie's uncle's, but with more imposing facades. Like her parents' home, some had wrought iron porches and well-maintained flower gardens.

Her knees quivered as she drew closer to her goal. Maybe this was a bad idea. Perhaps she should write a letter first, then come on a day when she was expected. Three more doors and she'd be standing in front of their house. Two more. Her palms moistened.

She reached the paved walkway, took a deep breath, and mounted the steps to the porch. Gripping the brass knocker firmly in one hand, she rapped on the striker. In a moment, the door opened and a young woman gaped at her. Her hair was covered with a ruffled cap, and she wore a full-length apron.

"Yes, miss? Are ye lost?"

Mama has a servant? "I . . . I'm here to see Mrs. Saxon. Is she receiving callers today?"

"No one here by that name."

Rosemary spread her fingers against her chest. "She has to be! She's my mother."

"Who is it, Birdie?" A gray-haired woman leaning on a cane moved toward them.

"I don't know, ma'am."

A sense of unreality swept over her as she watched someone other than her mother crossing the hallway of her childhood home. She took a step closer to the entry. "I'm Miss Rosemary Saxon. This is my parents' house."

"My husband purchased this property from Mr. and Mrs. Saxon a year ago." The older woman's words were cloaked in sympathy. "How is it you didn't know?"

"I've been . . . away. Please, can you tell me where they went?"

"Yes, certainly. It's a curious thing." She turned to Birdie. "Would you bring tea into the sitting room?"

After the girl scuttled away, the woman opened the door wide. "I'm Mrs. Thorndyke. Please come in. I'll tell you what I know."

The sitting room looked as it did in Rosemary's memory. Settee under the front window, matching chairs beside a tea table in front of the fireplace, bookcases along one wall. The difference was the furnishings weren't her mother's. Her sense of unreality increased as she took a chair across from her hostess.

"This is very kind of you. I apologize for intruding on your morning." She leaned back to allow Birdie room to place a tray between them on the table.

Mrs. Thorndyke poured tea into eggshell-thin china cups. "I'm happy for the company. With my husband at the bank all day, things are too quiet here." She stirred a lump of sugar into her beverage, took a sip, and added another lump. "Now. Your parents. I don't know the how or the why, but I'm told they sold most everything they had and hired on as caretakers at the disabled soldiers' home."

Rosemary froze in the act of stirring her tea. The spoon dropped from her fingers and clinked on the saucer.

"You must be mistaken. My mother would never do such a thing."

"The agent who arranged the property transfer is the one who relayed the information. My husband has known him for years. He wouldn't pass on an unfounded rumor." She reached her age-spotted hand across the table to pat Rosemary's arm. "The war has changed people, dear. Some of us see things differently now."

Rosemary stared at the amber liquid in her cup. Once an idea planted itself in her mother's head, she never changed her mind. Never. Yet Mrs. Thorndyke seemed so sure.

After a few minutes of polite conversation, Rosemary

stood and replaced her cup on the tray. "Thank you for the tea and the information. If you'll excuse me, I must be on my way."

Now that she'd begun her quest, she had to learn the truth, no matter where the knowledge took her.

As soon as Rosemary boarded a south-bound horse-car, she walked through the coach and stopped next to the driver.

"Can you please tell me if there's a line that goes west to the soldiers' home on Arsenal Road?"

"City don't run cars out there, ma'am. Too far away." He lifted the reins. "Best take your seat. We needs to be goin'."

She held up her hand. "Wait, please. Is there another means you could suggest?" She heard the pleading in her voice.

"Well, there's a livery stable down on Beabeau. Road from there goes out to Arsenal. You might could hire a buggy."

The cost of renting a buggy gave her a moment's pause. "Do you happen to know what they charge?"

He pushed his cap back on his head and seemed to see her for the first time. "I believe it's a silver dollar, but you tell Mr. Rush that Winston sent you. See if'n he'll cut you a bargain."

"Thank you."

As soon as she reached her seat, he snapped the reins and the coach moved along the track. Rosemary squeezed her arms around her waist. If she spent a dollar on a horse and buggy, she'd have to leave for Noble Springs tomorrow, whether or not she found her parents. She'd already used half the day on the journey to Roubillard Street. If they were no longer living at the soldiers' home, perhaps someone there would know where they'd gone. *Please, Lord, let me find them—today.* She folded her hands in an attitude of prayer. *And please help me know what to say.*

True to his word, the driver stopped at Beabeau Street and pointed to a wooden building with a corral on one side. "There you be, ma'am. Good luck to ya."

She thanked him again and strode toward the stable. The closer she got to her destination, the more pungent the air. Because her brother had spent months working for the livery owner in Noble Springs, she was accustomed to the smells. Still, she hesitated when she reached the open doors. Few women hired buggies. What if Mr. Rush refused to rent one to her?

"Help ya, ma'am?" A lean man with a weathered face walked out of the shadows. His manure-crusted boots testified to his occupation.

"Are you Mr. Rush?"

He tipped his hat. "The same."

"Winston—he's a driver on a horsecar—sent me. I want to rent a buggy for the afternoon." She drew a steadying breath. "A little runabout would be perfect, if you have one." She tried to conceal her nervousness and appear confident at the same time.

"Winston sent you? Well, guess I could find something you can handle. You want to wait over there in the shade, I'll get a rig ready." He disappeared inside the stable.

Thirty minutes later, she traveled west on Arsenal Road in a black runabout, thankful that Mr. Rush had charged her half price since it was past noon. The bay mare he'd provided was almost as slow as her brother's horse, Moses.

The road ran straight through flat terrain dotted with small farms. A multistoried brick structure rose in the distance, a tall bell tower in front standing several stories higher than the rest of the building. The stable owner had told her she couldn't miss her destination. He was right.

A trickle of perspiration slid along her temple, more from anxiety than the midday heat. She flicked the reins to spur the horse to a trot. Within a few minutes she guided the runabout onto a curved drive that ended at a columned portico. Other horses and buggies were tied to rails on both sides of the entrance. Several men milled about the grounds, while others sat in the sun. No one paid any attention to her arrival.

After securing the reins, she pushed open the heavy door and found herself in a large room lined with tall, narrow windows. The space reminded her of the lobby at City Hospital, except the aroma floating in the air smelled like ginger cookies rather than medicine.

She jumped when a voice spoke behind her. "You here to visit a family member?" A young man wearing a blue Union uniform smiled at her.

This was the moment. She could either say yes and proceed with her plan, or flee. Rosemary gripped her hands together until the nails bit into the flesh.

"Yes, I am. Not a soldier, though. I was told Mr. and Mrs. Saxon are employed here."

His eyes brightened. "They surely are. Mr. Saxon's out in the vegetable garden, but I believe Mrs. Saxon is in their apartment. She generally takes a rest after she sees to our dinner." He took a step toward a hallway leading to the left. "Want me to take you to her?"

"Please." She hated the way her voice squeaked.

She followed him to the end of the hall, where he tapped on a door. "Miz Saxon. Someone to see you." He bowed toward Rosemary and strode away.

The door opened. The welcoming smile on her mother's face paled to a look of astonishment. "What . . . what are you doing here?"

"I might ask you the same question, Mama." She tried to smile. "Mrs. Thorndyke told me where you were. May I come in?"

"Please do." Her mother's voice trembled.

When she stepped inside, her mother rested her hand on Rosemary's shoulder. A butterfly touch. "I'm so happy to see you. I was afraid . . . I didn't know how . . ." Her eyes glittered with tears.

Rosemary fought to keep her own tears in check. Swallowing the lump in her throat, she took her mother's hands in her own. Now. She needed to speak before her courage fled. She drew a long breath.

"I came to apologize. I was harsh and self-righteous when you tried to explain how your brother's death affected you. To have me leave you as well must have been a double blow." She bowed her head and focused on their joined hands. "I miss you so much. Can you forgive me?"

After a moment of hesitation, her mother gathered Rosemary in her arms. "I'm the one who was wrong. No proper mother sends her children away. To say I'm sorry isn't nearly enough. It never will be."

Resting her head on her mother's shoulder, she inhaled the sweet powdery scent that she remembered from childhood. They held each other tight for a long moment. Then her mother stepped back and led Rosemary to the sofa.

"Tell me everything. Where do you and Curt live? Is he

teaching again?" She drew a handkerchief from her apron pocket and dabbed tears from her cheeks.

Rosemary shook her head. "First, tell me how you and Papa came to be here. Caring for Union soldiers, of all things."

"The Lord's forgiving power is a wonder. When we heard of this place being built, my first thought was of my brother—wishing he'd survived. Then one day the idea came to me that these men are no different than he was. They just wear a different-colored uniform." She leaned forward, enthusiasm shining from her face. "Your papa and I prayed over this decision and felt led to come here. The war is over, praise God. We're doing what we can to help those who have no families left."

She remembered her mother caring for neighbors who were ill, and her father sharing his harvest up and down their street. A flood of love for her parents filled her heart.

"I'm proud of you, Mama."

Her mother looked away. "I was proud of you too, when you served at the Barracks." Her voice was a whisper. "But I couldn't bring myself to say so."

Rosemary scooted closer until their shoulders touched. "It's all past now." She kissed her mother's soft cheek. "Let me tell you about Curt." She related her brother's experiences in Noble Springs, first as a stableman, now as the mathematics instructor at the academy. "He married my best friend, Faith Lindberg."

Mama sat bolt upright. "Curt is married?"

"Last October. We wrote to invite you and Papa." She raised her eyebrows. "You didn't receive the letter?"

"We left Roubillard Street in June. Your message never reached us. I would have welcomed a reason to visit." Fresh tears seeped from her eyes. "Your father has been urging me to make the trip ever since we sold our house, but I was too afraid of our reception. You and Curt must have believed we were the worst parents in the world, to ignore such happy news."

Rosemary cringed. That's exactly what she and her brother had thought.

"It's not too late." *For either one of us.*

osemary stepped down from the train in Noble Springs. Her elation at the reconciliation with her parents subsided as she gazed between the station and the building where Elijah had his office. So much had happened since Monday morning, when she'd gone to work anticipating their wedding.

And now, five days later, she had the prospect of a job and a temporary place to live in St. Louis—and Elijah had Miss Mason. Her heart twisted as she contemplated spending the next week avoiding them. *Lord, please help me through this.*

A man driving a farm wagon traveled past the station. In the back, a brown and white dog wagged his tail when he saw her.

Her spirits lifted a bit. At least she'd have Bodie with her when she left next time. They'd make a new start together, as they'd done when she came to Noble Springs. Seizing the handle of her valise, she avoided Elijah's office by walking up Court Street to King's Highway. Then she turned right toward home. After changing into fresh garments, she'd go straight to the mercantile.

Within the hour, she locked her front door and hurried through the late afternoon humidity toward the center of town. Faith stood at the window rolling the shades down when Rosemary arrived.

She stopped in midtask and ran out onto the boardwalk. "I didn't expect you for another week!" She grabbed Rosemary in a hug. "I hope you changed your mind about staying in St. Louis."

"Quite the contrary. I have a promise of employment."

"That's not what I wanted to hear." Faith's shoulders drooped. "I'll miss you terribly." She grasped Rosemary's hand and led her into the store. "Tell me what occurred there. You don't sound very happy."

"So much happened I don't know where to start. Some good, some not so good. Would you like the exciting news first?"

"I can't imagine that anything about you moving away would be exciting." Faith leaned against a counter, her arms folded across her middle.

"I talked to my parents. They're coming to see Curt and meet you as soon as they can." She grinned at the astonished expression on Faith's face. "I told you it was exciting news."

Shaking her head, Faith dropped onto one of the chairs next to the woodstove. "This is the last thing I expected. You said you wouldn't visit them."

"Once I was in St. Louis, I couldn't get Mama out of my mind." She recounted passing Roubillard Street on her trip to Cassie's, and waking up the next day compelled to try for reconciliation. "Now I know how Jonah felt when the Lord sent him to Nineveh. Going to see Mama was one of the hardest things I've ever done—and it turned out better than I could have imagined."

"How did you get them to promise to come for a visit?"

"That's the best part of all. Their lives are so different now."

After describing the soldiers' home and her mother's new attitude, Rosemary concluded, "Mama said she'd been afraid they wouldn't be welcome after the way she behaved toward us." She squeezed Faith's hand. "They didn't receive the letter we sent before your wedding, or I believe they would have come then."

"Curt will be overjoyed at this news." Faith's cheeks grew rosy. "Our child will have grandparents."

It was Rosemary's turn to be astonished. "Are you . . . ?"

"I think so." Her eyes shone.

Rosemary pulled Faith to her feet and wrapped her in a hug. "A new little Saxon. What a blessing." She tried to hide the pain in her voice.

She'd be living in St. Louis when the child was born.

After locking the mercantile, Faith and Rosemary strolled toward Faith's home. While they walked, Rosemary explained her plans to leave the day after Amy's wedding.

"Mrs. Kenyon promised she'd find a place for me to live, and Dr. Harding is expecting me on the eighth."

"How will you ever be ready so quickly?"

"I don't have that many possessions. The house was already furnished when I came here last year to live with Curt. My plants . . . I'm hoping he can move the greenhouse to your backyard. I'll put as many of the herbs as I can in pots, and take them, but some varieties don't like to be uprooted." The more she thought about her plans, the more complicated they became. She didn't like to be uprooted, either.

Faith put a hand on her arm and stopped her in the shade of a maple tree. "We'll both do all we can for you, but are you sure you want to leave? Thaddeus told us that Dr. Stewart sent Miss Mason away on yesterday's train."

"He sent her away?"

"Yes. She's gone. Perhaps there's still hope."

"If he would dally with another girl's affections once, he'd do it again. I don't want to marry a man I can't trust." No matter how much she loved him.

"Rosemary—"

She freed her arm. "Let's go get Bodie. I'm anxious to see him."

They walked in silence until they neared the Lindberg home. Faith cleared her throat. "Bodie missed you. From what Thaddeus said, so did Dr. Stewart."

Rosemary sighed. "For today, I'll enjoy Bodie." She tried to keep her voice light. "I'll worry about Elijah some other time."

"Fair enough, but don't think for a minute I'm going to drop the subject." Faith grinned at her and climbed the steps to her porch. As soon as she opened the door, Bodie hurtled across the entryway and planted his front paws on Rosemary's skirt. His tail whipped in circles.

She dropped to her knees and hugged his wiggling body. "I'm glad to see you too." After a few moments of rubbing his ears and belly, she stood and gazed into the vacant sitting room. A pang shot through her when she saw the mantel and thought about the decorations she and Amy planned for Amy's wedding. Closing her eyes, she imagined walking across the same room to stand by Elijah's side. Then Miss Mason's face blotted out the scene.

"Would you like to help in the mercantile tomorrow?"

At Faith's eager voice, Rosemary banished Miss Mason from her mind and turned to her friend. "I'd love to. I want to spend all the time I can with you before I leave."

Rosemary took her time traveling the distance between Faith's home and her own. As she passed familiar structures, she slowed to take a second look, wanting to memorize the town she'd soon be leaving. Bodie sniffed each tree they passed, giving her ample time for reflection. When they reached Courthouse Square, she paused to admire Noble Springs's most imposing structure. Its three stories of stone reflected reddish orange light from the sunset that flared behind her. In St. Louis, the building would be one of many. Here, it stood apart.

"Rosemary! Wait." Footsteps pounded on the boardwalk behind her.

Her breath seized. Elijah.

She lifted her chin as she turned, and speared him with a chilly stare. "Dr. Stewart." Bodie jerked at his leash, his feet scrabbling to reach Elijah. She pulled the dog close to her side.

"Thank goodness I spotted you. I was sitting in Thaddeus's office when you walked by." He looked more appealing than she remembered.

"We have nothing to talk about." She kept her tone icy. "If you'll excuse me—"

He held up his hand. "Please, listen to me."

"I can't think of anything you'd have to say that I wish to hear." She took a step in the direction of her home.

He moved beside her and matched her pace. "Miss Mason is gone."

"So I heard." She walked faster. They passed the barbershop and crossed the street. Her picket fence glowed like a beacon in the setting sun.

"She was never my fiancée." Desperation filled his voice.

Rosemary stopped at her gate. "She wouldn't have come here without a reason. Good evening, Doctor."

"You are, without a doubt, the most stubborn woman I've ever met. Good evening, Miss Saxon." He strode away, his broad back ramrod straight.

The next week would be more difficult than she'd imagined.

When Rosemary left her house the next morning, Sheriff Cooper waited at the hitching post.

He lifted his hat. "Morning, Miss Rosemary."

She greeted him with a smile. "I hope you've come to tell me you caught the man who's been harassing me. Even with my doors locked, I didn't sleep well for worry." And for thoughts of Elijah, she could have added.

"I've got a good idea who it is but can't seem to find him." He rested his hand on his holster. "Anyway, Miz Faith said you was coming to the mercantile today. Thought I'd keep you company on the walk."

"Thank you." She bolted the gate and set off for town. Why couldn't the sheriff locate the man? He was probably so wrapped up in his upcoming marriage that he hadn't spent a moment paying attention to his job. She blew out an impatient sigh. Looking on the bright side, the move to St. Louis would end her uneasiness. Whoever the person was, he'd never find her in the anonymity of the city.

Once they reached the mercantile, he tipped his hat. "I'll stop by at day's end to see you home." He rode toward the jailhouse.

Rosemary stepped into the store, savoring the special mixture of aromas from oiled floors, dyed fabric, and dozens of other items.

Mr. Grisbee waved at her from his chair next to the checkerboard. "Miz Faith said you'd be coming in, just like old times."

"It's good to be here."

On the opposite side of the board, Mr. Slocum shook his head. "She told us you were moving to St. Louis. This town won't be the same without you."

Faith emerged from the storeroom. "Keep talking, Mr.

Slocum. Maybe you can change her mind." She crossed to Rosemary, giving her a one-armed hug. "But knowing how stubborn you are, Amy and I came up with an idea last night."

Rosemary grinned. "You're going to lock me away in a tower, like in a fairy tale."

"Hmm. I hadn't thought of that. First we need to find a tower." Faith giggled. "In the meantime, do you want to hear our plan?"

"Please."

"We want to have a farewell party for you next Thursday evening—Independence Day." She managed a smile. "The date seems to suit your departure."

"You can't do that. Nobody will come."

Mr. Slocum rose and stood beside Faith. "I'd be honored to attend. So would old Grisbee here. You got lots of friends, Miss Rosemary. You'll be sorely missed."

She saw him through a haze of tears. "I'll miss you too, Mr. Slocum." She looked at Faith and arranged her face in what she hoped was a convincing smile.

"Tell me about your plan."

For Rosemary, the next several days passed in a drift of time spent at the mercantile and evenings locked in her house sorting what she'd pack and what she'd leave behind. When she walked Bodie, she planned her route so she wouldn't pass Elijah's house or his office.

On Thursday morning, she waved good-bye to Sheriff Cooper and entered the mercantile. Faith stood behind the fabric counter deep in conversation with Clarissa French. When they saw her, they stopped talking. Rosemary sensed suppressed excitement in the air.

She took Bodie to his blanket, then tied her apron around her waist and busied herself with dusting while Clarissa made her selection and left the store.

Faith hurried over. "She's sewing clothes for Jolene's baby. Thank the Lord she's softened toward her."

"I knew she would in time. Jolene's a perfect daughter-in-law." She tightened her grip on the duster. One more person she would miss. Two more, counting Galen.

Tears stung her eyes, but she blinked them away. This was no time to wallow in regrets. This evening's gathering would be difficult enough without spilling tears now as well.

As if sensing her distress, Faith patted Rosemary's shoulder.

"Without you, I don't believe there would have been a happy ending to that story."

"We need to give the credit to the Lord. He guided each of us during that time." To change the subject, she swiped the duster over a counter. "When I finish this, I'll straighten the storeroom. I noticed a new supply of cookware arrived yesterday."

"Thank you." The bell jingled, and Faith turned toward the door.

Mrs. Wylie bustled in, stopping short when she saw Rosemary. "Oh! Miss Saxon. I didn't know you'd be here. Happy to see you, though." Her face flushed. She sidled over to Faith and pushed a slip of paper into her hand, then hurried from the store.

"What was that about?" Rosemary quirked one eyebrow at Faith.

"Nothing." She shoved the paper into her apron pocket. "Now that I think of it, the storeroom can wait. Today promises to be quiet. Why don't you treat yourself to a day at home? I know you have packing to do, and herbs to transplant." She plucked the duster from Rosemary's hand. "I'll send Curt for you this evening."

The prospect of spending a day alone held little appeal, but if Faith didn't want her here . . .

She fastened Bodie's leash to his collar and stepped into the bright morning. Buggies and riders on horseback filled the wide street. With this many people in town, Faith might be busier than she expected. Rosemary looked back at the store, then shrugged. Time spent working in her greenhouse might soothe the confusion in her unsettled spirit.

Without Sheriff Cooper to see her home, she dawdled along the boardwalk, looking in the dressmaker's window at a peach-colored traveling costume on display, then crossing the street to admire hats in the milliner's shop.

She knew she procrastinated. Sooner or later, she'd have to dig up her plants and pray they'd survive the journey. For today, she'd trim faded blooms and water dry roots.

After leaving the milliner's, she paused at the corner diagonally across from her block and waited until a farm wagon passed. Then she took one step off the walk and froze.

Her gate stood open. She knew beyond a doubt that she'd left it closed and bolted.

Bodie dropped his head and crouched into a stalking position. His body quivered.

Rosemary whirled back in the direction of town. Lifting her skirt above her boot tops, she ran for Sheriff Cooper, praying as she pounded along that he'd be in his office. Bodie raced beside her. Shoppers on the boardwalk turned to stare at them as they flew by the milliner's, then the dressmaker's, and on past the mercantile. Rounding the corner onto Court Street, she was relieved to see the sheriff's horse tied to the rail in front of the jailhouse.

She burst through the door. "Sheriff! Quick! There's someone on my property." She leaned forward to catch her breath. Perspiration trickled down her temples.

He jumped to his feet. "Are you sure?"

"Do you think I'd run all the way over on a whim?" Panting, she rested her hands on her hips.

"I reckon not." He flung open the door. "You wait here." He vaulted into the saddle and galloped east.

Ignoring his order, Rosemary tugged at Bodie's leash and strode the two blocks between the jailhouse and her home. Dust boiling behind the gelding's hooves marked the sheriff's passage along King's Highway. When she drew close to her house, she saw the horse tied outside the gate. Sheriff Cooper was nowhere in sight.

Bodie growled. She stopped outside her fence, pulse

pounding, and heard the sounds of a scuffle behind the house. After several tense minutes, the sheriff appeared, half-dragging someone by a rope binding the man's hands behind his back.

Stunned, she gazed into the burning eyes of one of Elijah's patients—Abraham Grice.

He spat on the ground at her feet. "You! You ruined everything with your witches' brews. Me and Bingham was doing fine before them women showed up."

"You mean Cassie and her mother? I had nothing to do with Mr. Bingham's marriage to Mrs. Haddon."

"You had everything to do with what happened after. Them potions you gave that woman put a spell on Elmer. Everything was 'Eliza this' and 'Eliza that.' He didn't have no time for me—until he got sick. Then that woman gave him more potions to drink, no matter how I tried to keep her away. Well, they finally killed him."

He shot her a look of pure hatred. "Only friend I ever had, and he's gone, thanks to you."

Horrified, Rosemary grabbed the fence for support. "Nothing I gave Mrs. Bingham could cause harm."

"Cooper's listening. Course you'll lie."

She cast a frightened glance at the sheriff.

"He won't bother you no more, Miss Rosemary. I'll see to that." He slung the struggling man over the saddle and led the horse in the direction of the jail.

Fighting to control the tremors that shuddered through her, she made her way into the house on shaky legs, then dropped onto the settee. Thinking of Cassie and her mother in the same house with Mr. Grice threatened to upset her stomach. No wonder Mrs. Bingham fled Noble Springs as soon as her husband died.

By evening, a bath and a rest had helped Rosemary regain her composure. She slipped into her gray silk dress and arranged her hair in a crown of braids, leaving a few curls loose beside her ears. She hadn't wanted a party, but now that the time had come, she looked forward to seeing the few friends she had in Noble Springs. Fortunately, the topic of the arrest of her tormenter would prevent the conversation from centering on her decision to leave.

She heard a knock and then Curt's voice called, "Time to go."

When she opened the door, her brother smiled down at her, handsome in a black coat and trousers. "I've been told you had an eventful morning."

"Indeed it was." She turned the key in the lock. "I'll tell you all about it on the way."

Her dress rustled when he helped her into his buggy. While they rode west she described the morning's events. As she talked, she shivered at the image of Mr. Grice's glare. "He hates me, Curt. I've never—" She gulped.

His warm hand covered hers. "He's locked up. You're safe now. Think how good it will feel not to worry when you step outside your door."

"You're right. I'm thankful." She bit the inside of her lip. Four more days and she'd step outside that door for the last time.

As they drew closer to Judge Lindberg's house, she noticed a number of horses and buggies tied to hitching rails. People milled about on the porch and spilled onto the walkway.

She put her hand to her lips. "Are all these people here for the party?" She tried to count heads but couldn't come up with a number.

Curt grinned at her. "They're here to see you. Faith has

been busy day and night arranging everything." He leaned over and kissed her cheek. "You're loved, little sister."

I will not cry. She clutched his arm. "Please stay close by. I'll need you to lean on."

"I'll stick to you closer than Bodie does." He jumped down and tied his horse next to another buggy, then swung her to the ground.

"There she is," a voice called.

"Miss Rosemary." Mr. Grisbee shuffled away from the crowd. He'd shaved his usual scruffy whiskers and slicked his hair down with scented oil. He crooked his elbow in her direction. "Let me escort you."

She gazed at the smiling faces greeting her. A number of Faith's customers were present, among them the Wylies. Mr. and Mrs. Haggerty, with their two daughters and their infant son—the first baby she'd helped deliver. Mrs. Fielder, from the restaurant. More than a dozen other patients she'd helped treat in Elijah's office.

Faith beamed at her from the open doorway. "Come on in, Rosemary. There's someone inside who wants to say hello too."

She assumed Faith referred to Judge Lindberg. With Curt on one side and Mr. Grisbee on the other, she mounted the stairs, smiling and murmuring greetings along the way. When she reached Faith, she threw her arms around her friend. "I don't know what to say." Tears slipped along her cheeks. She dashed them away with her fingers. "Nothing like this has ever happened to me before."

"You deserve all this and more." A masculine voice spoke from the entryway.

Her heart stopped. Elijah.

Eyes wide, she stared at Faith. "You didn't."

He stepped forward. "I invited myself." His hand closed

around hers. "Come with me. I have something to say and I won't let go of you until I've said every word. Then you can talk."

"I told you before, I'm not interested." She planted her feet and resisted his tug at her hand.

"It won't hurt you to listen," Faith murmured. "Go with him."

Elijah tugged again. This time she followed, trying to ignore the tingles that raced up her arm at the touch of his hand. He led her past the dessert-laden dining table, through the kitchen, and out to a bench under an oak tree in the backyard. Slanting shadows through the leaves gave an illusion of privacy.

"Please sit." He tapped the seat with his fingertips.

She complied, her posture stiff and her arms folded across her chest.

"Here's what happened in Chicago." He paced away from the bench, then turned and faced her. "Miss Mason's brother is going into practice with my father. At every formal meal, every play, every event my father insisted I attend, Miss Mason and her brother were there. I spent no time alone with her."

"Then why—?"

He held up his hand. "Please don't interrupt. Apparently after I left, she and her brother decided the practice would benefit from my name on the door. He sent her down here to persuade me. The idea that she was my fiancée was something she and her brother concocted, ring and all. Not a grain of truth to the whole story. I suppose they thought I'd return to Chicago if she could convince you to leave."

"Are you quite finished?" Her voice quavered.

He flung his hands out, palms up. "There's nothing more to add."

The tears in his eyes tore at her heart. She looked away,

knowing his words made sense. If only she hadn't been so hasty . . .

He dropped to one knee in front of her. "You're the woman I love and want to marry. If you don't say yes now, I'll ask you every day until you agree, even if I have to follow you all the way to St. Louis."

"Oh, Elijah! I've been so wrong. How can you still want to marry me after the way I treated you?" She choked back a sob. "I'm sorry for not listening when you tried to explain."

One corner of his mouth quirked in a smile. "Well, it's not as if I didn't know you were stubborn."

"But I've wasted so much of the time we could have spent planning our wedding."

"Is that a yes?"

Sounds of the guests' laughter and chatter floated from the front of the house. Her farewell party. What would everyone think if she didn't leave?

She leaned toward him. "Yes," she whispered.

His beautiful smile spread over his face. "What did you say?"

"I said yes!"

He lifted her from the bench. His dark gaze traveled straight to her soul. "My little Rosemary."

She melted into his arms and raised her face for his kiss.

She'd send telegrams to St. Louis later.

Acknowledgments

I'm beyond grateful to my writing support group. To name everyone who has helped with this completed novel would take too many pages, so I'll start with those most directly involved—the team at Revell who polishes my ideas and my words until they're the best they can be. To Vicki Crumpton, I offer my deepest thanks for originally signing me as a new author, and for her keen eye in improving each of my books since that day. Barb Barnes and her editing staff are truly gifted in finding and pointing out, oh so gently, errors in my work. Michele Misiak is one of the busiest people I know, yet she always has time to answer my questions. I've received many compliments on the cover for this book, and for those on each of my previous novels. All credit for that goes to Cheryl Van Andel and the art department at Revell. I'm truly blessed to be writing for such a supportive publishing house.

My agent, Tamela Hancock Murray, has been instrumental in guiding my writing steps, and she, also, is never too busy to answer my questions the same day I ask them. I appreciate you, Tamela!

Every author needs stellar critique partners, and mine are brilliant. Thanks to Sarah Schartz and Bonnie Leon, with special gratitude to Judy Gann and Sarah Sundin, who gave up weekend time to critique the final chapters when I was pushing my deadline.

Because of several life interruptions, this novel was in process right up to the last minute, and I owe a huge debt of gratitude to my husband for his patience and understanding during the final frenzy.

A book is nothing without readers, and to you, I offer heartfelt thanks for reading my novels and taking the time to contact me with your kind comments. I hope you've enjoyed Rosemary's story as much as I've enjoyed sharing her journey with you. For those of you who are familiar with St. Louis, you'll recognize the liberties I've taken with the history of your city. A National Home for Disabled Volunteer Soldiers didn't exist there, although several were built elsewhere around the country after the close of the War Between the States.

Most importantly, I know my writing wouldn't happen at all if the Lord weren't with me every step of the way. As I've often said, he holds me by my right hand—always.

Ann Shorey has been a full-time writer for over twenty years. She made her fiction debut with the At Home in Beldon Grove series in January 2009.

When she's not writing, she teaches classes on historical research, story arc, and other fiction fundamentals at regional conferences. Ann and her husband live in southern Oregon.

Ann loves to hear from her readers, and may be contacted through her website, www.annshorey.com, or find her on Facebook at http://www.facebook.com/AnnShorey.

Don't miss book 1 in
Sisters at *Heart* series!

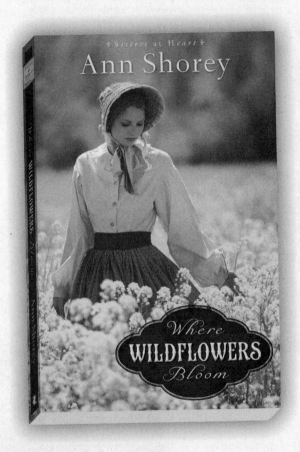

"*Where Wildflowers Bloom* invites you to settle down over by the checkerboard at Lindberg's Mercantile Store and get to know the people of Noble Springs as they put the sorrows of the Civil War behind them and embrace life and love anew."

—**Ann H. Gabhart**, author, *The Gifted* and *Words Spoken True*

AT HOME IN *Beldon Grove* series

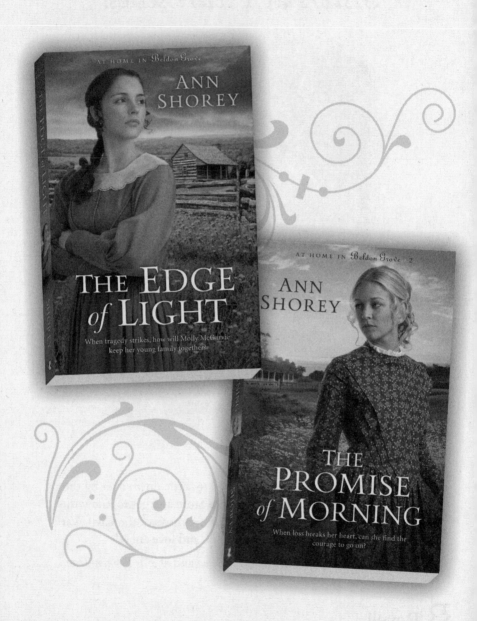

AT HOME IN *Beldon Grove*

ANN SHOREY

THE EDGE of LIGHT

When tragedy strikes, how will Molly McGarvie keep her young family together?

AT HOME IN *Beldon Grove* 2

ANN SHOREY

THE PROMISE of MORNING

When loss breaks her heart, can she find the courage to go on?

... will capture your *heart!*

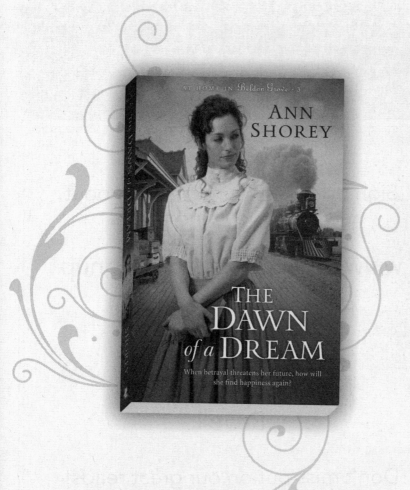

Ann Shorey weaves three emotional love stories of strong women who are determined to make it despite the difficulties of prairie life.